Jade Island

ELIZABETH LOWELL

Jade Island

AVON BOOKS  NEW YORK

This is a work of fiction. Names, characters, places
and incidents either are the product of the author's
imagination or are used fictitiously. Any resemblance
to actual events, locales, organizations, or persons,
living or dead, is entirely coincidental and beyond
the intent of either the author or the publisher.

AVON BOOKS, INC.
1350 Avenue of the Americas
New York, New York 10019

Copyright © 1998 by Two of a Kind, Inc.
Interior design by Kellan Peck
Visit our website at **http://www.AvonBooks.com**
ISBN: 0-380-97403-7

Library of Congress Cataloging in Publication Data:
Lowell, Elizabeth, 1944–
    Jade Island / Elizabeth Lowell.—1st ed.
        p.   cm.
    I. Title.
PS3562.08847J33   1998   98-22742
813'.54—dc21   CIP

First Avon Books Printing: October 1998

AVON TRADEMARK REG. U.S. PAT. OFF. AND IN OTHER COUNTRIES, MARCA REGISTRADA, HECHO EN
U.S.A.

Printed in the U.S.A.

FIRST EDITION

QPM   10   9   8   7   6   5   4   3   2   1

For
Nancy and Roger Kisner.
Wonderful neighbors, wonderful friends,
wonderful people.

Jade Island

prologue

The man was frightened.

His hands shook as he picked up pieces of jade and packed them into boxes. Precious jade, ancient jade, the Stone of Heaven . . . the dreams of man carved in rock with inhuman patience, inhuman skill.

Dreams that roused envy, greed, avarice.

Dreams that led to theft, betrayal, death.

His hands were colder than the jade he stole piece by piece, dream by dream, the soul of an entire culture passing through his clammy fingers. Here a dragon coiled in elegant designs that were three thousand years old. There a scholar stood wrapped in cloud-soft curves of creamy stone. In the corner a mountain loomed, the lives of the sages carved into its moss-green face, lives sculpted by artisans whose own lifetimes came and went before the creation was complete.

Dreams of beauty condensed into a thousand shades of jade, white sliding to ebony, green shimmering to blue, red burning to yellow; and all colors transformed harsh light into an ethereal glow, a soul lit from within.

Unique.

Priceless.

Irreplaceable.

Seven thousand years of culture stacked in gleaming array. Ancient *bi,* disks that represented heaven; equally ancient *cong,* hollow cylinders that represented earth. Ceremonial blades and armbands exquisitely carved with symbols whose real meanings were older than man's memory. Rings, bracelets, earrings, pendants, buckles, seals, bowls, cups, plaques, clouds, mountains, knives, axes, men, women, dragons, horses, fish, pigs, birds, the immortal lotus; everything a culture ever dreamed had been patiently, patiently, carved from the only gemstone that spoke to this culture's soul.

Jade.

"Hurry up, you fool."

The man gasped and would have dropped a fragile, ageless bowl if another hand hadn't shot from the gloom and grabbed the cool, hollowed-out hemisphere.

"Wh-what are you doing here?" the first man asked, his heart slamming frantically.

"Making certain you do it right."

"What?"

"Pillage the Jade Emperor's Tomb, what else?" replied the second man sardonically.

"I—not all—I—no! It will be discovered!"

"Not if you do what I say."

"But—"

"Listen to me."

Shaking, the first man listened. Hope and fear grew in him equally. He didn't know which was worse. He only knew that he had dug this grave with his own hand.

And he would do anything not to be buried in it.

As he listened, he didn't know whether to laugh or weep or hide from the devil who whispered coolly, gently, of absolute betrayal. It was so simple after all. It wasn't necessary for him to grasp the nettle of guilt firmly. The devil had found someone else to grasp it for him.

Understanding that, the thief laughed.

When he went back to packing the priceless jade, his hands were warm.

o n e

The pounding on Lianne Blakely's door made her sit straight up in bed, her heart beating rapidly. For an instant she wondered if she was dreaming all the noise. She certainly was tired enough to be dreaming. She had worked late last night, arranging and rearranging the beautiful jade pieces in her apartment until she was certain she had the right design for the Jade Trader display at tonight's charity auction.

The pounding increased in volume.

Lianne shook her head, pushed heavy waves of black hair out of her face, and stared at the bedside clock. Barely 6 A.M. She looked out the small window. Dawn had arrived in most of Seattle, but not in her old, west-facing apartment above Pioneer Square. Even if the morning had been clear—it wasn't—no sunlight would reach her windows until late morning.

"Lianne, wake up! It's Johnny Tang. Open the door!"

Now she really wondered if she was dreaming. Johnny had never been to her apartment, or to her business office, which was just down the hall. In fact, she rarely saw him at all unless she was visiting her mother in Kirkland.

"Lianne!"

Elizabeth Lowell

"Just a minute—I'm coming!" she called.

Grateful that there were no neighbors to complain about all the yelling on a Saturday morning, Lianne kicked off the duvet, grabbed the red silk robe her mother had given her last Christmas, and hurried to the door. Two locks and a dead bolt later, she yanked the door open.

"What's wrong?" Lianne demanded. "Is it Mother?"

"Anna is fine. She wants to see you before the auction."

Mentally Lianne rearranged her crammed schedule. If she did her own nails, she could manage a visit. Barely. "I'll swing by after I set up the Jade Trader exhibit."

Johnny nodded, but he didn't look like a man who had gotten what he came for. He looked restless, irritable, caged. Anger bracketed his full mouth and tightened the skin across his wide cheekbones. Despite that, he was a handsome man. Two inches under six feet, lean, quick of hand and mind, and with a generous smile when he was in the mood to use it.

"Do you have any coffee?" he asked. "Or are you still stuck on Chinese caffeine?"

"I have coffee as well as tea."

"I'll take mine black. Coffee, not tea."

Lianne stepped away from the door as Johnny walked in. She didn't know exactly how old her unacknowledged father was—close to sixty, surely—but he looked barely forty. Through all the years of Lianne's childhood, her mother's lover had aged hardly at all. Some silver hair was now mixed in with the black, a few laugh and frown lines had appeared, there was a slight blurring in the line of the jaw; small things, really, when Lianne thought of all the changes she had been through from birth to almost thirty years of age.

And never once in all that time, through all her changes, had Johnny Tang acknowledged that Anna Blakely's child was also his own.

Pushing the thought away, Lianne closed the door and shot the dead bolt home. What Johnny did or didn't admit was no longer the most important thing in the world to her. Jade was.

Tang jade. Her father's father's collection. Hundreds of pieces, thousands. All of them were precious, some were priceless, and each piece of jade gleamed with time and secrets and the luminous soul of art.

"Couldn't resist playing with them, huh?" Johnny asked, gesturing with one hand.

There were jade sculptures sitting on the small kitchen table, more objects lay on the floor, and some of the smaller pieces perched on the tiny counter.

"Playing? If that's what you call it," Lianne said. "They aren't exactly dolls."

He gave a crack of laughter. "Father would faint if he heard you say dolls and jade in the same breath."

"Wen knows I respect jade."

"Wen is using your skill and not paying you enough."

Lianne gave her father a startled look. "He taught me everything I know."

"Wrong," Johnny said impatiently. "Until seven years ago, he didn't know you were alive. Then you picked up some jade beads in a garage sale and he decided you had some kind of jade genius."

"Those beads were from the Western Zhou dynasty, three thousand years old, and were incised with dragons—a symbol of royalty. They were tied with a faded red silk cord that was older than the U.S. Constitution."

"If you had sold them and put the money in the stock market, you wouldn't be living in this dump. But no, you gave them to my father for his birthday."

At first Lianne was too surprised to answer. It wasn't like Johnny to talk about family. Certainly not with her. She looked at him out of the corner of her eye, measuring all the small signs that he was truly upset.

"I didn't know you disapproved of what I did," she said quietly.

"Would it have mattered?"

"Of course. I don't want to anger you or your family."

Lianne had never wanted that. She had turned herself inside out, learned Mandarin and Cantonese, worked seven days a week, fifty-two weeks a year, to prove to the family of Tang that she was worthy of them. She was still working on it, no matter how much she pretended to herself that she was simply trying to keep her own business healthy by staying close to her best clients—the widespread, international family of Tang.

"You should have done as your mother wanted and become a teacher," Johnny said.

"You woke me up at six A.M. to tell me this?" Lianne asked finally.

"No."

When Johnny didn't say anything more, she turned on the gas under the coffeepot and waited for things to start perking. In Seattle, percolator coffee was practically a sacrilege, but at the moment she didn't feel up to the intricate demands of the espresso machine she had bought on sale a week ago and still hadn't fully mastered.

While coffee perked in the tiny kitchen, Johnny paced several times through Lianne's small studio apartment. It was obvious she didn't spend much time there. Other than a framed print of the San Juan Islands and another one of Warring States decorative jades, there was nothing individual in the room. The subtle, unmistakable proof that Lianne was pouring herself into her work instead of her private life didn't please Johnny.

"Why are you living in this dump?" he asked.

"The rent is cheap."

"I give—" Johnny stopped abruptly. "Anna has enough money to see that you live in a better place."

"What she has is hers." Given to her by Johnny Tang. But that was something Lianne wouldn't say aloud. "I'm more than old enough to support myself." In fact, she would be thirty soon. She would be celebrating that landmark alone; Anna and Johnny were going to Hong Kong or Tahiti or somewhere on the other side of the Pacific to celebrate the thirty-first anniversary of their relationship.

"Anna says your business is doing well," Johnny said. "Why don't you do better for yourself than this?"

"The building belongs to your family. If you think it's a dump, complain to your oldest brother, Joe Tang. He's the landlord of record."

For a time there was silence. It wasn't a comfortable one, but Lianne made no attempt to break it. She didn't trust herself to. She might say something she shouldn't, something like *Why this concern for me all of a sudden?* The question wouldn't be entirely fair. Johnny had done better by his illegitimate daughter than many men did by their legal offspring. It wasn't his fault if Lianne hungered for the love of a family that didn't want her in any way except as a jade expert.

Old history, Lianne reminded herself. All of it. She couldn't change the past, but she could work for the future. And she was. Though the Tang family's patronage for her jade business was important, it wasn't the only reason she had beaten the odds and established her own business. A lot of the reason for her success was her own expertise and willingness to work ninety-hour weeks.

"Have you talked to Kyle Donovan yet?" Johnny asked.

"Is that why you came here for the first time, to find out if I've 'accidentally' managed to meet Mr. Donovan?"

"Why else would I come?"

Because I'm your daughter. Biting her tongue against the bitter words, Lianne reached for two mugs. The coffee wasn't quite ready, but she was more than ready for an excuse to do something with her hands.

"Coffee," Lianne said, handing Johnny a mug.

He took it and watched her, waiting. "Well?"

"No," she said, answering his question about Kyle Donovan.

"Why not?"

Lianne poured herself coffee and took a sip of the weak brown stuff.

"Are you involved with someone else?" Johnny pressed.

"No. And why would it matter? You asked me to meet Donovan, not to seduce him."

"Then meet him!"

"How?" she demanded. "Stick out my foot and trip him?"

"Come on," Johnny said impatiently. "Don't go all modest and fake Chinese on me. You're as American as your mother. Just do what the other girls do. Go up and introduce yourself. That's how I met Anna."

And look where it got her. Again Lianne bit back the bitter words. Her mind knew that it took two to make the master-mistress duo; her mother was a very willing participant in her second-class status. Lianne didn't understand it, but she was beginning to accept it. Finally. The cost of fighting it was just too high.

"He'll be at the auction tonight," Johnny said. "Do it tonight."

"But—"

"Promise me."

Lianne saw the emotion in her father's eyes, anger or impatience or something she couldn't name. Yet she knew it was real, as real as her fear of acting like what she had been called all her life—the daughter of a whore.

"Why?" Lianne asked, something she hadn't done before.

"Anna and I are going to Tahiti after the show. If you don't do it tonight, it will be too late."

"Too late for what? Why are you so eager for me to meet Kyle Donovan?"

"It's important. Very important."

"Why?"

Johnny hesitated. "Family business. That's all I can tell you."

Family again. Always.

But not hers.

"All right," Lianne said thinly. "I'll do it tonight."

"Let me summarize," Kyle Donovan said, staring in disbelief at his oldest brother. "You want me to seduce the illegitimate American daughter of a Hong Kong trading family in order to discover whether she's involved in the sale of cultural treasures stolen from China?"

Archer tilted his head as though thinking it over, studied the cold salt water beyond his brother's cabin in the San Juan Islands, and finally nodded. "Yeah, that's about it. Except for the seduction part. That's optional."

"I don't believe it."

"Fine. So seduce her."

"This is a joke."

"I wish."

Kyle waited, but his brother wasn't feeling talkative. Kyle was afraid he knew why. Archer hated involving family in any of the gray areas of his past. Uncle Sam was definitely one of those areas. But the U.S. government, like the past, never really went away.

"What's going on?" Kyle asked finally, shifting in his chair. "And don't give me any bullshit about hands across the water and international cooperation."

Archer glanced at his brother. Sunlight glinted in Kyle's tarnished blond hair and made his hazel eyes look more gold than green, but even sunlight couldn't brighten the dark rim around the iris. Nor could light take away the lines and shadows of experience, experience Archer would rather have spared his youngest brother.

"Would you believe business?" Archer asked neutrally.

"Monkey business, yeah."

Archer's smile was fast but real, like the anger narrowing his gray-green eyes.

Kyle simply waited. This time he wasn't going to be the one to break the silence.

Archer got out of his chair. He was tall, rangy, quick, a darker echo of his younger brother. Silently Archer prowled the cabin's homey main room, touching things at random: a computer that bristled with Kyle's Rube Goldberg additions, books on everything from international banking to five thousand years of Chinese jade, a Baroque flute, a small vase with a branch of rosemary in it, a letter opener that could slice to the bone, and a fishing lure that looked like a tiny hula skirt. Beneath the slithery, glittery skirt was a hook so sharp it would stick to rock. It certainly wanted to stick to flesh.

"You've changed," Archer said, smiling as he carefully set aside the lure. "Before that amber fiasco last year, you couldn't outwait me if your life depended on it."

"Does it?"

Archer's smile vanished. "Not as far as I know."

"Which brings up an interesting question," Kyle said. "What *do* you know?"

"Enough to worry. Not enough to do anything useful about it."

"Welcome to the human race."

For a moment longer, Archer stood near the window. He watched the windswept fir forest and the salt water beyond, where currents more powerful than rivers coiled beneath the peaceful surface of Rosario Strait.

"I don't know any more hard facts than I already told you," Archer said finally. "There have been rumors of a spectacular find, a Ming emperor's tomb. The emperor was a jade connoisseur. He creamed seven thousand years of Chinese jade and took it to his grave."

"Where was the find? Who made it? When? Does China—"

"I've told you most of what I know," Archer interrupted.

"Tell me the rest."

"My contact believes that Dick Farmer bought every important jade artifact in the tomb."

Kyle whistled. "Must have cost a lot."

"Close to forty million, one way or another."

"Even for a guy who's worth three billion—"

"Five, at last count."

"—that's a lot of money," Kyle finished.

"Money can be replaced. All it takes is a printing press, and God knows Uncle has one," Archer said bluntly. "But the contents of the Jade Emperor's Tomb can't be replaced. The Chinese are having an international hissy fit."

"No surprise. What are they doing to get Uncle's attention?"

"Not much." Archer's tone was as sardonic as his smile. "The Chinese just threatened to break off all relations with the U.S. if the Jade Emperor's treasure turns up on our soil."

Kyle's blond eyebrows shot up. "They *are* pissed. Will it turn up?"

"Worst-case scenario?"

"Is there any other kind?"

"It's already here."

"Where?"

"My contact didn't know or didn't say," Archer said. "Same difference, as far as the Donovans are concerned."

"Farmer isn't stupid," Kyle said slowly, "but he isn't the kind of guy to hide his glory under a bushel basket. He wants to be recognized as a big man in cultural circles, a true connoisseur as well as merely wealthy. If he has a coup the size of the Jade Emperor's Tomb, he'll strut it."

"That's what Uncle is afraid of. At this moment we have some very quiet, extremely delicate negotiations going on with mainland China."

"Trade, dope, immigration, or illegal arms?" Kyle asked.

"Does it matter?"

"Yes."

Archer smiled slightly. He and his brother were more alike than either one of them had realized until recently. "Illegal arms. The Chinese are making a bundle exporting munitions that are outdated by our standards, yet plenty high-tech by Second or Third World standards."

"Ah, civilization. Ain't it grand."

"It beats whatever is in second place. That's why Uncle is negotiating instead of shooting. Since it's China we're negotiating with, we've heard a hundred degrees of yes and none of no; but not a damn thing has been signed, sealed, or delivered in the way of promising to shut down the export of high-tech munitions."

"What does China want?"

"My contact didn't say. Obviously it's more than we're willing to give them so far. If this Jade Emperor shit hits the fan, we're going to end up looking as bad as we smell. Uncle will have to give up a lot more to China than is good for the long term, in order to get what we must have in the short term—less weapons in the hands of ambitious tyrants."

"Hand me the milk," Kyle said. He couldn't go back to bed and he sure as hell needed something extra to kick his butt into gear. Not to mention his mind.

He grabbed the milk carton from Archer and didn't stop pouring until the coffee in his cup was the color of the Mississippi in flood. He drank hard and fast, then waited for the caffeine to hit his brain cells.

"Okay," Kyle said. "So Uncle thinks the Tangs swiped the tomb goods and sold them to Farmer."

"That's one theory."

"What are the others?"

"SunCo is the second favorite."

"They're based in mainland China. If they did it, their government would be all over them like a cat covering shit."

"Probably. Depends on who SunCo is allied with in the mainland government. They have more factions than we have names to give them. Anyway, until further notice, the Tang Consortium is the favorite bad guy."

Kyle drank the last of his coffee, ran his hands over his bristly cheeks, and looked up at Archer with clear, hazel-green eyes.

"Since the Turnover," Kyle said, "the Tang Consortium has

been pretty well shut out of Hong Kong and the mainland. The Tangs need a strong U.S. ally. They don't get any stronger than Dick Farmer."

"Yeah. If it weren't for the arms negotiations, Uncle would let China, Farmer, and the Tangs slug it out. And we wouldn't be voting for the American. Farmer doesn't have too many friends in high places."

"You're speaking of the man most likely to start his own party and get elected President."

"It would mean a step down in power for Farmer. A big step. When the President wants to hold an international meeting, it takes protocol experts months to plan. When Farmer wants to hold the same meeting, everyone comes to Farmer Island and no one bitches about who has precedence."

"Yeah. I love that trick he plays with the lapel pins and the house computer. When you smuggled yours out after that last conference Donovan International attended, it took me months to reverse-engineer the chip and build one that would make the computer think whoever wore it was God."

"So you say. It's never been tested."

Kyle shrugged. He had done it, he knew it, and that was all that mattered to him. "Can you get a full description of the tomb contents? Otherwise we won't know what to look for."

"For openers, there's a jade burial suit. Intact."

Kyle was too surprised to say anything. When he wasn't surprised anymore, he still didn't know what to say. Absently he picked up the Baroque flute and blew a series of notes that were piercing yet sweet, random yet musical. Then he set the wooden flute aside and turned to his brother.

"Jade burial suits are extremely rare," Kyle said. "Nearly all that have been discovered are still in China. The very few that have gone overseas are in the hands of national institutions, not individuals."

Archer waited.

"What else was in the tomb?" Kyle asked.

"The usual stuff—jewelry, scepters, sculptures, dishes, screens."

" 'The usual stuff,' " Kyle muttered, shaking his head. "I'll need better descriptions than that. Size, color, age, that sort of thing."

"I'll try, but my contact was unofficial."

"Unofficial. Uh-huh. Do you really believe that?"

"Most of the real work is done that way. Off the record."

Subtly Kyle flexed his left shoulder, trying to work out the ache. The wound had long since healed, but the shock wave from an off-the-record bullet had done unhappy things to the nearby cartilage. When it came to predicting rain, he had a better average than the expensive weather guessers on TV.

"So this unofficial contact calls you," Kyle said, "and says that there are rumors of the type of cultural theft that will make diplomats reach for tranquilizers while governments beat the drum of nationalism and everybody with any sense heads for cover."

"Yes."

"Why did he come to you?"

"He didn't say, beyond the obvious."

"Which is?"

"Donovan International is in the right position and I know how the game is played."

"With real bullets," Kyle muttered.

"No. With real permits, passports, and other kinds of official paper. If we tell Uncle to bugger off, life becomes a lot trickier for Donovan International. It's hard to run an import-export business without the cooperation of the U.S. bureaucracy. Farmer can do it. We can't."

"And we owe Uncle one, don't we?" Kyle asked quietly. "For cleaning up my mess on Jade Island."

Archer shrugged, but the tight line of his mouth said a lot.

"Mother," Kyle said, disgusted. He had been afraid of that. "I tried to keep the family out of it."

"So did I."

Kyle flexed both hands, trying to work off the tension he felt every time he realized how close he had come to dying—and taking his sister Honor with him. "Let's go over it again, just to make sure I don't fuck this one up, too."

Turning suddenly, Archer looked straight at the big blond man who had once been his little brother and would always be his youngest brother. "What happened on Jade Island wasn't your fault."

"Yeah, right," Kyle said, disgusted. "I'm surprised you trust me with this."

"That's crap. The only one lacking trust around here is you, in yourself."

"Did your contact ask for me by name?" Kyle asked, changing the subject.

"No. But you're the one Lianne Blakcly has been watching for the past two weeks."

Kyle's odd, gold-green eyes widened. "What are you talking about?"

"The illegitimate daughter of—"

"Not that," Kyle interrupted. "The rest of it."

"Simple. She was looking at you and you were so busy looking at cold jade that you never noticed a warm woman trying to catch your eye."

"Jade isn't cold and I've never met a woman of any temperature who wouldn't crawl over my bleeding body to get to you."

Archer bit off the kind of comment that would spiral down into a sibling argument. He had never understood why everyone thought he was such a lady-killer. As far as he was concerned, Kyle was the best-looking of the Donovan brothers, with Justin and Lawe very close behind.

"Not this lady," Archer said. "Lianne was looking at you. That's one of the reasons I agreed to ask for your help in penetrating the Tang Consortium."

"Penetrating, huh? First the woman, then the whole damn

clan. You've got an overblown idea of my libido, not to mention my stamina."

Archer made a growling sound that was a combination of exasperation and humor.

"In any case," Kyle continued, "if the lady was looking at me rather than you, we can be sure of one thing."

"What?"

"It's a setup."

Archer blinked. "I'm having trouble following you."

"Take it one word at a time. In the last two weeks, you and I have gone to three jade previews together."

"Five."

"Two were so lousy they don't count. If Lianne saw past you to me, then it's because the Tang Consortium figures I'm an easier nut to crack."

"You don't think it's possible that Lianne prefers blonds?"

Kyle shrugged. "Anything is possible, but the last time a woman passed up a tall-dark-and-handsome type for me, I nearly got killed before I figured out exactly what kind of screwing was going on. That kind of lesson sticks with a man."

For a moment Archer didn't know what to say. Kyle was so certain that the only thing women wanted him for was to use him and lose him. Before last year, Kyle wouldn't have reacted like that.

At times Archer missed the old Kyle, the one who laughed easily, the golden boy bathed by a perpetual sun. But Archer never would have asked that golden boy to do anything more serious than match wines with meals.

"Maybe it's a setup," Archer agreed. "And maybe there's a different game entirely. That's up to you to find out. If you want to."

"And if I don't?"

Archer shrugged. "I'll put off my trip to the South Seas and take a run at the Tangs myself."

"What about Justin? He's blond. Kind of."

"Justin and Lawe are ass-deep in their own alligators, trying to get a line on a new emerald strike in Brazil. Besides, they're too young."

"They're older than I am," Kyle pointed out.

"Not since Kaliningrad."

Kyle smiled. It wasn't an open, sunny kind of smile. It was like Archer's, more teeth than comfort.

"I'm in," Kyle said. "When and where does the game begin?"

"Tonight. Seattle. Wear a tux."

"I don't have one."

"You will."

t w o

Lianne sat in her mother's elegant Kirkland condominium and watched Lake Washington's gray surface being teased by cat's-paws of wind. Never quite still, never predictable in its movements, the lake licked slyly at the neat lawns and sidewalks that crowded its urban shores. In balcony planters and along streets, tree branches were just beginning to shimmer with the kind of green that was more hope than an actual announcement of spring's return. The bravest of the daffodils were already in bloom, lifting their cheerful faces to the cloud-buried sun.

"Do you want green, jasmine, or oolong?" Anna Blakely called from the open kitchen.

"Oolong, please, Mom. It's going to be a marathon tonight. I'll need all the help I can get."

And all the courage, Lianne acknowledged silently. If Kyle Donovan was at the charity auction/ball tonight, she had to pick him up. Or try to. It would have been much easier if she wasn't attracted to him. But she was. Very. He made every female nerve ending in her body wake up and yowl.

Since she had never been attracted to a man like that before in her life, especially a big blond Anglo, she was afraid she would be all thumbs and blushes in his presence. That was why she had put off approaching him, and put it off, and put it off. She really didn't want to embarrass herself.

Now she had run out of time.

If she failed to pick him up, then she failed, Lianne told herself briskly. Her father would just have to chalk up one more disappointment from his bastard daughter. She didn't have the kind of recklessness or innate female confidence to approach a good-looking stranger with the idea of getting acquainted for business purposes, much less for sexual ones.

But Lianne was definitely the kind to repay a favor or keep a promise. Engineering a meeting with Kyle Donovan did both.

Her stomach hitched at the thought. She told herself that, despite what her father believed, Kyle wouldn't be at the ball tonight. He had no patience for that kind of arts-and-culture crush, and no need to siphon money from society's cream.

Lucky him.

Lianne wished there had been time for her to go to the gym and work out her nerves on a mat or with a partner. Nothing settled her mind and body like the intricate demands of karate—part ballet, part meditation, always compelling.

"Nervous?" her mother asked from the kitchen.

Lianne barely prevented herself from jumping up and pacing the room. "Of course I'm nervous. I chose every single piece of the Jade Trader display myself. Wen Zhi Tang never gave me that much responsibility before."

"Wen's eyes are going. Besides, the crafty old bastard wanted goods that would appeal to Americans as well as to overseas Chinese."

"And his bastard granddaughter is as close as he can come to American taste, is that it?"

The sound of a teaspoon hitting the polished granite countertop made Lianne wince, but she didn't apologize for her bluntness. She had spent too many years pretending that she was the daughter of a widow, while knowing full well that

Johnny Tang was her father, Wen was her grandfather, and since Anna had never been married, she could hardly be widowed.

Lianne was tired of the legitimacy charade, just as she was tired of watching her mother being treated like an unwelcome stranger by the Tang family. As far as Lianne was concerned, bastards were made, not born.

And the Tang family had made more than its share of them.

Anna Blakely walked into the room carrying a lacquered tea tray that held a bone china teapot and two elegant, handleless cups. She wore a brocaded peach silk jacket, slim black silk pants, low-heeled sandals. Pearls gleamed at her neck and wrists, along with a Rolex set with enough diamonds to glow in the dark. On her right hand was a diamond-and-ruby ring worth more than half a million dollars. Except for her height and glorious blond hair, she was the picture of a prosperous, semi-traditional Hong Kong wife.

But Lianne's mother was neither prosperous nor Chinese nor a wife. She had built her life around being the mistress of a married man for whom family, *legitimate* family, was the most important thing in life; a man whose Chinese family referred to Anna only as Johnny's round-eye concubine, a nonentity who didn't even know the names of her parents, much less her ancestors.

Yet no matter how often Anna came in at the bottom of her lover's list of family obligations, she didn't complain. Watching her mother's quiet elegance as she poured tea, Lianne loved Anna but didn't understand the choices she had made. And still made.

Bitterness stirred, a bitterness that was as old as Lianne's realization that she would never be forgiven for not being one hundred percent Chinese. She was too much an American to understand why any circumstance of birth, blood, or sex should make her inferior. It had taken her years to believe that she would never be accepted, much less loved, by her father's family.

But she had vowed she would be respected by them. Someday Wen Zhi Tang would look past her wide, whiskey-colored eyes and thin nose and see a granddaughter, rather than the unfortunate result of his son's enduring lust for an Anglo concubine.

"Is Johnny coming by later tonight?" Lianne asked.

She never called her mother's lover by anything other than his given name. Certainly not "Father" or "Dad" or "Daddy" or "Pop." Not even that all-American favorite for a mother's dates: "Uncle."

"Probably not," Anna said, sitting down. "Apparently there's a family get-together after the charity ball."

Lianne went still. *A family get-together.* And she, who had spent three months of her free time preparing the Tang Consortium's display, wasn't even invited.

It shouldn't have hurt. She should be used to it by now.

Yet it did hurt and she would never be used to it. She longed to be part of a family: brothers and sisters, aunts and uncles and cousins and grandparents, family memories and celebrations stretching back through the decades.

The Tangs were her family. Except for Anna, they were her only family.

But Lianne wasn't theirs.

Without realizing what she was doing, Lianne ran her fingers over the jade bangle she wore on her left wrist. Emerald-green, translucent, of the finest Burmese jade, the bracelet was worth three hundred thousand dollars. The .long, single-strand necklace of fine Burmese jade beads around her neck was worth twice that.

She owned neither piece of jewelry. Tonight she was merely an animated display case for the Tang family's Jade Trader goods. As a sales tactic, it was effective. Resting against the white silk of her simple dress and the pale gold of her skin, the jewelry glowed with a mysterious inner light that would act like a beacon to jade lovers, connoisseurs, and collectors.

The jewelry Lianne owned was less costly, though no less fine to someone knowledgeable about jade. She chose her personal pieces with an eye toward her own desire rather than their worth at auction. The trio of hairpicks that kept her dark hair in a swirl on top of her head were slender shafts of imperial jade carved in a style four thousand years old. When she wore them, she felt connected to the Chinese part of her heritage, the part she had spent her whole lifetime trying to be accepted by.

Distantly Lianne wondered if she would have been invited to the party if Kyle Donovan was her date. Johnny, Number Three Son in the Tang dynasty, seemed hell-bent on getting an entree into Donovan International. He certainly had gotten tired of waiting for her to screw up her nerve. *Come on. Don't go all modest and fake Chinese on me. You're as American as your mother. Just do what the other girls do. Go up and introduce yourself. That's how I met Anna.*

The memory of her father's words went down Lianne's spine like cold water. She couldn't help wondering if Johnny figured that what was good enough for the mother was good enough for the daughter—a life of guaranteed second best in a man's affections.

A mistress.

As Lianne drank tea from ancient, unimaginably fine china, she told herself that Johnny only wanted her to meet Kyle, not to seduce or be seduced for the sake of Tang family business. She also told herself that it was impatience rather than fear she had seen in her father's eyes that morning.

"Lianne?"

She swallowed the bracing tea and realized that her mother had asked a question. Quickly Lianne replayed the past few moments in her mind.

"No," she said. "I won't be staying for the ball. Why would I?"

"You might meet some nice young man and—"

"I have work piled up," Lianne interrupted. "I've spent too much time on Tang business already."

"I wish I wasn't going to the South Seas tomorrow at dawn. I'd come to the exhibit."

"No need." Lianne smiled and pretended she didn't know that her mother never went anywhere that she was likely to meet her paramour's family. Just as she pretended that she was an adult who no longer needed her mother's presence to mark important passages in life. "The hotel will be a zoo."

"Johnny appreciates all the hard work you've done with the jade. He's so proud of you."

Lianne drank tea and said nothing at all. Disturbing her mother's comfortable fantasy would only lead to the kind of argument that everybody lost.

"Thanks for the tea, Mom. I'd better get going. Parking will be impossible."

"Didn't Johnny give you one of the Jade Trader parking passes?"

"No."

"He must have forgotten," Anna said, frowning. "He's been worried about something a lot lately, but he won't tell me what."

Lianne made a sound that could have been sympathy and headed for the door. "If I don't see you before you leave for Tahiti or wherever, have a great time."

"Thanks. Maybe you could join us there for your birthday."

Why? Lianne thought acidly. *Did they need an audience while they screwed their way through a South Seas paradise?*

"You need a break after all your hard work," Anna said. "I'll have Johnny get a ticket for—"

"No," Lianne said curtly. Then she forced her voice to gentle. "Thanks, Mom, but not this time. I have a ton of work to catch up on."

Careful not to slam the door hard behind her, she headed out into the gusty night. As she walked to her car, she glanced around uneasily. Earlier that evening, when she had left her apartment, she had felt a chill, prickly certainty that she was being watched. She felt the same now.

Telling herself that she was just nervous about the cost of the Tang jewelry she wore, Lianne hurried around the side of the building, grateful for the motion-sensing walkway lights that flared to life at her presence and died away thirty seconds after she had passed the sensors. Her little red Toyota was right where she had left it. She got in and locked all the doors before she turned the key in the ignition.

The benefit ball for Pacific Rim Asian Charities was one of the big social events of the season in Seattle. Invitations were reserved for the rich, the powerful, the famous, and the merely gorgeous. Normally Kyle and Archer wouldn't have bothered attending this kind of show-and-tell in the name of charity and social climbing, but not much had been normal since Archer had received a call from the government. That was why they were pushing through the crowd just outside the hotel lobby.

"At least the tux fits," Kyle muttered. Except for the loose area just under the left arm, which had been tailored to fit seamlessly over a gun holster.

"I told you we were the same size, runt."

Kyle didn't say anything. He was still surprised that he fit into Archer's long-legged, wide-shouldered clothes. No matter how old Kyle got, part of him was still the youngest of the four Donovan brothers, the butt of too many brotherly jokes, the runt of the litter, always fighting to prove that he was as good as his bigger brothers in everything from fishing to gutter fighting to exploring the face of the earth for gems.

"You see her?" Kyle asked, looking past the herd of limousines to the glittery crowd filing into Empire Towers, Seattle's newest hotel. Dick Farmer's hotel, as a matter of fact.

"Not yet," Archer said.

"Not ever. I didn't know this many people owned tuxes.

Not to mention stones." He whistled softly as a matron walked by, wearing a diamond necklace whose central feature was a pendant the size and color of a canary. "Did you see that rock? It should be in a museum."

Archer flicked a glance at the woman and then looked away. "You want to talk museum pieces, try the companions of the Taiwanese industrialists who just walked in. Especially the woman in red."

Kyle glanced beyond his brother. The red silk sheath—and the body beneath it—was an eye-popper, yet it was the woman's headdress that sent murmurs of appreciation and greed through the crowd. A lacework cap of pearls encased her gleaming black hair. Teardrop pearls as big as a man's thumb shimmered and swayed around her face. A triple strand of matched teardrop pearls the size of grapes fell from the back of the cap down to the cleft in the woman's rhythmically swinging ass.

"Companion, huh? As in mistress?" Kyle said.

"It's common enough. When some well-heeled Asian men come to the States, they leave their wives at home with the kiddies and in-laws."

"Afraid their little women will bolt to greener pastures if they get the chance?" Kyle asked dryly.

"Wouldn't you?"

"I wouldn't be fenced like that in the first place." Kyle pushed through the hotel doors into the lobby. "Let's try the atrium. That's where the Jade Trader has its display. SunCo's stuff will be there, too. Ever since China took over Hong Kong, the Sun clan has been whittling away at the Tangs."

Archer smiled slightly. "Been doing some research?"

"If I had to do research in order to name the competition, I wouldn't be much good to Donovan International, would I?"

"You're really serious about dragging Donovan Inc. into the jade trade, aren't you?"

"I've been serious about it ever since I held my first five-thousand-year-old jade *bi*," Kyle said simply. "I'll never know why the piece was carved, but I do know that someone way back then was like me. He loved the smooth satin weight of jade. Otherwise he never would have tackled a stone that hard with little more than rawhide, sticks, and grit."

When Kyle would have turned and started toward the atrium, Archer put a hand on his arm, stopping him. "There's only a limited market for Neolithic jade artifacts," Archer said neutrally.

"The market is expanding every day. Even New York has caught on. Besides, there's a lot more to jade than Neolithic artifacts."

"Do you feel expert enough to advise us on the full spectrum of jade, to go one-on-one with the Pacific Rim's best?"

"Not yet. But Lianne Blakely is. Or didn't your contact mention that?"

"He didn't make a point of it. He just said she was a kind of back door into the closed world of the Tang Consortium."

"Back door, huh? Okay, let's see if I can learn more from sweet Lianne than she can learn from me before she's finished using me for whatever old man Wen Zhi Tang has in mind."

Archer blinked. "That's scary."

"What?"

"I understood you."

Kyle forged a way through the crowd with Archer at his side. Once inside the atrium, the crush of people broke into clots centered around various exhibits of the corporations that were donating pieces to the auction.

"Forget it," Kyle said, pulling Archer away from an exhibit of black South Seas pearls. "Lianne Blakely is into jade, remember?"

"Any harm in looking at something else?"

"If it's you and pearls, yes."

"As bad as you and jade?"

"Worse," Kyle said, looking around.

Against the towering greenery-and-glass backdrop of the atrium, people from three continents and several island nations revolved around the central fountain, creating a kaleido-scope of languages and fashion. The fountain itself was striking—a clear, cantilevered glass sculpture of rectangles and rhomboids where light and water danced with a grace people could only envy. The sweet music of the water blended with the languages of Hong Kong, Japan, and several regions of China, as well as with English accented by countries as distant as Australia or Britain and as close as Canada.

"The jade must be on the other side of the atrium," Kyle said.

"Why?"

"Most of the Anglos are right here, crowded around the rubies and sapphires from Burma or the Colombian emeralds or Russian diamonds. Jade is a more subtle, civilized taste."

"Bull," Archer said mildly. "Civilization has nothing to do with it. Jade was available in ancient China. Diamonds weren't. Same goes for Europeans. Clear gemstones were more available than jade. Tradition is created from the materials at hand."

Kyle and Archer continued arguing about culture, civiliza-tion, and gems while they circled around the glittering foun-tain. On the way to Asian jade, they passed museum-quality, pre-Columbian jade artifacts from Mexico and Central and South America. Fright masks of gold and turquoise grinned or snarled, scaring off demons whose names were known only to people thousands of years dead. Mixed in among the arti-facts were modern examples of gold and jade art.

Everything, ancient or modern, had a card in front of it naming the corporation which owned the object. Corporate display of support for the arts was as much the purpose of the evening as the charity auction that would precede the ball.

By the time the Donovan brothers came to the section reserved for offshore Chinese exhibits, Kyle was wishing he was aboard the *Tomorrow*, sharpening hooks and tying leaders for a dawn fishing raid. He snagged a glass of red wine from a passing waiter's tray, sipped, and grimaced. At a function like this, he had expected higher quality.

"Bingo," Archer said softly.

Kyle forgot the mediocre wine. "Where?"

"To the left of SunCo's jade screens, near the Sikh in the jeweled turban."

Though they were less than ten feet away, Kyle at first didn't see any woman. Then the Sikh stepped aside.

Kyle stared. "You're sure?"

"Positive."

"Hell."

Kyle didn't know what he had been expecting, but he knew Lianne Blakely wasn't it. With a combination of skepticism, disgust, and grudging male interest, he studied the sleek, petite young woman who supposedly was so smitten with him that she had been watching him from afar for two weeks.

Yeah. Right. He was standing close enough to admire the fit of her panty hose, and her patrician little nose was buried in an exhibit of Warring States jade ornaments as though she was alone in a museum.

Then Lianne turned and looked at Kyle. Her wide, tilted eyes were the color of cognac. She hesitated, almost as if she might have recognized him. Then she shifted the thin strap of her tiny white silk purse on her shoulder and went back to studying jade as though no one else in the room existed, certainly not a man she was interested in meeting.

"You're sure that's her?" Kyle asked quietly, praying it wasn't.

"I just said so, didn't I?"

"She doesn't look like an international art thief."

"Really?" Archer asked softly. "How many have you known?"

"Not as many as you, I'm sure. So tell me, is she?"

"A thief?"

"Yeah."

"They don't wear labels."

Kyle didn't say anything more. He simply watched Lianne Blakely.

Archer looked from his brother to Lianne, wondering why Kyle had come to a point like a bird dog scenting warm pheasant. Lianne was attractive, maybe even beautiful in an exotic way, but she certainly wasn't in the gorgeous–companion category. The simple white dress she wore fit well enough, but wasn't slit from hem to crotch or throat to pubic bone in order to draw and hold a man's eye. The jade bracelet she wore was doubtless Burmese and of the highest quality, as was her necklace, yet Kyle didn't seem to have noticed the jewelry. He was staring at the woman and ignoring the jade.

Not good.

"Maybe we should forget the whole thing," Archer said abruptly. "I'll put off the trip to Japan and Australia, give you more time to heal up."

"I told you, my shoulder is good as new," Kyle said without looking away from Lianne.

"Nothing is good as new after a bullet."

Kyle shrugged, then winced. His shoulder still ached when the weather was setting up for rain. In the Pacific Northwest, that was pretty often. "I know much more about jade than you do."

"Considering how little I know, that's not much of an argument for your participation in this little waltz."

Kyle smiled crookedly. The non sequitur hadn't even made Archer pause before he answered. That was the good thing about family: they knew you well enough to follow your thoughts.

It was also the bad thing about family. That kind of knowing could be claustrophobic when there were six kids. But Kyle had learned the hard way that running off to the other side of the world didn't prove anything except what he already knew.

He was four years and one century younger than his oldest brother.

"What's really bothering you?" Kyle asked, looking at Archer. "Afraid another woman will grab me by my dumb handle and lead me into trouble?"

"If you get hurt because of me, Susa will have my butt on a canvas stretcher."

"Our own mother? Ha! You're her favorite son."

Archer gave Kyle a look that would have backed off anyone else.

Kyle wasn't about to back up anywhere. He felt like he had just taken a sucker punch to the gut. Lianne Blakely was everything that appealed to him in a woman, and he hadn't even known it until he saw her. He had thought he liked big women; she was small. He had thought he liked blondes; she was dark. He had thought he liked outgoing, laughing women; she was quiet, poised around an inner stillness.

One thing Kyle did know for certain was that he never wanted to be at the mercy of his dick again. Yet he wanted Lianne in a way that had nothing to do with old knowledge, old learning, old promises. His sudden, primitive arousal made him furious. He must be a slow learner on the subject of being used by a woman.

Maybe he could be a fast learner on the subject of how to use one.

"Don't wait up for me," Kyle told his brother, starting toward Lianne. "I've got some monkey business to conduct."

three

Though Lianne pretended to be absorbed by the exquisite jades in the display case, she knew the exact moment Kyle Donovan began to walk toward her. Even before her father had made his surprising request, she had been watching Kyle out of the corner of her eye. It was easy. Kyle Donovan had the kind of athletic body and fierce blond looks associated with Vikings.

"We've got to stop meeting like this," he said.

Startled, Lianne glanced away from a Warring States jade buckle and into Kyle's eyes. They were the most unusual she had ever seen: a starburst of gold around the black pupil, then green all the way to a thin outer rim of glittering black.

"Excuse me?" she managed, trying not to stare at his eyes. "You didn't really say that."

"You're right. Must have been my evil twin brother. Got a match?"

"I don't smoke."

"Neither do I, but it seemed like a good way to strike up a conversation. I could have done something more timely, but you aren't wearing a watch."

Lianne groaned at the puns and was rewarded by an off-center smile. She blinked and wondered if he had any idea how welcoming his smile was.

"I'm Kyle Donovan," he said, holding out his hand. "You're Lianne Blakely. Now that we've met, you can tell me why you've been stalking me for the last two weeks."

Her amusement faded. For the first time, she noticed that his unusual eyes were watching her with the kind of remote, measuring glance usually reserved for unwanted relatives who showed up on the doorstep just in time for dinner.

"What are you talking about?" she asked.

"You. Following me. Tonight. Two days ago. Last week."

"Are you referring to the fact that we've both attended the same jade showings?"

"Yes."

"That constitutes following you?"

"A guy can hope."

"A guy can drop off."

Kyle shrugged. "Okay."

He turned and started to walk away.

"Wait," Lianne said before she could think better of it.

There were promises to keep. And there was the undeniable fact that Kyle Donovan interested her. Maybe she was finally getting over the man who had seduced her, married a proper Chinese maiden, and then had been surprised when Lianne didn't want to continue the relationship.

Like mother, like daughter.

Kyle turned back toward Lianne. And waited.

Lianne took a hidden, calming breath and glanced up through her eyelashes at the tall man whose shoulders were too wide for her comfort. The wineglass looked small in his big hand, yet he held the crystal with precision and delicacy. His inherent restraint and coordination reassured her. She repeated what had become her mantra in the past two weeks: *You can do it. Women do it all the time.*

Yet Lianne had never stalked a good-looking stranger. Until recently. And she had been caught. Now she wondered what to do next. Something subtle, perhaps indirect, certainly calm, preferably patient. Those were the qualities favored by her almost-family of Tang.

"I have a really big favor to ask," Lianne said baldly. Subtlety, indirection, and patience be damned.

"Decent wine?" Kyle asked.

She looked at her own half-full glass and almost smiled. She was so edgy tonight that everything tasted like vinegar and ashes. She set her glass aside, took a steadying breath, and smiled.

"Try the beer," she suggested, raising her voice to carry over a burst of Cantonese as three connoisseurs argued over the merits of a Ming statue. "The Chinese aren't noted for their understanding of wine."

"That explains it."

"What?"

"Last week. Bubbles in the burgundy."

Despite Kyle's dry words and crooked smile, his golden-green eyes were watching her with unflinching patience. He was waiting for her answer the way a cougar waited for a fawn to do something stupid.

A server came by balancing a tray of wineglasses both empty and full. He picked up Lianne's glass, accepted Kyle's, and took their refusal of more wine with an understanding smile.

"Bubbles in the burgundy," Lianne repeated, biting her lower lip and smiling almost sadly as the waiter disappeared into the crowd.

Silence grew. Kyle did nothing to break it.

"You know," she said, "it would be easier if you at least smiled again."

He did.

It wasn't.

"I'm not planning on sticking a nail file in your oversize chest," Lianne said, "if that's what is bothering you."

Despite his wariness of the intriguing Ms. Blakely, Kyle's

smile warmed a few degrees. The thought of the petite lady attacking him was amusing.

It was also arousing. The stirring of his body surprised him. He hadn't been much interested in women lately. Being set up to die by a former lover had had a chilling effect on his interest in the fair sex.

"What do you want from me?" Kyle asked bluntly.

Irritation jerked, replacing Lianne's uneasiness. He had no reason to act as though she was a criminal or a beggar asking for a handout.

"Do I have to have an agenda? Hasn't a girl ever come on to a big stud muffin like you?" she asked with cool sarcasm.

"Yeah. That's how I know you aren't. What do you want from me, Lianne Blakely, and what makes you think I can help you out?"

"You're big."

"So is a stuffed elephant. Want me to call a taxidermist?"

The idea of hauling a stuffed elephant to jade sales or to meet the Tangs would have made Lianne laugh, but the look in Kyle's unwavering eyes took the humor right out of the situation. The wishful thinking she had done about taking care of two problems at once—her promise to Johnny and her own protection—evaporated.

"Please do," Lianne said. "I think you would be charming stuffed. In fact, it's undoubtedly the only way you *could* be charming."

Without intending to, Kyle laughed. "Oh, I have my moments."

"I'm breathless."

He took her hand, raised it slowly to his lips, and brushed a Continental kiss over her fingers.

"Let's start over again," he said, putting her hand between his. "I'm Kyle, you're Lianne, we're both human, and we're both interested in Chinese jade. What else do we have in common?"

"My hand."

"A very nice hand," Kyle agreed without releasing it. "Small, clean, warm, elegant shape, nails buffed but not lacquered. That's another thing we have in common."

"Buffed fingernails?"

"Warmth," he said, running a fingertip lightly over her palm.

Lianne felt breath filling up her throat. "All right. You have moments of charm. May I have my hand back?"

"Sure you want it?"

"I'm very attached to it."

Kyle grinned. "And you wince at *my* puns."

He released her hand by letting it slide slowly from between his own. Hoping to conceal the slight quiver of her response to what felt very much like a caress, Lianne laced her fingers together as soon as both hands were free.

"All present and accounted for?" he asked dryly.

"What?"

"Your fingers."

"Oh. Er, yes. All ten. Thanks."

"You're welcome. I rarely eat digits on first acquaintance."

Lianne blew out her breath. She had a distinct feeling that the conversation was slipping right out of her control.

The combination of alarm and humor in her expression got to Kyle more deeply than her taut little body and wide cognac eyes. In some ways she reminded him of Honor and Faith, his younger twin sisters, who often started more than they could finish with their older brothers.

A burst of Mandarin came from behind Kyle. The only word he recognized was Lianne's name. Though she didn't move an inch, she seemed to withdraw behind a thick glass shield. Whoever was heading toward her wasn't someone she wanted to see.

Kyle turned and saw a thickset, middle-aged man bearing down on them. The two younger men walking behind him could have been his sons or nephews or cousins or business associates, but Kyle doubted it. Something about them smacked of bodyguards.

Then Kyle recognized the older man as Han Wu Seng and was certain that the other men were bodyguards. Seng was one of the People's Republic of China's foremost political facilitators. Anyone who needed a few million for a good political cause could come to Seng, trade favors, and walk away a richer man. No wire transfers, no paper trail. Cash only. Hence the bodyguards. He never knew when he would meet a hungry politician, so he was always prepared for business.

Seng strode up and stood very close to Lianne by anyone's cultural standards. By mainland Chinese standards, it was nearly a physical assault.

She stepped back as though turning to say something to Kyle, but it was just a polite excuse to put more distance between herself and Seng. He was one of the biggest reasons Lianne wanted Kyle at her side in the next few weeks, until Seng was called back to the mainland.

Seng wanted her. He was known for getting what he wanted, whether it was jade, political power, or a woman. What worried Lianne was that Wen Zhi Tang was eager to form a liaison with Seng, hoping it would lead to the Tangs being viewed with more favor by the mainland Chinese. While she didn't care about Tang ambitions, for both personal and professional reasons she didn't want to anger her grandfather.

"There you are," Seng said impatiently. "You were to be with the Tang Consortium exhibit, but no, you are flying like an autumn leaf around the building. Have you heard anything more about the contents of the Jade Emperor's Tomb? I was told there was a particularly spectacular piece of fellatio, a possible cunnilingus, a phallus for the instruction of young concubines, a—"

Lianne put a business smile on her face and calmly interrupted one of the PRC's most powerful capitalists. "Forgive me," she said in rapid Mandarin, "but I must introduce my companion, who speaks only English. It will be necessary for me to translate."

While Lianne made introductions in two languages, Seng looked at Kyle with shrewd black eyes. Though Seng shook hands with appropriate vigor, he didn't bother to hide his lack of interest in Kyle's existence.

Then the name Donovan sank in.

"Donovan International?" Seng asked in heavily accented English

Kyle nodded.

Seng's smile warmed. He began speaking in rapid Mandarin. Lianne translated, working only a few words behind him. Kyle focused on the English and looked at Seng. Seng focused on the Mandarin and looked at Kyle. Both men were accustomed to business meetings that were conducted in several languages. The trick was to get a good translator, one who was not only accurate but fast and seamless.

Lianne was very good.

Kyle listened to the usual compliments, returned as good as he got, and wondered what Seng wanted from Donovan International.

"Your father is a difficult man to meet," Seng said finally.

"The Donovan is noted for being difficult," Kyle agreed.

"That makes doing business very difficult."

"Not really," Kyle said, smiling. "His assistants are easy to reach."

"It is better to deal with Mr. Donovan himself."

"I've said the same thing to The Donovan many times. He doesn't listen to me. But then, I'm only Number Four Son. The Number One Son is Archer. Have you met him?"

"I have not had the opportunity."

Kyle glanced around. Archer was nowhere in sight. Kyle shrugged. "Maybe next time." He looked directly at Lianne. "If you want, I'll take a hike and—"

One of Lianne's hands wrapped around Kyle's wrist. Her

speed surprised him as much as the clenched intensity of her grip.

"It would be an unforgivable breach of etiquette not to make the rounds of all the exhibits," Lianne said quickly. "We promised, remember?"

The plea in her eyes was as naked as the pressure of her fingers on his skin.

"You're right, of course," Kyle murmured, putting a hand over hers. Then he asked softly, "Is he the reason you wanted a stuffed elephant?"

Lianne gave an odd crack of laughter and answered with half the truth. "Yes."

The other half was the man she thought had followed her from her mother's condo. The man she might have glimpsed through openings in the crowd when she looked away from a display unexpectedly. Medium height. Black tuxedo. Common Caucasian complexion and color. So unexceptional she couldn't even be certain she had seen him.

Yet no matter how she tried to ignore it, she had the uneasy sensation of being followed. Despite her years of karate workouts, she had zero desire to go one-on-one with a mugger or worse. The gym was one thing. A back alley was quite another.

"Much as I'd like to chat," Kyle said to Seng, "Lianne and I are on a short clock. There's so much to look at before the auction begins. I'm sure you understand. Next time I speak with The Donovan, I'll be sure to mention your name."

Lianne's fingers loosened, but didn't leave Kyle's wrist. Her translation took an unusual amount of time. Kyle kept smiling, for he suspected that she was smoothing a ruffled ego. Yet nothing in her eyes or posture suggested that she regretted brushing off Han Wu Seng, or that she was interested in touching him with anything more personal than words.

A year ago, Kyle would have felt simple masculine pleasure at being preferred over a man who could buy and sell countries, much less people. But any flicker of pleasure Kyle might have had was burned out by a much stronger curiosity: why had Lianne picked him as her white knight?

He looked at her slender, steel-hard fingers holding onto his wrist and decided that the answer was probably as simple as the Tang Consortium deciding that Number Four Son was indeed the easiest mark at Donovan International.

The only important question remaining was what the Tangs wanted.

"Thank you," Lianne said quietly, letting go of Kyle's wrist as Han Seng and his two shadows stalked off.

"Most women would be delighted to have Seng look at them the way he looks at you."

"Like a piece of merchandise?"

"Beautiful merchandise."

"Another pun?" Lianne said, but there was no laughter in her voice.

Kyle's bronze eyebrows rose in silent question.

"Beautiful merchandise," she said evenly, "is one of many Chinese euphemisms for a whore."

"Sorry. Want to begin all over? Third time's the charm and all that."

A quick smile changed the aloof lines of Lianne's face. "Let's keep the third time in reserve."

"You see worse misunderstandings ahead for us?"

"Life has taught me always to have something in reserve."

"You must have an interesting life."

"Not as interesting as this Warring States buckle." Lianne turned back to the exhibit she had been examining before Kyle approached her.

He hesitated at the transparent change of subject, then shrugged and decided to play it Lianne's way for a time. He stepped closer and looked over her shoulder into the case. Over the top of her head, actually. She didn't even come up to his chin. When he breathed in, a scent like rain and lilies came to him. When he breathed out, tendrils of hair which had escaped from the jade picks stirred against her ear. Then another breath and it was rain and lilies all over again, only warmer, because he was leaning so close now that he could feel the subtle heat of her body. And the unsubtle heat of his own.

With a silent, bitter curse at his hormones, Kyle stepped aside and focused on the very old jade ornament instead of on Lianne's fragrant flesh. The S-shaped dragon design was still vibrant and crisp after more than two thousand years of existence.

"Beautiful," Kyle agreed, yet he was looking away even as he spoke. "But it can't touch the sheer power of the ceremonial blade in the next case."

When Lianne glanced at the chisel-shaped jade that had captured Kyle's attention, she almost smiled. The long, narrow, nearly rectangular form of the blade was familiar to her from many hours spent listening to Wen talk about the aesthetics and ritual purpose of various Neolithic ceremonial objects.

"You sound like Wen Tang," she said. "He's quite passionate about his archaic jades."

"Are you talking about Wen Zhi Tang?" Kyle asked, though he knew very well she was.

Lianne nodded but didn't look away from the case holding the ancient blade. With a soft sound she leaned closer, so close that her breath clouded the glass surface of the case. Impatiently she backed up a bit and waited for the glass to clear.

"What is it?" Kyle asked.

Lianne didn't answer. She was holding her breath, examining the five-thousand-year-old jade object as closely as she could behind its glass barrier.

"Incredible," she muttered, narrowing her eyes. "Size I could understand. Color I could accept. Design, no problem. But to have similar burial stains in similar places?"

Frowning, she stared intently at the ceremonial blade.

"You'll get lines if you keep that up," Kyle said after a time.

"Only Americans are obsessed with youth," she said, not looking away from the jade.

"And Chinese are obsessed with age."

"Obsession is cross-cultural. Human. The object of obsession is cultural." As Lianne spoke, she walked around the case, viewing the jade from all angles.

"Thinking of bidding?" Kyle asked.

"Yes."

"Then I hope you or your client is wealthy. That's a very fine piece of Neolithic jade. The sort of thing that might be found in an emperor's grave."

Lianne barely heard Kyle's words. She was already mentally rearranging the contents of her checking and money-market accounts. She could cover the probable cost of the jade. Barely. If the rattle in her car turned into a problem, she would have to max out her credit cards. Either way, she would have to give up the exquisite Eastern Zhou pendant she had had her eye on, at least for the time being. Once she had solved the mystery of the Neolithic blade, she could sell it and balance her books again. Unfortunately, by then the lovely pendant would be sold.

With an unconscious sigh, Lianne said good-bye to the twenty-five-hundred-year-old bit of jade she had promised herself for her thirtieth birthday.

"You don't look happy," Kyle said.

"Excuse me?"

"Most collectors hot on the scent of a new acquisition look tight, glassy-eyed, panting to get their hands on whatever their obsession is. Sort of like Seng looking at you."

Lianne shot Kyle a sideways glance from eyes the color of very old whiskey. It didn't take her long to decide she would rather talk about Seng than about the Neolithic blade that she was almost certain belonged to her grandfather.

Or had. The card in front of the blade stated that it was owned by SunCo and had been donated for the auction.

"Mr. Han—"

"Seng to his friends," Kyle interrupted dryly, "and he wants to be your friend. A close one. Real close."

"Mr. Han," Lianne repeated, "has a variety of enthusiasms. For the moment, I appear to be one of them. It won't last. But while it does, I wouldn't mind having an escort of a certain type while I attend jade events."

"A certain type?"

"Large. Like you."

"Ah, we're back to the stuffed elephant."

"Your words, not mine."

Kyle examined Lianne as though she was a piece of jade that was on the market. "You're serious."

"About needing you? Yes."

"What do I get out of it?"

"The satisfaction of being a white knight," she shot back, embarrassed by the certainty that there was a flush climbing her cheeks.

"Sorry, but I traded in my metal underwear for good old cotton."

Lianne hoped her professional smile concealed her irritation. And her disappointment. "Understandable. I'm sure chain mail chafes something fierce. Excuse me, I have a lot of jade to see. Nice meeting you, Mr. Donovan."

For an instant Kyle was too surprised by Lianne's cool, swift withdrawal to do anything but stare. Before he had time to think it over, he was moving, cutting off her escape.

Lianne came to an abrupt stop. It was that or walk head-first into Kyle Donovan. Automatically she stepped to the right. He stepped to his side, cutting her off again. She moved to the other side. So did he.

"The dance is after the auction," she said in a clipped tone.

Kyle smiled. He liked the spark and snap of anger in her eyes much better than the blank, remote politeness that had been there when she brushed him off like dandruff.

"I have a suggestion," he began.

"Lovely. Get out of my way and I'll find someone who cares."

"My suggestion has to do with trading favors."

Lianne's eyelids lowered, concealing the dark whiskey blaze of her eyes. "Such as?"

"Every hour I'm a stuffed elephant for you, you'll give me an hour and teach me what you see when you look at various kinds of jade."

Her eyes widened in surprise, dark centers expanding. "What?"

"I have a fair working knowledge of ancient and archaic jades, but I could learn a lot from listening to the thought processes of an expert like you."

"I'm hardly *that* expert."

Kyle managed not to laugh out loud. If Wen Zhi Tang had an apprentice, it was Lianne Blakely. And when it came to jade, Wen was as expert as God.

"Then it's an even trade," he said easily. "I'm not an expert escort."

When Lianne hesitated, Kyle smiled lazily down at her. He had been told that he had a disarming smile, so he used it when being underestimated was a real benefit. In this atrium swirling with Asian and Caucasian sharks, he figured he needed all the help he could get. Six months of immersion in the study of Chinese jade artifacts didn't make up for a lifetime spent climbing over the face of the earth looking for minerals.

Lianne didn't relax as much under his smile as Kyle had hoped. If anything, she withdrew even more.

"Sort of you scratch mine and I'll scratch yours?" she suggested.

His smile widened. "Close enough. You game?"

"As long as all I'm scratching is your jade itch," she said bluntly. "How much do you want to know about jade?"

"I'll tell you if I get bored."

Lianne tilted her head to one side and looked up at Kyle.

"You're really serious about this, aren't you?" she asked, echoing his earlier remark.

"Yeah. I hate being bored."

She took a breath and thought of all the reasons she should turn and walk away from the man with the easy smile and beautiful, measuring eyes.

"All right," she said faintly. Then, more firmly: "It's a deal."

For the first time since Kyle had seen Lianne, his gut relaxed. He didn't know why it was important for him to stay close to her. He only knew that it was. In a woman, what he felt would have been called feminine intuition. In a man, it was called reasoning, experience, deduction, or, at worst, a hunch.

Kyle's hunch said there was more to this deal than a pretty lady asking a big male to keep the Seng wolf at bay.

"Where do you want to start?" Lianne asked.

"At the beginning, of course. The Neolithic blade."

Kyle was intensely curious about the jade artifact that had made her stare and then stare again, until finally something that looked like fear drained color from her face. But he didn't say anything aloud about the subject of fear. At this point their alliance was too fragile to take any kind of strain.

For an instant Kyle wondered what he had gotten himself into. Then Lianne stepped past him to the display case and he breathed in the heady, delicate fragrance of lilies and rain. It went through him like a combination of peace and adrenaline, soothing his mind and revving his body.

"This blade," Lianne said, "which many Chinese would refer to as a shovel—"

"Why?" he interrupted.

"Wen says that in ancient times people used digging sticks with an edge like that. Some academics say that it's more an adze than a shovel. In any case, we all agree that objects like this are modeled after a blade of some kind, an artifact that was important enough to the culture to be included in rituals."

Kyle nodded.

"This blade," Lianne continued, gesturing toward the case, "is *pih,* one of the eight traditional categories of jade colors."

"Green?"

"Moss green. Some might call it spinach. In any case, this blade is an excellent example of buried jade."

"Grave goods."

"Exactly. They have always been valued by Europeans. Among the overseas Chinese, the old mainland prejudice against collecting grave goods is almost gone. The stains on this blade are the result of thousands of years spent in a tomb. The Chinese have a long and exacting aesthetic tradition with regard to weathered jade."

The reverence in her tone when she said "stains" made Kyle's eyebrows lift. "Stains, huh? Aren't they valued simply as an indicator of age?"

"In some cases. For a Chinese collector, the true importance of these particular stains would be that they enhance rather than diminish the impact of the totemic patterns carved into the blade itself."

"So I've been told. But I have to say, that's one of the aspects of jade appreciation that eludes me."

"Why?" Lianne asked, looking up at him.

"The jade was selected, carved, polished, and buried by human hands. The stains just came along randomly, a byproduct of being stuck in wet earth near a corpse."

Lianne's eyes gleamed behind her thick black lashes as she smiled. "A very Western point of view."

"That's me, born and raised."

"Me, too. Wen has lectured me many times about my lack of subtlety in jade appreciation. The placement of accidental stains is one of the things I had difficulty with."

"Had?"

"Now I think of the stains in the same way the carver thought of the stone before he went to work."

Kyle looked from the blade to Lianne. "I don't understand."

"Every piece of jade is different. It's the carver's duty and joy to reveal the object hidden within the stone."

He nodded. "I get that part of it. Applied human skill and intelligence."

"And the stains," Lianne said softly, "are the condensations of time, as much a part of the jade today as the original stone or the carver's skill. If time blurs the design or breaks the stone, the value of the whole is diminished. If time enhances the object, the result is a magnificent, multilevel piece of art, like the one you can't keep your eyes off for more than ten seconds."

Almost guiltily, Kyle looked back at Lianne. Her smile turned her eyes the color of dark honey.

"I wasn't complaining," she said. "I love seeing someone who is genuinely fascinated by jade, rather than just collecting it to impress other people or because it's the latest investing craze."

"Even though I prefer unstained jade?"

She laughed. "Just remember that the placement of stains on buried jade is very important to the Chinese collector."

"What about Americans? Don't their preferences count?"

"They can love or hate stains on buried jade, but it doesn't change the fact that stains which add to the aesthetic power of a piece drive up the price, especially in a mixed Asian-Caucasian auction such as this."

"I see a plush future for the Pacific Rim Asian Charities," Kyle said dryly. "But I can't imagine a collector letting go of this Neolithic blade for anything short of disaster or death. It has to be one of a kind. Or is that just my relative inexperience talking?"

Broodingly, Lianne studied the extraordinary blade lying within the case. Stone, yet so infused with time and reverence that the jade fairly glowed.

"No, I can't imagine Wen letting go of it," she said softly, not knowing she had spoken aloud.

A feeling like winter slid down her spine. She wondered what calamity had struck the Tang family, what disaster was so great that Wen Zhi Tang had been forced to sell a piece of the jade collection that had been in the family since the time of the Ming dynasty.

No wonder her father had been too distracted to remember details like a parking voucher for her. No wonder that he was pushing her to provide an opening for the Tang family with Donovan International. If he just would have told her what was going on, she wouldn't have dragged her feet about approaching Kyle. The Tangs might not like admitting it to her, but they *were* family.

Her family.

"Lianne?"

She realized that Kyle had been speaking to her, but even when she tried, she couldn't remember anything he had said. Her thoughts were a turmoil of speculation and unease.

"Excuse me," Lianne said. "I was thinking about . . . jade."

And fear.

It wasn't impatience she had seen in her father's eyes when he talked about the need to contact Kyle Donovan. It was fear.

f o u r

The Sung dynasty jade bowl collected admirers like a magnet sucking up bright metal pins. Asian and Caucasian, collector and collected alike crowded around the single high display case and whispered in mingled awe and avarice.

Carved from a single piece of highly translucent white jade, with hints of pale green in the curves, the bowl was as simple as it was spectacular. It glowed like a dawn moon against the dark velvet of the case. The discreet card said two things: the jade belonged to Richard Farmer, and it was not for sale.

"Normally I don't care for Sung pieces," Kyle said, staring over the heads of several people at the case. "This one might rearrange my prejudices. Just as well it isn't for sale. It would take pockets as deep as Dick Farmer's to buy it. Is he one of your clients?"

"I've never dealt directly with him," Lianne said.

Kyle wondered if she was being intentionally evasive. Farmer could be a client of hers and still never have seen her face-to-face. A self-made multibillionaire in the gray world of international technology resale, Farmer had legions of people sweating with eagerness to take care of his business for him. And his billions.

"Do you know who acquired this bowl for Farmer?" Kyle asked.

"Chang Wo Sun would be my guess."

"Never heard of him. Is he a jade player?"

"No. He's a facilitator for SunCo."

"I didn't know SunCo had any deals going with Farmer."

"They don't. Yet. I suspect the bowl is part of a rather complex and very Chinese courtship ritual."

As Lianne spoke, she stood on tiptoe and tried to look over two men to see the Sung bowl. When her view was cut off by a casual shift of shoulders, she made a frustrated sound.

Then she made a startled one as the floor dropped beneath her feet until she was head and shoulders above the crowd, suspended between Kyle's big hands.

"Better view?" he asked blandly.

"Much. Um, thanks."

"All part of the stuffed-elephant service."

Lianne laughed even as she wondered if he felt the sudden drumming of her heart the way she felt the warmth of his hands locked around her ribs. She hoped he would assume that the sudden speeding of her heart came from surprise, rather than from a simple feminine response to the heat and strength of the man holding her.

After the first few breaths, Lianne decided that she liked the view very well indeed. Just below her, a woman's intricate hair ornament dipped and swayed like a pearl ballerina as the woman tilted her head from side to side, studying the elegant Sung bowl. Just over her shoulder, a man's head revealed a bald spot on top, a natural tonsure he tried to conceal by combing hair over it. A delegation from mainland China stood to one side of the case. In defiance of Seattle civic law, they had cigarette smoke like a permanent fog over their heads.

And when Lianne looked over her shoulder, she saw that the same man who had followed her in lockstep from her car was still behind her. He was trying quietly, quickly, urgently to fade out of her newly enhanced line of sight.

Gotcha.

Lianne smiled with grim pleasure even as anxiety prickled hot and cold over her skin. No doubt the man had thought keeping track of her discreetly would be easy—just follow the tall Anglo, and short, little old Lianne would never be far away.

"Don't worry, I won't drop you," Kyle said, feeling the sudden tension in Lianne's body. "I've carried packs heavier than you over high mountain passes."

"I'm not worried about you."

The man who had succeeded in pulling the crowd around him like a multicolored fog was another thing entirely. He worried Lianne. She stared at the people behind her for a minute longer, but didn't see him again. He had vanished as though he was no more than a product of her imagination.

And maybe he was. Maybe she was just jumpy about wearing nearly a million dollars in jade jewelry that wasn't hers.

"Thanks, I've seen enough," Lianne said.

Kyle lowered her to the floor, leaned down, and asked against her ear, "Did you recognize him?"

The flinch of surprise that she couldn't conceal told Kyle that he was right: her attention hadn't been on jade.

"I don't know what you mean," Lianne said.

Disappointment and impatience flared in Kyle. Apparently the little lady thought he was as stupid as a stuffed elephant.

"Right," he said, opening a path away from the Sung bowl. "What's next on your jade agenda?"

"The auction won't begin for two hours. What exhibits haven't you seen?"

"The buffet," Kyle said bluntly. "Or did you eat dinner before you came?"

"No. I was too nervous," she admitted.

"About what?" he asked casually, leading her out of the atrium toward the buffet that had been set up in the ballroom.

"The Jade Trader exhibit," she said, only half the truth. But she wasn't about to admit to Kyle that the thought of having to approach him had tied her stomach in knots. "It was my responsibility to choose the jades."

"I thought the patriarch would have done that."

"Wen?"

"Last time I checked, he was the grand old man of the Tang clan."

"He is. It's just that he's . . . awfully busy," Lianne finished weakly.

Kyle gave her a sideways look that said he wasn't buying that one, either.

She told herself that Wen's health was an open secret, one that Kyle would be sharing as soon as she introduced him into the Tang family.

"Wait," she said, pressing against Kyle's arm. Standing on tiptoe, she leaned close enough to speak without being overheard. "Wen's eyesight is very bad. Even his touch isn't reliable anymore. Arthritis, I guess, but no one speaks of it. Yet he still took part in the exhibit. Joe passed Wen's suggestions on to Harry or Johnny, who gave them to me."

Kyle tried not to let Lianne's unique scent distract him from the main point: one of the world's wealthiest trading families was undergoing a quiet change in leadership. Following the shock of Hong Kong's reversion to mainland China, Wen's increasing frailty must have had the many branches of the Tang family scrambling and clawing to see who would lead the clan through the profitable minefields of the twenty-first century.

"Joe? Harry? Johnny?" Kyle asked.

"Joe Ju Tang is Wen's oldest son. Harry Ju Tang is the second oldest. Johnny is his youngest."

"You know them well?"

"Yes," Lianne said, no expression on her face. "The Tang family is very interested in jade. They are among my biggest clients."

Kyle kept his face as blank as Lianne's while he guided her toward the tables of hors d'oeuvres. As he handed her a plate, he asked casually, "What does the Tang family have to say about the Jade Emperor's Tomb?"

She shrugged. "The same thing everybody else is saying."

"Which is?"

Lianne gave him a look, but his attention was on the spectacular variety of hors d'oeuvres, as though the conversation was merely polite rather than pointed.

"A combination of curiosity and naked greed," she said, reaching for some miniature pot stickers. The aroma lifting from the spicy morsels of sausage wrapped in thin dough had her mouth watering. "The collectors are dancing in place, dying to know whether their personal collections will be enhanced or diminished by the tomb goods."

"You think that fine blade might have come from the Jade Emperor's Tomb?" Kyle asked.

"I . . . don't know. Anything is possible, I suppose."

He put a tiny, incredibly delicate spring roll in his mouth and chewed, watching Lianne without seeming to. It wasn't exactly hard duty. Her cheekbones would have made a model weak with envy. Light shimmered and flowed like a lover's breath over her black hair. Her lips were full, ripe, inviting.

And she was lying through her white, even teeth about the Neolithic blade. She had a good idea where it came from. Kyle was as certain of this as he was that her heart had beaten very quickly beneath his hands when he lifted her above the crowd. He wondered if her response had come from fear or desire. Or both. Then he wondered if he would find out Lianne's truth before he found out the truth of the Jade Emperor's grave.

Lianne popped one of the pot stickers in her mouth and made a murmurous, humming sound of pleasure that drew Kyle's body tight with a hunger that no amount of hors d'oeuvres would ever satisfy.

"God," she said, almost shivering with pleasure. "Food like this must be against the law. Are the spring rolls nearly as good?"

"You tell me." He tucked one of the crispy morsels between her lips and watched while she chewed and swallowed.

"Incredible," she said, then added in dismay, "but I'll never be able to taste all of it before I'm full."

The look of distress on Lianne's face as she eyed the table of hors d'oeuvres would have made Kyle laugh, but he wanted too badly to lick up the tiny crumb of roll that was clinging to the corner of her mouth. The need twisted inside him with startling force. Even as he told himself he had been without a woman too long, he felt an unsettling certainty that he could have just crawled out of bed with a female and he still would want Lianne Blakely.

"You can stuff my pockets," he offered.

"Don't tempt me." She laughed, then looked at the table again and sighed. "If only we had some decent wine . . . What a feast."

"I know the chef. She understands wine. Obviously none of the wines here tonight were her choice."

Lianne's hand paused on the way back from an hors d'oeuvre plate. A small, ginger-spiced shrimp hovered on a bright toothpick next to her open lips. "You know the chef?"

"Yeah. Now eat that shrimp before I do."

The unsubtle threat in Kyle's voice surprised her more than the excellent food. Hastily, she offered the shrimp and several other tidbits besides.

"You should have told me you were starving," Lianne said when Kyle instantly polished off every scrap she gave him. "We could have come to the buffet first. Who's the chef?"

"Mei O'Toole. Her husband works for Donovan International. She and her sisters got tired of hearing about fusion cooking that ignored Asia and decided to show Seattle how Pacific Rim cooking should be done. They opened the Rain Lotus two months ago."

"I should have guessed," Lianne said, seeing for the first time the discreet card indicating which restaurant had donated the table of food. "I've been trying to get into that place since I heard about it. They're booked solid for the next six months."

"How about tonight after the auction?" Kyle asked. "Or were you planning on staying for the dance?"

"No, I wasn't, and what about tonight?"

"A late supper for two at the Rain Lotus."

Lianne simply stared at him. "You're kidding."

"Nope. All part of the stuffed-elephant escort service."

"I'd love any kind of supper at the Rain Lotus—early, late, or middle."

He smiled at her eagerness. Whoever said that the way to a woman's heart was a diamond bracelet hadn't met Lianne. Maybe he could feed her until she begged for mercy, and then he could quiz her on the Tang family and the Jade Emperor's stolen art.

"It's a deal," Kyle said. "I take you to supper and you tell me what you've heard about the Jade Emperor."

She shook her head. "Not you, too."

"Me what?"

"Part of the Jade Emperor craze."

"Why should I be immune to the hottest jade rumors since Chiang Kai-shek creamed mainland China's treasures on the way to Taiwan?"

"Unlike Chiang Kai-shek, there's no proof that the Jade Emperor ever existed, much less that he had a tomb filled with jade from all previous eras of Chinese history," Lianne pointed out.

As she spoke, she filled her plate with an anticipation and hunger she didn't bother to conceal. Idly Kyle wondered if she approached sex that way—directly, openly. When she tucked a bit of crab between her lips, then licked her fingertips, his curiosity took on a more urgent edge.

"Assume the Jade Emperor existed," Kyle said, turning away and filling his own plate at random. Anything that came from Mei O'Toole's kitchen was fine with him. "And assume his grave was found."

"When?" Lianne said, chewing and swallowing quickly. "Before or after Mao?"

"Does it matter?"

"If the goods left mainland China before Mao, the problem of rightful ownership is sticky but not insurmountable."

"Like your fingers?"

Caught with her tongue in mid-lick, Lianne managed to look both guilty and defiant. "There aren't any chopsticks, and the toothpicks are too slippery."

Kyle laughed and wished he knew Lianne well enough to lick those elegant, saucy fingertips himself. "But provenance is insurmountable after Mao?" he asked, watching her closely.

She nodded, hesitated, then calmly finished licking hoisin sauce from the side of her finger before she put another hors d'oeuvre in her mouth. Slowly her eyes closed while the flavors and textures melted through her.

"Unbelievable," Lianne said, and reached for another sliver of duck in a tiny nest of shredded raw vegetables. The second bite was even better than the first. She savored it as she reached for a third tidbit. "Addictive."

Kyle forced himself to look away from her intriguing sensual pleasure. "Why are things stickier after Mao?" he asked after a moment.

"Because it became illegal to export anything more than fifty or a hundred years old from China. Except people," Lianne added wryly. "They aren't considered cultural treasures."

"Since when has provenance become such a problem for collectors? An avid collector is the last one to look a gift horse in the mouth."

"Of course. But when the U.S. and China started to do the trade dance, provenance became a hot-button topic. You can still buy, sell, and own anything your morals are comfortable with; you just can't display black market goods publicly anymore."

Kyle wondered where Lianne drew the line on collectors

and ethics, but he didn't ask. That would have been as rash as sucking sauce off her fingers.

A large group of Japanese men approached the buffet tables. Despite the clots of people standing around the food, the men proceeded to go through the buffet as though no one else was in the room. There was nothing intentionally rude in their actions. They were simply accustomed to being at the top of the cultural pecking order.

"Good thing we filled our plates," Kyle said, guiding Lianne away from the sudden crowd. "So when was the Jade Emperor's Tomb found?"

"Who said it was found at all?"

"Lots of people."

Lianne didn't bother to argue. She was too busy enjoying a mouthful of lobster in a sauce that tasted like a rainbow with just a tiny bite of lightning at the finish.

"I've heard that the tomb was found during the civil war, before Mao was in power," she said, swallowing. "I've heard that the tomb was found twenty years later. And I've heard that it was dug up last year." She shrugged. "What have you heard?"

"I'm new to the jade game. I've just heard a few rumors. But if the tomb exists, it holds the result of a lifetime of collecting by a man whose bank account was as big as China and whose whim was law. Can you imagine it?"

"I try not to. I especially try not to think what he might have collected from the Warring States period, which is my special jade passion."

"Passion or obsession?"

"I don't have the money to be obsessive."

He smiled. "And I try not to think about what the Jade Emperor would have collected from Neolithic times, which is my passion. Yet I can't help imagining what it would be like to discover the greatest collection of Chinese jades ever assembled on earth."

"Dream on."

"Hey, it's free. But if a collection like that was found and smuggled out of China, how would it be sold?"

"That's what makes me think it hasn't been found," Lianne said simply. "There hasn't been a sale of that size."

"Maybe you weren't invited."

"Doesn't matter. It would be impossible to hide a concentration of previously unknown jade artifacts of that quality. Nobody gossips like collectors."

Kyle finished off his plate of hors d'oeuvres and started stealing from Lianne's. She threatened him with a scarlet toothpick. Since she gave him plenty of time to evade, he didn't take the threat seriously.

"How about stealing a few pieces at a time?" he asked.

"Are we talking about my food or the mythical emperor's jade?"

He smiled but didn't quit snitching her hors d'oeuvres. "Jade."

"Breaking up the collection would diminish its value, but . . ." Lianne beat Kyle to the last spring roll on her plate and chewed thoughtfully, considering the possibilities. "It would explain why no one is able to pin down the rumors."

"Want more?" Kyle gestured toward the Rain Lotus's buffet table.

"Am I breathing?"

His laughter made her laugh in return, but what she liked best was the way humor took the calculation out of his eyes, leaving only a beauty that appealed to her as much as jade. For a few moments she felt like a woman on a date with a very interesting man. With a pleasure that had nothing to do with anticipating more food, she watched him load their plates.

Then, Lianne saw Johnny Tang approaching her. Pleasure evaporated, replaced by a cool, yearning kind of reserve.

"Hello, Johnny," she said. "Come to check up on the Jade Trader exhibit?"

"Naturally."

She waited, but he didn't say anything more. "What did you think of it?" she asked.

"Excellent, of course. With Tang family jade and your feel for American tastes, how could it be anything else?"

"I didn't ignore Chinese aesthetics in the Jade Trader exhibit," Lianne said stiffly.

Johnny waved his hand, dismissing her instant defense of her knowledge and taste.

"The Tangs are known to the Chinese," Johnny said calmly. "It is the Americans who must be cultivated, especially since Hong Kong is no longer independent. Speaking of cultivating—"

"Kyle," Lianne interrupted swiftly, seeing him approach behind her father, "this is Johnny Tang. Johnny, Kyle Donovan."

Relief loosened Johnny's face for an instant, but when he turned to Kyle, nothing showed except polite interest.

"Mr. Donovan," he said, offering his hand.

Lianne took a plate from Kyle so that the men could go through the small, necessary social ritual of shaking hands.

"Did Wen come with you?" she asked Johnny.

"No. He's saving his energy for tonight."

"Ah, yes. The family gathering."

Kyle noticed the slight, biting emphasis Lianne put on the word *family*.

If Johnny noticed, he didn't show it. "My father would, of course, be happy to have you join us for our little party after the auction. Please bring Mr. Donovan with you." He turned to Kyle. "We Tangs admire the family of Donovan. I'm sure there will be much of interest to talk about."

Lianne hoped her expression was as bland as Johnny's. She had wondered what it would take for her to be invited to a Tang family gathering. Now she knew.

She didn't like it.

"Thank you," Kyle said, "but it's up to Lianne where we go after the auction."

"Then we will see you," Johnny said with satisfaction. "Lianne wouldn't disappoint Wen."

After another minute or two, Johnny excused himself and merged with the crowd that was slowly edging toward the auction room, as though sheer impatience could hurry the pace of the evening.

"Finished?" Kyle asked.

Lianne looked at her plate. It was as clean as her fingernails, yet she didn't remember eating even half of the hors d'oeuvres. "More importantly, are you?"

"Will there be food at the Tang party?"

"Oh, yes. Mountains of it. It's a necessary part of entertaining guests."

"Is the food any good?"

"That depends. Do you like traditional Asian cuisine as well as the fusion kind?"

"I'll pass on the hundred-year chicken embryos," Kyle said, "but I can nosh on poached chicken digits with the best of them."

"Great. I'll give mine to you."

"What about the hundred-year eggs?"

"In a word? Yuck. But the rest of the food is very good."

"Then I'll last until after the auction."

Kyle stacked their empty plates on a waiter's tray, tucked her hand over his arm, and led her back to the atrium.

"You don't have to go," Lianne told him.

"Look at more jade?"

"No. To the Tang party."

"The food is good and you wouldn't want to disappoint your best clients, would you?"

Clients.

Lianne tried to think of a simple, brief way to explain her long, complex relationship with the family of Tang. None came to mind. It was just one of the many awkward moments she had endured as the unacknowledged daughter of Johnny Tang.

"No, I wouldn't want to disappoint them," she said finally.

Then Lianne smiled sadly. What a joke. She had disappointed them since the instant of her birth, living proof of Johnny Tang's liaison with a foreign woman.

"Mind if I ask a question?" Kyle said. He felt the sudden tension in Lianne's hand on his arm and looked down at her. "Professional, not personal."

"About the Tangs?"

"No. About that tiny little purse of yours."

Lianne looked down at the slim silk envelope that swayed at the end of its long, thin strap. The purse weighed so little she had forgotten she was carrying it.

"What about it?" she asked.

"Most of the serious traders here tonight are making notes at each exhibit."

She nodded.

"Your purse is too small to hold a notebook," he said, "but it just might be big enough for a high-tech recorder. Verbal notes, as it were."

"I'll take your word for it. My purse is empty except for a car key and business cards." She didn't feel it necessary to add that she also had a small vial of pepper spray tucked away.

"Does that mean you aren't a serious trader?" Kyle asked.

"No. It means that I have a photographic memory."

"Good. Then you should have no problem describing the guy who's following you."

f i v e

*L*ianne thought about denying that she was being followed. Then she thought about facing the night alone if Kyle called her bluff and walked out.

"Caucasian, about five feet ten inches," she said, fighting to keep her voice even, "medium weight, clean-shaven, brownish hair, white shirt, black tuxedo that doesn't quite fit across the stomach, street rather than dress shoes, and an uncanny ability to melt into a crowd."

Kyle whistled softly. "Sounds like you've seen a lot of him."

"I saw him once, tonight, for about three seconds when you boosted me above the crowd."

"Photographic memory," he muttered.

"Yes."

"How long has he been following you?"

"Him personally? I don't know. Several times in the past few weeks, I've been certain that someone was following me."

"Why?"

"I don't know."

Kyle looked at Lianne as she walked next to him. Her chin was up in a stubborn line and her spine was very straight above the inevitable swaying of her hips. Jade jewelry glowed against white silk like spring against ice.

"Try again," he suggested softly.

Lianne's chin tilted up even more, but she couldn't conceal the frisson of unease that went through her body. "It's the truth. I don't know why I'm being followed."

"Guess."

"The jewelry, maybe."

"Have you worn it in the last few weeks?"

"No."

"Then guess again."

She tried to take her arm out of his, only to find herself held in place.

"I don't feel like playing Twenty Questions," Lianne said roughly. "If you're so worried about that man, all you have to do is walk away from me."

"Did you dump a lover recently?"

Her eyelids flickered as she remembered Lee Chin, now called Tang. But she hadn't seen him except in passing for two years. In any case, she hadn't dumped him. She had just declined to continue their affair after he married one of her Tang cousins and took the Tang family name for his own.

"No," Lianne said. "No recent lovers, dumped or otherwise."

"No outraged admirers?"

"Not a one."

"How about your family? Are they on anyone's shit list?"

"Recently?" She shrugged. "No more than usual."

"What's usual?"

"My mother is Johnny Tang's mistress," Lianne said neutrally. "She has been for over thirty years. That puts her high on the Tang shit list, but it's old news."

Kyle loosened his grip on Lianne's arm slightly. Though his hand still covered hers, his fingertips stroked over the backs of her fingers. He nudged her toward a quiet corner of the atrium, where examples of fine calligraphy were on display. Calligraphy was the Asian version of abstract art; without extensive education and training, most people didn't appreciate it. That meant an island of privacy in the teeming room.

"Have you bought or sold any hotly contested jades lately?" Kyle asked quietly. "Pissed off any shady collectors?"

Lianne shook her head and pretended to concentrate on the calligraphy. "I told you. I don't know why I'm being followed."

He shifted until he could see what was going on behind her. There were swirls of people around most exhibits, plenty of black tuxedos mixed in with the rainbow silks and gleaming gems, and more Caucasians than Asians. The man Lianne had described could be within fifteen feet of them right now.

He almost certainly was.

"What about Seng?" Kyle asked.

"If he has any Caucasian employees, I haven't met them."

"He could hire someone."

"It's not Seng's style."

"What isn't?"

"Sneaking around. He's the frontal-attack sort," Lianne said, her mouth thin.

"Has he attacked you?" Kyle asked sharply.

"Not exactly. But he's made it real clear that I should be delighted to warm his sheets for a night or two."

"What happened when you refused?"

"He barely noticed. All in all, Seng makes a sumo wrestler look like a mountain of subtlety."

When Kyle gave a muffled sound of laughter, Lianne looked up from the calligraphy and smiled slightly.

"No telephone calls, no notes, no presents, no threats?" he persisted.

"Nothing. Just a prickle at the back of my neck and a shadow sliding away at the corner of my vision."

"You should have gone for the great-white-hunter-type escort, not the stuffed elephant."

"You don't have to—" she began.

"Let's look at some more jade," Kyle cut in. "Maybe your mysterious admirer will get careless, trip over my big feet, and break his neck."

Startled, Lianne glanced at Kyle. He was smiling, but his eyes weren't. They were narrowed, measuring the nearby crowd. If she hadn't met Kyle at her father's urging, she might have been very wary of him, wondering if she had just stumbled out of the frying pan into the firing line.

"How about another look at that Neolithic blade?" Kyle suggested.

Lianne stretched her legs and kept pace with him. She was eager to see the piece again. She kept telling herself that it couldn't be from the Tang family vault. She must have been wrong the first time.

Must have, but couldn't be.

Doubt and certainty haunted her equally. Her visual memory had never played that kind of trick on her. Her uncanny accuracy was a lot of the reason she had gained a valuable reputation as an expert in all varieties and ages of jade.

The people milling around the SunCo display were concentrated on the intricate, decorative Han and Six Dynasties pieces, leaving the Neolithic items less well attended. Still hoping that she had been wrong the first time, Lianne inspected the ancient blade.

It took less than a minute for her to know that she hadn't been wrong. The picture in her mind and the blade in the case matched too exactly to be anything but one and the same artifact.

Unsettled and uneasy, Lianne watched while Kyle circled the case several times. The look in his eyes told her that he was completely under the jade's spell.

"You aren't thinking of bidding on it, are you?" she asked finally.

"Is that a problem?"

"I hope not."

"Are you going to bid on it?"

"I . . . yes," Lianne said, sighing. "I really don't have any choice."

"Why?"

She didn't answer. She simply turned away from the blade and went to stand at another SunCo display. This case featured Neolithic work as well, but it was thousands of years "younger" than the blade that haunted her.

Kyle watched Lianne, wondering what it was about the fine blade that brought unhappiness, perhaps even fear, to her dark cognac eyes.

"I thought Warring States jade was your passion," he said.

"As a rule."

"And this Neolithic blade is the exception that proves the rule?"

She made a sound that could have meant anything, then looked up at Kyle. "Have you seen this case? It has extraordinary examples of Shang work," she said carefully, "fully as exceptional as the blade."

Reluctantly Kyle shifted his attention away from the blade to the case where Lianne stood. Inside the elegant glass cage, two jade bracelets rested on burgundy velvet.

"Notice particularly the bracelet on the right," she said. "At some time in the past, the jade was burned, perhaps in a tomb fire, perhaps later in a collector's home that was destroyed by war."

"How do you know?"

"Nephrite—Chinese jade—only takes on that chalky, pale beige, 'chicken bone' color after it has been burned in fires as hot as one thousand degrees. The heat changes the chemistry of the jade. It becomes opaque, the original color fades to near white, but the carving itself remains as clear and distinct as when it first came from the artisan's hands. Time and fire have altered the main color, yet left the darker, veinlike patterning of the stone intact. The result is striking."

"Enhanced by time."

Her smile flashed briefly. "You're a quick student. Or am I going over things you already know?"

"Like I said, I'll tell you if I get bored. What else do you see when you look at the chicken-bone jade bracelet?"

"In profile, it would be slightly concave rather than straight."

Kyle looked more closely, then nodded.

"Not only is a curved profile more difficult to make than a straight one," she said, "but the carver was skillful and patient enough to keep the thickness of the bracelet the same no matter the degree of the curve."

He bent down, then sat on his heels to view the bracelet from another angle.

"In the machine age," Lianne said, "we take that kind of precision for granted. Yet this bracelet is from the Liangzhu culture, perhaps five thousand years old."

Kyle heard what she said, and he heard what she wasn't saying, too. She appreciated the jade bracelet, respected the tradition it sprang from, admired the result, and had no desire to bid on it herself.

"What makes the Neolithic blade superior to this bracelet?" Kyle asked.

"Nothing."

"Yet you're not going to bid on this bracelet."

"No."

"Why?"

"It's personal, not professional," Lianne said.

"In other words, none of my business."

"As I said, you're a quick student."

Kyle stood with a swift, fluid power that startled her into stepping backward.

"You're quick, period," Lianne said.

"Youngest brothers have to be, or they're chopped meat."

She stared for a moment, trying to imagine the tall, rangy man in front of her as a boy. "How many brothers do you have?"

"Three, all older than me. Two younger sisters."

Lianne smiled wistfully. "Five siblings. What fun that must be."

"Yeah, a regular six-ring circus."

Yet Kyle was smiling despite his dry words. He butted heads with his brothers on a regular basis, his independent and stubborn sisters made him crazy, yet he wouldn't have traded any of it for peace and quiet. At least not on a permanent basis.

Once in a while, though, he wanted distance. After the fiasco in Kaliningrad with the stolen amber, he had needed a lot of space to lick his wounds and think about all the stupid things he shouldn't have done and would never do again if he could help it. When thinking got too painful, he stepped aboard the *Tomorrow,* cast off, and went fishing, letting the hours and days slide away.

"Does your family live here?" Lianne asked.

"Some of them, some of the time. Mostly we're scattered all over the planet. Comes of running an international import-export business."

"Donovan International."

"In my case, Donovan Gems and Minerals," Kyle said. "The four brothers got together and went into business for ourselves. We're an independent affiliate of Dad's company."

"But still very close to him," she said.

"No help for it. The Donovan is as hard to get rid of as cat hair."

"The Donovan?"

"That's what we call Dad. Among other things."

Lianne frowned. "Don't you get along?"

"Sure. Usually at the top of our voices. Then Susa—that's our mother—spreads balm and cracks heads until peace is restored."

Lianne tried to imagine what it would be like to be part of a noisy, affectionate family. It was impossible. Her memories of childhood were quiet, almost adult in their tranquility.

Her mother had worked very hard to make her home an oasis of peace for her paramour. Not that Lianne had been neglected. She hadn't. She and her mother were quite close, more like lifelong friends than parent and child.

Slowly Lianne followed Kyle to another display case. This one held a variety of Western Zhou jade objects. The stone was very fine-textured, almost glassy in its finish. All but one piece featured bird or dragon designs on the translucent green surface. All glowed with the subtle inner light that only fine jade had.

"It must be wonderful, having a big family like that," Lianne said.

"It has its moments." Kyle's flashing smile said more than his words. "I think we've all prayed to be an only child at one time or another. What do you think of these?"

Reluctantly she looked away from Kyle's burnished blond hair and infectious smile to the jades. "If these are any example, I think SunCo has a fine collection of Western Zhou jades. The designs are very cleanly executed. Do you know why that era preferred birds and dragons for its motifs?"

Kyle shook his head. "I've had enough trouble learning the rudiments of Neolithic or 'cultural' jades. I haven't had time to appreciate the rest of the jade eras."

"Birds were a symbol of gentleness, and dragons of moderation."

His dark blond eyebrows lifted. "Moderation? *Dragons?*"

"The Chinese saw dragons differently than the Celts. The Celts saw violence and danger, death and the opportunity for man to test himself against sheer brute strength. The Chinese see dragons as immortal, patient, wise, and infinitely subtle."

"Sounds dangerous to me. Especially the subtlety. The Christian devil is immortal, reasonably patient, and as subtle as the ten thousand gradations of sin."

"But not moderate?" Lianne asked, smiling slightly.

"Nope. Are you going to bid on any of these?"

"At the moment, none of my collectors have a request in for Western Zhou jades."

"Who wants the Neolithic blade?"

"It would be unethical for me to discuss clients with you."

"Why?" Kyle asked easily. "I'm a stuffed elephant, not a client or a competitor."

"You're a stuffed elephant with a passion for Neolithic jade," she retorted.

"Right now, I'm a relieved stuffed elephant."

"Relieved? Why?"

"When you said your interest in the blade was personal, I was afraid you would be mad if I bid against you and won. But now that I know you have a client in mind . . ." He smiled and spread his big hands. "Business is business, and may the best bidder win."

Caught in a trap of her own making, Lianne gripped the strap of her purse more tightly. If she admitted that she didn't have a client, Kyle would want to know why she was bidding on a Neolithic blade when her personal passion was supposed to be Warring States jades. If she told him she thought the blade belonged to Wen Zhi Tang, that would open up a floodgate of questions, none of them comfortable or easily answered.

The longer she thought about the blade, the more it bothered her. An outright sale was the most likely explanation for the blade's presence in the SunCo display, but Lianne couldn't believe that a key part of her grandfather's Neolithic blade collection had been sold without her knowledge. Though nothing had ever been said outright, the care of the Tang family's extensive jade holdings had gradually passed to her as Wen's eyes and hands failed him. Yesterday, when she removed the jade pieces she had selected from the vault, the various collections had appeared to be intact.

Not that she had checked them piece by piece. There was no need, except on the rare occasions when the jades were being loaned for various exhibitions. The Tang jade collection was kept behind thick steel doors and heavy combination locks. Jade was a significant portion of Wen's personal wealth. More important, the collections were the heart and pride of the Tang family.

The simplest explanation for the Neolithic blade Lianne had seen tonight was that she had made a mistake in thinking that it was her grandfather's. In other words, her memory, talent, training, and experience had failed her. Completely.

It wasn't a comforting explanation. Nor was it one she could easily accept. The only way to be certain was to get her hands on the blade, take it to the Tang vaults, and see if it had a twin in Wen's collection. If it didn't . . . well, that would lead to more questions, questions whose answers would be as unsettling as the fear she had seen in Johnny Tang's eyes.

Kyle noticed Lianne's growing tension. Her slender fingers were wrapped around her purse strap with enough force to make her knuckles white. He didn't know why the Neolithic blade meant so much to her, much less why it made her unhappy just to think about it, but he was sure it did.

Undoubtedly Lianne knew more about the blade than she had told him. Yet. It was just a matter of gaining more of her trust. From what she had said about the Tang family, she was pretty much on her own. Vulnerable.

Easy prey.

The realization should have made Kyle feel good, because it made his job easier. *You want me to seduce the illegitimate American daughter of a Hong Kong trading family in order to discover whether she's involved in the sale of cultural treasures stolen from China?*

Yeah. Except for the seduction part. That's optional.

Unfortunately, the idea of seduction was appealing more and more to Kyle with every moment he spent inhaling the lilies-and-rain essence of Lianne. All he had to do in order to satisfy his hunger was to get his conscience to take a brief holiday. Maybe if he reminded himself often enough that she was the one who had begun the game, he wouldn't feel like a jerk for taking advantage of her.

"Relax," Kyle said easily. "I'm sure your client has a ceiling. If the price of the Neolithic blade goes over his limit, he can't blame you for not buying."

"I have to register for the auction. What about you?"

"Same here. I hadn't planned on bidding until I saw the blade."

Lianne's mouth tightened into a downward-turning arc, a reflection of the cold certainty that had settled in her stomach. The price she could pay for the Neolithic blade wasn't nearly as high as the price Kyle Donovan could pay.

s i x

During the pause between the second and third sessions of the auction, the auction room remained filled with people, whispers, perfumes, and the slithery whisper of silk dresses against synthetic panty hose. Spectators sat separate from bidders and enjoyed the drama. Inexperienced bidders sat with their catalogs dog-eared, note-ridden, and open to the piece they wanted. The bidding paddles they clutched were cream parchment with bold, stylized numbers on both sides.

Experienced bidders were more relaxed, or at least appeared to be. Their catalogs were closed, their paddles casually held. They already knew what they would bid on any given piece, and the line they wouldn't cross between profit and desire to possess. Auction fever was for innocents.

Whether it was due to charity or the rising international interest in Asian art objects, the bidding had been aggressive. No bargains were walking out of the hotel tonight. A Warring States bronze with gold, silver, and copper inlay had brought one hundred and fifteen thousand dollars. A large, very nice Ming vase had just sold for more than seven hundred thousand dollars.

A collective sigh went through the crowd when the palm-sized gong sounded, signifying that the bidding on the third session was about to begin. Catalogs rustled and shimmered in the bright light as pages were turned to the first group up for auction. As with the bronzes and porcelains, the bidding was brisk.

Seated down in front with the rest of the bidders, Lianne became progressively more nervous as piece after piece of jade was presented, bid on, and sold. The single piece of jade that Wen had agreed to part with for charity—a rather ordinary Ch'ing dynasty *shoulao,* or sculpture of an old man with a walking stick—had been bid up to a surprising seven thousand dollars before the gong sounded. The Shang dynasty bracclets had gone for six thousand dollars. Each. The Warring States buckle she had admired had sold on a preemptive bid of five thousand dollars.

The Neolithic blade was next up for auction.

Breathing a silent prayer that the bidding wouldn't go beyond four thousand dollars—preferably twenty-five hundred—Lianne sat back and tried to get a feel for the bidders who were interested in the blade.

The minimum opening bid listed in the catalog was one thousand dollars. Three paddles went up at once, beginning the auction. A single glance told Lianne that the eager paddles belonged to bottom fishers, not serious bidders. The real bidders would be like her, waiting to see who was earnest and who was simply using the auction paddle to fan his face.

"Fifteen hundred," the auctioneer said, scanning the crowd.

Two paddles lifted, then a third. The last one belonged to Charles Singer, the owner of an excellent jade shop in downtown Seattle.

"Two thousand."

Singer's paddle lifted, along with two others.

"Twenty-five hundred."

Again Singer raised his paddle. Only one other person was bidding against him now.

"Three thousand."

No one raised a paddle.

"Come, now, ladies and gentlemen," the auctioneer coaxed. "This is a very fine example of Neolithic artistry. The stone fairly glows with mystery, immortality, and six thousand years of secrets. Surely that's worth at least fifty cents a year to a discerning collector?"

The audience laughed. Singer raised his paddle in the manner of a man who knows he is paying too much but is willing to do it for charity.

"We have three thousand dollars. Will someone bid thirty-three hundred?"

Singer's paddle remained in his lap.

Kyle and Lianne raised their paddles simultaneously. So did a man in the back of the bidding section.

"Excellent," purred the auctioneer. "I just knew this room was full of civic spirit."

The crowd laughed while the bidding quickly rose to thirty-nine hundred dollars. Singer and the man in the rear of the section went head-to-head for another five hundred dollars' worth of bids. Then Singer dropped out, leaving only the anonymous man, whom Lianne couldn't see.

"Forty-five hundred. We have forty-five hundred. Do we have forty-six?"

Lianne held up her paddle. She could just barely afford forty-six hundred . . . if she ate oatmeal for a month and her car stopped using gas and her panty hose didn't run.

"Forty-six. We have forty-six hundred. Do we—thank you, Number One-oh-six. You are a man of civic virtue. We have forty-six hundred. Forty-six hundred. Going once. Do we see forty-seven hundred?"

Kyle looked at Lianne for the first time since the blade had gone up for auction. Behind her professional calm he sensed a seething kind of despair.

"Going twice at forty-six hundred. The next bid is forty-seven hundred, ladies and gentlemen."

In silent question, Kyle touched Lianne's wrist. She let her paddle drop into her lap. She was through bidding. She should have been through at four thousand.

"Going—"

Kyle flicked his paddle into an upright position.

"Thank you, Number One-ten. We have forty-seven hundred. Forty-seven hundred looking for forty-eight. Do we have forty-eight?" the auctioneer asked, looking toward the back of the bidding section. "Forty-eight, thank you. I'm waiting for forty-nine."

"Fifty-nine," Kyle said.

"Fifty-nine. I heard clearly? Fifty-nine hundred for the Neolithic blade?"

Kyle lifted his paddle in confirmation.

There was silence, then a scattering of applause. Though the money was less than many of the other articles had brought that night, the bidding on the blade had been more competitive, thus more entertaining.

As the gong sounded, ending the bidding on the blade, Lianne closed her eyes and wondered what she would do if she looked in Wen's vault and discovered that a very, very fine Neolithic blade was missing.

Wen wouldn't have sold it. The more she thought about it, the more certain she was. Though far from his most valuable piece, the blade was one of Wen's most cherished possessions. It was simply, incredibly, good. Even if he had needed cash desperately, there were other jades that could be sold, other ways to raise cash.

Cold washed through her, a chill that grew with her certainty that the extraordinary blade Kyle now owned had been stolen from Wen Zhi Tang.

"Thank you," the auctioneer said. "Before we move on to the final lot of the evening, Precious and Important Gems of the Pacific Rim, we have a special treat for you. Mr. Richard Farmer, whose white jade Sung bowl many of you admired in the atrium, has graciously agreed to preview some of the magnificent—quite literally *imperial*—artifacts he will be featuring in his soon-to-open Museum of Asian Jade. Indeed, after seeing just a few pieces of this extraordinary collection, I am tempted to crown Mr. Farmer the new Jade Emperor. Please welcome Richard Farmer, international businessman, humanitarian, philanthropist, and jade connoisseur of the highest level!"

Kyle's eyes narrowed at the words *Jade Emperor*. He glanced sideways at Lianne to see how she was taking the announcement. She didn't seem to have heard. Her skin was pale and her eyes were closed. He bent down so that he could speak in her ear, above the sound of applause.

"Lianne? Are you all right?"

She jerked, nodded, and opened her eyes, trying to pretend interest in what was happening around her.

The audience was beating its hands together with real enthusiasm. If it wasn't for Richard Farmer Enterprises Inc., the auction wouldn't have been held tonight and the charity wouldn't have benefited.

Though it was common knowledge that Farmer's philanthropy was as self-serving as his business interests, no one complained. There were too many businesses that didn't bother with philanthropy at all. The fact that Farmer was on his way to owning a considerable chunk of the free world and controlling a lot more through foreign licensing arrangements simply made people more grateful for his streak of charity, however lean it might be.

The lights dimmed dramatically, then came up again to reveal Dick Farmer striding toward the podium, which the auctioneer had abandoned. The curtains had been drawn across the small stage. Farmer's black tuxedo showed vividly against the heavy, lipstick-red velvet of the curtains. He was a man of medium height, unassuming looks, and supreme confidence.

"Thank you, thank you, thank you," Farmer said, picking up the cordless microphone from the podium and going back to center stage like a rock singer or a televangelist. "I'm delighted and overwhelmed to be among such generous patrons of the arts, especially the Asian arts."

Kyle shifted in his uncomfortable seat and wished he had known this was coming. He could have left before all the self-congratulations began. Usually that sort of babble was reserved for the end of a charity event, or the beginning, sometimes both. Pitches at intermission were left for public TV.

If he hadn't been interested in seeing Farmer's jades, Kyle would have stood up and left. And if Farmer blathered on for more than three minutes, Kyle would leave anyway. The Museum of Asian Jade would open in another week; he could see all of Farmer's artifacts then without having to listen to a canned lecture.

"Before I show my jades, I'd like to give those of you who are into painting and ceramics a brief overview of jade's importance in China."

Kyle managed not to groan out loud. Barely.

"As with all precious and semi-precious stones throughout history, jade was believed to have special, even spiritual, properties," Farmer said. "From the very earliest beginning of Chinese civilization, jade was the embodiment of various virtues we like to think of as Christian: loyalty, modesty, wisdom, justice, integrity, and, of course, charity."

The audience murmured appreciatively.

The sound Kyle made was guttural disgust. The closest Farmer came to any of the virtues listed was when he formed the words in his mouth. Farmer was a businessman first, last, and always. He had an unwavering, uncanny instinct for entering international markets at the moment when they were just emerging. He came in when he could buy land and workers for a handful of pennies. When he got out, he sold for a bucketful of diamonds. Governments bitched about the trade-off, but they lined up anyway to lure Farmer into business deals. He created value where nothing had existed before.

Kyle admired the man's marketing genius and jugular instinct. He didn't admire Farmer's efforts to represent himself as an international icon of charity and a gentle, genial prince among men.

"Naturally, when it came time for burial, jade was among the most important items in any grave offerings," Farmer continued. "Jade, the incorruptible stone, was believed to prevent corruption of the human body. Immortality, in a way. Thus, thousands of years ago, men of importance were buried with jade closing all nine openings of the body. In time, man, being man, decided that if nine pieces of jade were good, hundreds of pieces would be better. Thousands would be better still: an entire burial suit of jade plaques sewn together with threads of pure gold, rather like a medieval suit of armor made wholly from precious jade—jade from helmet to boots."

Kyle stopped shifting restlessly and began to listen. Really listen. He wasn't the only one. The room had gone still while Farmer paced the stage and spoke urgently, drawing people into his words, into the vision he was creating of an ancient time.

"That's what Han emperors were buried in," Farmer said. "Suits of pure jade, the Stone of Heaven brought to earth for man. All this at a time when it took months of an artisan's work simply to shape and pierce a single plaque of jade. And the burial shroud had thousands of such plaques.

"The lavish and lavishly aesthetic lifestyle of China's emperors and empresses is well known. What is less well known is that many princes and court functionaries also lived—and died—in ways that Egyptian Pharaohs could only have envied.

"The Han princes are a prime example. Their tombs were filled with the best that whole generations of contemporary and ancient artists could provide. Imagine it: the output of an entire kingdom channeled into providing a tomb to amuse its royal occupants throughout eternity. The cream of the artifacts of an entire civilization skimmed and buried forever."

Farmer let the audience's stillness build, then smiled like a boy. "Well, perhaps not *forever*. Many tombs were robbed before the royal corpses were cold. The fantastic grave goods were brought into the light again and sold to wealthy connoisseurs. But some tombs, a very special few, remained untouched for hundreds, even thousands, of years. The tomb of an individual we call the Jade Emperor is one of those. Or was."

The crowd stirred, as though everyone was sitting up and leaning closer. Kyle and Lianne were no different. They sat forward, afraid to miss a word.

"The Jade Emperor was a prince of the Ming dynasty who dedicated his life to the collection of one thing. Jade. With unlimited time, unlimited power, and the discriminating eye of the true connoisseur, he collected the best that China had to offer. When he died, he took everything to his grave. Of course, it isn't possible tonight for me to bring more than a few things from that tomb. More, much more, will be on view when I open my museum. Until then, ladies and gentlemen, *I give you the Jade Emperor.*"

The crimson velvet curtains parted suddenly. Alone on the stage, impaled by a vertical column of light, a jade burial suit shimmered in ageless shades of green.

Distantly Lianne was aware that her nails were digging into Kyle's hand and that he was holding her fingers hard enough to leave dents. She didn't care. She needed something solid to hang onto, something warm, something strong, something that could balance the queasy fear coiling through her.

In the whole world, she knew of only one jade burial suit in private hands. That suit was in Wen Zhi Tang's vault.

Or had been. Like the Neolithic blade.

Even as Lianne told herself she was crazy, the burial suit she was looking at now couldn't be Wen's, she knew she must examine Farmer's gleaming green prize for herself. Until she did, the sick fear inside her would grow into a nightmarish certainty.

The way it was growing now.

Even at a distance of twenty feet, the suit looked the same

as Wen's. It looked like it was made of plaques of imperial jade, not softer serpentine. Darker on the head, flowing to a pale, creamy green across the torso, deepening to moss on the feet. Gold thread winked everywhere, especially on the sections that covered the face and chest. There the thread was so thick it was like embroidery, a careful series of Xs criss-crossing and outlining each separate plate of jade.

It can't be the same suit.

Without knowing it, Lianne stood and leaned closer to the stage. She wasn't the only one. People in the audience were coming to their feet like corks out of champagne bottles. There was a restless shifting, then a concerted rush toward the stage.

Lianne didn't notice. She was staring at the patterns of jade and gold stitching on Farmer's prize. From where she stood, they were identical with her memories of Wen's suit.

Her throat closed around air that was too thick to breathe. She didn't know which would be worse: being mistaken in identifying the blade and the burial suit, or being right. She tried to get past Kyle, but there was no room.

"Let me by," she demanded urgently. "I have to see it close up."

"You and every other jade lover. I wouldn't mind taking a good look myself. But we're too late. There's a crowd six-deep heading for it right now."

"No, you don't understand. I must examine that suit. Get out of my way!"

He looked sideways at her. Her face was pale, strained, and her body was vibrating with the intensity that had her nails buried in his callused palm. She was tugging and push-ing, trying to get past him in the tightly packed crowd of people.

"Why?" he asked.

Lianne shook her head and said starkly, "Let me by!"

"Stay close. I'll break trail for you."

"Ladies and gentlemen," Farmer said loudly. "Please sit

down. The suit will be on display for the opening of my Museum of Asian Jade. It will remain on display thereafter. Everyone who wishes will have ample time to see the burial shroud."

Perhaps half the people heading for the stage hesitated. The rest just kept on going. Hard-faced guards wearing tuxedos materialized near Farmer.

Towing Lianne behind him, Kyle made for the side of the room. He ignored the startled curses and outraged looks from people whose feet happened to be in his way. Then he saw the guards form a ring around Farmer, who was yelling at them to protect the suit, not him. Soon the guards would become a solid barrier across the stage.

Kyle turned to Lianne. "Faint," he said quietly.

"What?"

"If you want to get close to that burial suit, *faint*."

Lianne crumpled.

Kyle grabbed her, lifted her in his arms, and began shoving roughly through the crowd.

"Get out of my way," he shouted. "She needs air. Clear a path!"

Quickly Kyle forced a way up on the stage, which was the only place in the auction room that wasn't crowded. Several guards started toward him, saw the utterly limp woman in his arms, and turned back to control the people who were still on their feet. The curtain thumped down behind Kyle's back, tangling the most eager members of the crowd in a combination of soft velvet folds and guards whose hands were a good deal harder.

"Stay away from the jade," a guard snarled at Kyle.

"Screw the jade. She has to have air."

Before the guard could decide whether to go after Kyle, one of the mainland China contingent staggered out from under the curtain. While the guard was trying to do a little hands-on, cross-cultural exchange, Kyle slipped around behind the coffin-sized pedestal that supported the jade suit.

"Wake up, Sleeping Beauty," Kyle said in Lianne's ear. "You've got maybe thirty seconds before a guard spots us. Ten seconds after that, we'll be out on our ear."

Lianne didn't need a second invitation. She twisted in Kyle's arms until she was facing the shroud.

It was barely two feet away, illuminated by a spotlight so intense that it seemed like a solid column of white. Gold threads twisted and glittered as though alive, but it was only Lianne who was alive, straining toward the immortal jade with an urgency that made her quiver.

"Hey! What the hell do you think you're doing!" yelled a guard.

"Take it easy," Kyle said. "This is the only decent air in the room."

"Take her outside," the guard said curtly, running across the stage. "Move!"

"We're bounced," Kyle murmured, heading for the exit.

Lianne didn't complain. She had seen enough. Too much. Dick Farmer's beautiful jade prize had once belonged to Wen Zhi Tang.

The certainty of it stunned her.

Belatedly she realized that Kyle was still carrying her. "Put me down."

"In a minute."

"But—where are we going?"

"Outside."

"Why? Is the guard still after us?"

"No, but I want to see if anyone else is. Got any objections?"

If Lianne did, she didn't have time to voice them. Kyle put her down and then hustled her through an outside door so fast her feet barely touched the floor. He kept going until they were beyond the well-lighted building and down a side walkway. Soon they were hidden in the shadows leading to the hotel's underground garage.

Kyle stopped and held Lianne motionless against his chest.

Over her head he watched the empty walkway they had just hurried down.

"What are you—" she began.

"Be still," he whispered.

Shivering in the chill, she waited quietly, watching his eyes for any sign that they were being followed. All she saw was a faint gleam of reflected moonlight in a face that was uncompromising, chiseled out of shadow and ice. He looked barbaric, cruel, an ancient Viking wolf dressed as a civilized modern lamb.

The part of Lianne's mind that wasn't shell-shocked over the jade suit told her that she must be out of her mind to trust Kyle Donovan.

She must be out of her mind, period. She would have to be crazy to believe that Wen had parted with the very core of his treasury—a jade burial suit, the only such artifact in private hands.

"Don't look so worried," Kyle said, his voice a bare thread of sound. "I won't let anyone get to you."

Lianne almost laughed out loud. *Don't worry.*

The only way she could do that was to shove all thought of Wen and stolen jade into a corner of her mind. She would worry about it later, when she was calmer. It would make sense then, when she knew more.

It would be all right.

Gradually Lianne's body became less tense as she fell into old patterns of handling trouble. The ability to divide her mind and then get on with the needs of the moment was something she had developed as a girl, when the hurt of not being accepted by her father threatened to tear her apart. She had honed the ability, and her self-respect, with karate, mental and physical control combined.

Yet even years of training couldn't prevent the shiver that rippled through Lianne a few minutes later. She told herself it was the cool wind or leftover nerves, but she knew it was the slow, slow journey of Kyle's fingertips down her spine.

Each time he touched a new indentation or slight ridge, his hand lingered as though memorizing it.

"Cold?" he asked quietly.

"You try standing around out here in silk underwear in March," she said under her breath. "Of course I'm cold."

"Underwear? I didn't—" Kyle stopped abruptly. He doubted Lianne would enjoy being told that he hadn't felt anything under his fingertips but a thin layer of silk and a much warmer layer of woman. "Sorry. I didn't think about the temperature. We'll go back in soon. It doesn't look like he took the bait anyway."

"Maybe there was no one to take the bait. Maybe I was just imagining things earlier and you were imagining things now."

"Maybe," Kyle said. But the watchfulness of his eyes said otherwise.

"What makes you so sure we're not imagining things?" Lianne murmured, her voice as low and secretive as his.

"My gut."

"Your gut?"

"Yeah. It's restless."

"Have you tried antacids?"

He laughed softly, shaking his head just a bit. Then he went completely still.

"What—" She couldn't finish the question. Her mouth was smack up against the black cloth of his tuxedo.

"Quiet," Kyle breathed.

Holding both of them motionless in the shadows, he watched the figure that came out of the side door and stepped immediately to the left. A man. Medium height. Black tux. No way to see how it fit him.

Light flared, then snuffed out. The match had been shielded in such a way that Kyle saw only a brief glow against the man's jaw. No beard. No mustache. The burning pinpoint of a cigarette went from red to gold to red again as the man sucked in smoke. He took several more quick drags, flicked the cigarette into some shrubbery, and went back inside.

Kyle waited until he was certain that the man wasn't coming back.

"Okay," he said quietly, releasing Lianne. "Let's go in before you freeze to death."

"Suffocate."

"What?"

"I would have suffocated before I froze. Do you have any idea what raw tuxedo tastes like?"

"Nope." Kyle smiled and barely caught himself before he smoothed his hand down Lianne's back all the way to her sleek, tempting butt. "I always have mine well done," he explained, leading her back onto the lighted path.

"Was he trying to follow us?" she asked, ignoring Kyle's teasing tone.

"Hard to say. He could have raced out to see where we were going, or he could just have been desperate for a nicotine fix."

"So we're back where we started."

"Not quite. You haven't told me why I bid too much on that blade."

"Auction fever."

"Try again."

"Ignorance."

Kyle's hand closed more firmly around her arm. "Again."

"I'm not a mind reader."

"Even your own? You wanted that blade, Lianne, and you wanted it bad. Why?"

Lianne's only answer was the eloquent angle of her chin. She wasn't going to say a word.

At a speed that forced her to stretch her legs, Kyle headed for the front door of the hotel rather than the side. "I can understand why you were climbing walls to get a look at the burial suit," he said, "but why was that Neolithic blade so important to you?"

"No," she said curtly.

"Are you telling me it isn't important?"

"I'm telling you it's none of your business."

He pulled her to a stop just outside the hotel entrance. "Does that blade have anything to do with the man who's following you?"

"What makes you think that?" Lianne asked, surprised.

"You've looked frightened over three things tonight. One was the man following you. The other was the blade."

She didn't need to ask what the third thing was. "There's no connection," she said hurriedly, not wanting to talk about the jade shroud in any way at all.

"How can you be so sure?"

"The Neolithic blade is Tang family business. The man is Caucasian. No connection whatsoever."

"There's you."

Lianne's only answer was silence.

Kyle's gut kicked into overdrive. He didn't know what was wrong, but he had no doubt that something was. His next thought was that, despite the tuxedo, he was underdressed for the occasion. The area under his left armpit was buck naked.

Without a word he grabbed Lianne and headed for his car.

s e v e n

Driving skillfully, Kyle shifted his glance between the car's various mirrors and the mire of Seattle traffic. The snarl didn't compare with those in cities like Manhattan, L.A., or even Vancouver, British Columbia, but a simple repair of one lane on First Avenue had backed up cars for six blocks. He looked in the mirror again, yanked on the wheel, and made an illegal left turn in the middle of the block. He shot through a half-full parking lot, went the wrong way down a one-lane alley, and popped out on a side street.

Nobody made the turn after him.

He would have felt better if his gut wasn't telling him that this was the calm before the storm. And it would be a hell of a storm if what Archer had said was true.

The Chinese just threatened to break off all relations with the U.S. if the Jade Emperor's treasure turns up on our soil.

He didn't know how Lianne was involved in the Jade Emperor mess, but he knew that she was. There had been a lot more than professional curiosity driving her to examine the burial suit. There had been desperation.

"And I thought Johnny was a bad driver," Lianne muttered

when Kyle executed another illegal turn and shot through another alley.

"What do you mean, bad? No scraped paint, no ticket, and a clear road ahead of us."

"What about lights behind us? The kind that come with sirens."

"None of them, either."

She let out a breath she hadn't been aware of holding and settled into the comfortable leather seat. "Lucky man. Where are we going, or are we just wheeling around to get my adrenaline count up?"

Instead of answering, Kyle asked a question of his own. "Where's the Tang party?"

"Back at the hotel we just left. The Tangs rented the penthouse suite."

"Same hotel, huh?" he said, thinking quickly. "Am I expected to show up in this monkey suit?"

"That's up to you."

Kyle didn't care whether he wore a tux or bib overalls to the party, but changing clothes was the best excuse he could think of to get back to his room. Or better yet, Archer's. His older brother was sure to have a nine-millimeter in the safe, plus a spare magazine or two.

Kyle really didn't like what his gut was trying to tell him, but he didn't ignore the warnings. The last time he had told himself that he was jumping at shadows like a kindergartner on Halloween, a Lithuanian thug had come within one blow of killing him. The blow that had made the difference was Kyle's. His attacker had gone head over heels out the cab of the truck and sprawled in the muck by the side of the road.

"I'll see what's clean in my closet," Kyle said.

"Suit yourself. Literally."

He looked at her. She wasn't as pale and tense as she had been at the hotel. In fact, she looked so calm that he wondered if he had been imagining her distress. Before he could talk himself into that cozy little reassurance, his gut let him know he was being a fool. Again.

Whatever was going on, Lianne was in it right up to her sexy lips.

Kyle turned the car into the driveway of one of Seattle's more upscale and less ostentatious condo complexes. The three buildings were under twenty stories high, designed around the waterfront view, and owned by the real estate subsidiary of Donovan International.

"Is this your place?" Lianne asked.

"My family's. Whoever is in town uses it."

"Nice."

"I prefer my cabin," Kyle said, "but I'm here and it isn't."

"Where is your cabin?"

"In the San Juan Islands."

He pulled an electronic unit from a compartment in the driver's door.

"Is that a garage-door opener?" Lianne asked.

"Sort of."

"It looks like a TV remote."

"That, too."

The handheld gadget Kyle used to get into the parking level had begun life as a suburban garage-door opener. Then he had started thinking about how useful it would be if it not only opened doors, but told him if anyone else had come looking for him while he was gone. The result was a soldering-gun marriage between a pager, a door opener, a TV remote, and a spiffy little computer chip that could store an organic chemistry textbook with room left over for the Oxford unabridged dictionary.

Archer had christened the bastard electronic unit a "gizmo snitch" and promptly ordered one for himself. As long as they remembered to replace the batteries regularly, the snitch was reliable.

The garage door unbolted automatically and lifted up long enough to allow Kyle's hunter-green BMW to slide through.

He looked at the display window of the snitch and saw a comforting line of zeros. Nobody in since he had left. No power interruptions. All doors in the condominium exactly as he had left them. Locked.

"Is that some kind of fancy security system?" Lianne asked as he put the unit away.

"Just a gadget I invented because I'm lazy."

She looked at him doubtfully. Nothing she had seen so far tonight—or in the past two weeks—had suggested that Kyle was lazy.

"It's true," he said, smiling at her as he shut off the engine. "Unless it involves fishing, I don't make a move I don't have to." Before she could ask any more questions, he changed the subject. "Ever been fishing?"

"I went out on a 'cattle boat' once during the salmon season."

"Hell of a way to fish."

"I caught one," Lianne said, eyes gleaming. "There's a lot of power in them, even the little ones."

"How little was yours?"

"Six pounds."

"That's pretty little," Kyle agreed.

"It didn't affect the flavor one bit," she retorted. She licked her lips, remembering. "Succulent, like lobster. The color was so vivid."

Kyle slid out of the car. It was either that or take Lianne up on the unconscious invitation issued by her tongue. At least he thought it was unconscious.

He leaned back into the car and looked at her intently. She wasn't posed like a siren with her skirt halfway up to her crotch. Though her coat was open, she wasn't fiddling with the jade beads that nuzzled against silk and taut nipples. If she was sending out sexual invitations, she was a hell of a lot more subtle about it than the women he was used to.

And she smelled like heaven, after a whiff of the garage's concrete-and-crankcase purgatory.

"You're welcome to come upstairs with me," Kyle said. "If going to the condo makes you nervous, you're welcome to wait down here. Your choice. Either way, I won't be long."

Lianne met his eyes without coyness. "If you were going to be a jerk, you would have tried something when I 'fainted' or while we were playing hide-and-seek outside the hotel."

He smiled slightly. "I thought of it."

"Was that before or after you counted every vertebra in my spine?"

Kyle's laughter echoed in the parking garage. He thought again how much his smart-mouthed little sisters would enjoy Lianne. His older brothers would, too, but somehow that thought wasn't nearly as appealing. All of his brothers were single and too damned good-looking.

He went around the car in time to close, not open, the door for Lianne. She was a woman accustomed to watching out for herself.

"This way," he said, putting his hand lightly on her back. Though her coat was a butter-soft wool, he missed the sleek texture of silk with a woman's heat burning softly through it. Unconsciously his fingers pressed more deeply, seeking her warmth.

"Counting vertebra again?" Lianne asked.

"Just wanted to be sure I didn't miss any."

"Is being part of a big family why you have such a quick tongue?"

"Doubt it. You're an only child and there's nothing slow about your tongue. Succulent color, too."

Lianne saw his teasing grin and wondered if she should have stayed in the car and faced all the worries she had shoved into a corner of her mind until "later," whenever that came.

Without realizing it, she shook her head; she didn't want "later" to be "now." She had the whole Tang party to get through. She couldn't do it if she was thinking about a Neolithic blade and a jade suit that should be in Tang vaults.

"Don't worry," Kyle said, seeing Lianne's faint frown. He stuck a key into the wall by the elevator. The door opened immediately. "I'm not going to do the Jekyll-Hyde thing."

She blinked, slammed the door to her worries shut, and concentrated on Kyle. It wasn't hard. The more she looked at him, the better she liked what she saw. And what she felt. It was an odd, pleasant feeling to be aware of herself as a woman again, a woman who was very aware of a certain man.

"You sure about the Jekyll-Hyde act?" Lianne asked.

"Relatively," he said, holding open the door.

"Pity," she said, stepping past him into the luxurious elevator. "I was hoping to get a chance to try out my pepper spray."

"Not in the elevator, sweetheart. Neither one of us would make it out alive."

While Kyle punched in a six-digit code on the illuminated keypad, Lianne admired the elevator. Recessed lighting. Tibetan rug in jewel colors. Panels of cherry and bird's-eye maple. A telephone made out of something space-age, matte-finished, and curved. A small TV screen.

"What, no wet bar?" she asked.

His eyebrows rose. "In an elevator?"

"Well, this has everything else a good limousine does, including a driver wearing a tux."

"You know," Kyle said calmly, "all that's standing between you and a good kissing is that pepper spray."

Lianne put her hand over her heart and fluttered it like a Victorian maiden. Then she laughed, surprised at herself. It was heady to simply enjoy a man's company without watching every word she spoke, everything she did. She had had to be very careful when she was with Lee Chin Tang. Her sense of humor and his hadn't overlapped much. In truth, beyond his interest in Chinese culture, international trade, and the family of Tang, not much about Lee and her had overlapped.

Well, one thing had. They both wanted very much to be accepted into the Tang family. Lee achieved his ambition, but not through Lianne. He married the granddaughter of one of

Wen's male cousins, changed his surname, and was now managing the Tang Consortium's Seattle office. She still saw Lee occasionally. It hurt a little less each time. The sting these days was to her pride, not her heart. Lee had wanted her connection to the Tang family much more than he had ever wanted her.

The elevator stopped. To Lianne's surprise, Kyle punched more numbers on the keypad. Only then did the door open.

"This way," he said.

The carpet in the hallway was a thicker version of the one in the elevator. The walls were a pale cream that seemed to glow from the inside out. Chinese silk paintings were spotted throughout the hall. Though Asian paintings weren't her area of expertise, Lianne knew these were excellent, and quite old.

"A code to get out of the elevator, too," she said. "Now I see why."

Kyle glanced at the paintings and smiled. "Archer won them in a poker game."

"He must be Chinese at heart."

"Because of the paintings?"

"No, the gambling. It runs like lightning through the Chinese culture. Every male over the age of ten bets, whether it's on mah-jongg, dogs, horses, or the next bicycle to reach the intersection."

"Good recipe for empty pockets."

"The hit to the pride is worse. Whoever lost these paintings also lost a lot of face with his family. These were once part of a family's cherished heritage."

"They still are. Just the name of the family has changed."

"That's a very Western point of view."

"That's because I'm a very Western guy," Kyle said, opening the door. "Come in and sit down."

In the course of her work appraising jades, Lianne had been in many expensive rooms. None had appealed to her quite so much as this one, with its high ceiling, colorful rugs scattered over an oak floor, and walls of windows overlooking a shimmering, rain-drenched city.

"How odd," she murmured, looking around.

"What do you mean?"

"I like it."

"That's a shock?"

"I've always been drawn to a more Oriental approach to living spaces."

"Mahogany screens, low tables, floor cushions, inward facing rather than outward, that sort of thing?" Kyle asked, turning on lights.

"Oh, I admit to liking chairs. It's just that a room of this size, this height, all this glass and space . . ." Lianne paused. "Usually the result is impersonal. Like a palace or big hotel lobby. But this is lovely, very welcoming."

"It's my parents' home away from home. One of them, anyway. The Donovan and Susa live a lot of the year near Cortez, Colorado. Unless they're traveling. We're all holding our breath on that subject. My mother is determined to paint the Silk Road."

"Paint it?"

In answer, Kyle touched another light switch. Impressionistic landscapes hung like muted thunder on the only wall that wasn't glass.

Lianne's breath caught. She felt herself sucked into the paintings, through them, a feeling like dizziness, the top of her head lifting off and worries flying out to make room for the incredible energy of mountains and distance, desert and silence, rain and renewal, endurance and storm.

"Who?" she demanded. "Who did these?"

Kyle looked over her head at the wall of paintings. "Susa."

"Your mother?"

"Yeah. Good, aren't they?"

"Good? They should be in a museum!"

"Some of them are. These are Dad's favorites. Go ahead,

you can get closer. The paintings change into pure abstraction, but they don't lose their power."

Lianne drifted away, drawn by the silent explosions of color.

"I'll check out my closet," Kyle said, "unless you want me to fix you a drink first."

She shook her head without looking back at him. "Nothing, thanks. These are enough. More than enough."

Kyle walked past her, stepped around a freestanding bookshelf and into a slate-floored corridor that was invisible from the front entrance. Six widely spaced doors opened off the corridor. Each door led to a separate suite. There were no locks on the doors except from the inside. Only family stayed here. If someone was feeling a need for privacy, he or she locked the suite door from the inside and enjoyed as much peace as was possible in the presence of a large family.

The door to Archer's suite wasn't locked, which meant he probably had stayed for the end of the auction. He rarely missed a chance to check out the Pacific Rim gem market.

Kyle locked the door behind him and went straight to the safe. It was the old-fashioned tumbler-and-dial kind that Archer could open even if The Donovan changed the combination without telling anyone. It had happened more than once. Kyle was forced to rely on more conventional methods to get in.

"Hope the old man didn't play with the numbers," he muttered, spinning the dial.

After a few turns, the door swung open. Inside lay a wad of money, a shoulder holster, a nine-millimeter pistol, and four spare magazines. Archer took after The Donovan—cash, carry, and shut up. After Kaliningrad, Kyle understood the wisdom of that approach to life.

He peeled off his tuxedo jacket, strapped on the shoulder holster, slid the pistol in place, and put one of the cold, heavy magazines in his pants pocket. The jacket went on over the holster without a wrinkle or a bulge.

As usual, Archer was right. The tux fit better this way.

Kyle went to the closet and looked at the various shoes lined up in regimental perfection on the floor. Not Archer's doing, but the housekeeper's. One of the pairs of shoes was black and much better worn than the dress shoes that were presently making Kyle's feet miserable. He kicked off the shoes without hesitation and put on the other pair. They didn't fit as well as the tux, but at least they pinched in different places than the dress shoes had.

Silently Kyle unbolted the hall door, opened it, and pulled it shut behind him.

Lianne was still standing midway across the room, utterly absorbed in and by his mother's art. He had seen many reactions to Susa's paintings, ranging from a polite "Interesting" to excited arm-waving about brush strokes and energy, color and genius; but he had never seen anyone simply give herself to the paintings the way Lianne did.

Kyle felt a sudden, fierce desire to pull her down on the rug and find out if she had the same reckless ecstasy in her soul as the paintings had. While he was telling himself that that would be an unusually stupid thing to do, even for him, the phone rang. Or rather, the phones. There were several in the big room.

Lianne jerked, startled.

The closest phone was on a low table near one of the walls of windows. Kyle picked up the receiver before the second ring.

"Hello."

"Everything all right?" Archer asked.

"Yeah."

"You took off out of that auction like you had diarrhea."

"Lianne was feeling, uh, faint," Kyle said.

"The jade suit?"

"Enough to make anyone faint."

"What did she say about it?"

"Some lecture Farmer gave, wasn't it?"

It didn't take Archer two seconds to catch on. "Shit. You're not alone."

"You got it."

"Blakely?"

"Yeah."

"Good work."

Kyle made a muffled sound. Lianne had turned back to study the paintings, but she was only ten feet away. She could hear every word he said.

"Going to stay the night?" Archer asked.

"You're half right," Kyle said.

"Sleeping single?"

"Yes."

"Too bad."

"Not all of us are drop-dead handsome."

"Yeahyeahyeah," Archer agreed with a total lack of conviction. "So why are you back home?"

"I decided you were right about the tux. It fits better now."

There was a half-beat pause before Archer asked, "Did you decide that before or after Farmer detonated his jade bomb?"

"Before."

Silence, then a soft whistle as Archer realized the ramifications: even before Farmer, Kyle had felt the lack of a weapon. Kyle, who wasn't particularly fond of guns. "Need any more help than I left in the safe?"

"I'm not sure I need this much," Kyle said. "But I'd hate to be the only one not dressed for an occasion."

"What was the tip-off?"

"Three is a crowd."

"Somebody following you?"

"Half right again."

"Lianne is being followed?" Archer asked.

"Yes."

"Does she know?"

"Yes."

"Did she recognize him? Or was it a her?"

"You know how it is with men," Kyle said smoothly. "In the dark, one looks pretty much like another."

"Did you get a look at him?"

"I suspect it came with a USDA stamp of approval."

"Interesting."

"Yeah. If you have time, ask around. I'd hate to accidentally eat Uncle's lunch."

"More likely you'd get eaten," Archer said.

"Have faith in your teaching."

"Faith is our sister, not a way of life. Stay where you are. I'll come and—"

"Thanks," Kyle cut in, "but we're headed back to the Towers. Penthouse party and all that."

"The Tang Consortium rented the penthouse floor."

"So I'm told."

"Come in the south door of the hotel. I'll check you for lice."

"Sounds good. Call me tomorrow, okay? We'll do lunch."

"Get stuffed."

"Now *there's* an idea."

"Did Lianne know ahead of time about the jade suit?"

"No."

"You're certain?"

"Ninety-five percent."

"Anything useful for me to feed Uncle?"

"No."

"Shit. Will you be able to talk to me at the hotel?" Archer asked impatiently.

"Thanks, but there's no need. Tomorrow is better."

"I don't like waiting. Not when you're wearing my gun."

"Get another. One size fits all."

"I think I'll stuff you myself."

Smiling rather grimly, Kyle hung up the phone before Archer did.

eight

Lianne didn't look away from the art when Kyle walked toward her. Instead, she slowly drifted closer to the vivid rectangles that were seething with color and energy. The paintings would have called to her at any time, but they were especially compelling tonight, when she needed a feeling of strength to combat the fear that came when she thought about the Jade Emperor, burial shrouds, and her unacknowledged grandfather, Wen Zhi Tang.

"We can give your party a pass," Kyle said, studying Lianne's expression. "We'll just have a drink, enjoy Susa's genius, and talk about wonton wrappers."

Lianne jerked as though she had been stung. "I just need another minute," she said without looking at Kyle. Then she added quickly, "I always thought I was a sculpture person. You know, satin jade against your skin and thousands of years of history echoing in your mind. But these paintings . . ." Her voice died.

After a minute, Kyle went over to the security panel near the front door and checked the readout. A lovely row of zeros and no blinking lights. That was what he had expected, but seeing it felt good. He had learned in Kaliningrad that the unexpected wasn't fun. Better to be a stolid, solid type than a dead, adventurous type.

"Would you rather talk about the Jade Emperor?" Kyle asked, walking back to Lianne.

She looked at the explosive, barely contained storm painting for a few more seconds before she turned toward him. "You have a remarkable mother."

So much for the Jade Emperor. With a mental shrug, Kyle accepted the change in conversation. He had the rest of the night to grill Lianne. "Remarkable is right. Susa is the only one on earth who can get The Donovan to do something he doesn't want to do."

"If she has half the energy of those paintings, she would be an irresistible force."

"Twice."

"What?"

"Twice the energy," Kyle said. "She runs us ragged."

"All six of you?" Lianne asked dryly. "I doubt it."

"Seven, including Dad."

Her glance strayed back to the paintings.

"Nope," he said, guiding her toward the front door. "If you get started again, you'll disappoint Wen Zhi Tang. Which reminds me—why do the Tangs use Western-style name order?"

"You mean given name first and family name last?"

"Yes." Kyle stepped out into the hall after Lianne and reset the security system.

"Wen's father decreed that his branch of the Tang clan would look to the east—to America, the Golden Mountain— for their future. They would learn English and use Western name order. They would even call their daughters by individual names rather than by the usual birth-order designation of First, Second, Third, or Fourth."

"A real radical."

"A real pragmatist," Lianne said, following Kyle to the elevator. "After the revolution, the Tangs were shut out of mainland China's power structure."

"Wrong politics?" Kyle punched in numbers on the pad to the right of the elevator door. It opened immediately.

"Partly," she said, stepping in. "And partly it was just that the Tangs have always lived pretty much outside of or parallel to whatever government existed, unless they *were* the government."

"Warlords and feudal chieftains?"

"That's a polite way of putting it. Various emperors might have called various Tangs brigands, ruffians, and outlaws. The names got more grandiose during the Ming dynasty, after the Tangs got rich enough to buy and sell lives like sacks of rice. The Chinese have a very, very keen appreciation of power, as opposed to mere wealth."

The elevator door whisked open. They stepped out into the smell of cold concrete and warm machinery. Though the place was unusually well lighted, there still were shadows. It was the nature of parking garages to have dark corners and dense shadows.

With a quick, comprehensive glance, Kyle checked the area for other people. He didn't see any.

"So trading with foreign devils made the Tangs very rich," Kyle said, opening the car door for Lianne.

"Trading, tax collecting with or without the emperor's permission, a monopoly on grave robbing and gambling, and, most of all, what the Chinese call *guanxi*."

"Connections," Kyle said.

"The English word barely touches the Chinese reality," Lianne said. "*Guanxi* is a web of interconnected enterprises, cousins and brothers, uncles and fathers; branches of a family from the richest court lord to the poorest peasant spreading human manure in a rice paddy."

Kyle closed the door firmly and went around to his own side of the car. "Every family has poor relations," he said, starting the engine and driving toward the exit. "So the Tang family fortune comes from illegal ventures?"

"Define illegal," Lianne said simply. "The Tangs have been

making money for centuries. I doubt if all of it was legal according to the dominant culture of any given time. Besides, what is or isn't legal in China often is a matter of opinion."

"And money buys favorable opinions," Kyle said neutrally.

She shrugged. "Of course. It's no different here. That's why corporations and associations make political contributions. Someone new gets elected, selected laws are bent or changed, a few new sources of wealth open up."

"Or old—very old—sources are winked at. Gambling, prostitution, drugs, whatever society has outlawed that people want."

Lianne glanced sharply at him. In the glittering wash of fine rain and colored lights that was Seattle at night, his expression was unreadable.

"The Tangs aren't some kind of Chinese mafia," she said curtly.

He glanced at her. "Sensitive subject?"

She blew out an impatient breath. "Only if you read Hong Kong newspapers."

"I don't."

"Well, I do. The new regime in Hong Kong is carrying on as though the name Tang is synonymous with *gangster*. The Suns, of course, walk on water, never have impure thoughts, and—"

"Their farts smell like rose petals," Kyle finished.

Lianne made an odd sound and then laughed out loud. "You've got the idea."

"I assume we're talking about the Suns of SunCo?"

"Yes."

"From what Dad and Archer say, SunCo is a real comer on the international trade scene."

"Only because they have systematically cut off the Tangs overseas," Lianne said bitterly, "with the full blessing of the new Hong Kong regime and the old mainland China regime."

"Nothing personal, sweetheart. Just business."

"It's personal to me when I see a very fine, very familiar

piece of jade with SunCo's name on it instead of—" She broke off abruptly, not wanting to talk about the Neolithic blade. It might lead to questions about Farmer's jade burial shroud. She wasn't ready for that yet. She had to be fully in control when she confronted her not-quite-family tonight. Thinking about the burial suit made her stomach clench. "When you lose out, it feels personal."

"Losing is always personal," Kyle said easily.

"Some times are more personal than others."

"Like the Neolithic blade SunCo donated? Or the stunning coup that Farmer pulled off by displaying his own personal jade burial suit to a roomful of jealous connoisseurs?"

Lianne shrugged and said nothing.

"Do you believe that Farmer really managed to get his hands on the Jade Emperor's Tomb?" Kyle pressed.

"On the basis of the jade burial suit?"

"Yes."

Lianne started to say no, then realized that her answer would raise more questions. "I don't know."

"What do you think?"

She closed her eyes. "I think whoever sold Farmer that suit will have a lot of questions to answer."

"Because of the cultural-theft laws?"

"Among other things."

"Such as?"

"Provenance is always a question, isn't it?"

"Yeah. Where do you think the jade suit came from?" Kyle asked.

"I don't know."

"You got a good look at it. Is it real or a modern fake?"

"A fast look is hardly enough to make that kind of decision."

"I'm not asking for a sworn document. Just an opinion."

"Why are you badgering me?" Lianne asked tightly. "I'm not the one who has the suit. Farmer is. Grill *him*."

"I don't have a barbecue big enough."

Kyle glanced in the mirrors. There were cars behind him. The light in front of him was yellow going to red. He gunned the BMW and shot through the intersection.

No one followed.

For a time, there were no sounds except for the occasional swipe of windshield wipers, a distant siren, and the swish of tires over damp pavement. Kyle was curious about what Lianne was thinking, but didn't ask. The flat lines of her mouth and eyebrows told him that her thoughts weren't especially happy. Her silence told him that she wasn't going to talk about it.

With a throttled curse he pulled into the valet parking area of the Towers and turned off the engine.

"Wake up," he said. "We're here."

Blinking as though she really had been sleeping, Lianne looked around, surprised that they were already at the hotel. "Sorry. I'm not keeping my end of the bargain, am I?"

"What's that?"

"I'm supposed to be teaching you about jade, but . . ." She waved her hand and shrugged.

"I'll just add an extra hour onto your tab," Kyle said, checking the mirrors one last time.

Still no one following. Or if they were, they were too slick to spot. It would be interesting to see if he and Lianne picked up anyone between the valet parking and the south door of the hotel.

"Let's go in this way," Kyle said, guiding her past the main entrance.

"Any particular reason?"

"Because I can."

She blinked, looked at him, and smiled suddenly. "That answer would cover a lot of questions."

"That's why I like it."

Casually Kyle glanced over his shoulder. No one had pulled into valet parking behind them. He opened the hotel door for Lianne, walked in after her, and quickly scanned the collection of luxury shops. All closed. All empty. Several people were smoking outside the main entrance of the hotel, but no one was conveniently puffing near the south door.

Inside or outside the hotel, Kyle didn't see Archer, but he didn't doubt that his brother somehow was in a position to see him. When Archer said he would do something, it got done. The only other person Kyle had met with Archer's combination of brains, integrity, and lethal training was his sister Honor's husband, Jake Mallory.

"The penthouse elevator is this way, just around the corner," Lianne said.

As they rounded the corner, a dark, slender, very handsome Asian man standing near the penthouse elevator burst into a cascade of enthusiastic Chinese. He took one of Lianne's hands and stroked it repeatedly. For a Chinese male, it was an unusual display of public affection, unless he had been raised among a very wealthy, fairly Westernized overseas Chinese family.

Lianne answered the familiar greeting with a professional smile that made Kyle appreciate just how much warmth was in the smiles she had been giving to him.

Maybe he wouldn't be sleeping single after all.

But first he would have to detach the incredibly good-looking leech from Lianne's hand. No matter the man's feline, almost feminine beauty, the signals he was sending out were heterosexual and as blunt as a hard-on.

"Kyle," Lianne said smoothly, "this is Lee Chin Tang. Mr. Tang is an executive with the Tang Consortium. He doesn't speak English."

"Am I pleased to meet him," Kyle said without inflection.

"Moderately, but not excessively. He's acting as official greeter for the party."

As Lianne looked at Lee's dark, liquid eyes and raven hair, she waited for the slash of regret or anger she always felt when she saw him. Nothing came but a bittersweet acceptance that whatever love she had once felt for him no longer existed.

With another polite smile, she removed her fingers from his grasp.

"Yes, the man with me is Kyle Donovan," Lianne said in clipped Cantonese. "Please take us up to the suite. Uncle Wen," she added, using the common Chinese honorific *uncle* as she would use *mister* or *sir* in English, "will be eager to hear about the results of the auction."

"You left early," Lee said. "Is it true the Jade Emperor's Tomb has been found and sold to a foreign devil?"

"Ask Wen Zhi Tang," Lianne retorted before she could think better of it. "He knows more about jade than I do."

"Why did you leave the auction early? Where did you go? Was this man with you?"

"There was no need to stay at the auction," Lianne said, answering the only question she would. "Like me, Uncle Wen is not interested in Pacific Rim gems."

Strong, narrow fingers caressed her hand, her wrist, the soft skin beneath. "I have missed you."

"How kind of you to say so."

Beneath the polite answer, old anger flared for an instant in Lianne. Even six months ago, she would have given the earth to hear those words from Lee's full lips. Now it was all she could do to act professional.

Well, not entirely professional. There was a very personal, very female part of her that was delighted to encounter Lee while she was on the arm of Kyle Donovan, a man who drew a woman's eye whether the woman was Chinese or Caucasian. Glancing up at Kyle through her eyelashes, she smiled with frank, female approval.

Both men registered the difference in her smile. Suddenly expressionless, Lee let go of Lianne, stuck a key in the elevator, and motioned them inside.

"Good thing I don't wear glasses," Kyle said softly as the doors swished shut. "That smile you just gave me would have fogged them up inside and out."

Lianne's smile widened into laughter. She felt years

younger, almost giddy. It was a great relief to file Lee Chin Tang under "Old Business," shut the mental drawer, and be fairly certain that she wouldn't open it again in the middle of the night, when memories were especially cruel.

"Should I take the smile personally," Kyle asked, "or were you just trying to piss Lee off?"

"I wasn't trying to make anyone mad. I was just glad to be here and now instead of there and then."

"Would it help if I asked what you were talking about?"

"Nope."

"Just checking."

"No problem." Lianne tucked her arm through Kyle's and grinned up at him. "Has anyone ever told you what a fine, handsome, really world-class stuffed elephant you make?"

"Trust me, you're the first."

"I'll bet you say that to all the girls."

He grinned. "Only the ones who might believe me."

The elevator stopped with stomach-curdling speed. Lee punched the Door Open button and held it down.

"To your right," he said in Chinese. As Lianne walked by him, his left hand shot out and wrapped around her free arm, stopping her. "Better that you be my cherished concubine than a foreign devil's whore."

"I am neither concubine nor whore. Let go of me. Johnny won't be pleased if his honored guest, Kyle Donovan, is late."

"Johnny is only Number Three Son."

"Far better than zero," she said coolly. "That is your number, Lee. Zero. You married a distant, undistinguished cousin of Uncle Wen's and changed your name to Tang. You are no man's son."

"Do not speak so to me, female spawn of a foreign whore!"

"It would be my pleasure not to speak to you at all."

Lee's smile was as cold as his eyes. "May your fondest wish come true."

It was an old Chinese curse. Lianne's eyes narrowed and

her chin went up. She looked at Lee's hand on her arm and thought of the pepper spray in her purse.

The elevator beeped, announcing that it had been held open too long.

"Put a hustle on, sweetheart," Kyle said blandly. "That snack we ate at the auction just wore off."

"Sorry, I—" Lianne's breath caught when she looked up at Kyle. His voice had been so neutral that the cold anger in his eyes was totally unexpected.

"Why don't you tell this elevator jockey to take his thumb off the button?" Kyle asked in the same calm tone. "Or should I just pick him up and carry him along for you like a pet?"

The beeping became a buzzer.

Kyle glanced at Lee. Slowly Lee released Lianne's arm.

The elevator kept buzzing while Lianne and Kyle walked toward the penthouse suite. He felt Lee's black eyes measuring him for a shroud every step of the way. Not a jade shroud, either. The good old-fashioned linen kind.

Laughter, a woman's voice wailing a Chinese song, and cigarette smoke flowed out of the Tang suite into the hallway. Lianne's steps slowed. The noise surprised her. In the past, whenever she had been with a member of the Tang family, the atmosphere had been calm, almost silent, little but the whisper of Wen's soft slippers against wood or the dry rustle of his words as he described jade pieces that had been carved five thousand years before the birth of Christ.

"Second thoughts?" Kyle asked.

Lianne winced as a man's off-key voice joined the woman's in dreadful harmony. "I'm wondering if Wen's hearing has failed along with his eyes."

"Don't worry. Family gatherings are always noisy."

"I wouldn't know. I've never been to one."

Surprised, Kyle looked down at her. She was visibly composing herself, pulling what Americans would call her "game face" into place, her emotions retreating behind a coolly polite facade. For her, a family gathering was obviously more a battlefield than a place of safety and relaxation.

Lianne stepped into the smoky room and scanned it quickly for familiar faces. Two things registered immediately. The first was that only Tang men had been included in the party. The second was the nature of the women who had been invited to serve the men. All were young, striking, and for hire.

At that moment Lianne was intensely grateful her mother hadn't been included in the roster of female attendants. The humiliation would have been intense. And intentional.

"Looks like a lively family," Kyle said, glancing at the fifteen or so men of all ages and the handful of young women who were scattered around the penthouse's large living room. "Where do we start? Or is it just a free-for-all?"

Lianne wanted to start by turning around and heading back to the elevator, but it was too late. Johnny was already walking across the foyer. His left hand held a nearly empty plate. His other hand was out, American-style, ready to grasp Kyle's.

"I knew I could count on Lianne's sense of duty," Johnny said with a big smile, shaking hands. He nodded to Lianne and then focused again on Kyle. "Come in and meet everyone. I'll translate for you."

Kyle looked at Lianne. Hunch and intelligence together told him that she was certainly angry and very probably hurt, but her game face was excellent. If she resented being dismissed by her father like an employee, nothing showed on her face. Perhaps she felt nothing. Perhaps she was simply an errand girl whose errand was finished. She had produced Kyle Donovan for the Tangs, and now they had no further need of her presence.

Then Kyle saw the pulse beating hotly in Lianne's neck and knew she wasn't nearly as unaffected by Johnny's brush-off as she appeared.

"No need to take yourself away from your family," Kyle told Johnny. "Lianne is an excellent translator."

"Of course. I keep forgetting that she spent a couple of years in Hong Kong." He turned to Lianne and spoke in rapid Cantonese. "You did well, but do not monopolize our guest. I want Harry to meet him."

"After Uncle Wen, I will of course introduce Mr. Donovan to Number Two Son," she said.

Impatience thinned the line of Johnny's full mouth, but only for a moment. "So very proper and Chinese."

"You are very gracious."

"After we make the necessary introductions," Johnny said, "help the others serve drinks. I will act as translator for Kyle Donovan."

Lianne's eyelids flinched, the only outward sign of her sudden fury. "I think not, Mr. Tang. I am not a trained companion. Nor am I an untrained one."

"So very proper and American," Johnny said.

"You are kind to notice."

"You would do better to remember that you are here at the sufferance of the family of Tang. Do not make your mother lose face by showing less than the manners she would expect."

Chinese culture dictated that Lianne accept the reprimand with bowed head and many apologies. Part of her intended to do just that; then she saw a willowy young female kneel at the feet of Harry Tang and offer tidbits to him with a pair of ivory chopsticks. He didn't even look away from the man he was talking to. It was typical of the treatment women expected in Asia.

And Lianne was damned if she would bow her head and take it like a good Asian girl. Not here. Not in America.

"I have an excellent memory," she said, meeting her father's eyes squarely. "It is my only value for the family of Tang. As for my manners, they are what one would expect from the daughter of an adulterer and his paramour."

n i n e

Kyle didn't understand the words father and daughter were speaking, but the body language needed no translation. Lianne looked icy. Johnny looked like a man who had just taken a slap across the face and was about to return the favor.

"Sweetheart," Kyle said, smiling engagingly at Lianne, "I hate to interrupt, but I'm hungry enough to go back and eat that damn elevator jockey. Think it would be possible for you to translate all those buffet dishes for me?"

Lianne turned away from her father. Her expression softened as she spoke to Kyle. "Of course. You're the Tangs' honored guest. Johnny will explain to Uncle Wen how hungry you are. Won't you, Johnny?" she asked carelessly.

An odd combination of hope and anger crossed Johnny's handsome face. Then he nodded curtly and headed back across the room to a place where an old man sat with a beautiful girl at his feet. She was playing tunes on a *yueqin*, a Chinese "moon guitar." Neither the tonal scale nor the style of singing owed anything to Western traditions.

As Johnny started talking to Wen, another young, lithe woman hurried over to take the nearly empty plate from

Johnny's hand. Without a word from him, she went toward the buffet.

"I suppose it was rude of me to insist on being fed before the introductions," Kyle said.

"No more rude than Johnny speaking to me in Cantonese in front of you." Or dismissing her as though she was a badly trained employee.

A corner of Kyle's mouth turned up. "That's kind of what I thought."

As they crossed the room to the buffet, Lianne recognized two of the young men as her half brothers, Johnny Jr. and Thomas. She didn't wave or speak in greeting, for the simple reason that she had never been introduced to them. Johnny's sons, along with cousins of various degrees, were debating the uses of corruption on mainland China, the relative worth of political contributions in America as opposed to outright bribes in Hong Kong, and the merits of Chinese versus American or Canadian banks.

"What's that all about?" Kyle asked, gesturing toward three particularly passionate debaters.

"The young man on the left is trying to convince his uncle to put more money into mainland Chinese banks in order to win favors in bidding for construction jobs or import permits."

Kyle was familiar with the argument. The Donovan clan tended to divide along age lines when it came to international finance. "What does his uncle have to say about it?"

"He doesn't want to leave any money hostage to the next political turnaround on the mainland," Lianne said. "He would rather buy a few key bureaucrats outright and get favorable treatment that way."

"The nephew is a lot louder."

"That's because he's losing and he knows it. The older the man, the more experience he has with China's always unpredictable, sometimes self-destructive politics."

"Once burned, twice shy?"

"If you've only been burned once, you haven't been doing business in China very long."

The buffet was enough to make a hungry man salivate, but Kyle was the only man there. The other males were all being served food wherever they sat or stood.

"Bet I lose face by serving myself," Kyle said indifferently, reaching for a plate.

Quickly Lianne took the plate from him. "I should have thought of that. I'll serve you."

Casually he looked around the room, not missing any detail of the interaction between the men and the young women. He turned back to the buffet and took another plate for himself. "Thanks, but I'll serve myself. I haven't hired you for this night or any other."

Though red flared on Lianne's cheeks, she spoke without emotion in her voice. "The customs in Asia and America are quite different."

"Some are the same."

"Please, I don't mind serving you."

"If we really were in America, instead of in Hong Kong East," Kyle said, helping himself to a mound of garlic chicken, "who served whom would be a matter of convenience, not sexual politics and individual face. But we're in a different place."

"That's why I should—"

"If I serve myself tonight," he continued, gently ignoring Lianne's attempt to talk, "it's no skin off my, um, face. If you serve me, it says something about you that I'd deck a man for saying out loud."

"You're—"

"Very American," Kyle interrupted. "We settled that earlier. Want some garlic chicken, if only in self-defense?"

"Yes," she said quietly. An odd feeling expanded through her, both gratitude and something more. Something hungry. She touched Kyle's wrist, taking a very female pleasure in his heat and leashed strength. "Thank you for understanding what very few people would have."

"No thanks needed," he said, piling chicken on her plate. "All part of being a stuffed elephant."

"I think it has more to do with being American, and male. And . . . good."

The husky hesitation of Lianne's voice made Kyle want to put down the plates and take a loving bite out of her instead. Instead, he gave her a lazy kind of smile that had nothing to do with being good.

Breath filled her throat and yearning emptied her mind. She realized it would be very, very good to lose herself in passion with Kyle Donovan. No more fear, no more worry, no more Jade Emperor looming like death on her personal horizon.

"Kyle . . . ?"

"Any time," he said, watching her. "And if you keep looking at me like that, the time will be now."

Startled, Lianne looked from Kyle's mouth to his eyes. It was a mistake. She could see herself too clearly in them. She could see other things, too. The two of them naked, her hands clenching on his biceps as he lifted her and slid into her, filling her until pleasure overflowed.

Harsh words cut across her fantasy. Johnny Jr. was arguing in Cantonese with his younger brother, saying that he would have to wait a few more years before their father would approve of any marriage at all, much less one to a foreign ghost. Better that they do as their father had—marry Chinese and go whoring in whatever cultures and races tickled their cocks.

"Hey," Kyle said, smiling despite the sexual heat flooding his body. "Don't go all pale on me. I won't really ravish you among the egg rolls."

"What?" Then Lianne understood, laughed, and shut out the wrangling of her half brothers and all that it implied. "How disappointing. I was having this really tasty fantasy of you, me, and lobster sauce."

"I'd ask you to tell me more, but I'm afraid of embarrassing myself."

She glanced down the length of Kyle and smiled. "Embarrass yourself? Why? There isn't a man in the room who wouldn't be strutting if his pants fit like yours."

Kyle snickered, then threw back his head and laughed without restraint, like the Westerner he was. She laughed with him and tried not to think about a time in the near future when he would ask and she would answer and his strong, warm hands would slide up the inside of her thighs.

"I knew we should have stayed at the condo," he said.

Lianne's eyes widened and laughter fled at the hunger in Kyle's. "I don't—we don't know each other."

"You won't be able to say that tomorrow morning."

"No," she said quickly. "It's—too much. Too soon."

"Then the next morning after. I'm a patient man."

With that, Kyle proceeded along the buffet, helping himself and her to the mostly traditional Cantonese fare. The only overtly Western foods were the desserts. They had been chosen more for their sweetness than for their elegance. Cookies crusted with cracked sugar were clear favorites.

"The Chinese have a sweet tooth," Lianne said, seeing the direction of Kyle's glance.

"I picked up on that."

She smiled slightly. He had "picked up on" quite a few things tonight. Yet he seemed oblivious to the glances from the Tang men as he served her. Nor was he reacting to the frankly inviting smile being lavished on him by the young woman who was waiting a few feet away with an empty blue-and-white plate in her hands.

The girl had the kind of beauty that was both vivid and ethereal. Black hair, golden skin, full red lips, cat-slanting eyes, a waterfall of straight black hair that went just below her hips. The skirt of her tight black dress was the same length as her hair, which made for a rather startling view from the rear.

The fact that she had Johnny's plate in her hands did nothing to make Lianne feel more charitable.

"Hi," the girl said, walking up and standing close to Kyle. Very close. "I don't think we've met."

"I'm Kyle Donovan. This is Lianne Blakely."

The smile the young woman gave Lianne was a lot cooler than the one she had given to Kyle. After a scant second, she fixed her big black eyes on Kyle again and reached for the plate he was holding.

"It would be my pleasure to serve you," she said, her voice low, erotic, "in any way."

"Thanks," Kyle said casually, "but I'm in the mood to serve myself."

The girl ran the tip of her index finger around the edge of his plate and smiled slowly at him. "If you change your mind, just whistle."

"Are you a dog to be whistled to heel?" Lianne asked in curt Cantonese.

"If whistling awakens the sleeping turtle head," the hostess retorted in the same language, "I will be honored to find it a warm, snug refuge from a cold world."

Lianne grimaced. "Turtle head" was one of the less reverent Chinese names for penis. "Attend to the men who hired you," she said.

"You refuse to attend the handsome foreign ghost yourself, yet you send me away. Why is that, sister?"

Lianne thought of Kyle's universal answer and smiled thinly. "Because I can."

The hostess gave a very American shrug to Lianne and a smile that didn't require translation to Kyle. "It was a pleasure to meet you, Kyle Donovan. Perhaps we can meet again. Soon."

As she walked away, the black waterfall of her hair stirred and shimmered in time to the lithe hips swinging invisibly beneath. The legs weren't invisible and were well worth watching.

"Whew," Kyle muttered. "That's quite a hood ornament." He turned back to the buffet. "Do you want to drink wine, beer, or this orange stuff?"

Lianne sent another hard look after the friendly, bilingual hostess. "Remember our earlier discussion about wine and China?"

"Good point." He picked two beer bottles out of the crushed ice and opened them. "That should hold me for a few minutes. What about you?"

She looked down at her plate. While she had been thinking about the gorgeous, available girl, Kyle had piled her plate high with food. "This should hold me for a week."

"Don't worry. I'll help you out."

"Translation: if I don't eat fast, there won't be much left for me."

"You got it. Hold these for a minute," he added, handing her the beers. As soon as she took them, he snitched a spring roll off her plate and ate it before she could object. "Better stop talking and start eating, or all you'll get out of this is a dirty plate," he said, licking his lips and reaching for another roll.

When Lianne realized she couldn't eat because her hands were full, and Kyle was rapidly devouring her food, she laughed out loud and forcefully handed the beers back to him. Her open, quintessentially American laughter made several heads turn. She didn't even notice. She was having too much fun with her sexy, surprising stuffed elephant.

Kyle winked at her as he gently, efficiently, herded her away from the buffet table. He chose a place where he could stand with his back to a wall and still be close enough to the doorway for a fast exit. It was Archer's First Rule of Parties: *Pick where you want to be when the fighting starts.* Kyle didn't really expect a brawl to begin any time soon, but there was no percentage in being a naive, trusting stranger in a strange land. In short, an American outside America.

The Towers might have been in Seattle, and Seattle in the U.S.A., but right now the penthouse was a ripe, smoky slice of Hong Kong before the Turnover.

Letting the gusts of Chinese flow past him, watching the party, willing his aroused body to relax, Kyle ate quickly. Though the language, music, and food were uniformly Chinese, everyone—even the bent, white-haired ancient at the other end of the room—was dressed in Western clothing. Kyle didn't have to understand the words to see that there was a clear pecking order among the men. Yet none of them acted like a bodyguard or employee.

The furniture was Western, with couches, overstuffed chairs, and coffee tables. The design of the fabric was a stylized cloud pattern that could have been taken right off an ancient Chinese robe. Nondescript incense burners added to the smoke in the living room without managing to cover the harsh smell of tobacco. Young women circulated like bright, honey-seeking butterflies. Though there was no difference in the richness of male plumage, each girl knew who was where in the pecking order.

Wen was first. He had a girl playing the guitar at his feet and, as often as not, another hostess at his elbow feeding him. In Wen's case, the service was probably necessary; the hands that rested on an intricately carved, jade-headed walking stick were gnarled and enlarged by arthritis. Holding chopsticks would have been difficult for him. If the way he stared straight ahead was any indication, seeing the plate would have been impossible.

The second most important man in the room was never far from Wen. Whether this man sat or stood, a hostess was always at his elbow, ready to fetch food or drink as required. She looked older than the others, more woman than girl. And a stunning woman at that. Elegant limbs and a richly curved body. She wore a spectacular diamond-and-ruby bracelet that almost equaled her own physical beauty.

"The man in the corner," Kyle said quietly to Lianne. "The one close to Wen. Who is he?"

Lianne glanced over. "That's Harry Tang, Wen's Number Two Son."

"And from the look of it, his Number One Girl is right next to him," Kyle said, biting into a dumpling filled with pork and ginger.

"I don't know her name. Assuming she has one."

He didn't miss the flick of anger in Lianne's voice. "If that bracelet she's wearing is any sign," he said, "Harry has known her name for a long time."

Mentally Lianne gave herself a shake. She had to stop reacting to this "family" gathering like a child who had just found out why she didn't have a live-in father. There was no need for her to be so raw about the circumstances of her birth. Her mother had made her choice long ago, a choice that her daughter didn't have to understand but had to live with anyway.

As though they had nothing to do with her, Lianne looked coolly at Harry and his beautiful ornament. Kyle was right. This woman wasn't a one-night hostess. She knew Harry well enough to anticipate his demands and still have enough attention left to oversee the rest of the girls in the room. She wasn't the wife of Number Two Son, but she was ruling the roost tonight.

And the bracelet she wore was worth a good deal more than Anna Blakely's ring. But then, Johnny was only Number Three Son. His mistress would naturally have less costly jewelry than the woman who belonged to Harry.

"It isn't unusual for wealthy men to have mistresses," Lianne said neutrally. "Before the revolution, it was expected. And before Christianity, a Chinese man had a wife and as many concubines as he could afford. As for the women, there was more prestige in being a wife than a concubine, but often the concubine had more actual power."

"Yeah, you grab a man by his dumb handle and he'll follow you anywhere."

When Lianne understood what Kyle meant, she barely managed to swallow a mouthful of garlic chicken without choking. "Dumb handle," she said, clearing her throat. "I've never heard it called that."

"What do they call it in Chinese?"

"Oh, many things. Reverent things. 'Jade stem' is a favorite. 'Jade flute,' sometimes."

"Jade, huh? The Stone of Heaven."

"Um. Perhaps." She tried not to snicker, but the light in Kyle's eyes made it difficult. "I hadn't thought of it that way."

"What did you think the jade in 'jade stem' referred to?" he asked dryly.

"Texture and, ah, rigidity."

"Are you saying a man's best buddy isn't heavenly and immortal?"

Lianne gave up trying to eat and laughed openly again, not caring that she drew glances from various Tang men. Smiling, Kyle slid his empty plate under hers, took both in one hand, and began eating. By the time she had subsided into snickers, her plate was nearly clean.

"You're amazing," Lianne said, looking at the few crumbs that remained of her food.

"Just eating for two."

"You and who else? Me?"

"Nope, my buddy. Be amazed how much energy it takes to keep him up to expectations."

Shaking her head, trying not to add to the wicked light in Kyle's eyes, Lianne handed her half-drunk beer to a passing hostess and glanced around the room once more.

A torrent of Chinese burst out of a corner where two older men sat eating salted nuts.

"Another difference of opinion?" Kyle asked.

"No, they're unanimous. SunCo has to be kept from getting any more leverage in America."

"That could prove difficult."

Lianne looked at Kyle. He was studying the room, his unusual gold-and-green eyes taking in faces and body language.

"Why do you say that?" she asked.

"SunCo and Dick Farmer are rumored to be cutting a trade deal that would benefit both China and America."

"I'll bet it benefits SunCo and Dick Farmer more."

"That's like betting that the sun will come up in the east," Kyle said. "So who's third in the pecking order here?"

"Johnny Tang. He's Number Three Son. Joe Tang, the Number One Son, isn't here tonight. I think Harry said something about Joe going to Shanghai on family business."

Without appearing to, Kyle watched Lianne as she talked. If he hadn't already known that Johnny was her father, nothing in her actions—or in Johnny's, certainly—would have given away the relationship. It was the same when Lianne talked about her uncles. If there was anything filial in anyone's feelings, it didn't show on the surface.

"After Johnny, the order of precedence begins to blur," Lianne said. "The older men are cousins or brothers-in-law who are employed by the Tang Consortium. The younger males are sons and nephews of the Tang brothers."

Kyle looked at the well-dressed young men and tried to pick out which ones were Lianne's cousins and which were her half brothers. He was tempted to ask her, if only to break the professional mask that she had pulled so seamlessly over her feelings when he started asking questions about her secret family. But the thought of seeing her without defenses in this den of Tangs stopped him.

"Finished eating?" he asked.

"I never started."

"Want to?"

Lianne shook her head. "I'm not hungry. Nerves, I guess."

"The Jade Emperor?"

She flinched subtly. "Among other things."

"Was the auction that important to you?"

"It was an honor to be chosen to select the Jade Trader's display," she said. What she didn't say was that she had spent her entire lifetime working toward being accepted into her father's family. "One way or another, most honors are nerve-racking."

As Lianne spoke, she thought of Kyle's newly purchased Neolithic blade and of Wen's superb collection of ceremonial blades, of Wen's secret jade burial shroud and Farmer's very public one. Beneath her calm face and easy conversation, fear and urgency coiled, making her stomach clench.

She had to talk to Wen. Tonight, if possible. If not, then tomorrow, when she returned the exhibition jades to the Tang vault in Vancouver.

But right now she had to take care of Johnny's business with Kyle Donovan.

"Are you ready to meet Wen?" she asked.

"I don't know. Am I?"

"Yes," she decided. "You're ready."

She led Kyle across the room. Nobody greeted her, though one of the young men certainly looked her over with a thoroughness that raised Kyle's hackles. He wondered if the guy knew he was leering at a first cousin or a half sister.

When Johnny saw Lianne walking toward Wen, he shed his beautiful companion without a backward glance. He went over to his father, motioned the dainty guitar player into silence, and spoke in rapid Cantonese.

Wen nodded and tried to focus on the stranger who was now standing in front of him. All he saw was a tall shadow with a golden nimbus around his head, like an angel in an old Christian hymnal. A very large angel. The familiar scent of Lianne's perfume told Wen that she was the vague, pearly shadow standing at the stranger's side.

No sooner had Johnny finished the introductions than Harry appeared. More introductions followed. At a gesture from Johnny, three chairs appeared and the girls vanished to wait on other men. Harry's companion walked up on small, high-heeled feet. She stood to the side and behind him, waiting to be needed.

Wen spoke in the papery voice of an old man.

"He asks that you sit," Lianne translated for Kyle. "He is no longer able to stretch his neck to see the top of such a tall tree."

Kyle looked around for a chair. Johnny had already taken one, and Harry another, leaving the last one for Kyle. There was no chair for Lianne.

"Please," she said softly, understanding why Kyle didn't sit down right away. "As you pointed out earlier, we aren't in America. In any case, Wen's voice is very soft and speaking tires him. To hear, I must stand very close to him."

Kyle shrugged and sat down. Even seated, he was head and shoulders above Wen and half that much above his sons.

Lianne thanked Kyle with a smile, positioned herself so that she could hear her grandfather's frail voice, and pulled the impersonal role of translator around her like a welcome armor.

Kyle watched and listened while the Tang family paid court to him in the leisurely, gracious, indirect manner of the Chinese culture. All except Harry. The Number Two Son's attitude made it clear that he wasn't quite convinced that Kyle should be a guest, much less an honored one.

After the initial round of pleasantries, Wen settled back wearily in his chair. As though that was a signal, Harry and Johnny switched to English. Lianne continued to translate, but for Wen's benefit, not for Kyle's.

It was half an hour before the conversation passed from politely trivial to perhaps—just perhaps—meaningful.

"Wen understands that you are a connoisseur of archaic jade," Harry said.

"Specifically Neolithic," Kyle responded, looking at Lianne's unacknowledged uncle.

Harry looked older than Johnny by at least ten years,

clean-cheeked, and thicker through the shoulders and thighs. He had as much silver as black in his hair. His English was stilted but serviceable. He moved in the abrupt manner of a man accustomed to wielding power. His companion, who hadn't been introduced, lit his cigarettes, refreshed his beer, and kept a dish of salted nuts within his reach at all times. She did the same for Wen, Johnny, and Kyle, but it was Harry she looked to for instructions.

"My father is also interested in jade," Harry said.

"So I'm told," Kyle said. "Wen Zhi Tang's collection is the envy of everyone who has heard of it. Although now, I suppose, Dick Farmer will be the king of jade connoisseurs. A modern-day Jade Emperor. I presume you heard about Farmer's spectacular jade burial suit?"

A flick of Harry's immaculately manicured hand dismissed Dick Farmer, the Jade Emperor, and Kyle's question. "Is your father interested also in jade?" Harry asked.

"No."

"What are his passions? Gambling? Politics? Women?"

"He's a one-woman man."

Harry blinked. "Oh? Well, it is that way for some men, I am told. So he is a man with one passion and no, ah, hobbies?"

"Donald Donovan's hobby is the finding, mining, and refining of metallic ores. His four sons prefer precious and semiprecious gemstones. In my case, jade."

Harry nodded and lifted his right hand in the direction of his silent companion. Moments later a lighted cigarette appeared between his fingers. He puffed, blowing smoke in a long stream that blended with incense and other cigarettes. When he spoke, he appeared to choose his words carefully.

"Is that why your esteemed father's important company lacks any jade, ah, arms?" asked Harry, releasing another burst of smoke.

"Or feet, either. If you can't mine it and smelt it, The Donovan couldn't care less about it." Kyle's voice was cheerful, as if he didn't sense any darker currents coiling beneath the smooth surface of the conversation. "But I'm working on it. Every chance I get, I bend the old man's ear on the subject of jade."

Harry's companion slid a cigarette between Wen's raised fingers. He stuck the cigarette in his mouth and sucked in smoke with short, fast bursts while Lianne translated into Cantonese. Harry listened closely, too. Though he prided himself on his English, he needed a translator to grasp Kyle's rapid, idiomatic speech.

Johnny didn't have to wait for understanding, but it was Harry who was doing the talking. Johnny's job was to keep the discussion on track despite Harry's reluctance to reopen negotiations with the Donovans. If Harry had his way, the Tang Consortium would put all its money into overseas Chinese communities in the form of casinos, banks, hotels, and shipping.

But Harry didn't have his way. Nor would he. Though the Number One Son didn't share Wen's obsession with jade, he recognized that the Donovans were an international power. If Kyle's interest in jade could become the basis of an alliance, Joe was for it. So was Wen. The Tangs badly needed international allies.

"Ah, jade, that is good," Harry said to Kyle, letting out another round of smoke. An ashtray appeared just beneath his hand. He dropped the half-smoked cigarette in and waved it away. "You speak to your esteemed father about jade. To those who understand, Tang and jade are like this," he added, hooking his two index fingers together and yanking to prove the strength of the connection. "To know one is to know the other."

"That's what I said, but The Donovan keeps saying something about SunCo. Now, I have to admit they had some really sweet jade on display tonight. Not up to Tang quality in most cases, and not a patch on Farmer's stuff, but high end isn't the only end of the jade trade." Kyle sent a flat, white smile in Harry's direction. "I'm hoping Lianne will have some ideas that will make my father focus on Tang jade. She's a real pistol when it comes to jade. More ideas than a dog has fleas. Am I speaking too fast for you, buddy?"

Johnny shifted impatiently in his chair. He had the look of a worried man, or one with indigestion.

Kyle didn't care which. Johnny was only Number Three Son, Wen was half asleep, and Harry was running the show. Harry, whose contempt for any man's Number Four Son didn't need translation.

Lianne shot Kyle a warning look.

He gave her a smile that was all sharp edges and no warmth. If Harry figured that Lianne had snagged the easy mark in the Donovan clan, Kyle wasn't going to get in the way of the game, whatever it might be. And he no longer doubted there was one.

Just as he didn't doubt that Lianne was in that game right up to her stubborn chin.

t e n

Archer walked into Kyle's suite without knocking, shook him awake, and waved a copy of *USA Today* under his nose. After another shake, Kyle opened one eye, saw the clock, and turned his back on Archer without a word. Like his sister Honor, Kyle believed that early morning should be greeted with both eyes closed tight.

"Not this time," Archer said, stripping off the covers with a quick jerk of his arm. "Talk to me. I've been fielding unhappy phone calls for three hours."

"It's only six A.M."

"They start early in Washington, D.C., especially when China is chewing ass about stolen cultural treasures. Get up."

"I didn't get to bed until two, you woke me up at three—"

"For all the good it did me," Archer muttered.

"—I told you to drop off and went back to sleep," Kyle finished, ignoring the interruption.

"So what are you whining about? You slept four hours."

"Not enough."

"It will have to be. While you were partying with the Tang Consortium, word of Farmer's jade burial suit went straight to the People's Republic. The People aren't amused."

Cool air ate at the edges of Kyle's comfort. The covers were out of reach, he was bare-ass naked, and Archer wasn't going to go away like he had last night. With a curse Kyle shot out of bed and into the bathroom. The door slammed.

Smiling slightly, Archer went to get Kyle's reward—a cup of coffee that could etch steel.

Kyle didn't believe in cold showers. If a man was going to get up before the sun, the least he deserved was enough hot water to fog up a gymnasium. He was well on his way to steamy bliss when Archer opened the shower door and shut off the hot water, leaving on the cold.

Two seconds later Kyle leaped out, cursing.

"Dry up," Archer said, dumping a big towel over his brother's head. "Coffee's ready in the kitchen."

"Food."

"What do you think I am, room service?"

"You don't want to know what I think you are."

"Read the paper while I burn some eggs for you."

"You burn 'em, you eat 'em."

"Read," Archer said with the impatience of a bright-eyed dawn raider for the sleep-in rest of the world.

Kyle pulled on some old sweats and went into the suite's cheerful lemon-yellow kitchen. Beyond the window, low clouds, wind, and sun fought for control of Seattle's skies. At the stove, Archer was cracking eggs into a bowl. Barefoot, wearing old jeans and a blue work shirt, he looked younger than the thirty-five he had recently turned.

"Coffee," Kyle said, yawning.

"Open your eyes, runt. It's on the table."

"Runt you," Kyle muttered. "I wore your tux, didn't I?"

"And my dress shoes."

"They pinched."

"That's how you know they're dress shoes. Did you use the rest of the outfit or just wear it?"

"Just wore it."

"Good. Uncle would rather not have to clean up any more bodies."

Kyle felt the same way, but it was too early in the morning to be agreeable. "Then Uncle shouldn't pressure us to play full-contact sports."

"Drink your coffee before I do."

Kyle went to the long chopping table that occupied the center of the kitchen. Two wrought-iron, cafe-style stools ran along one side, for family members who didn't feel like sitting in the semi-circular breakfast nook that overlooked the sound. Near one of the stools, coffee steamed in a big mug that announced that the worst day of fishing was better than the best day of working. He reached for the mug, not caring if it held the black, bitter stuff Archer preferred.

The instant Kyle actually saw the coffee, he knew something serious was on Archer's mind; there was cream in the coffee. Kyle really got worried when he saw that Archer was grating cheese and slicing mushrooms for an omelet.

"That bad, huh?" Kyle asked, swallowing coffee.

"What do you mean?"

"Cream in my coffee and now an omelet instead of scrambled eggs. You want something from me."

"Read," was all Archer said.

"Aren't you going to Japan? Or was it Australia?"

Archer gave Kyle a look.

Kyle sat down and picked up the newspaper. When Archer's eyes went from gray-green to plain old steel, a smart younger brother shut up.

The headline on the news brief was "Emperor's Tomb Bought by Billionaire." Beneath that was a page number. Kyle turned to the page and saw a muddy color photograph of a Han burial suit. The caption read, "Precious jade shroud for an ancient emperor." The one-paragraph article gave the approximate age of the tomb as six hundred years, but named no individual or institution as its discoverer. No specific locale in China was named. "Spectacular" and "priceless" grave goods were mentioned, but there were no useful facts about what kind of artifacts actually had been recovered.

"You got me up for this?" Kyle asked. "Like I told you last night, Han burial shrouds are rare, very rare, but not unique. As for the tomb the shroud came from, maybe it is and maybe it isn't the Jade Emperor's. That will be up to the scholars to decide. When they do, it won't be from reading a newspaper article."

The eggs hissed as they hit the hot pan. Kyle's stomach gave a hungry rumble. The coffee was wonderfully potent, but it wasn't food.

"What did you hear at the auction?" Archer asked.

"Bids."

"You want to wear this omelet or eat it?"

"Even before Farmer strutted his new suit, I asked Lianne about the Jade Emperor's Tomb. She said she didn't think it had been found, much less robbed."

"Why?" Archer asked without looking up from the omelet he was cooking.

"Mainly because she hasn't heard about anyone having a big sale of top-quality grave goods."

"Maybe the thieves are just selling it off a piece at a time."

"That's what I said."

Archer pulled a warm plate from the oven, slid the omelet onto the creamy white surface, and put the plate in front of Kyle. "What did Lianne say?"

"Before or after Farmer's stunt?"

"Before."

"She said a piecemeal sale would lower the value but keep things quiet."

"What do you think?"

Kyle leaned back until the stool rocked on two legs, grabbed a fork from a nearby kitchen drawer, and attacked the omelet. He talked and ate at the same time, figuring if Archer didn't like the view he could shut his eyes.

"I think there's more going on in her mind than is coming out of her mouth."

Archer poured himself a cup of coffee, leaned against the counter, and gave Kyle his full attention. "Anything in particular, or just another one of your famous hunches?"

"Han artifacts, even spectacular ones like the jade shroud, aren't Lianne's passion, but she was ready to take on the whole crowd and Farmer's guards to get close to it."

Archer shrugged, unimpressed.

"Then there was a piece of buried jade at the auction," Kyle continued. "It was worthy of an emperor. A blade about eight inches long, not a chip or a crack, moss green with just enough yellow in it to show off the pattern of the stone. Lianne told me the stains were in the right place to please Asian tastes."

"Did she think it might have come from the Jade Emperor's Tomb?"

"She said anything was possible."

Archer grunted and sat down opposite Kyle. "Not much help there."

"Maybe. But she bid on the blade."

"It was an auction."

"Her personal passion is Warring States artifacts," Kyle said around a mouthful of omelet. "The blade was Neolithic."

"So she had a client."

"Maybe."

"But you don't think so?" Archer said, drinking coffee and watching his brother over the rim of the mug.

"I'd bet she was personally unhappy, not professionally, when she was outbid."

"Another 'feeling' of yours?" Archer asked.

"Yeah. Don't you wish you had them?"

"I'd rather count on something tangible."

"Like a gun?" Kyle retorted.

"Like family. How many of the Tang Consortium brass did you meet?"

"Of the immediate family?"

"Yes."

"Every male but Joe, the Number One Son."

"What did your gut tell you about Harry?" Archer asked.

"If I were Joe, I'd watch my back. Harry likes being in charge."

"What about Wen?"

"Old and getting older. Eyesight is very poor. Hands are gone to arthritis."

"You can finesse hands and eyes. What about his mind?"

"I don't speak Chinese, so I can't really judge. But Harry was real attentive to his daddy, which makes me think Wen's mind is just fine."

Archer looked into his coffee. It was black as hell and almost as bitter. "Wen is ninety-two."

Kyle whistled softly. "How old is Joe?"

"Sixty-three."

"Harry didn't look much older than fifty. Some gray in his hair, but not a whole lot more than you, old man."

"You aren't going to have a head for hair to grow on if you don't stop baiting me," Archer said without real heat. "Harry is fifty-eight."

"Johnny?"

"Fifty-seven. There are eight girls. The youngest is forty. The oldest is seventy-one. I could give you their names, but it wouldn't matter. In some ways the Tang family is very old-fashioned. When the sisters married, they stopped being Tangs."

"Lianne is what—twenty-two?"

"Almost thirty."

Kyle's bronze eyebrows lifted. "Must be something in the Hong Kong water. A regular Fountain of Youth."

"Lianne was raised in Seattle."

Metal grated on the slate floor as Kyle rocked his stool back on two legs. "Where was the rest of her family raised?"

"Anna Blakely lived in a series of foster homes until she was thirteen. Then she ran off to the big city. She was barely fifteen when she had Lianne. Johnny was twenty-seven, married to a Hong Kong Chinese woman, and the father of two boys and a girl."

"Busy man," Kyle said.

"He stayed that way. Lianne has seven half siblings."

"Lianne's mother stayed close with Johnny while he was busy making more Tangs?"

"Close as skin."

"Was it the money?"

"You'll have to ask her," Archer said. "All the file said was that Johnny kept her in good-to-great style from the day he first saw her. If she ever had another boyfriend, no one knew about it."

"Till death do them part, is that it?"

"It works for some people."

Kyle brought his chair forward with a snap and held his mug out for more coffee. Without comment, Archer poured. Kyle sipped, shuddered, and sipped again. He only took cream with the first coffee of the day. After that, he figured he could do without lactose crutches or go back to bed for the sleep he needed to get through the day.

"What do you know about a good-looking guy by the name of Lee Chin Tang?" Kyle asked.

"Why?"

"He'd like to kill me. I'd like to know why."

Archer looked up from the coffee he was pouring for himself. "Is he the reason you came back for my gun?"

"No, but I was particularly glad to be wearing it after I met him."

"What does he look like?"

"Thirty-five to forty, Chinese, movie-star beautiful, doesn't speak English, and his eyes could drill holes in steel."

"Nobody mentioned him to me, which means he's not one of the major players in the Tang Consortium."

"He'd like to be a major player in Lianne's bed."

Archer's left eyebrow rose in a swift, questioning arc. "How did she feel about it?"

"She gave him ice burns."

"Told you she preferred blonds," Archer said smugly.

"What about the guy following us?" Kyle asked, ignoring his brother's grin.

"Was he blond?"

"You tell me."

"Someone might have followed you out of the auction. It was hard to be certain. There was a lot of pushing and shoving to get close to or away from the jade suit." Archer stretched and rubbed the black stubble that he hadn't had time to shave yet. "I know for damn sure that no one followed you back into the hotel."

"Then why was Uncle all over you like a rash this morning?" Kyle asked after a minute. "And don't give me a load of crap about the newspaper article."

Archer drank deeply, then stared at the silty remains of his coffee. "I asked her the same question. Several times. No answer worth repeating."

"Her? Did they ring in what's-her-name again?"

"Who?"

"Jake's old playmate."

"Oh. Lazarus. No, this is an agent I haven't met. She knows you, though. Must have been at the auction. She was surprised that you were sleeping here last night. Alone."

"Mother," Kyle muttered. "I could get real tired of Uncle's cold nose poking up my ass."

Archer didn't say anything. He didn't have to. If he had liked the covert business, he would still be in it.

Kyle looked at his watch.

"You have something on today?" Archer asked.

"Jade instruction."

"Come again?"

"Lianne is going to give me five hours and fifty-one minutes of her jade expertise."

"But who's counting, right?" Archer asked dryly.

"Wrong," Kyle retorted. "I'm counting. So is she."

"Why?"

"We cut a deal. For every hour of stuffed-elephant service I give, she gives me an hour on the fine points of jade buying and selling."

"Stuffed elephant," Archer said neutrally. "That means something, I suppose."

"I'm big."

"You're a runt."

"Compared to Han Wu Seng, I'm a—"

"Seng! What does he have to do with this?" Archer demanded.

"You know him?"

"No, but Uncle does. He's a major contributor to U.S. political parties. He's also the funnel between polite Chinese society and the overseas arms of the Red Phoenix triad, which has a lock on heroin distribution from Vancouver to Hong Kong."

"Nice guy."

"Compared to some, yes."

Kyle's eyes narrowed. His brother was quite serious. Kyle shook his head. "I don't want to know."

"Neither did I, but sometimes you don't get lucky. How did you meet Seng?"

"At the auction. He's the reason Lianne gave for wanting to get to know me. I'm big."

"So she needs a knight in shining armor to chase off the big bad Seng dragon, is that it?"

"If she does, she's out of luck. The knight business is a hell of a lot more trouble than it's worth."

Archer lifted his coffee mug in a silent toast of agreement, and drank the bitter dregs. "Don't forget dinner tonight."

"What about it?"

"Honor knew you'd forget. Mom and Dad's thirty-sixth anniversary."

Kyle's broad palm smacked his forehead. "Damn! I've got to get them something."

"Honor took care of it. She'll bill you later."

"Thank God for little sisters."

"They have to be good for something."

"Funny," Kyle said, "that's what Faith and Honor were always saying about big brothers."

"Speaking of Faith . . ." Archer's face became expressionless. "She's bringing her intended to the party. Anthony Kerrigan. Word is she'll be wearing a diamond."

Kyle hissed something under his breath that was as unhappy as the slant of his mouth.

"I don't like the son of a bitch, either," Archer said evenly, "but that's our problem. Since Honor got married, Faith has been lonesome as hell. If Tony makes her feel good, so be it. Be here at seven with a passable smile on that pretty face of yours."

"I'm supposed to have a date with Lianne."

"Bring her."

"Wonderful," Kyle said sarcastically. "Bring the Tang family spy into the bosom of the Donovan family to meet the shit-eating insect Faith is going to marry."

Archer raked his fingers through his dark hair. "If I thought it would do any good, I'd take good old Tony hiking in Alaska and feed him to a grizzly."

"I'll buy the plane tickets."

"Did it ever occur to you that maybe we're being just a little too protective of our little sister?"

"No. Tony is a loser. He thinks Faith is a lifetime ticket to a place in the fast lane. When he figures out that she won't take a dime from the family that she didn't earn, things will go in the toilet real quick."

Archer didn't argue. "If I thought it would speed the process, I'd give her the results of Tony's background check, but she wouldn't—"

"Give them to me," Kyle cut in. He already knew Faith

was stubborn, especially if she thought her older brothers were interfering.

Which they were.

"Tony's good at wooing and bad at long term. There's an ex-wife in Boston who's suing him for nonpayment of child support. A girlfriend in Las Vegas who had two abortions. Another one in Miami who thinks Tony is going to marry her because she's two months away from delivering his son and heir."

There was a long, tight silence before Kyle spoke. "So good old Tony's dying to know how the other half lives? I'll show him. I'll take him fishing in Kamchatka. Big country. Wild. Empty. As they say in Australia, no worries, mate."

Archer's smile was as thin as a blade. "I'll keep it in mind. But first, let's give Faith a chance to figure it out for herself."

"Too late. You said she was showing up with a diamond."

"Engagement ring, not wedding. Not yet."

"Not ever," Kyle said flatly. "I mean it, Archer. Women like Faith and Honor are an endangered species—decent, generous, and honest. Honor has Jake to protect her. Faith just has us."

"Faith isn't stupid, just stubborn. Hormones and wishful thinking won't last long. Sooner or later she'll see Tony for the amorous, fertile weasel he is."

For a minute Kyle said nothing. He simply watched cloud shadows slide over the kitchen's lemon-yellow walls. "It's obvious that Tony likes knocking up his women. What if Faith gets pregnant before her common sense takes over?"

"Then we'll have a niece or nephew to spoil," Archer said softly. "And that lucky baby will have as many fathers as there are Donovan men."

Kyle's breath came out in a hissing sigh. He finished his coffee and smacked the mug down on the glass table. "I'll be here at seven. With Lianne."

"You're picking her up?"

Kyle nodded.

"Let me know when you're leaving," Archer said. "I'll follow you."

"That will be a switch, knowing who's following me. What if someone is already following Lianne?"

"I'm counting on it."

The predatory anticipation in Archer's eyes almost made Kyle feel sorry for whoever was following Lianne. But what he really regretted was that he wouldn't be around to help Archer ask questions.

"Sounds like you might be late for dinner tonight," Kyle said.

"Depends."

"On what?"

"If the tail's license plate goes back to Uncle, I'll be on time."

"Why would the government be following Lianne?"

"To find out where she goes."

"Kiss mine, Archer. You know what I mean."

Archer shrugged. "Maybe they want to know if she's clean or dirty. I sure as hell would."

Kyle started to say that Lianne was clean. Then he shut up. Just because his gut said she wasn't a thief didn't mean dick to the rest of the world.

And it shouldn't mean dick to him.

"What if the license plate doesn't come back to Uncle?" Kyle asked evenly.

"Then life gets interesting."

eleven

Lianne slowed at the U.S.-Canada border, pulled into the Pace Lane, and slid across the international boundary with no more ceremony than a nod and a wave. Cars that didn't have frequent-entry stickers on their windshields were stacked four across and twenty deep at the customs booths while people answered questions about plants, pepper spray, tobacco, alcohol, firearms, and other forbidden fruit.

She checked her watch as her car bumped over the thick "sleeping policemen" that slowed traffic coming away from the border booths. Off to the right side of the wide asphalt area, unlucky Canadian drivers stood around with trunks and doors open while Canadian customs officers went over their vehicles. The most frequent violation was undeclared U.S. merchandise, whether socks or cigarettes. The high taxes in Canada made personal-use smuggling by otherwise honest citizens not only tempting but inevitable.

The trunk full of jade artifacts in Lianne's red Toyota wasn't "dutiable." No taxes or declaration required. Nor did she need guards, armor plate, guns, or any of the other hoopla essential to people whose cargo was money, plain and very spendable. The jade she carried was priceless, which wasn't the same as easily converted into cash.

Even so, Lianne kept watching her mirrors. After the auction last night, she was more than a little jumpy. Yet, despite the restlessness that made her edgy, she didn't really believe she was being followed. No car had latched onto her bumper and stayed with her no matter what she did. Several other cars got off I-5 with her at Blaine to gas up, but that meant nothing. Gas in Canada was easily twice the price it was in the States. Smart motorists planned ahead.

Beyond the Canadian border buildings, traffic was quickly shunted onto B.C. 1. Painfully new housing tracts—bedroom communities for the booming city of Vancouver—competed with milk cows for possession of the salt-grass flatlands that lay between the international border and the muscular curves of the Fraser River. The city itself was on the far side of the river, a dense band of white buildings sandwiched between bold black mountains and cold blue sea.

As always, Lianne was struck by the beauty of Vancouver's physical setting. San Francisco bragged about its scenic wonders, but Vancouver had more, and more spectacular, scenery, up to and including a breathtaking bridge spanning the entrance to a deep, protected harbor. All the city lacked that San Francisco had was the San Andreas Fault. On the whole, people in Vancouver got along quite nicely without the extra adrenaline provided by earthquakes.

As for Lianne, she didn't need adrenaline at all. Her dreams last night had been a tangle of ageless jade shrouds and the immediate sexual reality of Kyle Donovan. If she hadn't been so determined to speak alone with Wen, she would have broken a lifelong rule about first dates and sex and gone home with Kyle.

Her mouth turned down in a wry, unhappy line. For all the good it had done her to stay alone, she should have accepted the invitation in Kyle's beautiful eyes and spent the night with him. She wouldn't have gotten any less sleep than she had, and she would have had a lot more fun. She was certain of it.

That was one of the reasons she hadn't slept well. The other was Harry's curt refusal to let her drive Wen back to Vancouver when she returned the jade to the Tang vaults. Instead, Harry had driven his father home after the party.

The Tang family compound fronted on the heavy traffic of Grenville Street. From the exterior, the compound was as inviting as a jail. All the way around a city block, high, solid, windowless residential walls of varying color and composition came right out to the sidewalk. Though it looked like there were at least four separate homes with abutting walls and separate entrances on each block, only a few of the entrances actually opened onto anything. The rest were like the false fronts on old Western buildings, show without function.

Inside the real entrances lay another world. A beautiful, serene one. In a central courtyard, spring bulbs bloomed beneath rhododendron and azalea, pine and dwarf maple and juniper. Birds drank from a pond where huge koi held station like lazy, colored flags. The smell of early lilies and sweet rain filled the silence.

In summertime the courtyard shimmered with bees and the laughter of children. In fall it burned with all the colors of maple and Autumn Joy sedum. In winter the courtyard slept gracefully, like a black-and-white cat storing up energy for the tumult of spring.

Lianne had seen the courtyard in all its moods, but never had she joined the Tang women who sat and laughed and talked while their children chased butterflies and each other. It wasn't the language barrier that kept Lianne apart. It was the much more subtle, much more insurmountable social barrier. She was an employee, not an acknowledged member of the Tang family.

A distant, aged Tang cousin who also acted as houseboy waited by the side door. He called out to her in Chinese.

"Uncle Wen is still sleeping. The celebration last night tired him. Daniel will help you replace the jade."

Lianne's heart hesitated, then beat steadily again. Daniel was Johnny's Number Three Son. Her half brother. She had seen him at a distance many times but had never been within speaking range of him. In truth, other than the party last night, Lianne couldn't remember a time when she had been close enough to her half brothers to have a conversation.

Before she could refuse help, Daniel came rapidly down the stairs to the service entrance, where she had parked. Though Lianne had never met him, she had learned about him as she had learned about her other half siblings. Daniel had been raised in Hong Kong until he was ten, when he was sent to live with relatives in Los Angeles. At twenty-six, he had a fine arts degree from the University of Southern California, a law degree from Harvard, and utter ease with two very different cultures.

But what struck Lianne was how much he looked like his father. Her father. *Their* father. He had inherited Johnny's athletic body, handsome face, and strong hands. He was eight inches taller and seventy pounds heavier than she was.

And a single look at his face told Lianne that Daniel despised her.

"Open the trunk," he said curtly. "I'll put the jade back in the vault. You don't have to come in."

Lianne forced her voice to be businesslike and nothing more. "That's kind of you," she said as she walked around to the trunk and opened it, "but it's my responsibility to make sure everything is replaced exactly as Wen left it."

"Listen, Ms. Blakely, there's no need for you to hang around waiting for Wen's approval. Just send your bill to the Jade Trader. My grandfather doesn't need you underfoot."

A rush of anger mingled with shame tightened Lianne's throat; her half brother was treating her like a door-to-door insurance salesman. For an instant she couldn't say anything.

Then her chin came up and she met Daniel's cold glance with one of her own.

"Wen Zhi Tang gave me the honor and responsibility of handling the Jade Trader exhibit in Seattle," she said in a clipped voice. "That includes putting every piece of jade back into the vault myself. If that bothers you, don't watch."

"You'd like that, wouldn't you? Being by yourself with all that jade."

"It would hardly be the first time."

"I know. That's what worries me."

Lianne went cold. "Are you implying that I can't be trusted?"

"Hey, you're sharp, aren't you? But I already suspected that. I knew it for damn sure a few months ago."

"What are you talking about?"

"Save the innocent act for someone who doesn't know where you came from," Daniel said bluntly. "From now on, every time you walk into the Tang vault, you're going to have me at your elbow. If I'm not here, you're shit out of luck. And I'm not going to be here a lot of the time."

"Let's go to Wen right now and—"

"You're through going to Wen," Daniel said, cutting off Lianne's words. "He's tired and old. He deserves rest. From now on, you deal with me. I'm the Tang family jade expert."

"What does Joe Ju Tang have to say about that?"

"What do you care? *It's not your family.*"

Before Daniel could say any more, a whispery yet strong voice came from the doorway.

"Lianne, is that you?" Wen asked in Chinese.

"Yes, Uncle Wen," she said, looking away from Daniel with relief.

The old man stood in the doorway. Wind tugged at his clothes and lifted his collar-length, thinning white hair. Barely taller than Lianne, weighing only a few pounds more than she did, he nonetheless commanded attention. The dark gray suit he wore was a fine blend of wool and silk; it had been tailored impeccably to fit his frail frame. His shirt was silk, as was his sedate burgundy tie. His shoes were handmade of a leather so soft it could have been used for gloves.

"Why are you standing outside when it is warm inside?" Wen asked impatiently. "Come, come! The spring wind is unkind to old bones. Qin? Qin, are you near?"

"I am here," said the houseboy patiently.

"Bring tea to the vault. Cookies, too. I am hungry."

"Grandfather," Daniel said in Chinese, "do not trouble yourself with this matter. I will see that each piece of jade is returned to its rightful place."

"Trouble?" Wen gave a harsh, papery laugh. "At my age, jade is the only trouble worth having. Help Lianne return my children to the vault. If you listen and look well, you might finally learn something useful about the Stone of Heaven."

Daniel's face darkened, but his voice didn't change. "Thank you, Grandfather. I have much to learn from you."

"Best be quick about it," Wen muttered. "The husk of my body dries more with every day. Soon the wind will take me."

"It would not dare," Lianne said, smiling. "Though you would make a fine fighting kite."

Wen's face wrinkled into a huge grin. Laughing silently, he turned back to the house. Then he stopped and glanced over his shoulder, seeking the small, bright-colored shadow that was all he could see of Lianne.

"Let the boy bring the jade," Wen said curtly. "Come, girl. Come and tell me once again how my children look in their nests of silk and satin and velvet."

Lianne sensed more than saw the whiplash of anger followed by rigid control that went through Daniel. Yet when she looked at him, he was bending into the trunk of her car, lifting out cartons of jade, and setting them carefully along the driveway as though he wanted nothing more in life but to do Wen's bidding.

"I am coming, Uncle Wen," Lianne said, hurrying up the steps. "It is always an honor to be your eyes."

The trunk slammed hard enough to bend metal. Lianne winced and said nothing. She was used to encountering indifference in the Tang family, but outright hostility was new. She found herself wishing that her very own stuffed elephant was by her side. The thought made her smile, chasing the chill of her half brother's blunt rejection of her and his doubts about her honesty.

The door led to the kitchen. Like the rest of the house, the kitchen was a smooth blend of Oriental and Occidental. The colors, use of space, flooring, and art were largely Asian. The furniture, lighting, appliances, and plumbing were Western. The scent was unique, a blend of incense and the Pop Tarts that Wen loved.

During their slow progress through the kitchen and down a corridor to the vault wing, Wen started questioning her about Dick Farmer's jade suit.

"My grandsons could tell me nothing," Wen said irritably. "They think only of stocks and banks and real estate. Did you see it?"

"Yes."

"Ah!" Wen waited, but she said no more. "Is anyone nearby?" he demanded.

Lianne looked over her shoulder. They were alone. "No."

"Is the suit as good as mine?" Wen asked impatiently.

She was too shocked to answer. A few years ago, she accidentally had discovered the suit when she was doing the yearly inventory and inspection of the Tang vault. She had been in one of the deep closets inspecting the trays of jade thumb rings and archer's cuffs, when the vault door opened. Joe and Wen walked in, arguing about Joe's love of horses and ancient calligraphy.

Lianne decided to finish the archery inventory and hoped that the men were through bickering before she announced herself. A few minutes later she heard a crash. She rushed out of the closet and spotted Joe braced against the weight of what looked like a steel door.

When she saw what was in the small, hidden room beyond the door, her mouth dropped. While Wen berated Joe for drunken clumsiness, Lianne stared, unnoticed, at the type of jade treasures she had only dreamed of seeing if she was ever permitted inside mainland China's state collections.

But of all the things Lianne saw in that first, unguarded instant, it was the jade shroud that was engraved on her mind. Until that moment, she hadn't known that any such treasure existed in private hands.

Then Joe had noticed her. He had shouted at her to get out, but Wen intervened. He went to her, saw both her shock and her reverence as she stared at the suit . . . and he smiled to see his love of jade and history shining in her eyes. He dismissed Joe, swore her to secrecy, and spent some of the most pleasant hours of his long life showing her the soul of the Tang treasures.

Lianne had kept her vow and the secret of the priceless jade shroud. She had seen it only once since then, when Wen had been flushed with illness or rage and demanded to be left alone with her in the vault. He showed her how to open the concealed door, then stood in silence with his hands on the suit as though drawing strength from the immortal properties of jade. An hour later they left the vault.

Neither of them had spoken of the jade suit then. Or ever. Until today.

"Did you hear me, girl?" Wen demanded. "Is his sacred jade suit superior to mine?"

Lianne's heart squeezed into her throat. She didn't want to lie to her grandfather, but the truth was unspeakable. "I could not examine it closely," she said finally.

"Why have the gods cursed me with a useless female?" Wen growled. "If I had been at the auction . . ."

His voice died. If he had been at the auction, he would have seen nothing. It had been months since he could see even a hand in front of his face.

"But," Lianne forced herself to say, "if you would let me

examine your suit now, I could give you an opinion as to which suit is better."

"Not today. Daniel is here."

She bit back a protest. Arguing with Wen simply made him more determined to get his way. "Yes, Uncle. But soon?"

Wen grunted. "Hurry with the locks. My feet are tired."

Lianne walked around a priceless screen made of lacy jade plaques set in small, densely carved mahogany frames. The screen separated the vault wing from the rest of the house. Grumbling, Wen waited while Lianne went to work on the combination that allowed the big, fireproof steel door to swing open.

Some of the jade objects inside were on display to be touched, admired, loved. Much more jade was held within steel drawers and cabinets. And in one very special, very small steel room, there was a coffin-sized pedestal supporting the Tangs' most extraordinary treasure—an intact jade burial suit from the Han dynasty. The tiny room was opened rarely and spoken about even less. Only the First Son's First Son knew of the suit's existence, and so the secret had been passed from generation to generation.

Once it had been Wen's pride and pleasure to have sole access to the Tang treasure room. When Joe turned thirty, Wen had given the combinations to him with much ceremony. Joe had looked around the jade vault without real interest. Patiently he listened to Wen's fervent lecture on the social, political, philosophical, religious, and monetary importance of the Stone of Heaven. Then Joe went back to his racehorses and his study of the history and practice of the ancient art of calligraphy.

Lianne had turned out to be a much more satisfactory acolyte at the Stone of Heaven's altar. Sixteen years ago, when Wen had decreed that the Tang Consortium headquarters be moved from Vancouver to Hong Kong, the Tang patriarch discovered that Johnny's backdoor daughter had an instinctive, rare, and deep understanding of jade. Wen had seen nothing like Lianne's innate skill since his grandmother, who had been the force behind his grandfather's and father's wide renown as jade connoisseurs.

When Wen finally despaired of training a son in the love and lore of jade, and it was too late to mold his own daughters in that role, he began Lianne's schooling. She would never be a Tang, but that didn't mean her gift for jade appreciation had to go to waste.

Then Daniel had matured. Though he lacked Lianne's experienced eye and uncanny instinct for jade, he had other, very important qualities: he was a Tang, he was a male, and he was fascinated by jade. Hoping to find in a grandson what he had never found in a son, Wen had spent much of the past year passing on his knowledge to Daniel.

Along with that knowledge came all but one of the combinations to the vault. Though Daniel thought it was long past time to upgrade the old dial-and-tumbler locks, he was fully aware of the honor his grandfather had given him. If Daniel wondered what lay behind the locked steel door at the west side of the vault, he never asked. No matter what time of day or night Wen felt the need to commune with his treasures, Daniel went without complaint to the vault, opened the many combinations to the various compartments, and sat with his grandfather, listening and learning.

Wen wished that his Number One Son showed half Daniel's diligence. It galled Wen to give over control of Tang destiny to a son who had little knowledge and less love of jade. But slowly, inevitably, Wen's increasing frailty had forced him to hand over many of his responsibilities to Joe.

Power didn't slip easily from Wen's aged hands. He hated giving up control to anyone, especially to an eldest son whose head was in calligraphy and whose heart quickened for racehorses more than for jade. Nor did Joe show any desire to live in the Vancouver compound for longer than a few days at a time.

An emotional preference for Daniel didn't sway Wen from

his duty to Joe, any more than emotion had swayed Wen from wedding the flat-footed eldest daughter of a rich merchant. Beauty could be purchased. Power had to be married.

In any event, not only did custom decree that Wen's eldest son assume command, he was the most suitable of the lot. Harry was too recklessly ambitious for the clan's good and Johnny was too emotionally tied to America. Despite his shortcomings in jade appreciation, Joe was Wen's best hope of taking the Tang Consortium to new heights of power and prestige in the twenty-first century.

All Wen had to do was hang on until SunCo's sails had been trimmed and the Tangs were welcome back in Hong Kong. After that, Joe could be trusted to carry on with the rest.

"This last lock is sticky," Lianne said, frowning and beginning the combination all over again. "Have you had the tumblers checked?"

"Daniel will see to it," Wen said, turning toward the jade screen. "Tomorrow, yes?"

"Yes, Grandfather," Daniel said from the far side of the screen.

Wen grunted in satisfaction. His eyes might be gone, but he had a despot's ability to sense people walking up behind him.

The last lock finally gave way to Lianne's deft fingers. The vault door swung open. Cool, incense-scented air washed over her. The area just beyond the vault door had once been an entire single-family home. Now it was a two-story, steel-walled, fireproof vault that was crammed with special drawers, cabinets, closets, and chests. This was the repository of Tang pride, the focus of Wen's personal wealth and obsession. Jade.

"Watch that worktable," Lianne cautioned, lightly holding Wen back. "It has been moved since I was last here."

Wen grunted and suffered himself to be led around the table he could no longer see.

With a mixture of hope and fear, Lianne looked toward

the west corner of the room, where the priceless Han burial shroud was stored behind yet another locked door. As long as Daniel hovered nearby, she couldn't bring up the Tang treasure unless Wen did. And Wen had made it clear that he wouldn't.

"Sit down, Uncle," Lianne said, leading the old man to the only chair in the vault. A small table stood by the comfortable chair. The table held a white jade bowl that needed no special lighting to display its beauty. It was the equal, if not the superior, of the bowl that Dick Farmer had so proudly displayed at the auction last night. "Your favorite bowl awaits you."

Wen laughed dryly. "Are you still wishing that it had been part of the Jade Trader display?"

"Of course."

"Only a fool advertises his wealth to the envious."

"Yes, Uncle."

Yet Lianne couldn't help wishing Wen had allowed the bowl to leave the vault. The jade piece had a flawless shape and spectacular, luminous simplicity. A perfect fusion of art and function, the bowl would have stolen the show.

Except, perhaps, for the Neolithic blade. It, too, had fused art and purpose, ceremony and function, into a single gleaming whole. And it had done so nearly seven thousand years before the Ch'ing dynasty bowl that was one of Wen's favorite objects.

Lianne gave a sidelong glance to the north side of the vault, where Wen kept his collection of Neolithic blades. As much as she needed to reassure herself that she had been mistaken, that the precious blade was still in the Tang vault, she had no excuse to go to the fourth cabinet from the right, open the fifth drawer from the top, and look inside.

While she helped Wen to the chair, Daniel carried a box into the vault and set it on a worktable. Five other boxes appeared rapidly, brought by servants who left as silently as they had come.

Daniel didn't leave.

A single look at his handsome, hard face told Lianne that he didn't plan to step out of the vault as long as she was inside. Searching out the truth of the Neolithic blade—and the jade shroud—would have to wait. With a soundless curse, she reached for the first box and carefully began opening it. It held the Burmese jade jewelry she had worn last night. The pieces belonged in one of the cabinets whose drawers were thin, shallow, and plushly lined.

"Let Daniel replace the jade," Wen said, motioning abruptly to Lianne. "Bring to me . . . the Tang camel. It has been too long since I last held my old friend in my palm."

She glanced quickly at Daniel. He was ignoring her, unpacking another box of jade as though he was alone in the vault.

And then he looked at her. The emotion in his eyes was so violent that Lianne stepped back before she could stop herself.

"Girl," Wen said in a raspy voice, "did you not hear me?"

"Yes, Uncle. I will bring the camel."

Feeling Daniel's contempt every step of the way, wondering what she had done to earn it, Lianne crossed to the east side of the vault. Drawers went from floor to ceiling. She ignored the stepladder, stood on tiptoe, and reached up to open the drawer that held Wen's most prized Tang dynasty pieces. The depth and breadth of the camel collection was unparalleled, even in China.

The drawer opened on silent, oiled runners. Daniel might have happily stuck a jade dagger in her back, but Lianne had to admit that he was taking good care of the vault. Unable to see into the drawer because of its height, she patted around on the silk bottom of the drawer, where she expected to find the jade camel. She found several, but none of them felt exactly right to the touch.

"Have you had the camel out since I last brought it to you?" Lianne asked.

"Were you not listening?" Wen demanded. "It has not been in my hands since you placed it there many weeks ago."

Daniel stopped unpacking and stared at Lianne. Though he was tall enough to reach the drawer much more easily than she could, he didn't offer to help. He simply watched while she dragged the stepladder over, climbed up three steps, and looked inside the drawer.

An exquisite array of palm-sized sculptures nestled in the padded silk lining of the drawer. Each camel was in a reclining position, curled around itself, with the long, supple neck turned back and the head resting on the body. The jade ranged in color from cream to pale yellow-green to spinach green to mink brown, often in the same sculpture. The artists had used the natural color variation in the jades to suggest movement and vitality. The animals had been so skillfully carved that light moved over them as though they were relaxed, breathing slowly.

"There it is," Lianne said. "Someone must have shut the drawer too quickly and sent the camel sliding."

"Bring it, bring it," Wen said.

"Just the one?"

"Can you not hear my words?" Wen muttered.

"It is hard to choose among such wonderful pieces," she said wistfully, running her fingertips over another camel.

This one was carved from a piece of creamy jade that had tiny brown veins running through it. The jade itself had the prized quality of luminous translucence, yet it somehow managed to evoke the dusty monotone of the interior deserts of China where camels carried the dreams of men on their backs.

Lianne eased her fingertip beneath one of the camel's creamy, curled legs. Tang sculptures were carved in the round, meant to be held more than viewed. If memory served her—and it always did—on this sculpture the separation of the camel's toes had been carved carefully, deftly. The result was faint nubs where the bottoms of the feet were, as though they had been worn almost smooth from weary miles packing trade goods along the fabled Silk Road.

Smiling in anticipation of once again feeling the hidden,

almost secret nubs of the toes, Lianne ran her fingertip across the bottoms of the camel's feet.

Nothing greeted her touch but a smooth, gently concave surface.

Frowning, she turned the camel over. All four feet were smooth rather than slightly nubby where toes would be. She peered into the shadowed back of the drawer, looking for another pale, brown-veined camel sculpture.

Daniel's hands gripped the reinforced side of a cardboard carton with enough force to leave wrinkles. Eyes narrowed until only glittering black slits remained, he watched her bending down to get her face even closer to the drawer.

"Girl," Wen said curtly. "You may have time in front of you, but nearly all my time is behind me. Bring the camel to me without delay. I will hold it while you remind me of the glory I no longer can see."

Or feel. But Wen was too proud to admit that aloud.

With a reluctance that only Daniel saw, Lianne climbed down the ladder, holding the sculpture that Wen demanded. Yet it wasn't the sculpture. Not quite. The difference was as subtle as the bottoms of the camel's feet. She doubted that it was a difference Wen could still appreciate.

As soon as Lianne took her hand out of the drawer, Daniel went back to unpacking jade, examining each piece with great care. She had no doubt that he was looking for signs of careless handling. She also knew he wouldn't find any.

"Here, Uncle Wen," Lianne said.

She set the lustrous brown-and-pale-green sculpture in his lap and put his contorted fingers around the camel's unchanging, timelessly graceful curves. Gently guiding his hands, she described the jade aloud, but she didn't mention its most distinctive feature, the bare suggestion of toes, a detail that set it apart from the vast majority of camel sculptures.

"The stone is of the highest quality. Its luster is gentle and unclouded, as smooth as a lotus petal. The humps are yellow and the rest is the color of rich, wet earth. The carving is intact, completely. There is a fine Cloud Spot on the left rear foot. The carving itself has the quality of elegance so often sought in jade sculpture and much less often found."

While Lianne's soft voice continued to describe the jade, using the traditional Chinese evaluation method called the Six Observations, Wen sat motionless except for an occasional nod when he particularly approved a point she made.

Daniel was listening, too. His hands moved more and more slowly as he unwrapped jade treasures and lined them up on the worktable. From time to time he stole quick glances at the small jade cradled between Wen's bony thighs, as though Daniel was comparing Lianne's words with the reality of the camel sculpture. While he moved around the vault, replacing the jades that had been in the Seattle exhibition, he wished bitterly that he had enjoyed the benefit of Wen's wisdom before his eyes and touch were clouded by age. Instead, that priceless learning had been lavished on a bastard grand-daughter.

"Ah, that is just so," Wen said to Lianne in his whispery voice, nodding. "You make my eyes live again."

"It is a small thing for all that you have given to me."

Wen grinned, revealing yellowed teeth that were still strong despite their ragged spacing. "Replace the camel and bring me something truly archaic, something as old as Chinese memories, older, something . . ."

"Buried jade?" Lianne suggested.

"Yes. Bigger than the palm, but not too big for my old hands."

"A blade, then," she said quickly. "I know just the one. It is magnificent."

"Ah, the emperor's blade." Wen nodded. "Bring it to me, that I may know again its excellence."

Hurriedly Lianne put away the camel with the mysteriously smooth feet and went to the north wall of shelves, the ones reserved for Neolithic jade. Even before she pulled out the fifth drawer from the top, Daniel was all but standing on top of her, watching her.

"Get out of my way," she said in curt English, pushing past him.

"I have more right to be here than you do."

"Take it up with your grandfather. He's the one who gives orders around here, not you."

Daniel's full lips curled in a smile that was more insulting than a raised middle finger. "You think you're invulnerable. But I know just how vulnerable you are, and why." He gestured to the drawer with the back of his hand. "Go ahead, you silly bitch. Play out your charade."

Lianne's heart raced and her hands tingled with adrenaline. She wanted to claw the sneer off her half brother's face, but didn't even try. She had been called worse names in the past, when her schoolmates had found out from their parents that Lianne's mother was a married man's whore.

"You're very brave hiding behind the fortress of your grandfather," she said evenly. "Grow up, little boy. Come out in the real world, the world that neither one of us made, but we have to live in it just the same."

"You—"

"Get out of my face," Lianne interrupted with quiet savagery.

Wen made a querulous sound. "I am waiting."

Daniel looked at his grandfather and stepped out of her way.

Shielding the trembling of her hands with her body, Lianne opened the drawer wide. An array of exceptional Neolithic blades gleamed beneath the overhead lighting. Her first thought was how much Kyle would have loved to see these jades.

Then a vise closed around her heart. The moss-green blade with the fine stains was gone.

She spun around and found herself staring into Daniel's

murderous black eyes, eyes that were horrifyingly like her father's.

"Girl, why are you so slow today?" Wen said in a raspy voice. "Are my requests not simple? A buried blade, that is all. You know my favorite. Bring it."

"Yes," Daniel whispered in English. "Take it to him, little bastard girl. If you can."

Chills coursed through Lianne. *Daniel knew the blade was gone.*

His hand shot past her shoulder so fast that she flinched aside, expecting a blow. He grabbed a piece of jade out of the drawer, holding the blade as though it was indeed a weapon.

"The third blade from the left, second row, is that not correct, Grandfather?" Daniel asked in Cantonese.

"Yes, yes. Have you forgotten, Lianne?"

She shook her head before she remembered that Wen couldn't see. "No, Uncle. I have not forgotten."

She looked from the drawer to Daniel's hands. He had taken the third blade from the left, second row, but it was *not* the blade Lianne remembered putting there. Numbly she walked away from the drawers while Daniel placed the false blade in Wen's contorted hands.

Lianne didn't recognize the jade, except that it was the same size and likely the same weight as the blade that Kyle had bought last night. This blade's color was a shade or two off the fine green of the auction blade. It was translucent, but not particularly luminous. It had burial stains, but they weren't pleasing. Its carving was clean and distinct. What she could see of the jade's surface appeared unblemished, with neither cracks nor chips nor gouges to mar the even flow of stone.

"Ah," the old man said. "Smooth, neither warm nor cool, satin. A clean weight. Another old, old friend. Describe it to me, Lianne."

She opened her mouth but no words came. The blade Wen

held was a very good artifact, but not an excellent one, much less a great piece.

And Wen could no longer tell the difference.

"I will describe it, Grandfather," Daniel said.

With triumph rippling through his voice, he began talking about the Neolithic blade in ancient, almost poetic terms. Wen nodded and made murmurous sounds of pleasure, as though communing with an old friend.

If Lianne closed her eyes, she, too, could see the blade Daniel described. It was the one Kyle Donovan now owned.

twelve

Kyle paced around the small waiting area of Jade State-ments, Lianne's business. She had set up shop in a third-story loft fronting Pioneer Square. Other than a discreetly lettered sign in Chinese and English on the door at the top of a flight of well-worn stairs, there was nothing to announce a commercial presence. Plainly, clients came to Lianne through word of mouth.

If potential clients weren't sold on her talents to begin with, the waiting room decor wasn't intended to impress the undecided. The walls were bare of framed certificates of expertise or self-congratulatory plaques listing awards won or civic virtue rewarded. The room was clean and furnished with a restrained, Pacific Rim flair. The small tables held Sotheby's catalogs or auction catalogs in Chinese, rather than slick Hong Kong color portfolios touting jade collections that Lianne had appraised or bought or sold.

Yet if the harried receptionist was any sample, Jade State-ments didn't lack for clients. The phone hadn't stopped ringing in the fifteen minutes that Kyle had been waiting for Lianne to appear. Most of the time the telephone conversation was in Chinese. The few times it had been in English, all he could overhear were descriptions of jade and repeated denials that the owner of the establishment knew anything about the discovery of the Jade Emperor's Tomb.

Kyle looked at his watch. Seven o'clock. Lianne had told him to be here at six-thirty to pick her up for dinner at the Donovan penthouse. He shoved his hands in the pockets of his dark, casual slacks and made another round of the waiting room. Nothing new. He would give her three more minutes before he sent up a flare to Archer.

The telephone rang again. The receptionist picked it up, resettled his glasses on his nose, and barked into the receiver in English. Then he looked up and motioned to Kyle.

"For you."

Kyle crossed the room in a few swift strides and took the phone. "Yes?"

"She there yet?" Archer asked.

"No. Maybe you better check with Uncle, see if something unexpected came up."

"I did. Her car license was put into the computer as a southbound entry through the Pace Lane at three forty-eight."

Kyle thought quickly, balancing distances with time of day. "She's probably stuck in traffic on I-Five north of the Ship Canal Bridge."

"That's what I figured. I called the condo and told them you would be late and I'd be later."

"I'll save a bone for you to gnaw on."

"If that's all you save me, you'll be gnawing on my knuckles."

Smiling, Kyle handed back the phone, picked up an auction catalog, and began thumbing through it. The Burmese jade choker featured in the catalog was very beautiful, almost mesmerizing with its inner light. Its sale price was also mesmerizing: more than seven million dollars U.S. Burmese jade seemed overpriced to someone raised in a culture that valued clear gemstones such as rubies, emeralds, sapphires, and diamonds. Yet for Asians, no stone was as prized as jade.

Kyle looked at the glossy pages of the *Highly Important Jadeite Jewelry* catalog without a desire to possess any of it. For him, beauty came from history, worth came from history, and rarity came from history. The rest was simply pretty.

The door opened just behind Kyle. He didn't need to look up to know that Lianne had arrived. The clean scent of lilies, rain, and woman curled around him like a caress.

"Sorry," she said tightly. "My appointment ran overtime."

"No problem." Kyle's swift glance took in the sleek lines of her teal business suit, the no-nonsense clip holding her hair at the nape of her neck, and the tension around her eyes and mouth. "Long day?" he asked.

"Very."

"We can call off tonight."

For an instant Lianne was tempted. She was still raw from Daniel's contempt. Worse than that was the fear that just kept growing the more she thought about the Neolithic blade, the pale Tang camel, and the jade burial suit. Though she had stayed several hours longer than she had planned, hoping to do a fast check of the inner vault and the burial shroud—or at the very least to open drawers to see if anything else was missing or replaced by less valuable goods—there had been no opportunity.

Every time she got close to a drawer, Daniel had loomed over her like a vulture. As much as she had wanted to inventory the vault, she hadn't wanted to explain her actions to a man who watched her with hatred and contempt crackling in his black eyes. Nor could she open the room with the jade suit as long as he was there.

Grimly Lianne locked away in her mind what she couldn't change and concentrated on the present. "Just give me a minute to comb my hair and put on some lipstick and I'll be ready to go."

Staying home wouldn't do her any good. She had had more than three hours to think during the drive from Vancouver to Seattle. Plenty of time.

Too much.

The more she thought, the more certain she became that something was horribly wrong. Then there was the fear she couldn't deny and couldn't ignore; Daniel either blamed her for the missing jade or was planning to put the blame on her.

Lianne's stomach clenched as she fought back tension and a surly nausea that wouldn't be banished. She had worked a lifetime to prove her worth to the family of Tang. Now she was being treated like a thief.

Little bastard girl.

Kyle watched the tight lines around Lianne's mouth deepen as her mouth thinned. Her skin was pale, almost waxy. When she wasn't gripping her black briefcase, her fingers trembled.

"Lianne?" he said, touching her shoulder.

She jerked.

"Why don't we just get a quiet dinner at the Rain Lotus?" he asked. "You don't look up to a Donovan family brawl."

Her nostrils flared as she took a quick, deep breath, forcing the iron bands around her lungs to loosen and allow air in. "No. I had all the quiet I can take on the drive down from Vancouver." And it hadn't done her a bit of good. She turned to the receptionist. "Anything that can't wait, Fred?"

"Mrs. Wong wants to know when you'll be available to appraise her father's collection for insurance purposes."

"You have my calendar. Put her on it."

"That's the problem. Mr. Han—"

"Not again," Lianne muttered.

"—has edited his collection and brought with him the pieces he wants to sell. Mr. Harold Tang, uh, requests—"

"Requests? Harry?" she interrupted. "That would be a first."

"Yeah," Fred said, sighing. His thin white hair was a stark contrast to his unlined face. His employment records said he was fifty-five. His face looked at least a decade younger. His eyes were much older. He had been a U.S. government liaison in Taiwan until he put in his twenty years and decided there was more to life than bureaucracy. "However, the Tangs are your best clients, and they know it. Mr. Tang wants you to pick up the Han jades soon as possible. The Jade Trader has pieces ready to swap for whatever parts of his collection that Mr. Han wishes to deacquisition. They will be brought to you."

"Deacquisition?" Kyle said. "Is that a word?"

"Only among museum types who have trouble with the truth," Lianne said.

"Which is?"

"Some acquisitions just don't hold up well over time. Or perhaps you find a better piece and you don't want both. You keep the better one and—"

"Deacquisition the inferior one," Kyle finished.

"Yes."

"*Unload* has fewer syllables," he pointed out.

Lianne smiled for the first time since she had left the Tang compound. "That's why *unload* isn't used in these circumstances. The more syllables the word has, the more important the object, and the more important, the bigger the price."

"*Junk* is a one-syllable, four-letter word, is that it?"

"In my business, yes." Lianne's smile became laughter. She felt like giving Kyle a hug for no other reason than being glad to see him. He looked at her with approval rather than contempt.

Fred cleared his throat and looked up from the calendar he had opened. "Mr. Tang was a, um . . ."

"A pain in the ass?" Kyle suggested.

The receptionist tried not to smile. "You could say that. I couldn't." He looked at his boss. "Mr. Han is expecting you tomorrow at six o'clock."

"In the morning?" she asked, startled.

"Evening."

"But the ferries don't run after—"

"Arrangements have been made for you to stay overnight," Fred said quickly. "You'll take the ferry to Orcas Island. A boat from the institute will pick you up, shuttle you out to the institute, and take you back in the morning."

Lianne's amusement vanished. The memory of Seng's greedy eyes crawled over her skin like insects. "No."

"Mr. Tang said it was vital to—" Fred began.

"No," she broke in, her voice flat. "Make another appointment, one that will allow me to go home for dinner."

"I tried. Mr. Han's calendar is filled." Fred flipped a steno notebook open and referred to his notes, which were a mixture of Chinese ideographs and Western script. "He leaves for China the day after tomorrow, and has meetings tomorrow from five A.M. until eight P.M. He'll try to join you sooner, but is confident of your ability to deliver the Tang jade, just as he—Han Seng—is confident that Mr. Wen Zhi Tang will choose appropriate pieces for the trade."

Closing her eyes, Lianne thought hard about what Fred had told her. Obviously Harry and Seng were continuing to finesse the problem of taxes, money transfers, currency exchange, and the like by trading jade for jade. It wasn't an uncommon thing. Dealers did it all the time. Trading up, trading down, trading sideways; none of that was taxed.

More important, if Seng was in meetings, he wouldn't be rubbing up against her like a tomcat with a rash.

Even as Lianne told herself that Seng's overbearing manner didn't mean that he had a little forced sex in mind, she knew she didn't want to be alone with him. Period.

"Which island is Seng on?" Kyle asked.

"It used to be called Barren Island," Lianne said. "Now it's called Farmer."

Kyle knew the place. It was close to Jade Island, where he sometimes camped and once had almost died. "Guest of Farmer's Institute of Asian Communications?"

"Yes. How did you know?"

"Not hard. Seng is one of the best-connected capitalists in mainland China. Farmer is a multibillionaire who is slavering to get a foothold in a market that holds one-quarter of the world's population."

"How about Donovan International?" Lianne asked. "Is it 'slavering' for a piece of the Chinese market?"

"Interested, not slavering. We don't handle electronics re-sale the way Farmer does. Why don't I come with you?"

She blinked. "You want to see Seng's jade rejects?"

"Dying to," he said laconically. "We can tie up at the institute's dock, you can do your thing with jade while I watch, listen, and learn, and then we can come back."

"Minus a ferry?"

"I have a boat."

"Oh." Lianne thought about it, then smiled with a combination of relief and malice. The relief came from being able to placate Harry at a time when she was afraid she would need all the Tang goodwill she could muster. The malice came from the thought of Seng's disappointment when she appraised his jade and walked off into the night on Kyle Donovan's arm. "This is above and beyond the call of duty, even for a stuffed-elephant escort service."

"Any excuse to get aboard the *Tomorrow*."

"Is that your boat's name, *Tomorrow*?"

"I called her that because I was always going to have more time to go fishing—"

"Tomorrow," Lianne interrupted, smiling.

"Yeah. Then a few months ago, I realized that tomorrow would never come unless I made plans for it today."

"You're sure it isn't too much trouble to take your boat?"

"To Farmer Island? Hell, no. I'll have to check the tides, but if we leave early enough, we might be able to catch some fish for dinner along the way."

The light in Kyle's eyes and the sudden eagerness in his expression made him look years younger than thirty-one.

"You catch it, I'll cook it," Lianne said.

"How about cleaning it?"

"How about eating out?"

He snickered. "Go put on your lipstick. We'll argue on the way to the condo."

As soon as Lianne closed the door of the inner office behind her, Kyle turned to Fred.

"Confirm that Lianne will be at Farmer Island tomorrow at six," Kyle said. "Don't say anything about me, my boat, or not staying the night."

Fred started to ask why, decided it was none of his business, and picked up the phone.

"Wait," Lianne said as Kyle reached for the door to the Donovan condo. "I'm a mess."

"Quit fussing," he said as she smoothed her teal skirt and tugged at her jacket bottom in a futile attempt to get rid of wrinkles. "You're gorgeous."

"Oh, right," she muttered. "You'd never guess I spent twelve hours in these clothes, seven of them sitting in a car."

Ignoring her complaints, Kyle started to push the door open. "Susa will probably be wearing paint-crusted jeans and one of Archer's old sweatshirts."

"Susa isn't here yet," Honor said, pulling the door wide open and giving Kyle a big hug. "If you get any better-looking, I'll have to buy you a guard dog."

"You're thinking of Archer," Kyle said, returning his sister's hug with interest. "He's the one who needs a guard to protect him from women."

Lianne looked at the tall, slender woman who had Kyle's unusual eyes and a smile that could light up a cave. She was wearing a thick, soft, sage-green sweater that was just like the one Kyle had on, size included. Unlike him, the black pants she wore fit like another skin, showing off long, long legs beneath the baggy sweater. On Kyle, the sweater didn't bag, but his shoulders were at least half again as wide as Honor's.

"Lianne Blakely, this is Honor Donov—oops. Mallory. I'm having a hard time getting used to the new name."

"Hi, Lianne," Honor said. "The name isn't that new, Kyle is just that slow."

"After thirty years, six months is new," Kyle retorted. "So when are you going to make me an uncle?"

"You want kids to spoil, you go and get them the old-fashioned way," Honor retorted. "Come in, Lianne. Welcome to the Donovan zoo." She turned back to her brother, who was closing the door. "Susa and The Donovan called just before Archer did. He got hung up with a currency exchange problem—Dad, not Archer—and Susa got bored and started painting sunset reflected in fog, and—"

"They're late," Kyle finished. "What did I get them for their anniversary?"

"I'll play your silly game," Honor said, wide-eyed. "What did you get them?"

The look of distress on Kyle's face made Lianne laugh even as she reached out to touch his arm in sympathy. "Your sister is teasing you."

"No!" Kyle said with mock horror. "How did you guess she's my sister?"

"Your sweaters match, like your eyes. Only hers are beautiful."

Honor snickered. "Guess she told you. I stole this sweater from Justin's dresser. Kyle must have swiped his from Lawe's. They're twins. Justin and Lawe, that is. Kyle is one of a kind, thank God."

"Swiped? I just borrowed," Kyle said, defending himself. "I wasn't expecting to spend several days in Seattle. Besides, Justin and Lawe are in South America. They won't know about sweater swiping unless you tell them."

"I won't tell if you won't," Honor promised. She grinned at Lianne. "Come in and meet my husband. Jake, where are you?"

"Marinating the salmon," called a deep voice from the rear of the condo. "I could use a hand chopping herbs."

"We're on the way," Honor said.

"Salmon." Lianne sighed and licked her lips unconsciously. After a quick, comprehensive look at the wall of landscapes that were calling silently, vividly, to her, she politely followed Honor into the condo's huge kitchen. Good manners became enthusiasm when she inhaled the scents of fresh food being prepared. "I'm in heaven."

"Not likely," Jake said, looking up from the lemons he was squeezing. "Too many Donovans."

"Only one," Kyle retorted. "Me."

"The prosecution rests," Jake said. He switched his smile to Lianne. "You must be Ms. Blakely. I'm Jake Mallory."

"Hi. Only it's Lianne." She smiled at the big, dark man whose hands made lemons look the size of limes. "Where are the herbs?"

"In the vase," he said, gesturing with his chin toward a counter.

"Knife?"

"Behind me in the right-hand island drawer."

"Chopped herbs coming right up." Lianne opened the drawer and pulled out a wicked chef's knife.

Honor and Kyle watched in fascination as Lianne smoothly, efficiently reduced the herbs to fragrant green flakes with rapid motions of the knife.

"Whew," Kyle muttered to Honor. "Remind me not to get between her and something she wants."

With a deft motion of the knife, Lianne heaped the chopped herbs onto the wide blade and turned to Jake. "Where do you want them?"

"You're better than a Cuisinart." Jake smiled and lifted his hands away from the pan of salmon filets. "Here, dump 'em on the fish."

Lianne bent over the shallow pan that held long red filets that were two inches thick. She inhaled discreetly, then with more force. Nothing came to her nostrils but a vague scent of cold and brine. Exactly what fresh fish should smell like and almost never did.

"Fantastic," she said reverently. "Where do you get fish this fresh? Even Pike Place Market isn't this good."

"Caught it this morning," Jake said.

She looked up into his blue-gray eyes and saw that he wasn't joking. "Are you a commercial fisherman?"

"Nope. A stomach fisherman. And Honor was the one who nailed this baby."

"Where?" Kyle asked instantly.

"Off Fildalgo Head," Honor said. "All eighteen pounds of him. The fish, not the headland."

"Blackmouth?" Kyle asked.

Honor nodded. "A real beauty. Fierce and feisty. His teeth raked my finger when I was getting the hook out." She showed a ragged red line along her right index finger. "But I figure he had a little of my blood coming. After all, we're eating him. You should have seen it," she said, her face lighting up with excitement. "He hit the lure like a runaway train and then—"

"My wife hates to fish," Jake interrupted, deadpan. "Just ask her."

"I can tell," Lianne said, hiding her smile. "I caught a salmon once. A little one. But it tasted so good I've never forgotten it."

"This one will be better," Honor said confidently. "Nobody does salmon like Jake. And I *did* hate to fish before I met him."

"I always wondered about that," Kyle said, turning to his brother-in-law. "How did you convince her that fishing wasn't slimy, scary, and disgusting?"

"No problem. I let her use my rod."

There was a beat of silence before Kyle snickered.

Color burned on Honor's cheekbones. She tried not to laugh, but couldn't stop herself. She gave Jake a slow-motion cuff on his shoulder that turned into a caress halfway down his arm. He gave her fingers a lingering, lemony squeeze and a smile that transformed his hard features.

Smiling rather wistfully, Lianne scattered fresh herbs over

the filets. As she admired the contrast of vivid green herbs and red-orange flesh, she thought of her years with Lee. She had never had that kind of sexy teasing and easy camaraderie with him. Perhaps the difference was cultural. Perhaps it was personal. Whatever, it was real.

The front door of the condo opened.

"Archer?" Kyle called as he started for the door. He was impatient to know if anyone had been following Lianne. And if so, who the tail worked for.

"No," called a woman's voice. "It's Faith and Tony."

Lianne wondered if Honor and Jake noticed the subtle hardening of Kyle's features. Lianne certainly did.

"Faith is my twin," Honor said over her shoulder as she rushed out to the living room, her smile just a bit too big, too welcoming.

Kyle and Jake exchanged a brief, sideways look, but neither said a word.

"Hey, it's your gorgeous sister," said a male voice. "Good thing you're spoken for, babe. I love the way you fill out a sweater."

Whatever Honor said didn't reach the kitchen.

"Drizzle some olive oil over that," Jake told Lianne. "I'd better go see that Faith and Honor don't get in trouble between the front door and the kitchen."

"The two of them are like puppies," Kyle explained. "What mischief one doesn't think of, the other does."

Lianne lifted silky black eyebrows. "I suppose you and your brothers never egged each other on into trouble?"

He fixed her with innocent, gold-and-green eyes. "Me? Trouble? I was altar boy of the year."

"I'd be impressed if I believed you."

Honor came into the kitchen arm in arm with her sister. Honor had sun-streaked chestnut hair; Faith's was a golden blond. Honor was an inch taller and more roundly built. Faith was a willow. Honor's eyes were the same striking color as Kyle's. Faith's eyes were the color of fog just before it thins into clear sky—silver with a hint of blue. Both sisters had slanting, pronounced cheekbones, a stubborn chin, a light-up-the-room smile, and a leggy, easy stride.

The man walking next to Jake was a big, brown-eyed blond who looked like he lifted brick outhouses for the hell of it. He was bigger than Kyle, bigger than Jake; Tony had been a nose tackle in college and a third-round draft pick for the pro circuit. Then he brought his foot down the wrong way on Astroturf and fractured every bone in his right ankle. An orthopedic surgeon put it all back together with titanium pins and screws, but Tony's career was over. It took a second break in the same ankle, more surgery, three months on crutches, and six more on pain pills to convince him, but he finally gave up his dreams of gridiron fame and took a job with his father's PR firm.

"There's my man! Kyle, gimme five. How 'bout them Sea Hawks?" Tony asked triumphantly.

Kyle and Jake looked blank. So did everyone but Faith. Football season was long over.

"Whatta play!" Tony said. "Pulled it out in the fourth with the kind of pattern I used to run when I played pro ball."

"What game?" Kyle asked.

"The one last night on the sports channel. They ran it all with commentary from a Sea Hawks trainer."

"I didn't catch the rerun," Kyle said. "Lianne, this is—"

"You missed it?" Tony asked in disbelief. Then he smiled slightly. "Oh, yeah. I keep forgetting you didn't play in college, big guy like you. You were in what, golf?"

"Synchronized swimming."

Honor's smile faded.

Faith's became more determined.

Kyle took a better grip on his uncertain temper. Faith was wearing a diamond the size of Wisconsin on her left hand. Or left fist, at the moment. He didn't give a damn what Tony thought, but he loved his little sister.

"Lianne Blakely," Kyle said, showing a double row of white teeth, "my sister Faith and her fiancé, Tony Kerrigan."

Lianne smiled, shifted the chef's knife to her left hand, and offered her right to Faith. Tony whistled, gripped Lianne's hand before Faith could, and glanced at Kyle.

"You've been holding out on me, buddy," Tony said. "Where did you pick up this exotic number?"

"Actually," Lianne said, notching her smile up to full industrial strength, "I picked him up." She retrieved her hand and held it out to Faith. "Hi, Faith. Glad to meet you."

"Same here," Faith said, smiling with a combination of relief and natural warmth as she shook hands. "How did you pick Kyle up?"

"With a crane."

The anxiety around Faith's eyes relaxed into laughter. Her left hand relaxed. The motion sent shards of light dancing off the diamond.

Even as Kyle told himself to get over it, that Faith had made her choice, he wondered whose credit had purchased the rock—Faith's or Tony's. The only way Tony could have bought it would be if he had gotten pig-lucky betting point spreads.

Honor didn't need a weather map to know that storm clouds were gathering. With the ease of a sister used to negotiating the unpredictable moods of older brothers, she deftly assigned Jake the job of setting up the barbecue and listening to Tony talk about his football glory days. Kyle was delegated to get charcoal from the storage area in the garage downstairs.

The ringing of the phone barely penetrated the laughter as Susa told about the one time she had coaxed her husband into posing for her and had ended up with more paint on her than on the canvas.

"That's when Faith and Honor were conceived," Archer said dryly, reaching for the phone. "It explains their artistic bent."

The Donovan just smiled, lifted Susa's hand to his lips, and tickled her palm with his mustache. Or perhaps his tongue. Lianne couldn't be sure. All she knew was that Susa laughed and looked at her husband with loving hazel eyes.

"She'll be right down," Archer said, hanging up the phone. He glanced at Lianne. "Your taxi is here."

"That was fast."

"Twenty minutes is fast?" Archer asked.

"Was it that long? Seemed like two or three." She looked at Kyle, who was sitting next to her, his long legs stretched out in front, his body warm against her hip and thigh. More than warm. Burning. She had never been more physically aware of a man in her life. When he shifted to stand up, she put her hand on his thigh. "Don't get up. Enjoy your family."

"They'll be here when I get back. Since you won't let me drive you home, the least I can do is see you safely to your taxi."

His thigh muscle flexed against her palm as he stood up, pulling her after him. Arm around her waist, he waited while she made her good-byes. He was the only one who noticed Archer's eyes narrow when Honor and Faith gave Lianne the kind of hug that said come again soon.

"You have a great family," Lianne said as the elevator door closed behind them. "Thanks for sharing them with me."

"You sure? Most people would have been overwhelmed by all those Donovans at once."

Lianne's laughter lit up her clear whiskey eyes. "I wish your parents had twenty kids."

Kyle smiled and shook his head. "The mind quails."

He laced his fingers slowly, deeply, with Lianne's and tried not to notice the heightened beating of the pulse in her throat. Just like he tried not to notice the sway of her breasts beneath her business suit, the inward turn of her waist, the rich promise of her hips, and the elegant shape of her legs.

He might as well have tried to stop his heart from beating.

The elevator stopped and the door whisked open. Just beyond the small, luxurious foyer and beveled glass doors, a taxi waited by the curb.

"I'll send him away," Kyle said, "and take you home myself."

Temptation snaked through Lianne, but she shook her head. She knew if Kyle took her home, she wouldn't sleep alone that night. No matter how sexy the man, she didn't do one-night stands. Perhaps it was because of being a bastard, perhaps it was simply pride, perhaps she just didn't have a high sex drive.

Whatever, she wasn't going to bed with a man who wanted nothing more from her than any whore could give him.

"Thanks again," Lianne said, standing up on tiptoe to brush her lips against Kyle's. "I can't remember when I enjoyed an evening so much."

The touch of her lips was too brief. He bent to give her another kiss, a kiss he meant to be as casual as the one she had given him. But something happened along the way. It was the tip of his tongue rather than his lips that met her smile, traced it, caressed it until she made a ragged sound and let him in. His arms locked around her, lifting her, holding her so tightly that neither one of them could breathe. Their tongues mated in a hungry, stabbing dance.

Kyle didn't know how long the kiss lasted. He knew only that when the impatient honking of the taxi finally got through the red haze of lust that passed for his brain, he was crushing Lianne between the elevator wall and his urgent body, and she was fighting to get even closer to him, making throaty whimpering sounds that begged him to strip her naked and fuck her blind.

"Jesus," he said, letting her slide slowly down his body, feeling every female inch of her. "Sweet Jesus Christ."

Her feet hit the elevator floor, her knees buckled. Her eyes were wide, dark, dazed. She made a ragged sound that could have been a laugh or a curse. Then she shook her head, trying to clear the overwhelming thunder of her heartbeat from her ears.

"What happened?" she asked shakily.

Before Kyle could answer, she twisted free of his arms and ran to the taxi.

"Tomorrow," he called after Lianne. "I'll pick you up at ten and we'll drive to Anacortes."

"No. Honor gave me your Anacortes address. I'll meet you there. Two o'clock."

The taxi door slammed. Red taillights surged into the night, blended with other city lights, vanished.

The service elevator chimed softly. The doors opened and Archer stepped out. He didn't have the look of a happy man.

"What's wrong?" Kyle asked.

"I was going to ask you the same. Did the elevator jam?"

"What do you think?"

Archer's steel-gray eyes went from Kyle's finger-combed hair to his kiss-reddened mouth and then to the blunt bulge in his crotch. "I think you need a cold shower."

"Why don't we do a little one-on-one in the downstairs gym instead?"

"Don't tempt me."

"Why not? You've been looking for something to thump on since you walked into the condo. And it wasn't just the rock on Faith's hand that set you off, was it?"

"Lianne's shadow was government," Archer said curtly.

"No surprise there. We knew Uncle was interested."

"So am I. I had a little chat with the tail. He made a call, gave me a number, and I made a call."

Kyle's eyebrows went up. "Why do I feel you're leaving something out? Like how the guy felt about making the call in the first place."

"He wanted his face. I wanted a telephone number. How either of us felt about it wasn't on the table."

"How long had he been following her?"

"He didn't say. It doesn't matter." Archer lifted his hand,

cutting off Kyle's attempt to speak. "He saw her come and go several times from the city of Vancouver and the Tang family fortress with trunkloads of jade."

"So what? She handled the Jade Trader exhibit last night. Stands to reason she would be shuttling back and forth with jade in her trunk."

"Some of what she handled stayed in her trunk. She's about one step away from being arrested."

"What does that mean?" Kyle demanded.

"Just what it sounds like," Archer said flatly. "Uncle has a wire into the Tang family. Some stuff has gone missing from the Vancouver vault."

"Too bad, how sad, shit happens. Has anyone seen Lianne with the missing stuff? Has anyone bought it from her?"

"Yes to the first. They're still looking for the second."

"Pretty thin. What makes them think Lianne is so stupid that she would steal pieces that were certain to be missed?"

"Not stupid. Very, very shrewd. She's been creaming old man Wen's collection, selling it, and substituting inferior goods so that no one noticed the holes."

"It doesn't fly. Wen would have noticed."

"A few years ago, yes. Things change. Wen's eyes and hands sure did. The substitutions were clever. Good, but not as high a quality, not as rare, not as aesthetic, not as old, whatever. The sort of things only an expert would notice, but they have a hell of an impact on the bottom line."

Kyle thought of Wen's gnarled hands and cloudy eyes. Then he thought of Lianne's clear eyes and sensitive fingertips. "I don't like it."

"Did someone ask you to? She never would have been caught if one of her half brothers didn't have a good eye for jade."

"Why would Lianne rob Wen?"

Archer gave his brother a look of disbelief. "The usual reason. Greed."

"Not her style." Kyle's voice was certain. His mind and his gut were in complete agreement on this one.

"Greed doesn't have a style," Archer retorted. "But if you don't like that motive, there's always revenge."

"They haven't done anything to Lianne except give her a lot of clients and an entree into the closed corridors of the jade world."

"Bullshit. Think with your brain instead of your dick. How do you suppose Faith would react if she knew she was as much a Donovan as any of us, and everyone from Dad on down treated her like a bad smell? But, hey, the girl is useful. Real talent. So the Donovans just use Faith like any other employee, except—"

"Lianne—" Kyle interrupted.

"Shut up and listen. Except we always knew she was desperately hungry to belong to the family, and we used that, too, dangling little rewards like candy in front of a starving kid. Someone with Faith's guts and temperament and hunger would keep trying and trying and trying to prove that she was worth being loved . . . until she grew up and realized that she was being as thoroughly screwed as her unmarried mama, and the pay wasn't nearly as good."

Kyle's fists and shoulders bunched with tension. He wanted to argue with Archer. His gut kept saying Lianne was innocent.

But his mind understood the need for revenge all too well. Lianne was both intelligent and proud. A dangerous combination in some circumstances.

"I won't argue the point," he said evenly to his brother. "I won't agree all the way, either. I can't."

Archer let out a long breath and a hissing curse at the same time. "What's the problem—your mind or your dick?"

"My gut."

"Hell." Archer crossed his arms over his chest and leaned against the wall. "You have a better idea how to explain the missing jades? And they *are* missing."

"Soddi," Kyle said succinctly.

A sardonic smile deepened the already bleak lines of Archer's face. "Soddi, huh?"

"Yeah. Some other dude did it."

"That only works for defense lawyers."

"It works for me until something better comes along."

"Parts of Japan are real pretty at this time of year," Archer said. "The Mikimoto showings are among the most spectacular gem displays on earth. Rooms of pearls, all sizes, all shapes, gleaming like heaven come to earth. And those South Seas black pearls have to be seen to be believed."

"Enjoy your trip."

"You enjoy it. I'm staying home."

"Send Faith. Separate her from Joy Boy upstairs."

"I'm considering it," Archer said. "The two of you would have a great—"

"No."

A year ago, Archer would have argued. A year ago, he would have won.

It wasn't a year ago.

"I'll do it your way," Archer decided. "For now."

"And then?"

"I'll do whatever it takes."

t h i r t e e n

Kyle was still thinking about Archer's words the next day when he and Lianne set off aboard his boat for Farmer Island.

Whatever it takes.

It wasn't a threat. It wasn't a promise. It was simply Archer stating a fact. A year ago, Kyle would have been nervous about the *whatever.* Today, he was simply wondering if he would have been closer to the truth about the Jade Emperor if he had screwed Lianne senseless last night.

It had been a near thing. The screwing, if not the truth. What had started as a casual, polite good-night kiss had burned like a fuse on the way to nuclear meltdown. He had barely stopped himself from ripping off her clothes and taking her in the open elevator with her taxi waiting twenty feet away. When he finally forced himself to let go of Lianne, she was trembling. It wasn't from fear. She was as hungry as he was.

What happened?

Kyle hadn't had an answer to Lianne's question. The realization of how fast and deep she had gotten under his skin was like a bucket of ice water thrown in his face. He shouldn't want any woman that much. He sure as hell shouldn't want *that* woman when he knew Uncle was drawing up an arrest warrant for her.

On the other hand, maybe a few sweaty hours between the sheets would loosen her sexy, hungry tongue. He hadn't had much luck prying anything useful out of her with questions and answers since she had met him at the little dock that was just below his cabin. When he brought up the jade burial suit, she shut down. Then she changed the subject. When he brought the topic back to jade, she asked about fishing.

So he took the pretty little thief fishing.

Except she just didn't look like a thief. Especially now, playing tug-of-war with a rockfish and so excited that she was dancing in place on the *Tomorrow*'s deck. She was wearing one of his fishing jackets over her businesslike suit. The waterproof jacket hung halfway down her legs. She should have looked ridiculous. Instead, she looked edible. She definitely didn't look like a woman on the verge of being arrested as an international art thief.

Archer was wrong. Or the government was. Or . . .

What's the problem—your mind or your dick?

Archer's sardonic question echoed in Kyle's memory. He told himself that he was too old and too smart to be led around by his dumb handle again. And he had proved it last night. He had been the one to end the kiss, not Lianne.

Besides, there were good reasons why Lianne could be innocent. The fact that there were good reasons why she could be guilty just made the game more interesting. And that was all it was. A game.

If Kyle didn't want to play, there was the uncomfortable fact that he owed the government a favor that Archer shouldn't have to be the one to repay. Let his brother go count pearls in Japan or Australia or Tahiti; Kyle was determined to find out if Lianne was a thief and he was a dick-brained idiot, or if she was mostly innocent and he wasn't a complete fool.

Laughter and the flash of dark cognac eyes distracted Kyle from his edgy thoughts. He checked the position of the *Tomorrow,* saw that nothing had changed, and went back to watching Lianne. The twenty-seven-foot powerboat didn't need much attention at the moment. It was anchored up close to Jade Island, at the foot of a steep cliff.

He had chosen the island's remote, stony presence for three reasons. The first was its proximity to Farmer Island. The second was the near certainty of snagging a rockfish among the eddies and swirls where the north side of the tiny island rose sheer and stark from the dark green sea. The third reason was that he had almost died here. The severe beauty of fir and rock, wind and sea, would remind him that there were some mistakes a man could get killed repeating.

Thinking with his dick was one of them.

Lianne blew strands of black hair out of her eyes, settled her feet more securely on the gently rolling deck, and shifted her grip on the rod.

"Is it another dogfish?" Kyle asked.

"How would I know? I can't see it. Maybe it's a salmon."

"Doubt it."

There hadn't been enough time to make a serious run at trolling for salmon, and the tide was wrong anyway. Fortunately, rockfish were tasty and they weren't as picky about what and when they ate as salmon were.

"This is great," Lianne said gleefully, reeling as hard as she could. "When I went out on that cattle boat, it took forever to find any fish at all. I've had two so far."

"They were dogfish. That's why we shifted fishing spots."

"In China we would have eaten them."

"In China you eat anything that doesn't eat you first. Keep reeling. I'm hungry enough to eat a big rockfish all by myself and look around for more."

"Aren't you going to fish?" Lianne asked, frowning as she reeled line in.

"I figure I'll be kept busy baiting hooks for you."

And pulling hooks off the bottom, replacing hooks after dogfish swallowed them, untangling snarls, and fixing all the other minor disasters that came while learning how to catch bottom fish.

Lianne laughed in sheer excitement as the rockfish fought against being reeled in. Watching her, Kyle kept trying to convince himself that she was a clever thief bent on revenge, no matter what the cost to family and country. He didn't make much headway on the project because he was caught in a three-cornered argument with himself: his mind had no problem with guilt, his dick didn't care either way, and his gut was hanging tough for innocence.

"This fish must be huge!" Lianne said, bracing herself again as the *Tomorrow*'s deck shifted almost lazily beneath her feet.

"Doubt it. Rockfish hit hard and give up easy."

"When does the give-up begin?" Lianne asked.

"Real soon."

"Is that a pun?"

"Bite your tongue."

The weight of the unhappy fish dragged the top of the rod into an arc. Long and limber, the rod was designed to let the fisherman feel every twist and wriggle of the fish, and to give the fish a fighting chance to throw off the hook. The reel was also designed with sport in mind, which meant that Lianne was having to work for her fish. Most reels were double action—one crank of the handle equaled two turns of line around the reel. Eight inches of line came in at a time. But Kyle used a mooching reel. One turn of the handle equaled one turn of the line around the reel, period. Four inches, not eight.

Suddenly the reel turned easily. Lianne made a dismayed sound. "It's gone."

"Nope. It just gave up. Keep reeling."

As Kyle had predicted, the fish came docilely to the boat and wallowed on its side.

"How do you know so much?" she asked.

"Legacy of a misspent youth. See those red spines along the back?"

"Yes."

"Stay away from them. Now wrap your hand around the line and swing this baby aboard."

"What about the net?"

"Nets are for salmon."

He got a pair of pliers and a cosh and waited for Lianne to lever the fish into the stern well of the boat. After a few false tries, she leaned way over the gunwale, wrapped the line around her hand, and yanked the fish aboard.

Kyle wished Lianne had several fish to play with. She looked good bent over the gunwale, her skirt and his jacket riding high enough that he could see that her nylons came only to mid-thigh and were held in placc by their own elastic tops. They made a sexy, smoky-gray contrast against her golden skin. He couldn't help thinking how plain damn good it would feel to slide his hands up nylon to flesh, then to stroke and probe until she was wet and so was he.

What's the problem—your mind or your dick?

Kyle grasped the rockfish's lower jaw with the pliers and coshed it on its tiny brain. Though he expected Lianne to flinch, she didn't. She just watched him as she had when he explained how to handle the mooching reel.

"No screams over killing something?" Kyle asked, removing the hook with a quick twist of the pliers.

Lianne looked at him with wide, dark eyes. A smile teased the corners of her mouth. "Disappointed?"

He laughed, opened the fish box, and threw the rockfish in. "Maybe a little. Honor and Faith used to make the most incredible high noises. It was half the fun of fishing, at first."

What he didn't say was that cleaning fish or accidentally threading a hook through a baitfish eyeball had made him queasy the first few times it happened. Same for all of his brothers, but you could have roasted them over a slow fire before they admitted to such weakness in front of their baby sisters.

Before Kyle could thread another limp herring on the hook, Lianne took it and skewered the little bait fish neatly just behind the eyes.

"You sure you weren't already a fisherman?" he asked.

"Fisher*san,*" Lianne corrected instantly. "That's what Honor told me last night. Fishersan is the proper usage, neither male nor female."

"Honor is as full of stuff as a Christmas goose."

"I liked your sister. Both your sisters. They're so close," Lianne said with unconscious wistfulness. "And your parents were great. Putty in each other's hands and solid rock in anyone else's. Best of all," she added, dropping the baited hook over the side and letting it spiral rapidly down into the green water, "Susa is smaller than I am. I was beginning to feel like a midget."

"Only because Tony kept towering over you."

"That's what I like about you. You're big, but you don't loom."

"How about your mother?" Kyle asked. "Big, little, in between?"

"Same size as I am. Small."

"Small? You're just—keep your rod tip up! That's a salmon!"

"How can you—"

"Watch your knuckles!" he interrupted.

Kyle's warnings and the wildly spinning handles of the reel connected with Lianne at the same time. She cried out, shook the hand that had stinging knuckles, and hung onto the rod with her left hand.

"You okay?" he asked.

She nodded and went back to reeling. Or trying to. The fish kept taking off, stripping line from the reel in a long, sustained scream of friction, pulling the handles right out of her grasp.

Kyle whistled. "That's a nice salmon."

"Are you sure it's a salmon?" she asked, struggling to control rod and reel. "It feels like a killer whale."

"It's a salmon. Blackmouth. I'll bet you picked it up just off the bottom."

"I didn't pick this boy up. He picked me up. Hard."

Grinning, Kyle watched Lianne fight to keep the fish from taking off any more line.

"Keep the rod tip up," he told her. "Let the fish fight the rod, not you."

"Easy for you to say. This sucker has a mind of its own."

Slowly she reeled the fish in closer and closer to the boat. "I can see it. Get the net!"

"If you can see the fish, it can see the boat, which means—"

Suddenly line screamed off the reel. Lianne yelped and snatched her knuckles away from the carnivorous handles. The fish headed for Farmer Island, which was a green blur several miles away.

"Which means the fish will bolt," Kyle finished with satisfaction. "You've got a blackmouth, sweetheart. And it's big enough to keep."

"How do you know?"

"You can tell a lot about a fish by the way it fights. I'll bet this one stops taking line real soon, then sits and sulks."

She blew her hair out of her face. "I hope so. I feel like I'm trying to reel in a Land Rover."

"Want me to take it?"

"Not on your life," she said fiercely. "This one is mine."

"It must be. This is the wrong place for a salmon, the wrong time, wrong tide, and wrong method. Beginner's luck beats skill every time."

Lianne was too busy trying to get four inches of line around the reel to listen to Kyle's complaints.

He judged the tension on the line, the deep arc of the rod, and her tight-lipped determination as she reeled. Or tried to.

The salmon was way down deep, sulking over the herring snack that was fighting back.

He looked at the western sky. Soon the sun would be a blazing orange disk dragging day behind it into the ocean's blue-black night. They might be late getting to the Institute of Asian Communications and Han Seng.

The idea didn't bother Kyle a bit.

"Remember what I told you about pumping the rod?" he asked.

"No," she said, panting.

"Like this."

Kyle stepped up behind Lianne, reached around her left side, and put his left hand above hers on the rod. His right hand came around her and eased the butt of the rod until it was snug against her torso.

"If that hurts," he said, "brace the rod against your hipbone or the top of your thigh. Honor does it one way and Faith the other."

"How do you do it?"

"Upper-body strength. You don't have it."

"Drop off," Lianne muttered. "Brawn isn't everything. Leverage counts more."

Kyle grinned and almost nuzzled the nape of her neck. She looked like a determined, grumpy cat. "So use leverage," he said against her ear. "Like this."

He settled the rod butt in the crease between her torso and her left thigh. "How's that?"

"Better. Now what?"

"Pull the rod toward you with your left hand. If you can't do it with your elbow bent, straighten it."

"Leverage," she said breathlessly, pulling.

"That's the idea."

She pulled harder, braced herself against Kyle, and pulled again. The rod didn't move much.

Kyle wished he could have said the same for his own rod. Surrounding Lianne like a blanket while her sweet little butt rubbed over his crotch was having a predictable and immediate effect.

"Move your hand up higher," he said. "More leverage that way."

More than her hand moved. Her whole body did. He gritted his teeth and thought about anything but the unintentional, fiercely sexual friction that came every time she changed her position even a bit.

And she changed it often.

"Got a good grip on the rod?" he asked.

"Yes."

"Straighten your arm, lean back with your whole body, then quickly lean forward and reel like hell at the same time. I'll steady you until you get the rhythm."

Lianne rocked back, then forward, and reeled like hell, gaining about a foot of line.

"Again," Kyle said.

Breathing hard from exertion, she repeated the maneuver again and again. After a few minutes he was breathing deeply, too, but exertion didn't have anything to do with it. The smell of her flushed, perfumed skin, the heat of it, the feel of her body rubbing against him from chest to thighs, all added up to the kind of sustained sexual torture he hadn't endured since his heavy petting days in high school.

If he had touched her like this last night, he wouldn't have had the control to let go of her. The only thing that was helping him now was that she was completely focused on the fish rather than on the man who was wrapped around her.

"I think I'm gaining on it," she said breathlessly.

"Good," he said through clenched teeth. "Keep pumping the rod. That's it."

"When do you get the net?"

"Soon," Kyle prayed beneath his breath. "I hope." Breath hissed between his teeth as her butt rubbed against him like a cat in heat. He bit off a groan.

"What?" Lianne asked.

"Pump!"

She pumped, cranking in a foot of line at a time. She didn't know she was panting and laughing and panting some more. All she knew was that something powerful and alive was on the other end of the line, something that was going to test her strength and determination before it gave up and became dinner.

It never occurred to her that she would lose.

Lianne wrestled the fish up to the boat again, only to have the salmon turn and race away once more. A hundred feet of line peeled off in a screaming blur. She shifted position like a boxer heading into the final round and began pumping all over again.

Kyle didn't know whether he was happy or sad. Crazy, yes. He knew about that. So crazy that he was hoping the salmon had at least one more good run in it.

The third time Lianne got the fish near the boat, it made a halfhearted run. Grinning fiercely, she reeled in line.

"I'm letting go to get the net," Kyle said. "Okay?"

Only then did Lianne realize that he had been wrapped around her like a lover, helping her to keep her balance while the fish moved from one side of the boat to the other. Heat shot through her, the same fire that had prowled through her all the long, restless night.

"I'm okay," she said. "I'm braced."

Unwillingly, he removed his arms. He stepped back just a little, steadied her, and reluctantly accepted that he had no more excuse to touch her. She was doing just fine on her own.

"Watch the weight," Kyle said suddenly. "Stop reeling!"

Lianne stopped, looked, and saw that the weight was at the rod tip, stuck in the eye of the first line guide. The tip was only a few feet above the water. Four more feet of line was underneath. At the end of that was a hook and a very unhappy salmon.

From the corner of her eye she saw Kyle take a big black salmon net out of its holder. Slowly he wetted the net in the sea, watching the tired turning of the salmon just out of his reach. The fish was big, deep, its scales shimmering with life.

"He's a beauty, twenty pounds if he's an ounce," Kyle said. "When I tell you to, back up and keep your—"

"Rod tip up," Lianne finished with a breathless laugh. "I have that part memorized."

"Don't stumble on the engine cover when you back up."

"Are you going to net my fish or order me around?"

"I'm an older brother. I can do both at the same time."

"Kyle, hurry up," she pleaded. "I don't want to lose it!"

"You won't. Back up some more. A little more. Keep going. Good!"

A quick swoop and flex of Kyle's arms, a rush of seawater pouring through the net, and the fish was aboard.

Lianne made a husky sound and dropped to her knees, reaching for the salmon. It was blue-black on top and burning silver underneath. Except for the net, the fish was free. It had thrown the hook the instant the pressure of the line was off.

She touched the salmon. It was as cold and elemental as the ocean itself.

"You aren't going to go all sentimental on me, are you?" Kyle asked warily.

Lianne didn't say anything, just looked at the fish.

"Oh, well," he said, "I had fresh salmon last night. I'll throw it back."

Her head snapped up. "What?"

"I thought you were having a round of fisherman's, er, fishersan's regret."

Lianne licked her lips. "Actually, I was thinking of how many ways I know to prepare salmon."

"You sure? You looked—"

"I'm sure," she cut in. "When I'm in Vancouver or Hong Kong, I go to restaurants where the fish are swimming in a tank. You pick out your dinner and it's killed and cleaned while you watch. That's how you know the fish is fresh. As for this salmon, the only regret I have is that I can't eat the whole thing right now, while it's so shiny and fresh and beautiful."

He glanced at his watch. "If we hurry, we can eat a hunk of it before we go see Seng."

"What are we waiting for? Hand me the cosh."

"I can do it."

"And I can learn."

"Cleaning, too?"

She sighed. "Yeah, cleaning, too."

"You're in luck. Salmon are a lot easier to clean than rockfish."

Kyle watched Lianne dispatch the salmon with a few quick strokes of the cosh. He wished that all of life's little problems could be solved so neatly. But they couldn't.

Even so, the thought of taking a cosh to the lecherous Mr. Han Seng had real appeal.

fourteen

The guard at the Institute of Asian Communications dock was unarmed, polite, and immovable until an invitation came from Han Seng for the *Tomorrow* to tie up. Then the guard escorted them to the executive pavilion, rang the bell, and waited for someone to come and take the visitors off his hands.

Gleaming in the twilight, the pavilion was a surprisingly successful combination of glass walls, cedar pillars, and Oriental rooflines. The evergreen-scented air was clean and crisp, with a delicious tang of ocean. The view to the south was two hundred degrees of salt water, complete with commercial shipping lanes, navigation buoys, pleasure craft, and rugged, fir-covered islands. The closest islands were uninhabited; Jade Island was one of them. Other than passing ships and a few houses on the shores of distant islands, little light showed except the moon rising through slate-colored clouds.

"Nice view," Kyle said, resettling a heavy carton of jade in his arms.

The guard didn't answer.

Neither did Lianne. She was wondering just where Seng was throwing his party. The executive pavilion had a few lights on. So did another part of the institute's complex, but there was none of the noise that she had expected. Either the soundproofing was as spectacular as the view or the party was a dud.

A middle-aged man whose clothes weren't up to the expensive standards of the institute cracked the pavilion's heavy cedar door and peered out. As the door swung fully open, the smell of Chinese tobacco rolled over Kyle and Lianne. There was another man sitting ten feet inside the door, a younger man, Chinese, unsmiling. Even though his clothes were flamboyantly expensive, the tailor hadn't been able to conceal the cannon under the man's left arm.

"Entry here is pleasure," the middle-aged man said in barely recognizable English. "I to Mr. Han are cousin."

Lianne answered in Mandarin. "Thank you. There is no need to disturb Mr. Han. I know he is very busy tonight and we are early in any case. Just take us to the room where he has set out his jade for me to see."

"No possibly," the man said in English, turning away. "Stay."

Lianne tried Cantonese, but he just kept walking.

The other man, the one with the badly concealed gun, didn't move from his chair. He simply watched them with black, unflinching eyes.

"No common language with the cousin?" Kyle asked Lianne quietly.

"Several," she said in a clipped tone. "That's Han Ju, Han Seng's shirttail cousin and personal assistant. Ju speaks Mandarin and understands Cantonese. He's simply being rude."

"Does that mean Seng isn't thrilled that you came on your own boat with a colleague?"

"Probably."

"Tough."

Lianne glanced up at Kyle. The open pleasure he had shown in her and the salmon was gone. Now his expression was shuttered, measuring everything and everyone with a probing intelligence that made no allowances for human frailty. He seemed older, harder, colder. Like Archer, who had been the only Donovan not to accept her with real warmth last night.

"You look like your brother," she said.

"Archer?"

"Yes."

"Hardly. He's drop-dead handsome."

"And you aren't?" Lianne retorted before she could think better of it.

Kyle gave her an amused, sideways glance. "No, I'm not. Trust me on this. I have the word of dozens of women on it."

"That's what comes of hanging around the Braille Institute," Lianne muttered, shifting the small box she carried. "Not handsome? What a crock. Your smile would stop traffic. Archer's would stop clocks."

"You didn't like him."

She shrugged. "It's hard to like somebody who doesn't like you."

"It takes time for him to warm up."

"It would take a blowtorch."

A burst of Chinese kept Kyle from having to answer. Seng came striding up to the pavilion entrance wearing a scarlet brocade smoking jacket, a Rolex Oyster, a world-class jade ring, Gucci loafers, and black silk slacks. He was combed, buffed, and perfumed like a gambler or a bridegroom.

Lianne took one look and was grateful to the soles of her feet for Kyle's presence. Unconsciously she moved closer to him, so close she was standing hip to thigh.

"The complete party animal," Kyle said under his breath.

"You're half right," she said quietly.

"Animal?"

"I'm afraid so." It was the simple truth. Part of Lianne was afraid of Han Seng. She knew that he was a very important contact for the Tang family. If she insulted him, Harry would be furious.

And if Seng made a hard pass at her, she would insult him and then some.

A curt order from Seng had his assistant taking the box from Lianne. The bodyguard stayed where he was, but he no longer watched Kyle with predatory interest.

Chattering in Chinese, Seng grabbed Lianne's arm and started down the hall without so much as a look in Kyle's direction. Kyle didn't mind the rudeness for himself, but Seng's grip on Lianne was hard enough to leave dents.

Just as Kyle started after them, she stumbled against Seng and caught herself in a flurry of hands and elbows. He made a whooshing sound, grabbed his stomach, and bent over. With a smooth motion Lianne recovered her balance and stepped beyond Seng's reach.

Before the bodyguard could get off his chair or Seng could straighten up, Kyle was standing between Seng and Lianne and she was apologizing in rapid Chinese for her clumsiness. Seng was too busy trying to breathe to listen.

"While the boss is gasping and flopping like a beached fish, maybe his assistant wouldn't mind showing us where the jade rejects are," Kyle said. "This carton is getting heavy."

Seng's cousin gave Kyle a glittering black look that suggested the man understood English a lot better than he spoke it. Seng barked something and gestured to Kyle.

"He wants you and his assistant to take the jade to Seng's suite. Then you're to wait aboard your boat."

"What about you?"

"Seng will personally show me his jades in the main conference room. He has everything set up."

"Where's this party of his?"

"Good question. I don't have an answer."

"Do you want me to wait on the boat?"

"No," Lianne said distinctly. "It's been a long few days. Very long. I want to wrap this up and go home."

"Sounds good to me. This way."

Kyle started down the hall as though the Hans and their bodyguard didn't exist.

"Where are we going?" Lianne asked.

"To the conference room."

"Do you know where it is?"

"Down the hall, turn left, third room on your right. Move it, sweetheart. The host is hell-bent on his own agenda, but I don't think he's prepared to be nasty about it."

Lianne didn't need to ask what Seng's agenda was. She had a very good idea. Too good. Despite all cultural bias, subtlety just wasn't Seng's long suit. It wasn't even his short one. He had made it quite clear that she was expected to lick his feet and any other part of his anatomy he generously bared to her.

Seng gave curt orders to his assistant, told Lianne with equal curtness that he had other matters to attend to, and turned on his heel. Lianne breathed a silent thanks that Seng was leaving and started after Kyle. Ju hurried to join them.

"How do you know the institute's layout?" Lianne asked when she caught up with Kyle.

"Farmer is big on hands-across-the-water functions. One way or another, the Donovans have come to lots of IAC conferences here in the past four years. Dad even rated the executive pavilion. That was when we had more clout in China than Farmer did. SunCo was courting us at the time."

"What happened?"

"Archer talked The Donovan out of an exclusive alliance with SunCo."

"Why? Wasn't the corporate mix right?"

Kyle was very aware of the assistant's footsteps behind them, and the fact that Han Ju's English was much better than he wanted his guests to believe. "He didn't tell me."

"Did you ask?"

"You met Archer, what do you think?"

"You didn't ask."

"There's the conference room," was all Kyle said. "The one with the solid gold lotus on the door."

Lianne beat the assistant to the door, opened it, and walked in. On a long, massive conference table, pieces of jade gleamed beneath muted overhead lights. An inventory sheet listing the number and characteristics of each artifact also lay on the table.

"Put the carton over there," she said to Kyle, gesturing to the table. Then she repeated the order in Mandarin.

Impassively, Seng's assistant put the second carton on the table.

"Do you want me to open them for you?" Kyle asked. The heavy twine and white paper wrapping, complete with many red wax seals, had intrigued him from the moment he saw Lianne carrying the boxes down to his dock.

"No," Lianne said. "The wrapping is Wen's way of assuring that what someone takes out at this end is what he packed in the Tang vault."

"Trusting soul."

She shrugged. "He's no worse than others I've worked with."

"I meant you. How do you know what's in the boxes?"

"It's not necessary for me to know," she said, tucking a loose strand of hair behind her ear. "But in this case, I know several of the pieces that will be offered in trade. Joe left instructions that I give a written appraisal of those items before they were packed."

"What about the rest of them?"

"I wasn't asked to appraise them."

"Odd."

"Chinese methods of doing business often seem odd to Americans."

Kyle looked at the boxes. There was no way to get into them without destroying at least one of the many red seals. It was an ancient, low-tech, highly effective way to prevent tampering.

"I'll need more light to examine the jades," Lianne told Kyle as she set her shoulder bag on the table.

"It is not necessary," Han Ju said in blunt Mandarin. "All is as agreed. The honorable Han Seng merely wished to display for you the quality of the jades. If you would wait, he will generously share his knowledge of the finer points of appreciation with you."

"I am flattered," she said indifferently, "but like the honorable Han Seng, I am caught in many conflicting demands." Then, in English: "Do you see any light switches?"

Kyle went over to a wall panel that would have looked right at home on a rocket ship and dialed up the illumination. The result was like sunrise in the tropics—quick, hard, and eye-hurting bright.

"Enough?" he asked Lianne blandly.

"I should have brought my bathing suit," she said, pulling out a pen and a tablet from her bag. "I could tan while I work."

"I'll dial down the ultraviolet. How about music?" Kyle suggested, turning back to the panel. "Classical, Celtic, Chinese opera, country, blues, New Age, classic rock, reggae, rap, European opera. Or natural sounds. Rain, thunder, surf, river, more birds than Audubon, jungle at dawn."

"Silence works for me."

"Tropic scents, then? Orchids and waterfalls?" Kyle offered. "Heat and sand from the eternal desert? Noon in the jungle? Afternoon in a field of flowers? Twilight in an evergreen forest with snow coming on? Good old salt air?"

Lianne made a noise that could have meant anything and bent over the first piece of jade. The closer she looked at it, the less she was impressed by what she saw.

"If the neutral walls don't appeal," Kyle said, "I can give you everything from murals of Xi'an and the Forbidden City to Manhattan at night and the Rocky Mountains at any time. If you're feeling academic, I can dial in paintings from every museum on earth. If you're feeling kick-back, there are movie posters and scenic wallpaper. If you're feeling kick-butt, there's a selection of sports clips from every country in the world, including Mongolian goat roping."

Lianne glanced away from the jade. "What are you, a tour guide?"

"I've hardly begun."

Beneath Ju's black gaze, Kyle strolled over to Lianne, leaned his hip on an Australian jarrah-wood conference table the size of an aircraft carrier, and crossed his arms on his chest.

"If we were real guests instead of peons," he drawled, "we'd be wearing lapel pins that would instruct the computer in each room to change the lighting, temperature, music, fragrance, and decor according to our preprogrammed preferences."

"What if our preferences didn't agree and we were in the same room?" she asked.

"Then we'd find out who's a VIP and who's butt-wipe. The highest-ranking lapel pin rules the computer." Kyle turned to Seng's assistant. "Good-bye, Han Ju. If we need anything, you'll know as soon as we do."

The man looked at Kyle for a long count of three, then walked out of the room. The door closed softly behind him.

Kyle leaned down until his lips were very close to Lianne's ear. "Don't do or say anything you wouldn't in Han Seng's presence. The place is wired and taped."

Lianne's eyes widened but she didn't say a word. She didn't even nod. She simply went back to the jades. The sooner she was out of Farmer's high-tech playpen and away from Han Seng, the happier she would be.

As she bent over the first jade again, she wondered if pepper spray would put the guard out of commission before he could draw his gun and shoot. Somehow she doubted it.

"Did you hear me?" Kyle breathed into Lianne's ear.

She nodded, then jerked slightly when she felt the faint, brushing warmth of his fingertips as he tucked in the strand of hair that insisted on coming free of her bone hair clip.

"I'm going to have to get a better barrette," Lianne said.

"Not on my account."

"You're distracting me."

"Should I apologize?"

"Only if you're sincere," she retorted.

He laughed.

Lianne gathered her fragmenting thoughts and concentrated on the jades Seng was offering in trade to the Tangs. Although the light looked good, she had a more reliable index than visual memory. She reached over to her purse, took out several examples of jade whose color was known to her, and set them on the table to see what the lighting did to them.

"Good," Lianne murmured. "Full-spectrum daylight. The color you see now is what you'll see at noon tomorrow somewhere else."

"You sure? This is pretty much a Mediterranean style of light. I can change the mix to pure Pacific Northwest."

Shaking her head, Lianne picked up the first jade, which rested on a card with the number 1 on it. The piece was a pendant half the size of her palm. The exterior of the pendant was a medium-green jade lattice of peach leaves and twigs. Inside the lattice was a peach that was a mottled white-green. The natural indentation of the peach had been exaggerated so that it was an accurate, if rather graceless, representation of a vulva.

"You're supposed to be thinking out loud," Kyle said. "Remember?"

Lianne nodded. She was also remembering that everything she said or did was being taped.

"So what are you thinking?" Kyle asked.

"I can see why Seng is editing this piece out of his collection."

"What's wrong with it?"

"It's an example of how a collector's particular passion can limit the quality of the pieces he collects."

Kyle looked at the pendant. "I'm listening."

"Han Seng has chosen to collect Chinese jade erotica from all dynasties. It's a difficult choice. Even though erotica was an accepted and expected part of Chinese life—at least until Christianity and the People's Republic—the vast majority of Chinese erotic art was in paintings."

"Visual aids, huh? Not much new there."

"Some things transcend cultural differences," Lianne agreed dryly. "Unless an emperor or a prince or a very wealthy bureaucrat commissioned jade erotic objects, they simply weren't made, or they were made by average craftsmen from average stone."

"Like the pendant you're holding?"

"Yes."

"So it's not the subject matter that's the problem?"

"That's your Puritan cultural background talking," Lianne said, smiling slightly. "Puritanism was a very late comer to China's cultural mix. The fact that Western museums display only Chinese household goods and landscape paintings says more about our society's reluctance to address sexuality than China's. China has a long and rich history of erotica."

"Most societies do."

"But China's wasn't kept in the closet. The frequency and duration of an emperor's visits to his wives and concubines were as much a source of public concern and discussion as his imperial decrees. In fact, satyriasis was a condition much admired in a ruler."

Eyebrows raised, Kyle looked down the row of jade artifacts depicting variations on the theme of human sexuality.

"Shocked?" she asked, watching him from the corner of her eye.

He smiled slowly. "Just thinking about what would happen if a museum put these jades in the lobby. Bet attendance would go through the roof."

"So would the local politicians."

"Yeah. As you say, different cultures." Kyle looked back at

the pendant. "So the only problem with this is in the execution and the quality of the stone, not the subject matter?"

Lianne nodded. "The Tang family has many exquisite variations of the peach leaves-and-fruit theme. The pieces are very sensual, suggesting the pleasure to be found within a woman's body, as well as fertility with its promise of a man's immortality through his sons."

"Well, the carver got the sex part of the pendant right. But the rest . . ." Kyle shrugged. "It's more clinical than evocative."

"Exactly. I wish I could show you one of the pendants in the Tang vault. It's this size and a bit better in color, but the skill of the carver was incredible. He used every minute variation in the jade's natural color to enhance the theme. In fact, the first time I saw that pendant, I wondered if the fruit in Eden wasn't a peach rather than an apple."

"You sure that's supposed to be a peach?" Kyle said, eyeing the pendant Seng hoped to get rid of. "Looks more like a body part."

Lianne gave him a sideways look. "In China, the peach is a symbol of the vulva."

"A jade peach for a jade stem, is that it?"

"Actually, the feminine form is more often called a jade pavilion. 'Pleasure pavilion' is another favorite. 'The one square inch' is also common."

Kyle tried to think of something neutral to say. He couldn't. Of all the conversations he had expected to have with Lianne today, this wasn't one of them.

"In any case," Lianne continued, "the pendant is supposed to be a Sung dynasty ornament for a concubine."

"Supposed to be? Don't you think it is?"

Lianne hesitated, remembering that everything she said or did was being monitored. She set down the pendant, rummaged in her shoulder bag, and pulled out a magnifying glass that came with a battery-powered light.

"What are you looking for?" Kyle asked. "Tool marks?"

"After a fashion. Before the age of machine power tools, the work went quite slowly. As a result, the designs were very clean, very distinct. Power gets the job done quicker, but not better. Overlapping corners in designs are a common result. The incised curves aren't as clean or as smooth."

"Couldn't stop the machinery before they overshot the mark, is that it?"

"Yes. Look here, just inside the lip of the peach. It should be a single sensual curve. But it isn't. It's more a notchy ripple than a true curve."

Kyle picked up the magnifying glass and the pendant, looked, and saw the ragged incised line.

"I think this piece was turned out by modern technology," Lianne said, "not Sung dynasty craftsmen working with foot treadles and crushed garnet abrasive."

"So what do you think this jade is worth?"

"A hundred dollars if you're too busy to bargain. Ten if you find a hungry shop owner. There are stores in Hong Kong and Shanghai that stock racks of similar stuff. All modern."

"New jade. That's what it's called, isn't it? Anything made after the nineteenth century."

"New jade," she agreed, then smiled wryly. "Even if it's a century old."

"That's a quarter of American history."

"And, depending on how you count it, a fiftieth of China's history," she said, taking back the pendant. "To confuse matters even more, there are many Chinese who call all jade after the Han period 'modern.' "

"Everything for nearly the last two thousand years is *modern?*"

"To the Chinese, yes."

Lianne set down the pendant, made notations on her tablet, and went on to the next jade. She worked quickly, efficiently, talking in phrases and single Chinese words that spoke volumes of her knowledge. "*Pih,* moss green. No particular artistry. Good polish. Subject not unusual."

"It looks like a man with his hand up a woman's dress," Kyle commented.

"As I said, not unusual." She picked up another jade, using both hands, for the piece was as big as a cantaloupe. "Several shades lighter than *pih*. Good artistry. Good-to-excellent use of the natural variation of the stone. Good polish, though modern. Too bad. If the polish had been done the old-fashioned way, by hand rubbing, the piece would be worth more. Hand rubbing gives a deeper luster."

"What about the subject?"

"Not unusual." Lianne set the jade aside, made notes, and continued down the table.

Kyle stared at the jade she had just put back. Both figures were fully robed. The woman lay on her back in a languid posture, her hips in the lap of her lover and her legs over his shoulders. Something about the woman's face suggested that she liked the position. The man certainly did. His head was tilted back as he climaxed.

By the time Kyle caught up with Lianne, she was five jades ahead of him.

"*Pi,* indigo," Lianne muttered, translating for Kyle's benefit. "Good color, very good carving. Unfortunately, the overall impact is static rather than dynamic. I'll tentatively accept a Tang date."

While she made notes, Kyle glanced at the jade. It was another maiden with her toes pointed to the sky. From the look on her face, the man between her thighs could have been giving her a pelvic exam. He didn't look too thrilled, either.

Kyle took the magnifying glass from Lianne and examined the sculpture more closely. Despite its lack of artistic or emotional impact, it was a beautifully carved piece. The curves were even. When a design turned a corner, it turned cleanly, no overshooting or overlapping with previous designs.

"*Kau,*" Lianne said.

"What was that?" Kyle asked, looking up.

"Yellow. Not the best example of the color. The carving is

after the style of Three Kingdoms, but the symbolism and subject matter are more common to the Sung dynasty."

"Meaning?"

"During the Sung dynasty, there was a revival of Three Dynasties styles. Perhaps this piece came from that time. Perhaps it's more recent. May I have that back?"

Kyle handed over Lianne's magnifying glass.

"Quite modern," she said after a moment. "It's hardly cooled from the mechanical polishing process."

She made another note, picked up another piece, and turned it slowly in her hands. *"Chiung,"* she said. Then, before Kyle could ask: "Cinnabar red. Unusual subject matter. I suspect this piece, too, is quite modern."

Kyle looked at the piece slowly revolving in Lianne's strong, slender hands. The people's robes were in disarray. The man's head was between the woman's thighs.

"Excellent form," she said blandly. "Wonderful polish. Not at all static. Outstanding technique. That's one happy concubine."

Kyle laughed out loud. "How do you know she isn't his wife?"

"She won't get pregnant that way."

"But she sure will be pleased," he retorted.

"If you listed the ten things that were most important to traditional Chinese males," Lianne said, making notes quickly, "the sexual pleasure of their wives would be number thirty."

She set aside her notes and concentrated on the next piece of jade, and then the next and the next. The pieces were invariably modern. The quality varied from good to fair, with much more of the latter.

Yet at least three of the jades Lianne had brought with her from the Tang vault, the three she had appraised herself, were excellent to superb. Whatever trade the Tangs were making was going to be very one-sided.

And her name would be the one signed on both Han and Tang appraisal sheets.

Unease rolled heavily in Lianne's stomach. Her skin prickled. Sweat condensed coldly in her palms, down her spine. She told herself that she was overreacting; she was simply following the instructions of her client. Whatever trade Han Seng and the Tangs had worked out was none of her business.

But her name would be on the bottom line just the same.

f i f t e e n

"Is he really sucking on her foot?" Kyle asked.

Lianne jerked, took a breath, and focused on the jade piece she had been looking at without really seeing. The man indeed had the woman's tiny, carefully maimed foot between his lips. The other foot was half unwrapped and pointed toward the sky.

"He really is," she said. "During the centuries that the Chinese practiced foot-binding, 'golden lilies' were considered the most sexually exciting part of a woman's body."

"Golden lilies? Her *feet?*"

"Not just any feet. Golden lilies were the culmination of a lifetime of pain. When a girl was four or five, her toes were bent down and bound to her heels, breaking the arch of the foot. In adulthood, the result was a maimed foot no bigger than a lily bud just before it opens. Three to four inches, max."

Kyle blinked. "This was sexually exciting?"

"To a Chinese male of those times, yes. The golden lilies were the only part of a woman's body she didn't bare in the presence of others, even the servants who attended her bath. The only exception was a woman's husband or, if she was a prostitute, a particularly favored client."

Kyle whistled tunelessly. "Well, that sexual stimulus doesn't transcend cultural differences for this boy."

"You'd feel different if it were her breasts."

"I sure as hell would."

"That's cultural."

"God bless America."

Lianne smiled despite the anxiety that was closing clammy fingers around her stomach. As she picked up the next jade, she hoped that the rest of the pieces Seng was trading to the Tangs weren't as lackluster as the batch she had already seen.

"Soochow," she said instantly. Then, under her breath: "Damn."

"Something wrong?"

"The older a piece is, the less likely it is to actually be jade," Lianne said. "Historically, the Chinese categorized stones based on their color rather than on the chemical composition of the stone itself. A lot of green stones were called jade, from soapstone to serpentine."

"They're easier to carve than jade," Kyle pointed out. "A whole bunch easier, in the case of soapstone."

"And the carvings don't last as long. Time softens the edges, the designs, until not much is left. Like wax left in the sun. Especially with soapstone. And nothing takes a polish like true jade."

"Is that jade you're holding?"

"After a fashion. It's called Soochow jade. Do you know the difference?"

"Soochow jade is serpentine, not nephrite," Kyle said. "Serpentine is softer than nephrite, has a lower specific gravity, and is more fragile."

"Should I assume that you understand the distinction between nephrite and jadeite?"

"Nephrite is a silicate of calcium, magnesium, and iron. Also known as a tremolite-actinolite. Jadeite is a different kind of silicate. Aluminum, sodium, and iron. Also known as a pyroxene. When it is emerald colored and highly translucent, it's called Burmese jade, imperial jade, jadeite, or *fei-ts'yu*. Does that cover the high points?"

"And some of the low ones as well. Why are you hanging around me?"

"I was a geologist before I got interested in jade. Chemistry is great for some things, but it lacks a sense of history. Chinese jade, no matter what its internal chemistry, is a condensation of Chinese history. In other words, I'm following you so I can find out how you know the woman in the sculpture you're holding is a bride rather than a prostitute."

"Look at the designs on the stand."

Kyle moved closer, so close that he could sense the warmth of Lianne's body. "Looks like carved, polished mahogany to me, the usual base for a Chinese jade sculpture."

"The wood is shaped to suggest a sleeping pallet. There are stylized bats on the ends—symbol of happiness as well as night—and her robe is etched with peonies, which symbolize renewal, spring, love, and happiness."

"Wedding stuff."

"Stuff? Spoken like a true Western bachelor," Lianne said, laughing. "To the Chinese, weddings were a weaving together of families, villages, dynasties, and destinies. Weddings were the point where the past flowed through man into woman and created the future."

Kyle bent down to look more closely at the palm-sized sculpture Lianne held. The bride's face was blank, barely differentiated from the stone. Beneath her hands, her robes divided just below her navel and rippled down the outside of her spread thighs. She wore no underclothes to conceal what awaited her bridegroom. The tightly folded vulva was much more detailed than anything else about the woman.

"She's ready for the future, all right," Kyle said.

"Or something. Again, the carver's skill wasn't up to the complex symbols and resonance of the culture. This is merely a woman with her legs spread." Lianne set down the sculpture and moved on.

"You know of a more, um, delicate variation of that theme?" Kyle asked.

"The Tangs have a carving that is identical in size and subject," Lianne said absently, studying the next jade. "The effect is quite different. The girl obviously won the marital sweepstakes and got a man who cared about her pleasure. I call the sculpture Bride Dreaming, although I'm certain from her expression that the consummation has already occurred."

"How?"

"What do you mean, how?" Lianne looked up at Kyle blankly. "The usual way, I suppose. Penetration followed by ejaculation."

He did a double take, then laughed in delight while red climbed her cheeks.

"I figured out the mechanics shortly after kindergarten," he said, stroking the back of his hand down her hot cheek. "What I meant was, how can you tell it was after rather than before?"

Trying to act as though she wasn't blushing like a bride or a first grader, Lianne leaned over the table and stared hard at another piece of jade. "It just . . . well, it just looked like it."

"Not much help there." Kyle breathed deeply, inhaling Lianne's scent. Between the jade erotica and the warm woman, his body was in testosterone overload. "Any chance I could further my education by getting into the Tang vault and comparing the jades?"

She shook her head. "No one outside of immediate family—and me, of course—has ever been allowed into the vault. But I might be able to bring you a selection of erotica, if that's what you want."

"I want to learn nuances. If erotica helps, I'm all eyes and tongue."

Lianne hid her smile and hoped Kyle couldn't sense the too-rapid beating of her pulse. She had discussed and acquired erotica for several clients, including Han Seng, without being in the least disturbed by the nature of the pieces.

It was different with Kyle. She didn't know why. She just knew it was. Not that she was uncomfortable or embarrassed, except with her own unruly thoughts. She kept thinking about what it would be like to lie sated, watching Kyle as he admired the one square inch they had so recently enjoyed.

"But I have to admit," he said, "I'm having a hard time seeing Wen Zhi Tang as a collector of jade erotica."

"It isn't his first passion, but he never passes up a chance to increase the breadth or upgrade the quality of his grandfather's and his great-great-grandfather's collection of erotica. They had superb taste, by the way. Many of their acquisitions are, quite simply, art."

"Like *Bride Dreaming?*"

Lianne closed her eyes and saw in her mind the utter relaxation of the sculpture, the sated smile, the softly swollen lips, the rare cat's-eye shine of the jade between the bride's thighs.

"Yes," she said in a husky voice. She cleared her throat. "Like *Bride Dreaming.*"

Hastily she picked up the next jade, which was resting in a silk-lined lacquer box. The sculpture was slightly longer than her hand and in the shape of an erect penis. She turned the piece over, noted the quality of the stone and the carving, and returned it to the box.

Kyle leaned over Lianne's bent head and tried not to notice the fragile, very female scent that curled into his nostrils. "You're not talking."

She froze, then relaxed. He was so close to her ear that his breath stirred wisps of her hair against her skin, raising goose bumps. "Not much to talk about. That's either a device to instruct prostitutes in fellatio or a rather uninspired sculpture, or both."

"I suppose the Tang vault has a better one?"

"Offhand, I can think of at least five. The jade stem was a favorite subject of erotica as well as, possibly, a ritual object in ancient times."

Rapidly Lianne finished surveying the jade pieces Seng had offered in trade. Nothing she saw made her feel better about the trade she had been told to carry out.

Kyle sensed Lianne's increasing tension and wondered what was bothering her. As she put aside each jade, she made quick, almost slashing notes. After the last one, she flipped to a new page and wrote quickly. When she was finished, she ripped out the sheet and left it on the conference table.

"You haven't said anything for fifteen minutes," he pointed out.

"Add it to what I already owe you."

With tight, jerky motions she stashed the tablet, magnifying glass, and pen back in her big purse. As she shouldered her bag, she tried not to think how angry the Tangs would be with her.

But she was damned if she would put her name on the bottom line of such a thinly disguised bribe.

"Aren't you supposed to take this jade back with you?" Kyle asked, gesturing to the pieces Lianne had just examined.

"Yes."

"Then we'd better round up some packing material."

"That won't be necessary." Lianne picked up the smaller of the two boxes that she had brought with her. "Get the other one, would you?"

Kyle's eyebrows shot up, but he did as she asked. "Now what?"

"Now we leave."

"No trade?"

"Not as far as I'm concerned."

"How will Seng feel about it?"

"Like he was shown a ham and given a weenie."

Kyle grunted. Behind the cover of the box he had picked up, he drew his gun and flicked off the safety. Only then did he head out of the conference room.

Lianne was close on his heels as he strode down the hall.

Neither of them bothered to say good-bye to the guard who was still seated near the front door.

Just as they opened the door, someone started yelling from the back of the pavilion. The guard reached under his coat, only to freeze when he saw Kyle's gun pointing right at him.

Han Ju burst around a corner, raced toward the front door, and skidded to a stop. He began berating the guard in Chinese.

"Ju," Kyle said curtly.

The man turned toward him.

"Pick up that phone and call the guard at the dock. Tell him you need him here to escort Seng's guests back to their boat. Speak in English. And don't stand between me and your pet kick boxer unless you want to get caught in the crossfire."

Ju didn't argue or lie about his understanding of English. He picked up the phone carefully, told the marina guard to come to the executive pavilion, and hung up.

"Kyle—" Lianne began.

"In a minute," he interrupted without taking his eyes off Ju. "Does Smiley understand English?" Kyle asked, indicating the guard.

"No," Ju said.

"Lianne, tell the guard to slowly put his gun on the floor and slide it over here. If I see the barrel of his gun pointing at anything but his chest, I'll shoot him."

Lianne spoke rapidly.

Without looking away from Kyle, the guard drew his gun. Slowly. He set it on the polished marble floor, butt toward Kyle. A nudge of the guard's foot sent the gun sliding toward Lianne. The metal gleamed like water in the gentle light of the hallway.

"Do you know how to handle a gun?" Kyle asked her.

"With great care."

"That's a good start. Pick it up."

Awkwardly, still holding onto the carton of jade, Lianne picked up the gun and looked at Kyle. He flicked a glance at the gun she was holding.

"Okay," he said. "It's on safety. Tuck it out of sight and head for the boat. I'll be right behind you."

The sound of Lianne's footsteps faded rapidly.

"Ju," Kyle said, "tell the guard to lie facedown, feet pointed toward the front door."

The guard was moving before Ju stopped talking.

"Now lie on top of him," Kyle said.

Ju started to object, then stopped at a motion of Kyle's gun. Muttering in Chinese, Ju lay on top of the guard.

"The first man who looks toward the front door is going to piss me off," Kyle said calmly. "I'll be in the bushes by the front door, waiting for the marina guard."

Quietly, his boat shoes soundless on the shiny floor, Kyle went backward out the door. The motion-sensing lights along the path to the marina were still burning from Lianne's passage. When Kyle caught up with her on the second turn in the winding path, his gun was nowhere in sight.

The guard nearly ran them down on the third turn.

"Thanks for coming," Kyle said to him, "but I told Ju we knew the way. Hurry along, sweetheart. We want to catch the tide."

Lianne lengthened her stride. Kyle followed right on her heels. The guard looked uncertain, then stuck to his primary orders: never leave guests unescorted on the island. He walked behind Kyle and Lianne to the dock, watched as they stepped onto the *Tomorrow,* started the blower, and prepared to cast off.

Just as Kyle fired up the engine, the guard's beeper began to shrill.

"Time to go," Kyle said to Lianne. "Get in the cabin, but leave the door open."

He cast off the lines and drove the boat from the aft station instead of from the wheel in the cabin.

By the time the guard started yelling, they were several hundred feet off the dock. Kyle switched to the forward helm station in two seconds flat. With a deep, throaty roar, the *To-*

morrow came up on plane and raced away. Its newly installed bow lights split the darkness, searching for the floating logs that were a hazardous fact of navigation in the San Juan Islands.

Lianne sat in the pilot seat across the narrow aisle from Kyle. She looked shut down and wired tight at the same time. If she had anything on her mind, she wasn't talking about it.

"Mind telling me what that was all about?" he asked.

"Not yet. Please. I have to think. God, what a mess. Wen will be furious. The Tangs need Seng's goodwill."

"So they offered a bribe? Good jade for bad?"

Her hands clenched even more tightly in her lap. She wasn't happy with her decision not to go through with the jade trade, but she didn't know what else she could have done. What she *did* know was that she was very grateful she hadn't gone to meet Seng by herself. Without Kyle, she was certain that she wouldn't have gotten the Tang jades off Farmer Island.

Not to mention the problem of Seng and his expectation of screwing her among the mediocre visual aids.

"Talk to me, Lianne. I need to know what's going on."

"I didn't want my name attached to such a one-sided trade," she said flatly. "All of Seng's jades put together didn't equal one of the three Tang pieces I appraised for this trade."

Frowning, Kyle brought the speed down to a safer night-time pace. "How many of these sealed-box trades have you brokered for the Tangs?"

"With Seng?"

"With anyone."

Lianne hesitated. "I'm not sure. Six, perhaps seven. The most recent ones have been with Seng, here in Seattle. A while back, there was a Taiwanese trader and a mainland Chinese collector."

"Do you do this for other clients, or just for the Tang family?"

"Just for Wen, actually. I began doing it about six months

ago, when his eyesight failed and he wasn't strong enough to travel anymore."

"Is this the first trade you've refused?"

"Yes."

"Were the others more even?"

Closing her eyes, Lianne tried to relax her clenched hands. "I don't know," she said starkly.

But she was afraid she did. She sat with her hands gripped in her lap and her mouth a thin, tight line. Silence pooled in the cabin as thickly as night.

Kyle started to push for more information, then decided against it. Navigating the waters of the San Juan Islands after dark was tricky enough without trying to pry information out of a reluctant suspect at the same time. He would wait until Lianne was back at his cabin.

Then he would get some answers.

"Watch your step," Kyle said as he finished tying off the stern line of the *Tomorrow*. "The dock can be slippery."

With an easy motion, he lifted Lianne from the well of the boat to the dew-slick dock beside him. She made a startled noise and hung onto his arms until she felt the dock supporting her feet.

"Progress," he said. "Good."

"What?"

"You made a sound. Two sounds. One of them might actually have been a word."

She flushed. She knew she hadn't been much company on the ride back from Farmer Island. "I'm sorry. I don't want you to think I'm not grateful for all you've done. I am. Without you . . ." She shivered. It didn't bear thinking about. "I was just wondering about . . . jade."

"Jade, or bad trades?"

Lianne would have turned away, but she couldn't. Kyle was too close.

"Then how about an even trade?" he asked. "Better yet, a *good* one."

Suddenly his breath was warm against her lips, his mouth even warmer. Hot. Savory. Hungry.

And there was no taxi waiting.

She told herself that she shouldn't, even as she reached for him, needing him in too many ways to deny herself the reckless oblivion she sensed waiting for her in this one man.

Kyle meant to go slowly, to seduce Lianne with the kind of finesse that would have her begging for more. A few kisses on the dock with the wind blowing sea-scented and mysterious around them, a few more kisses along the path where fir trees whispered to the night, a glass of wine in front of a fire, a languid unraveling of clothes and mind . . .

Then he tasted her, deep and long and hard. He made a thick sound and thought of nothing but sinking into her, dragging her against his body, drawing heat from her, the hottest kind of fire. He bit at her lips, dove into her with his tongue, fought through clothing until he found her breasts soft and hot, her nipples hard, begging to be plucked by his fingers and his mouth.

Too late Kyle realized that Lianne was half undressed and his hands were all over her, his mouth pulling at her, devouring her. He tried to lift his head, to stop, but Lianne's fingers were locked in his hair, holding him tight against her breast while husky, hungry sounds rippled out of her. With the last of his self-control, he managed to turn his head aside.

"The house," Kyle said hoarsely.

Lianne's only answer was the arch of her back, her hips seeking him blindly. She wanted more of him and she wanted it now, before she remembered all the reasons she shouldn't have him at all. But she couldn't say that, because she couldn't think of anything except the heat twisting through her, tangling her mind, burning through logic to the elemental need beneath.

"Now," Lianne said raggedly. *"Now."*

Kyle's last logical thought was that it was a good thing his cabin was isolated and the dock private. Because after the next breath neither one of them would care if they were on the hood of a car in a traffic jam. With one hand he unfastened his pants. His other arm wrapped around her bottom and lifted her until her hips were level with his.

"Put your legs around me," he said. And then he fastened his mouth on hers.

When Lianne felt Kyle's hand between her thighs, she shuddered and tried to get even closer to him. The feel of his fingers maddened her. Stroking, testing, probing slickly. It wasn't enough. Nothing could be enough. She needed everything and she needed it all at once, right now.

She twisted against him, trying to tell him what she must have. Words were impossible. Their mouths were fused together, teeth and tongues and hunger raging to be fed. She whimpered when his fingers slid in. The first wave of pleasure rocked her, yet it still wasn't enough. It was moonlight when she needed the fires of hell. She wanted him deep, wanted him hard, wanted him forever.

His grip shifted, opening her thighs until he could take her with a savage movement of his hips. After he filled her he pushed deeper, stretching her, demanding that she take all of him. Her slick core clenched around him, drenching him as she made a keening sound of ecstasy. The fierce satin grip and release of her climax demanded that he give himself as completely as she did. With a throttled cry he drove hard and deep, pumping himself into her until the world went darker than night around him.

And then there was nothing but the sound of two people fighting to get breath into their bodies.

After a time Lianne slumped against Kyle, utterly relaxed except for her legs still locked around his hips. Her breath came out in a shuddering sigh.

"Did you get the license number of whatever hit us?" she asked huskily.

He laughed. The motion moved him inside her. He felt the ripple of her body, the shivering, clenching, shivering, and heard her low, shocked cry as she climaxed again. His arms tightened, pulling her hard against his crotch. His hips pumped once, twice, then again for the sheer hellish pleasure of feeling her heat drench him, her body slack but for the sweet fist holding him deep.

Hunger sank its bittersweet claws into Kyle, but his teeth were a white flash of laughter in the moonlight. He felt like a magician or a god or a very, very lucky man.

Finally Lianne made a husky, incoherent sound, sighed, and bit his chest with lazy sensuality. Heat snaked through Kyle, tightening him inside her. She tightened around him in turn.

"Oh, no, you don't," he said, releasing her, letting her slide down his body. "I want you in bed next time."

"Next time?" she asked. Then she saw the gleaming length of his erection standing out from his clothes. "Oh. Next time."

And she smiled.

With a distant, shocked part of her mind, Lianne realized that she was standing on a dock in business shoes and thigh-high nylons, her skirt bunched around her waist, her bikini briefs askew, and salt air cool between her legs. If she had had the energy, she would have been embarrassed. But she felt much too good to worry about it.

"And if I don't cover you up," Kyle said huskily, "the next time will be right here."

Before Lianne knew what he was doing, he knelt and very carefully eased the narrow crotch of her thong-cut panties into place. Through the dark nylon lace he kissed flesh that quivered at his touch. Quickly he smoothed down her skirt and stood before he lost his head again. Then he licked his lips, tasted her, and was lost. He sank back down on his knees.

It was a long time before they made it up to the cabin.

sixteen

*B*eneath leaden skies and a fitful wind, the Pace Lane was backed up heading into Canada. Normally Lianne would have been impatient, but today she was simply relieved. The last thing she wanted to do on the morning of her thirtieth birthday was to go to Vancouver and confront Wen over a business deal she had refused to carry out.

No, it was the *next*-to-last thing she wanted to do. The last thing would be to hand over excellent jade, accept lesser goods, and sign her name to the appraisal sheets.

Cars crept forward. The Pace Lane went marginally faster than the rest of the traffic. To pass the time, Lianne studied the signs of returning green along the highway and admired the fresh plantings in the Peace Park. Anything to take her mind off the upcoming confrontation in the Tang family compound.

Family. But not hers. Not really.

Clients, she reminded herself. *Think of the Tangs as clients and everyone will be happier. Actually, think of them as former clients.* Because in a few hours, they probably would be just that. Former.

Lianne forced her thoughts away from the Tangs and

thought of last night instead. And this morning. What a wonderful way to turn thirty. An iridescent thrill shot through her from her breasts to her knees as she remembered lying in bed with Kyle's beautiful eyes, smoky from desire, looking at her. Just looking at her.

She had felt sensitive all over, fully alive, loved. Or at least enjoyed. Thoroughly. She had never known a lover like Kyle— hungry, intense, sensual to the soles of his feet, giving as much as he took. Giving more. One night with him, and every man she had ever known, even the one she had once loved, was now in a category labeled "BK: Before Kyle."

And after Kyle . . . ?

The thought of "after" didn't appeal to Lianne. She was thirty years old now, more than old enough to understand that men like Kyle Donovan were rarer than imperial jade. She knew she should prepare herself for the emptiness to come, but this morning she simply didn't have the energy. She felt too good, especially the sweet ache that came when she thought about holding him hard and hungry, so deep inside her she felt like part of him, same breath, same heartbeat, same sleek, sweaty skin.

And Kyle did care about her outside of bed. He wanted to help her.

Lianne, we've got to talk. Are you in some kind of trouble because of these jades?

There's nothing to be done for it, Kyle. I'll take the jades back to Wen and tell him that I don't want to broker any more blind trades for the Tangs.

And then what?

Kyle's question echoed in Lianne's memory. She hadn't wanted to think about the future, much less talk about it, so she stopped his questions by the oldest method of all. She slid her hands down his wonderful, naked body. And then she slid her mouth.

A polite tapping on the driver's window startled Lianne out of her sultry memories. She saw a middle-aged man in a dark gray suit. He held a badge in his hand and motioned for her to roll down the window. When she did, cool air gusted in, lifting tendrils of her black hair.

"What is it?" she asked. "Is something wrong?"

"Could I see some ID, ma'am?"

"Driver's license? Passport?"

"Either one would be fine, ma'am."

She took her purse from the passenger seat and pulled out her wallet. Her Washington driver's license wasn't in the first place she looked, or the second. She finally found it stuck in her checkbook, where she had last needed it for identification.

"Here you are," she said, handing over the license.

The man glanced at it, measured her against the color photo, and said, "Ms. Blakely, would you get out of the car, please?"

"Why? Is something wrong with the license? I just renewed it a few weeks ago."

The man opened her door and waited. Frowning, Lianne slid out of the car and stood up.

"Ms. Blakely, you're under arrest for grand theft, smuggling, and sale of stolen goods."

At first Lianne thought he was joking. Before she could do more than make a startled sound, he had turned her around and cuffed her hands behind her back. A woman in a neat business suit appeared at the man's elbow. With smooth efficiency, she searched Lianne for weapons, found none, and hustled her into an unmarked sedan that was parked nearby.

When Lianne managed a fast look over her shoulder, she saw the man who had arrested her leaning over her trunk. He popped it open, reached in, and lifted out the first carton. Bright red wax seals gleamed against the white wrapping paper.

Kyle ignored the first four rings of the phone. Beneath a bright light, working with the aid of a big magnifying lens, he was assembling tiny silicon wafers on a circuit board. If all went well, the result would be a modem-activated control for the security system he had built into the Donovan penthouse.

At the fifth ring he swore, set aside his tools, and grabbed the phone.

"What?" he barked.

" . . . Kyle?"

The voice was so strained and hesitant that he almost didn't recognize it. "Is that you, Lianne? You sound like you're in another country."

"I feel like it." She took a ragged breath. "I'm sorry to bother you, but my mother is on her way to Tahiti with Johnny and I didn't know who else to . . ." Her voice frayed into silence.

The last of Kyle's impatience vanished when he realized it was emotion rather than a bad connection that had thinned Lianne's voice into a stranger's.

"What's wrong, sweetheart?" he asked.

"I've been arrested and I don't know what . . ." She cleared her throat painfully.

Kyle didn't like the mixture of emotions that shot through him, rage and regret and a prowling hunger he hadn't even begun to appease, so he ignored emotion and focused on finding out what had happened. "Where are you?"

"Seattle."

"What are the charges?"

"Theft, smuggling, sale of stolen goods, and some other stuff that I don't understand," she said bleakly.

"What kind of goods?" he asked, even though he had a cold certainty that he already knew.

"Jade. They think I stole from Wen Zhi Tang. I didn't, Kyle! I never would steal from—"

"Do you have a lawyer?" he interrupted curtly.

"A lawyer? Where would I get a lawyer? I don't even know one!"

"Take it easy. I'll get you one. Don't talk to anyone else

until you talk to Jill Mercer. Jill Mercer. Got that? No one. Is there an officer nearby?"

"Yes."

"Put him on."

"Her."

"Whatever. And Lianne?"

"Yes?"

Kyle wanted to tell her not to worry, it was all a mistake, he would straighten it out and she would be free; but he suspected it wasn't a mistake, she wouldn't be free, and he was worried as hell himself.

"I'll see you as soon as I can," he said finally.

"Sure. And thanks, Kyle. I just didn't . . . have anyone else to call."

The last words were spoken in a voice so low that he almost didn't hear them. And then he wished he hadn't. The thought of her being that alone cut him in ways he didn't want to deal with. Especially after last night, when she had given herself to him without reservation, taking him higher each time, going with him; and the shock in her eyes telling him that she had never been there before. Not like that.

He wondered if the same shock had been in his own eyes.

"I'm glad you called me," Kyle said. "Remember, don't talk to anyone until you've talked to Jill."

"I . . . hurry, if you can. Being held like this, handcuffed, locked in . . ." Her breath fractured as she swallowed the fear that was clawing at her.

Kyle's eyelids flinched in a pain she couldn't see and he couldn't admit. "Put the officer on. I'll be there as soon as I can."

"What did the lawyer say?" Archer asked Kyle.

"Nothing good." He looked out the window of the penthouse without really seeing the wind-burnished surface of Elliott Bay. Despite a strengthening wind, the mid-afternoon sunlight was losing its battle with time and clouds. Unless the wind won, there would be a long twilight before true dark came. "About all the Feds haven't charged Lianne with is spitting on the sidewalk."

"Standard operating procedure. The more charges, the higher the bail."

"Half a million high. She doesn't have the money for even a tenth of it."

Archer whistled. "Half a million? Not bad for someone with no priors and a clean driving record. The judge must have had a case of the ass."

"Or he had folks whispering dirty stories in his ear."

"It happens. Especially when the suspect had a part in smuggling the Jade Emperor's burial shroud out of China."

"Nobody said anything about that to Lianne."

"Yet. But we both know that's why the Feds are in on it. They don't give a rat's hairy ass about Wen's collection of erotica."

"Which leads to an interesting question," Kyle said, turning back to Archer. "The Feds were following Lianne because they thought she would lead them to the Jade Emperor, right? Once they had the burial suit, they could move in and defuse the international explosion."

"That's the way I see it."

"But the Feds know where the jade suit is now."

"So do the Chinese. They've demanded that the U.S. return it."

"Sounds good to me," Kyle said.

"Farmer says he got it from Taiwan, not mainland China."

"What does Taiwan say?"

"They'll get back to us," Archer said.

"Mother."

"Smart money says that Taiwan will step up and say they were the seller of the suit or the victim of a thief who stole the suit."

"Why?"

"It's a great way to stick a thumb in China's eye," Archer

said. "China is yelling at Uncle to seize the burial suit because it was stolen from China, either by Chiang Kai-shek during the revolution or, more recently, by a person or persons unknown. If Uncle doesn't return the stolen property, it will seriously strain relationships between China and the U.S. Human rights will be the first to go. The Chinese government is already screwing down on students and newspapers in Hong Kong."

Kyle made a disgusted sound. "The only way China will ever have any human rights worth mentioning is when they have more GNP or less humans. It has nothing to do with a jade burial suit."

"Grow up," Archer said impatiently. "Politics isn't about reality, it's about what you can make people believe is real. If you didn't learn that in Kaliningrad, you never will."

Kyle looked away from his brother's cold, intelligent eyes. Archer was right. Kyle just didn't want to hear about it. "What is Taiwan's version of reality?"

"It's yelling at the U.S. that Taiwan is a legitimate, *separate* Chinese government and if Uncle gives anything back to China it will seriously undermine democratic Taiwan in its long, underdog battle against the overwhelming might of the Chinese Communists."

"Bullshit."

"You're eighty percent correct," Archer said, his voice as cold as his eyes. "The other twenty percent is why Uncle is tiptoeing and praying the whole thing will just go the hell away."

"Which side are you betting on?"

"I'm keeping my money in my jeans. Unless something breaks soon, it's going to be a hell of an international pissing contest, the kind nobody really wins."

"They're big boys. All I want to do is get Lianne out of the yellow rain."

"Good luck," Archer said ironically. "Choosing between the legitimacy of Taiwan and China is a nettle that Uncle really doesn't want to grasp. If the Feds can pass the nettle off to someone else—anyone else—they will."

"Lianne hasn't earned it."

"Maybe. And maybe Uncle tagged the right thief."

"No," Kyle said curtly.

Archer closed his eyes for an instant, then opened them again. Life had taught him that bad news didn't go away just because you didn't look at it. "Any particular reason you're so sure of her innocence, or do you just like fucking her?"

"Don't talk about her like that," Kyle snarled.

"Bloody hell," Archer said savagely. "Bloody, *bloody* hell." His fist slammed down on the nearby end table with enough force to make a heavy bronze lamp jerk. "I should have yanked you out of the game the instant I saw you watching the sexy Ms. Blakely like you'd never seen a woman before."

"I'm not the one at risk. Lianne is. She's not hard enough for this game, Archer. She was as shocked as anybody when she saw Farmer's jade suit."

"Do you really believe that was the first time she had ever seen it?"

Kyle started to say yes. Then he remembered the way she had demanded to see the burial suit up close, and then the fear she hadn't been able to conceal when he gave Lianne her wish.

"She didn't know Farmer had the suit," Kyle said. That, at least, he was sure of.

"But the auction wasn't the first time Lianne saw that suit," Archer said neutrally, "was it?"

"I don't know."

"I think you do. I think you just don't like it."

"Damn it, she doesn't have the apparatus to pull off a theft the size of the Jade Emperor's Tomb!"

For the first time, Archer smiled. It was thin and cold as a slice of ice, but a smile nonetheless. "Glad to see all of your brain cells haven't sunk to your crotch. That's why Uncle wants someone close to Lianne. To find out who else is involved."

"Are you saying that the Feds don't really want her locked up?"

"Not particularly."

"Then why did they arrest her, cuff her, and haul her off?"

"They didn't have much choice. They desperately needed a bone to throw China. Someone gave them Lianne and jade."

"Who wants her off the street that bad?"

"Wen Zhi Tang."

"But why?"

Archer bit back a cutting remark. He would rather have Kyle's cooperation than the head-thumping brawl his youngest brother was asking for. "People tend to get pissed off when more than a million dollars' worth of jade goes missing."

"I don't think Lianne stole anything. I think she was set up."

"You think? You *think*? With what? Your hyperactive dick?"

"Shove it, Archer. I'm serious."

"So am I!" And this conversation was going nowhere fast. He glanced at the mess of electronics on the kitchen table, where Kyle had been working when Lianne called. "Looks like you dropped something."

Kyle refused the chance to change the subject. "Listen to me, Archer. I know how it feels to be set up, on the run, not knowing who to trust except family. But Lianne doesn't have any family."

"What about her mother?"

"Anna and her lover are on the way to Tahiti. Lianne is all alone. Even if I wanted to, I can't just turn my back on her. She's alone. And she's scared."

"Shit," Archer hissed. He raked lean fingers through his thick, already unruly hair and reined in the desire to give Kyle the fight he was begging for. "Okay. Who set her up?"

"Whoever stole the jades."

"Breathtaking," Archer said sardonically. "Any other brilliant insights?"

"I need to talk to Lianne."

"So do it. You know where she is."

"Not in a cell. Here."

"I thought you said she didn't have the fifty grand cash against the bail."

"She doesn't," Kyle said, heading for the front door. "But I do."

"Take the money to Vegas. Your odds of coming out a winner are much better."

Kyle's answer was a middle finger over his shoulder.

Archer's fist hit the table at the same instant the front door slammed behind Kyle. The lamp jerked, shivered, and settled back into stillness.

"So," Wen said in his dry yet strong voice, "the ungrateful female has been arrested."

Harry and Joe exchanged looks. Neither one of them was in a hurry to speak. Lianne's treachery had hit Wen harder than they had expected.

Daniel was young enough not to understand the risk of being the bearer of bad news. "She is in custody. I am sorry, Grandfather. Not for the arrest, but for the pain of having given so much ancient, honorable knowledge to a dishonorable slut."

Saying nothing, Wen shifted on the garden bench and tilted his face toward the afternoon sun. He felt the light more clearly than he saw it. The increasing darkness of age was difficult enough; having Lianne use his failing sight to dupe him was a pain approaching agony.

He had trusted her with the Stone of Heaven. She had betrayed him.

"You were correct in insisting that Johnny and his concubine be far away when this happened," Wen said, turning toward his Number Two Son. "There is enough pain. I would not have a daughter's treachery turn son against father. Against family."

"Thank you," Harry said quietly. "We would have spared you, Father. We would have waited until you joined our ancestors. Such waiting was not possible."

"She was too greedy," Daniel said. "In a few more years she would have bled us dry. Our jade treasury would have been plundered down to the velvet lining of the drawers."

Wen said nothing. He simply sat with his face tilted up to the sun he could see only as a faint lessening of darkness.

"When Daniel came to me and told me about the substitutions," Harry said, "I waited until Joe returned. Then we decided that no good would come of pretending that nothing had happened. You are the head of the family of Tang. It is your right to be informed."

Wen's gnarled fingers settled on the cool jade carving that was the head of his walking stick. He had never felt so old, so weak, so foolish.

"She will be jailed," he said. "She will enter the house of Tang no more. Ever. See to it."

"Yes, Father," Joe said, speaking for the first time. He was glad his father's eyes were hazed with age. Wen had always been too shrewd, too clever, too quick to find fault in his sons. He never allowed for errors or simple humanity. He would never forgive Johnny's bastard daughter. "I will see to it. If she so much as looks toward Vancouver, I will know."

Wen sat motionless for so long that the others thought he had fallen asleep. Then he lifted one hand and dismissed his sons and grandson with a jerky motion.

The three men left. Wen sat in the spring sunshine, head tilted back. There was no one to see the slow tears coming from his blind eyes.

"What do you mean?" the man said, squeezing the other man's arm like it was an enemy's throat. Everything had gone so well up to now. Jade flowed out, money flowed in. Nothing threatened him or his pleasures. "She was arrested!"

"Kyle Donovan arranged bail," the second man said simply.

"I was assured that bail was impossible."

"The United States government influenced the decision. They want Lianne Blakely to be free."

"Why?"

"To lead them to the Jade Emperor's Tomb. To *us*."

The first man put his head in his hands and wished he had never thought to rob from one in order to pay another. "I am doomed."

"You have less courage than a woman," the second man said, turning away in disgust. "I will see that she talks to no one."

"How?"

"Do you care?"

The first man said no more. All he cared was that the threat go away. He told himself what he always did when he found himself without money and thugs were breathing down his neck demanding payment of loans.

Just one more time. Just this once. Then I will stop and no one will ever know.

s e v e n t e e n

Lianne looked pale and much too tightly strung as Kyle helped her into his car. Her own little Toyota had been impounded. It would stay that way until the smuggling charges against her were dropped. If she was convicted, the car belonged to the Feds. Vehicles used in smuggling were routinely seized by the law.

"Thank—" she began.

"If you thank me one more time," Kyle cut in savagely, "I'm going to gag you."

He might have felt less guilty if Lianne hadn't lit up like a Christmas church the instant she saw him walking toward her. She wasn't able to hug him because of the handcuffs, but she had burrowed against him like a small animal seeking shelter.

Even while he had held her, wanting to comfort her, part of Kyle knew that he was using Lianne as much as he was setting her free. The knowledge had put a brutal edge on his temper. Telling himself that he had to find out what she knew in order to help her didn't ease his guilt. Or his anger.

Wind raked through his hair, the same wind that had surprised the weather guessers by clearing the skies, turning spring gloom into a luminous golden afternoon.

Kyle slammed the passenger door and went around to the driver's side, telling himself to take it easy every step of the way. Letting loose his anger wouldn't help a bit. He had almost decked the officious prick who insisted on keeping Lianne in handcuffs until the last sheet of paper was signed. The bureaucrat hadn't been in any hurry to get the paperwork done, either. It had taken an unreasonably long time to get Lianne her freedom.

If Kyle had been a suspicious, untrusting, cynical sort, he would have thought the Feds were doing everything they could to drag out the process. Like maybe they needed time to set up a 24-7 tail on her. Even Uncle had to shuffle things around to put a watch on someone twenty-four hours a day, seven days a week.

And even if Lianne didn't end up dragging Uncle's agents behind her like a ball and chain, she wasn't really free. Set one foot beyond the boundaries of the U.S. and she would be back in jail again.

But at least she wasn't wearing handcuffs.

Kyle just managed not to slam the car door after he got in. He jammed his seat belt on, shoved the key in the ignition, and looked over at Lianne,

"Fasten your seat belt," he said. His voice was too rough, but Lianne didn't seem to notice. That bothered him most of all. She was too grateful to tell him to shove it when he chewed on her for no better reason than she was there and he was mad clear through.

Lianne reached for the seat belt, then stopped, staring at her hands as though she didn't recognize them. Despite a lot of scrubbing, the ink that had been used to fingerprint her still lay like a thin black moon along the undersides of her nails. She curled her fingers to hide the shameful stains.

"Seat belt, Lianne."

When she simply kept on staring at her hands, Kyle reached over and fastened her belt himself. She smelled more institutional than fresh, more like disinfectant and fear than rain and flowers. The black pantsuit she had taken from her overnight case this morning at his cabin was crumpled from use and vaguely dusty, as though some of the places where she had been sitting lately weren't very clean. Her hair was in disarray around her shoulders. Her jade hairpicks had been confiscated until their true ownership could be determined.

Lianne looked at her hands. Fists, really. They ached from being clenched. Like her jaw. Like her throat, closed around screams of rage and pain and fear.

The grandfather she loved and had worked so hard to please believed she was a thief.

"I didn't do it," she said hoarsely.

"That's what we have to talk about," Kyle said, turning on the engine. "Mercer can keep the Feds at bay for a while, but in order to mount any defense worth mentioning, she'll need a lot of information from you."

Numbly Lianne nodded.

Kyle started to ask a question, took another look at her, and decided to wait. She was quivering like a wild animal in chains. She probably felt like one. He certainly had in Kaliningrad, when a question arose about his passport and he was seized without warning and thrown in jail before Jake could straighten out the mess. To someone raised with the unquestioned belief that a good citizen's freedom was as reliable as oxygen in the air, being grabbed off the street, handcuffed, put in a locked room, and treated like dogshit was as shocking as rape.

With an effort, Kyle loosened shoulder muscles that were bunched for a fight. As he left the parking lot, he automatically glanced in the rearview mirror.

A tan Ford Taurus pulled into traffic right behind him. The agent's maneuver was about as subtle as turning on red lights and a siren. Obviously fifty grand and signed assurances about the rest of the bail hadn't been enough to comfort the good guys. They planned to keep an eye on Ms. Lianne Blakely.

And they were letting her know it.

"That does it," Kyle said through his teeth. "Time to talk, sweetheart. What the hell is going on?"

Lianne turned and gave Kyle a confused look. "I told you, Wen Zhi Tang thinks I'm a thief."

"Not good enough." Kyle goosed the accelerator and shot through a yellow-going-red light. Might as well make the tail work for his salary, benefits, and early pension. "You were accused of stealing—what, a million bucks' worth of jade?"

Lianne's eyes squeezed shut, like her lungs, her throat, her hands, everything. She desperately wanted a bath, a cup of coffee, and the clock to turn back to a time when Wen had trusted her, when she had believed that someday she would be accepted by the Tangs as a member of the family.

"Yes," she managed. "A million dollars."

"Even if you sold all the jade at face value—not frigging likely, because hot goods are always heavily discounted—your bail is still way out of line."

"What do you mean?"

"Bail is supposed to reflect the severity of the crime and the likelihood of flight. The theft was hefty, but not violent. You aren't likely to flee for the simple reason that you have nowhere to go that you wouldn't be extradited. Contrary to popular belief, a million bucks cash won't buy freedom in a Third World country. Ten million, maybe. The price goes up every month."

Lianne opened her eyes and looked at the dazzling, late-afternoon sky. It had turned into the kind of yellow-and-blue spring day people prayed for and rarely got. "They took my passport," was all she said.

"And gave you a tail."

For a moment she didn't understand. Then she glanced in the side-view mirror. An American car with a suit behind the wheel was locked on Kyle's bumper like a tow job.

"Not very subtle," she said.

"Yeah. It's enough to make a tax-paying citizen wonder what the hell the Feds are really after."

Lianne's expression told him that she didn't understand.

"Look," Kyle said impatiently, "I know of murderers, child molesters, rapists, and drug traffickers who aren't considered important or dangerous enough to warrant a full-time tail. So I'll ask you again: what are the real stakes in this game?"

"A million dollars in jade isn't enough?" she asked in disbelief.

"No."

"Then what is?"

"Christ," he muttered. "Lianne, I can't help you unless you trust me. What in hell is really going on?"

"I don't know!" She took a broken breath and shook her head as though to clear it. "This morning I woke up smiling and you made love to me like I was a goddess. An hour later I'm in handcuffs and treated like a criminal. Happy thirtieth birthday."

"Today is your birthday?"

"Yeah. Bake me a cake with a file in it." Lianne started to laugh, didn't trust herself to be able to stop, and shivered violently instead. She wished her mother wasn't on the other side of the world with her lover. "God." She shivered again. "The things you learn when you're arrested."

"Like?"

"How alone you are. I never thought I'd turn thirty with no one to care if I'm in jail and the key is lost. No husband, no children, no real friends, no lover, no—"

"There's me," Kyle interrupted before he could think better of it.

"One night." Her smile trembled on the edge of turning upside down. "And what a night. But there are the days, aren't there? All the days. I thought it was enough to be independent, owing nothing to anyone, building my own business so that no man could wave his hand and kick me out on the street if he got tired of me."

Kyle didn't have to be a mind reader to know what Lianne

was talking about. "Johnny Tang and your mother have been together longer than a lot of married couples."

"I'm sure that comforts her when Johnny spends Chinese New Year with his family, shows up for their birthdays and christenings and misses ours, gets his wife pregnant as often as he likes . . ."

Another violent shiver racked Lianne, the only outward indication of how hard she was holding onto her self-control. "How they hate me," she whispered.

"Your mother?" Kyle asked, shocked.

"No. My father's family. They would send me to hell with a smile."

"What about your father?"

"What about him?" Lianne asked wearily. "His money raised me, clothed me, educated me. That's more than some fathers do for their legitimate kids. As for the rest, it's my fault."

"What is?"

"Isolation. Building Jade Statements took every bit of my time and energy. While I was doing it, I didn't regret it. I might have been alone, but I wasn't lonely. Besides, I was always going to get to a point in the business when I would have time for a personal life. Someday. Now . . ." Lianne cleared her dry throat. "Now I'll have time, all kinds of time. My business won't survive the loss of my reputation."

"Assuming you're guilty."

"Why shouldn't people assume it? Wen does. Johnny's youngest son does. And so do you."

"I didn't say that."

"You didn't have to." Lianne turned away from the bright sunlight pouring through the windshield. "You just keep watching me with those cool, measuring eyes and asking me what really is going on."

"That's—"

"No," Lianne cut in, lifting her hand abruptly as though to ward off an attack. "I'm not complaining. You barely know me, yet you got me out of handcuffs. It's a lot more than I had a right to ask of a one-night fling."

"Is that how you feel?"

"No. It's how *you* feel."

"Right now, all I feel is pissed off."

For a time only random traffic noises disturbed the strained silence. Kyle drove with an unconscious expertise that left him plenty of time to think. Too much. He kept remembering Kaliningrad and how he had nearly died. Then he remembered how the Donovan family had closed ranks around him. He hadn't asked for their help. In fact, he had been determined to go it alone. Yet he had always known that help was there, waiting.

Then he thought of Lianne. *You barely know me, yet you got me out of handcuffs. It's a lot more than I had a right to ask of a one-night fling.*

Kyle let out a hissing breath. "My gut believes you're innocent. My mind is asking questions."

And his dick still didn't care.

Lianne lowered the window and let the cool air wash over her. It wasn't a bath, but it was the best she could do for now.

"Ask away," she said finally, pushing hair back from her eyes. "You might get lucky. I might know something useful. But I doubt it. None of the people who questioned me seemed happy with the answers I gave them."

Kyle's mind said there were two explanations for that. The first was that she didn't know anything, so she could hardly help. The more likely explanation was that she knew exactly what everyone wanted and had no intention of sharing.

The Feds were a lot of things, but rock stupid wasn't usually one of them. Unless politics were involved. Then everybody's IQ dropped off the scope.

The Jade Emperor's Tomb made for a nasty bit of politics.

"Did you get a list of pieces that are missing from Wen's collection?" Kyle asked.

"Ms. Mercer requested it."

"And?"

"The Tangs are working on a complete inventory." Lianne smiled brittlely. "That will be hard."

"Why?"

"Other than me, Wen is the only person who knows each and every piece of the collection on sight. Or did. Now he can't tell the real from an inferior substitute."

"Substitute? Are you saying that the pieces of Tang jade aren't really missing, that the Feds just made up charges out of thin air?"

"I don't know what they're doing. I do know that at least two pieces of Wen's jade collection have been taken from the vault and similar, less valuable pieces have been left in their place."

Three, if she counted the jade shroud. Assuming that there had been a substitution at all.

She didn't know. The only way to find out would be to get inside the vault and have a look around. That would be hard to do when the Tangs didn't trust her and the Feds would arrest her if she crossed the border into Canada.

"Are you certain about the substitutions?" Kyle asked.

"Yes," Lianne said bleakly. "Turn left after the next light. My apartment is in the same building as the Jade Trader."

"Just two pieces have been substituted?" he persisted.

"There could be others. I don't know. I didn't even know about those two until yesterday. That's why I was so late meeting you for dinner. I kept waiting for Daniel to leave so I could do a fast check of a few other drawers in the vault. But he didn't leave."

"Daniel?"

"Johnny's youngest son. Wen is teaching him about jade. I think Daniel must have been the one who put Wen up to filing charges."

Kyle filed that fact as he dodged a bicyclist, pulled around a stopped bus, and decided against pushing the stoplight. It was already red.

The tan Ford stuck with him through all the urban maneuvers.

"So Daniel believes you stole from Wen?" Kyle asked.

Lianne remembered the hatred and contempt in Daniel's eyes. "Yes."

"Why?"

"He knew about the Neolithic blade. It was Wen's."

Kyle's glance snapped away from the rearview mirror, where the Ford grew like a tumor on the BMW's bumper. "The one at the auction?"

Lianne nodded.

"The one I bought?" he demanded.

"Yes. That's why I wanted to buy it. I was nearly certain it was Wen's. Now I *am* certain. I've seen the drawer in the vault where the blade was kept. Another blade was in its place."

"An inferior one," Kyle said.

It was a statement, not a question. Any blade he had ever seen would have been inferior to the one he now owned.

But he wouldn't own it for long. By law, stolen goods were returned to the owner upon discovery. The buyer, however innocent, lost out.

"It will be interesting to see if that blade turns up on the list of stolen jades," he muttered.

"I can't imagine it not turning up."

Kyle accelerated quickly away from the light. The Ford caught up again halfway down the block.

"What about the other piece of jade?" he asked. "You mentioned two that you were sure of."

"A recumbent camel from the Tang dynasty. The one that was substituted lacks the very subtle toe pads on the undersides of the feet. But Wen's hands and eyes are too bad for him to notice the substitution."

"How much were the replacement pieces worth, the blade and the camel?"

"It would depend on the collector. At a guess, I'd say perhaps one-third to one-half what Wen's original jades were."

"A thousand each for the substitutes, maybe more?"

"Probably a lot more. I can't be certain. I didn't examine them for sale."

"The Feds didn't mention substitution, did they?"

"They dropped some hints. I ignored them."

"So a million in jade is missing and a third to a half million in jade has been substituted?"

Though Kyle's voice was carefully neutral, Lianne sensed his skepticism. Why would a thief bother to spend money leaving decent substitutes? "I don't know about the rest of the missing pieces," she said, "whatever they are. I only know about two."

"The camel and the blade?"

"Yes."

"We'd damn well better find out about the rest, hadn't we?"

The word *we* went through her like a shot of neat whiskey, making her light-headed. Until that moment, she hadn't admitted to herself how much she didn't want to be alone in this tangle of family, lies, jail, and jade.

"Why?" she whispered.

"Because until we find out, we won't have the faintest idea what's going on with the Tang jades."

"No, not that. Why are you helping me when you don't really trust me?"

"Good question. I'll let you know when I have a good answer."

It was less than Lianne wanted and more than she had any right to expect. It was much more than she should take from a man who had nothing in common with her but jade and great sex, a man she liked, respected, and could too easily love.

That would be stupid of her and unfair to him. If she truly cared about Kyle, she would keep him as far away from this mess as possible. He had done nothing to deserve the grief that was coming her way.

She took a slow breath and put away the temptation to lean on Kyle, and in doing so, drag him down into the mud with her.

"This is the corner," Lianne said quietly.

Kyle turned and waited for a bus to get out of his way. He was frowning, because he was looking at Lianne's neighborhood with new eyes. What he saw wasn't good.

Despite the rich, slanting sunlight and pigeons cooing and crapping everywhere, it wasn't the kind of place where a good-looking single woman—or man, for that matter—should live. Pioneer Square might be a tourist attraction, but it was also smack in the middle of an area that could most charitably be described as colorful. Panhandlers, the homeless, and the not-so-gently insane lay in wait for marks who believed that a handful of change could turn someone's life around, or at least make the mark feel like he had done penance for the sin of not being poor.

"I hope you have good locks," Kyle said.

"The rent is cheap, the space is large, and you can't beat the commute to work. But yes, I have very good locks."

"And pepper spray. Don't forget that."

"I left it at home. It's illegal in Canada."

"Ah, yes. The Canadian motto: good government and plenty of it."

Lianne surprised both of them by smiling. "Turn into that alley," she said, pointing. "There's a cramped little parking area just after the first building."

Kyle turned in and parked in the last miserable slot, ignoring the signs that guaranteed towing by the first truck to arrive with a hook. The Ford Taurus stuck with him like a license plate. There was no place to park, so the tail simply backed out and parked across the street, where he could watch Kyle's car.

"Why were you carrying your passport with you to Canada?" Kyle asked as Lianne reached for the door handle. Which was a roundabout way of asking her if she had been planning to go overseas from Vancouver, taking the jades with her to one of the best jade markets on earth: Hong Kong.

"Even with the Pace stickers," Lianne said, opening her car door, "sometimes I'm stopped by U.S. Immigration officials on the way back into the States."

Kyle got out of the car and quickly caught up with her. "Why? Do you have a past violation of some kind?"

She unlocked a scarred, grubby alley door that led to a gloomy hallway. Curling linoleum and dirt fought for ownership of the floor. She was so accustomed to the uninviting entrance that she no longer noticed it.

Kyle did.

"A lot of Asians came to Canada on British passports when Hong Kong changed governments," Lianne said, turning back to Kyle. "Free access among colonial countries is a perk of the former British Empire. Sometimes the Asians who come to Canada decide to live in the U.S., but don't want to go through all the tedious immigration formalities."

"So they just drive south and stay?"

"Yes."

"And immigration types who can't tell the difference between Amerasians, Chinese, Vietnamese, or Koreans hassle you."

"At first, yes. Now most of them know me, but every time a new one comes on, I get a chance to chat while they check out my accent."

"And your eyes," Kyle said.

Lianne looked at him. "My eyes?"

"Yeah. Agents are trained to look for signs of nervousness. A big one is refusal to meet the agent's eyes."

"Is that why one of them asked me to take off my sunglasses?"

"Probably."

"Would you take off yours?"

"Now?" Kyle asked, surprised.

She nodded.

He pulled off his sunglasses and looked curiously at her. "Why?"

"It makes you less . . . distant." Lianne smiled oddly. She stood on tiptoe, bushed a swift kiss along his jaw, and quickly stepped back out of reach. "Thanks for being my knight, Kyle Donovan. I'll let Ms. Mercer know if I think of anything that might be useful."

Kyle realized that Lianne was planning to walk into the dingy hallway and out of his life. "Wait," he said, grabbing her arm. "I'm not through with you."

She looked at him out of eyes that were very dark in the dim interior light. "I'm not sure I like the sound of that."

Kyle muttered something under his breath and forced an easy smile onto his lips. "What I meant was, I'd like to take you to dinner. We could put our heads together and see if we come up with a way out of this mess."

"That's very kind, but your way out is simple. Drive away and stay away."

"And leave you alone?"

"I'm used to it."

"But—"

"No. You've helped me more than enough. Now help yourself. Get out before your reputation is as ruined as mine."

"Screw my—"

"Good-bye, Kyle," she said, talking over him and the siren that was wailing closer to Pioneer Square with every second. "And thank you. Nobody else cared."

The weathered door shut hard behind Lianne. It locked automatically.

Kyle fought an impulse to kick the door off its hinges.

Then he heard Lianne scream.

eighteen

The heel of Kyle's foot crashed into the door before his mind even registered what he was doing. It took four solid kicks to make the wood splinter away from the old lock. He shoved through the door, ignoring the sound of yelling that came from behind him. All he cared about was the chilling silence that had followed Lianne's single scream.

The switch from sunlight to gloom forced him to stop inside the doorway for an instant. It was long enough for him to see two shadows struggling in the hallway. There were pants and grunts and the scrape of shoes on the floor, a hissed word in Chinese as a heel connected with flesh.

A knife shone in the dim light.

Lunging forward, Kyle grabbed the attacker's hair in one hand and the fingers holding the knife in the other. Spinning the wiry Asian man away from Lianne, Kyle slammed the attacker face-first into the brick-lined hall. An instant before his nose hit the wall, the man kicked backward, trying to break Kyle's knee.

At the last second Kyle turned to take the karate kick on his thigh instead of his knee. The movement threw him off-balance, preventing him from breaking the attacker's wrist on the first try. Kyle yanked the Asian's knife hand up between his shoulder blades and slammed him headfirst against the wall again. This time the man's wrist broke and the knife fell to the floor.

Despite being disarmed, the assailant was far from harmless. Or beaten. He fought back in every way he could, twisting and kicking in unexpected directions, yelling in Chinese.

For Kyle, it was like wrestling with a basket of muscular steel snakes. Ducking heels and elbows every inch of the way, he hung on grimly and body-slammed the Asian into the hallway wall hard enough to echo.

"Give it up, asshole," Kyle panted, launching him into the wall one more time. Hard. "I don't want to kill you, but you're pissing me off."

The Asian twisted sharply. Blood made Kyle's hands slippery. The attacker managed to get his good wrist free. The edge of his hand started toward Kyle's throat with blurring speed.

Lianne lashed out in a high kick that smashed into the man's forearm, knocking it off target. An instant later the edge of Kyle's hand thudded against the attacker's neck. He was unconscious before he hit the floor.

Kyle let him land like a sack of wet cement, kicked the knife out of reach, and watched the man like the deadly little snake he was. The Asian didn't move.

"Nice kick," Kyle said, breathing hard, watching the wiry man. "You okay?"

Lianne was fighting for breath, too. "Yes. I guess."

"First the kitchen knives and now karate. Hell of a combination. Thank God I haven't pissed you off yet."

She laughed a little wildly. "Same goes for you."

"I'm big, sweetheart, but that son of a bitch is a lot better than I am in the clinch." Kyle let out a long breath and rubbed his thigh where he had been kicked. "Hope I didn't kill him. I tried to pull my punch, but I was getting tired of wrestling."

"I hope you didn't kill him, too," a voice said from the doorway. "The paperwork is a bitch kitty."

Kyle and Lianne both spun around, adrenaline pumping, ready to fight again if they had to. A man in a dark suit stood silhouetted against the doorway. His hands were empty.

"You drive a tan Ford?" Kyle asked.

"Yes."

"Then you have a radio. Why don't you do something useful for a change? Call the cops."

"I am one."

"You're a Fed. We need a city uniform."

"I'll call a medic while I'm at it."

"Yeah, I suppose the little shit needs one," Kyle said.

"I was thinking of you."

Kyle looked down at his right arm where the knife had somehow managed to cut him during the brief, vicious fight. His forearm burned like hell and blood had made his hand slippery at an inconvenient moment, but everything still worked. "I'll be okay."

"Just a scratch?" the agent said dryly.

"It's a long way from my heart."

Laughing, the agent turned around and went to call in the assault.

Kyle waited until the agent was out of sight before he knelt down, grabbed a handful of the Asian's T-shirt, and methodically began slapping his face.

"What are you doing?" Lianne asked.

"Delivering a wake-up call. Did he say anything before he attacked you?"

"No. One second I was alone in the hall, the next instant a door opened and he came at me."

"Was that his knife or yours?"

"His."

Kyle's big hand smacked against the man's cheek with a sound like a gunshot. "What happened next?"

Distantly, Lianne knew she was running on an adrenaline

high that would eventually drop her off a very tall cliff. But for the moment, she could leap skyscrapers and catch bullets in her teeth.

If only she could stop shivering.

"Lianne? Don't fold up on me now."

Smack went Kyle's hand on the attacker's reddened cheeks.

"I screamed and kicked him," Lianne said. "He turned so that I missed his crotch, but I got a piece of his midriff. It slowed him down a little. I got an elbow into his kidneys before he got set again. After that, things went to hell real quick. He's a lot better trained than I am. He was just getting ready to use the knife on me when you grabbed him and started hammering him into the wall."

Smack.

The attacker groaned.

Kyle slapped again. Hard. The thought of what would have happened if Lianne had been truly alone was eating at him. So was the gut certainty that there was more to this assault than a spot of daytime mugging.

When the Asian didn't come around after a few more slaps, Kyle stripped off the man's leather jacket and searched for ID. There wasn't any, unless you counted the tattoos marching up and down his muscular arms.

Feeling more uneasy than before, Kyle returned to his first method of getting information: slapping the man into consciousness. The attacker groaned, tried to raise his hand to protect himself, and cried out in pain at his broken wrist.

Fist bunched in the Asian's black T-shirt, Kyle dragged the man into a sitting position. His head lolled forward. Thick black hair slithered over his forehead and ears. There was a lot of blood on his face, compliments of Kyle and the rough brick wall.

"Did he say anything while you fought?" Kyle asked Lianne.

"Do Chinese curses count?"

"What flavor is he—mainland, Hong Kong, Taiwanese?"

"Mainland. He's been over here long enough to dress Western, but the haircut is mainland."

"How can you tell?"

Lianne ignored the shivers of adrenaline spurting through her blood and tried to concentrate. "You ever stay overseas longer than a vacation?"

"Yes."

"Where?"

"Kaliningrad, among other places."

"If you saw someone from there on the street here, would you notice differences?"

"Okay," Kyle said. "He's mainland Chinese. Nice tattoos."

"Triad or tong, I would guess."

"Yeah, that's what I figured. Did he try to rob you? Rape you?"

"I don't know what he wanted. He never said a word. He just jumped out and grabbed for me."

Kyle's hand landed heavily on the man's cheek. The attacker's eyes quivered open. They were black and glazed.

"Ask him who sent him," Kyle snapped.

"But—"

"Hurry. We don't have much time."

Lianne asked something in rapid Chinese. The man simply stared through her.

"Ask him again," Kyle said, smacking him sharply.

Lianne repeated her question. The man continued his silence.

"Close your eyes," Kyle said to her.

"What?"

"Close your eyes."

She did.

Kyle reached for the assailant's broken wrist.

Lianne heard a groan and some broken phrases in Chinese.

"What did he say?" Kyle demanded.

"No one sent him."

"Yeah. Right. He got all that body paint at Pike Place Market, too, along with fresh veggies." Jaw clenched against the queasy flip of his stomach, Kyle reached for the man's wrist again. He had learned in Kaliningrad that the price of civilized ignorance was death. "Ask him the name of his triad or tong or whatever he calls his tattoo buddies."

The man answered just as Kyle's fingers closed around his wrist.

"Red Phoenix," Lianne translated. "Can I open my eyes now?"

"You'd rather not. Trust me."

An instant after she looked, she decided that Kyle was right. She would rather not have known what he was doing. But she did. She drew a deep breath and reminded herself that the assault hadn't been her idea. The man had been looking for trouble.

He certainly had found it.

"Ask him why he was trying to kill you," Kyle said without looking away from the Asian.

Lianne was speaking in Chinese before Kyle had finished with his question. The answer was longer in coming.

"What did he say?" Kyle asked.

"The Chinese equivalent of 'Fuck you and your ancestors, too.' "

"Not real useful." Kyle's finger's tightened on the sinewy, rapidly swelling wrist. "Ask him why he was told to kill you."

"I already did."

"He might be feeling more talkative now. Ask him."

The attacker jerked.

Lianne's breath came in with a ripping sound and went out in a rapid stream of Chinese.

Cold sweat stood on the assailant's face.

Cold sweat ran down Kyle's spine. Nausea clenched viciously. Silently he cursed his weak stomach and the Asian's grim ability to endure pain.

Abruptly the man went slack.

"Shit," muttered Kyle. He thumbed back one of the attacker's eyelids. Only white showed. "He's not faking it."

Sirens cried in the distance. A different siren screamed a lot closer, then shut off. The city cops had arrived.

"Don't mention the man in the tan Ford unless the cops do," Kyle said, standing up. "Ditto for being out on bail. It will just confuse things."

The cop who strode through the door was a middle-aged heavyweight whose uniform collar cut into the slack flesh of his neck. There was nothing slack about his eyes. After a fast, comprehensive glance at the sprawled, unconscious suspect, the cop took in everything at the scene, from the blood on Kyle's arm to the pallor on Lianne's face to the knife kicked halfway down the dirty hall.

"Let's start with names," the cop said, pulling out a notebook. "Ladies first."

Lianne gave her name, handed over her driver's license for ID even though the law didn't require it, and generally tried to be a good citizen while not mentioning that she was out on a half-million-dollar bail and had a permanent, unwanted federal tail.

Two paramedics rushed in, one male, one female. With cool efficiency and latex exam gloves, they checked the unconscious man's vital signs and determined that he was in good shape, all things considered. They trussed him to a backboard just in case and carted him off on a gurney for the best medical care the free world and the taxpayers of Seattle could provide.

While the male medic began attaching tubes and sensors in the back of the ambulance, the female medic returned. Saying little, she began working on Kyle.

When it was Kyle's turn to field questions from the cop, he did the same as Lianne had, answering whatever was asked and offering nothing that wasn't. The questioning was a little more awkward in Kyle's case because the medic was peeling him down to the waist, taking his blood pressure and pulse, listening to his heart, and swabbing his cut arm with stuff that left a yellow-brown stain.

The cop scribbled, asked questions, scribbled, and asked more questions.

"So you kicked in the door, not the perp," the cop said to Kyle.

Lianne blinked. "Perp?"

"Perpetrator," Kyle explained. "You should watch more television. Yeah, I kicked it in. She was screaming and I didn't have a key."

The medic looked up. "How does your foot feel?"

"Like I kicked in a door."

"Better have it X-rayed."

"I'm standing on it, so it's not broken."

The cop looked at his watch and decided he had better call his ex-wife on the way back to the station and tell her he would be late picking up the kids for the weekend. Filling out paperwork on this one would take hours, especially with a wounded citizen and a perp who didn't speak English and whose only ID was tattooed all over his skinny, rope-muscled body.

Kyle glanced at the doorway, wondering where the federal tail was. He couldn't see much of the small alley from the hall. The city cop's partner had leaned the door upright to keep out the street people. Idly Kyle wondered if the drunks would see the door as hanging straight or if it would look even more drunkenly askew than it did to the sober citizens.

"Your pulse was pretty high, ma'am," the young paramedic said to Lianne.

"My heartbeat still is," she retorted. "I'm not used to being attacked in dark hallways."

The med-tech nodded slightly. "All the more reason to come in with me and get checked out thoroughly."

"No, thanks."

"What about you, sir?" the medic asked, turning to Kyle.

"Ditto."

The medic duly noted on a form that both citizens had refused to go to the hospital against the advice of the medic at the scene.

"Sign here," she said, holding out a form and a pen to Lianne. "It just says that you refused further medical aid. Something to keep the legal types happy."

Lianne signed. So did Kyle.

By the time the cop had finished asking questions and filling in all the necessary bureaucratic blanks, Kyle was bandaged, dressed, and more than a little impatient to wrap things up. The longer they stood around in the drafty hall, the better the chance that whoever had sent the triad thug would find out that things hadn't gone according to plan.

Whatever the plan had been.

Kyle had a feeling he knew. It wasn't a comforting sensation. His gut was in overdrive.

Finally the cop put away his notebook, gave the hallway another look, and left to call his ex-wife.

"How long will it take you to pack?" Kyle asked Lianne.

"Pack what?"

"Whatever you need for as long as it takes to sort this mess out."

"But—"

"Argue while you pack," Kyle said, taking her arm and urging her down the hall.

"Why should I go anywhere?"

"You'd rather stay and wait for the Red Phoenix boys to get lucky and kill you?"

Kyle's certainty that the man had meant to kill her was like a blow to Lianne. She stumbled, then caught herself against his arm. "Sorry."

"It's the other one that's cut." He stopped in front of an elevator decorated by graffiti whose only pretense to originality was in leaving the *c* out of *fuck*. "Which floor?"

Automatically Lianne punched the button to call the elevator. She wasn't thinking about the elevator or her apartment, but about Kyle's words.

You'd rather stay and wait for the Red Phoenix boys to get lucky and kill you?

The elevator cage stopped four inches short of the hall floor. The doors opened anyway.

"Are you saying that attack wasn't just random?" she asked tightly.

"What do you think?"

"I want it to be random."

"Before I grew up I wanted to marry Tinkerbell. Which floor?"

"Top."

With a hand that still shook at odd moments, Lianne swept her hair back from her forehead. When the doors opened, she started to step out into the hall. Kyle pulled her back into the elevator.

"Which way?" he asked.

"Left, down the hall, then right."

"Opposite your office?"

"Yes."

"Give me your key."

She went still. "You think someone is lying in wait inside my apartment?"

"I think it's possible. They don't call them gangs because they hunt solo."

"But—"

"The guy who attacked you didn't have to kick in the door. He had a key or picked the lock. He may have had a buddy, too." Kyle held his hand out, palm up. "Key."

She slipped past him into the hall. "You're hurt. I'll go."

"Christ."

Kyle grabbed for Lianne, only to have her evade his hand with a supple twist of her body. Swearing, he strode down the hall after her. When he reached her, she had the key in the door. When she started to push it open, he yanked her aside, kicked the door open, and flattened her between his body and the hallway wall.

The door slammed open with enough force to echo. There was no other sound.

"I'm going to check the place out," Kyle said in a low voice. "Stay here."

"It's my apartment and you're hurt."

"Were you born mule-stubborn or did you just practice a lot?"

Lianne's chin came up and her mouth opened to tell him more than he had asked about. He bent and gave her a swift, hard kiss. Her pulse and breathing spiked.

"Stay here," Kyle said. "I won't be long."

She waited just long enough to be out of his reach before following him through the apartment door. Heart scrambling, she glanced around the single room.

Empty.

The relief was so great that dizziness swept over Lianne, followed by a not-quite-sane desire to laugh as she watched Kyle systematically search every place that was big enough to hide a man—including under the Murphy bed that she had left open.

Kyle went into the bathroom, checked swiftly. Then he stood on the toilet seat and looked out the open window into the alley. No one in sight, unless he counted the tan Ford with the suit behind the wheel, talking on a cell phone.

With a heartfelt obscenity, Kyle stepped off the toilet and went back to Lianne.

"Do you usually leave the bathroom window open?" he asked.

"Only in the summer. Why?"

"It's open."

She raced past him to the bathroom, then stopped and stared at the window. It was open. All the way open. And it was jammed so tightly in that position that she couldn't close it no matter how hard she yanked.

"I'll do that," Kyle said. "You pack."

"But—"

"I don't want to hear it," he interrupted bluntly. "Pack. And if you give me any more crap about going it alone, I'll stuff a sock in your mouth and haul you out of here like dirty laundry."

Lianne opened her mouth, closed it, and started packing.

n i n e t e e n

When Dick Farmer was working instead of impressing CEOs and politicians, he didn't bother with an office building, a brace of assistants, an archaic wooden desk the size of Lake Michigan, or any of the other modern corporate power symbols. He simply packed up his hard drive and his only personal assistant who was worth a damn, stepped into his private plane, and ordered the pilot to fly them to his own personal island.

Today Farmer was working. He had just arrived on his island, ready to grapple with the new, prickly opportunity that life had given to him. At this point the opportunity looked more problematic than promising, but the difficulties energized rather than worried him. He had made his fortune taking on deals that others had avoided as too risky.

Farmer didn't want to surrender his prized jade burial suit, but he would. For a price. Until the price was agreed on, the suit would stay on Farmer Island, not in the unopened museum that had become a target of too much official interest.

The sun was only a rumor on the eastern horizon when Farmer entered a remote wing of the institute. With his lapel-pin battery pack blanketing any other signals, doors sprang open, lights came on, and music followed him everywhere he went. He hated silence almost as much as he hated dogs, cats, and tweety birds.

Mary Margaret, his personal assistant, went immediately to her station in a small room with an adjoining door. She didn't wait for orders or requests; most of the time she knew what her boss wanted before he did. She just booted up her computer and got to work on whatever messages had followed or preceded them to the island.

Farmer walked into a nearly closed circle of surplus and/ or slightly outmoded electronic wonders, settled into a rotating chair that had been made for him as carefully as an astronaut's couch, picked up a standard-issue telephone, and punched his assistant's intercom button even though he could reach her by raising his voice.

"Did that Chinese jade expert call here while we were in the air?" Farmer asked.

"No, sir," Mary Margaret said, reading the computer log quickly. "Mr. Han Seng did, on behalf of Sun Ming, who is the Chinese government's jade expert."

"SunCo, hmm? Those fellows do get around. Any message?"

"Yes, sir. 'There are details of the offer to be discussed.' "

Mentally Farmer cursed the stiff-necked mainland Chinese bureaucrats who wouldn't know a good deal if it grabbed them by their tiny little balls. "What details? I have the jade suit, they want it, and they have something I want. I named my price. They can ante up or get out of the game."

"Yes, sir. Is that the message you wish to be passed on to Mr. Han Seng?"

"Shit, Mary Margaret, you know me better than that. Is Seng still here on the island?"

"Yes, sir. I canceled his plane reservations before we left Seattle."

"Yeah? When's he going back to China?"

"He didn't say, sir. Do you wish for me to inquire?"

"Not yet. Where is Seng now?"

There was a pause while Mary Margaret asked the main-frame to search for the guest wearing lapel button 9-3.

"The east terrace room, sir. He just ordered breakfast."

"Send some bagels and cream cheese and coffee to the terrace for me. I just can't warm up to pickled cabbage and green tea before dawn."

"Yes, sir."

Farmer hung up, hitched up his jeans, and headed for the east terrace. His running shoes made little squeaky noises on the marble floors, but he rarely noticed. His lapel pin was programmed to spread music wherever he went.

He passed the main conference room but didn't look in. He just crossed his fingers and hoped that Seng had finally packed up his sleazy jades. Seeing all that stone pussy spread out on the conference table had made Farmer uneasy. Screwing women was one thing. Looking up their skirts while you did it was another.

Pale predawn light filled the sky along the east side of the terrace room. Han Seng was seated at a sleek mahogany dining table. Printouts from various international newspapers were spread in front of him. As always, Han Ju and the bodyguard were nearby. The latter two men came to their feet immediately when Farmer walked in. Seng took his time standing up.

Farmer noted the lag. It told him that he was in for a rough negotiation. Silently he damned the Chinese trait of saying a polite yes and meaning a flat no. He wondered if he would ever learn all the Asian gradations of *yes* that meant *Not in this lifetime, asshole.*

"Good morning, Seng," Farmer said in English. He was one of the few people on earth who knew that Seng spoke and understood that language very well. "Sorry I couldn't join your jade party last night. I got held up in Seattle. I trust all the arrangements were satisfactory?"

Seng bowed slightly. Nothing in his expression showed that

the party had been a bust and the host had gone to bed without the delectable Ms. Blakely to lick his turtle head.

"Mary Margaret told me that the Chinese government has assigned you to cut a deal with me over the jade suit," Farmer said bluntly.

"The government of China has complimented me with their trust, yes," Seng said. "It is a very serious matter, this theft of part of the Chinese soul. My government wishes to be sure you understand just how grave the situation is before irreversible mistakes are made."

Farmer managed not to sigh. Just barely. Experience had taught him that when Seng got all formal, the price went up. The more words, the higher the price.

"You know me, Seng. If this wasn't important—goddamn important—I'd have sent someone to negotiate for me, the way SunCo did."

"My government appreciates your deep concern," Seng said, ignoring the reference to SunCo. He doubted that an American could understand the subtle, profound entanglement of family and politics in China. In some matters, SunCo *was* the Chinese government. In other matters, it was simply SunCo, a powerful and profitable business. And always there was the fact of *guanxi,* a web of connections that no Westerner could understand. "You do my government much honor by your personal presence."

Farmer smiled thinly. "I sure as hell do." He hooked a mahogany side chair with his foot, flipped the chair around, straddled it, and said, "What's on your government's mind?"

Seng sat again, sipped tea, and wondered if he would ever understand Westerners. Not only were the women arrogant and without manners, the men showed little grasp of ceremony and less of civility. Always in a hurry. Yet, Seng acknowledged as he carefully replaced his cup on its thin white saucer, all the Western rushing about had its uses. People who hurried were often careless.

"We are much heartened by your offer to return the jade

burial suit to its rightful and legal owners," Seng said. "The international community of citizens shares our . . ."

Without changing expression, Farmer pretty much stopped listening. He had already heard the answer to his offer: no. But unless he appeared to listen to the counteroffer, China would be insulted. That would turn a problem into a disaster.

Five minutes later, Farmer held up his index finger. Just that. It was enough.

Seng fell silent and waited.

"Let me summarize," Farmer began.

It wasn't a request. Still, Seng nodded agreement.

"Your government thinks the jade burial suit is the most important cultural icon since Christ," Farmer said, "but they won't give me fifteen years as the exclusive purveyor of computer equipment to mainland China in order to get the suit back. They won't even give me ten years."

"The point is rightful ownership," Seng countered bluntly, "not exclusive deals for any amount of time."

Farmer almost smiled. It was worth pissing Seng off just to cut through the bullshit. "That may be China's point, but it isn't mine. I have no doubt about who owns that jade suit. Me."

"Archaeological treasures belong to the country in which they originated. American law on that point is quite specific. I'm sure your government—"

"Who said anything about archaeology?" Farmer cut in. "I didn't dig up anything. I bought a private collection. The suit was part of it."

"The jade burial suit was stolen from China. It must be returned. Immediately."

"No deal."

"Have you discussed this with your government?"

"I pay a buttload of taxes. That's all the discussion my government gets."

Seng's surprise showed only in the slight lifting of his eyelids. "Even you are not entirely independent of your own government."

"Entirely? No. I still have property in the U.S."

Seng nodded and smiled.

"But," Farmer added, "I also have friends in Congress. A lot of them. American political campaigning is terribly expensive, as your government knows. Care to match China's political contributions against mine?"

Seng was silent.

"Smart," Farmer said. "Now let's try it again. I have something China wants. China has something I want. There are three days until I open my museum. Talk to me, Seng. Tell me why I should give you my very valuable jade suit and get nothing more than an international pat on the head in return."

Seng started talking.

Fifteen minutes later, Farmer got up and walked out.

The door to the condominium shut behind Archer. Kyle's code had appeared on the gizmo snitch, so Archer wasn't surprised to see his brother at the kitchen table, waiting for the coffee to finish brewing. But after what Archer had just learned from Uncle, he was surprised to see Kyle alone.

"Where's the Blakely woman?" Archer asked bluntly.

"Where I'd like to be. Asleep."

"With her?"

"If I was with her, I wouldn't be sleeping."

"Still thinking with your dick?"

"If I was, I wouldn't be with you."

"You're in a fine mood, aren't you? Let me see your arm."

"How did you find out about—oh, hell, never mind. I'll bet your informant drives a Ford Taurus. How much do you know about what happened?"

"Is Blakely sleeping in your bed?"

Apparently Archer wasn't answering questions right now. Kyle didn't feel like answering them, either. He looked out the kitchen window of the Donovan apartments. Dawn, such as it was, hovered like a coy date, smiling just beyond reach. The lights of Seattle gleamed amid patches of fog. Above the fog, rising in a silver majesty men could only envy, the Olympics waited for whatever mountains wait for.

"Kyle?" Archer said impatiently.

"Shut up and pour coffee." Kyle rubbed his unshaved face and grimaced at the sandpapery sound. "Yes, Lianne is sleeping in my bed."

Kyle's tone didn't invite questions or idle conversation. Archer ignored the attitude and poured coffee. He was used to surly siblings at dawn. At the moment, he was one himself.

"Do you think that's smart?" Archer asked.

"It beats the alternative."

"Just because she bandaged your manly wounds—"

"The med-tech took care of that," Kyle interrupted. "Give me the damn coffee."

Archer set a mug in front of Kyle. He drank, grimaced, and got up to look for milk in the refrigerator. Archer watched with cold steel eyes while Kyle poured milk. His brother didn't have the relaxed, sated look of a man who had spent the night screwing his latest lady. Instead, he looked like a man who was worried.

Or afraid.

"Let's have it," Archer said.

Kyle put the milk away, stirred the coffee with his finger, and drank deeply despite the scalding heat. Then he held out the cup for more.

Archer poured coffee.

"It's pretty simple," Kyle said. "Someone wants Lianne dead."

"The city cops say it was a mugging. Homeless illegal immigrant with a knife. Single woman with a purse."

"That's crap."

"So are a lot of things. The guy's lawyer got him out an hour after he woke up."

"Lawyer?" Kyle said in disgust. "What would a 'homeless illegal immigrant' know about lawyers?"

"Enough to call one," Archer said dryly.

"Who?"

"Ziang Lee."

"Is he a freelance ambulance chaser?"

"No. Ziang and his partners specialize in Asian Pacific law. They also have a reputation for taking care of triad business in the Pacific Northwest."

"What kind of business?" Kyle asked.

"The usual. Prostitutes, gambling, drugs, loan-sharking, trafficking in parts of endangered species."

Kyle looked blank at the last category.

"Asian medicine," Archer explained. "The Chinese will pay a lot for potions made out of bear gallbladder, tiger penis, that sort of thing."

"It's too early in the morning for this discussion."

"Stop whining. I've been up all night."

"Why?"

"A game of Twenty Questions with Uncle."

"Who was asking and who was answering?"

"We traded off," Archer said.

"And?"

"You want an omelet before we talk?"

"That bad?" Kyle asked.

Archer didn't answer. He just started cooking.

After a few minutes Kyle made toast and more coffee. The brothers sat down together just in time for sunlight to slide through the east window and across the breakfast nook that was positioned to take advantage of dawn.

"You keep trying to butter me up and I'm going to get fat," Kyle said, diving into a plate heaped with cottage fries and a Spanish omelet.

"Just stay alive and I won't complain."

Kyle's fork hesitated. "I don't like the sound of that."

"Who said anything about liking?"

Archer went through his breakfast like a man who knew it could be a long time before he had another decent meal. When he was finished, he poured himself the last of the coffee and started talking. He focused on Kyle as though force of will alone would make his brother understand that getting emotionally involved with Lianne Blakely was a mistake of potentially lethal proportions.

"The so-called mugger is a lieutenant in the Red Phoenix triad," Archer said. "He's part of an informal cultural-exchange program. Uncle Sam locks up or deports one triad man and they send two to take his place."

Kyle dripped honey onto the last piece of toast and listened, knowing he wasn't going to like what he heard.

"The particular snake you tangled with is a triad terminator," Archer said. "Need someone killed? When the next flight out of China or Hong Kong or Singapore lands in Seattle, off comes the bad-luck man. He kills the target and is on a plane out of the city before anyone knows what happened."

"Not this time."

"You were pig-lucky," Archer said flatly. "Qiang Qin—your bad-luck man—isn't a virgin. He's been dropping bodies for the Red Phoenix triad all over the Pacific Rim countries. Six in Hong Kong alone, and that was a slow year."

"Busy boy," Kyle said casually. But even with honey, the toast suddenly tasted like sawdust. The thought of Lianne alone in that hallway with a triad hit man made Kyle sick. "How did you find out about him?"

"How do you think?"

"Either you took off our tail's face or Uncle decided to be friendly."

"Friendly it is."

"Shit. Better you had taken off the guy's face. When Uncle gets friendly, I get nervous. What does our dear government want from us now?"

"Same thing it did before—inside the Tang family."

"So why are you complaining that I brought Lianne home?"

"Because," Lianne said from just beyond the doorway, "Archer wishes Qiang Qin had done his job and killed me."

Archer and Kyle spun toward the door with identical looks of surprise and anger on their faces. Lianne would have laughed, but she was too hurt and much too angry. She had been so pathetically grateful when Kyle helped her out.

Now she knew why he had. The knowledge stuck in her throat like a jagged piece of ice.

She had been so easy.

So stupid.

She had believed that a man like Kyle Donovan might be interested in a woman with no family, no money, no connections, nothing but a knack for jade and the stubbornness to pursue it no matter what life threw at her.

"That's not true," Archer said calmly. "I don't want you dead."

"Yet," Lianne shot back, her voice as even as his. "Not until I act as a Judas goat and lead my family off to slaughter."

"Your *family?*" Archer asked, his eyes narrow. "Funny, when the chips were down, it was the Donovan family that came to your rescue. The Tangs were hot on your heels, baying like hounds closing in for the kill."

Lianne's chin came up subtly. She didn't like hearing the truth, especially from a man who disliked her, but she wouldn't deny it. She was a survivor. Survivors accepted the truth even when it came at them like a sword.

"Back off," Kyle told Archer. "Lianne doesn't owe us anything."

"The hell she doesn't. Without our money she'd still be in handcuffs or behind bars."

Kyle surged to his feet. "It was *my* money, not the family's."

"Sit down."

Kyle leaned forward and spread his big hands flat on the table. "Back off, Archer, or Lianne and I are out the door."

"Just like that? You go to bed with a woman for one night, and then you go to war against your family for her?"

"Why are you being such a prick?" Kyle snarled.

"Because it pisses me off to watch a piece of ass lead my brother around by his dick."

With startling speed, Kyle reached for Archer. With equal speed, Archer knocked his brother's hands aside and leaped to his feet.

"Stop it," Lianne said, shoving between them. "There's no need to tear up the kitchen just to put on an act for me."

Kyle stared at her.

Archer stared, too, but there was speculation rather than surprise in his eyes.

It was Archer's look Lianne met, Archer she spoke to, Archer she tried to convince. She didn't want to look at Kyle and remember her foolish abandon, her eager mouth and hands, her abandoned response to his expertise.

"I have something you want," Lianne said, her voice as flat as the line of her mouth. "You have something I want. I'm sure we can reach an understanding."

"You're in no position to be making a deal," Archer said impatiently.

"Wrong. If you didn't need me, you'd have left me in jail."

"It's not too late for a return trip. Or do you think your father will come running back and make everything right with his family? *His* family, Lianne, not yours. A child born out of wedlock doesn't have a family."

"That's it," Kyle said coldly, reaching for Lianne. "We're gone."

"No." With a lightning motion Lianne wrenched free of Kyle's hand. Her eyes never left Archer's. She smiled without a trace of warmth. "Baiting me won't work, Archer. I don't lose my temper and do stupid things. Not since third grade, when I knocked a boy on his ass for calling me a slant-eyed bastard and my mother a Chinaman's whore."

"I'm not baiting you," Archer said, his voice even. "I'm telling you the truth. No one from your so-called family will help you out of this one."

"I know that better than you do."

"Lianne," Kyle began. But he couldn't think of anything more to say, and she wouldn't look at him. Slowly he lifted his hands to her shoulders. He began kneading muscles tight with the rage and pain she didn't reveal in any other way.

"Don't," Lianne said, shrugging off his hands and moving aside, away from both men. "You pretended you cared about me before. Now I know why. No need to go on with the farce."

"Talk about farce." Archer stepped in front of Kyle before he could reach for Lianne again. "You followed Kyle for two weeks before he walked up to you at the auction. So let's cut the crap about who did what to whom and see if we can find a common ground. Coffee?"

Lianne's eyes widened. It was the last thing she would have expected from Archer. "Please," she replied automatically.

He smiled. "There, I knew we could get things back on a civilized basis. Sit down, brother."

"I'd rather hit you."

Archer's steel-gray glance flicked over Kyle, who bared his teeth in a smile that was more like a curse.

"But see how civilized I am?" Kyle asked through his teeth. "I'm smiling."

"Good," Archer said gently. "That way you have a fall-back position."

"I sure as hell do." Kyle looked at Lianne. She was watching both of them the way she would watch poisonous snakes. "Want some food with your coffee?"

"No," she said.

"You sure? Archer makes a mean omelet."

"I'd be astonished if he made a friendly one."

Archer laughed, drawing another surprised glance from Lianne. His laughter was as genuine as his anger had been. And, like anger, laughter transformed him.

For an instant she wished they could have been friends rather than enemies. Then she looked into the clear, cold depths of his eyes and knew she might as well wish that Kyle had been drawn to her as a woman rather than as a back-door connection to the family of Tang. Both wishes were equally painful, equally pointless.

"Cream, sugar?" Archer asked.

"Black," Lianne said in a low voice. "Very, very black."

With false calm she sat down, pushed up the sleeves of her red satin bathrobe, and waited to see what kind of deal the steel-eyed devil would offer her.

t w e n t y

Kyle sat down next to Lianne in the breakfast nook, hemming her in against the cedar wall. She gave him a cold sideways look, the kind she would give a stranger who took up too much of the bus seat next to her.

She didn't know what else to do. How did you treat a man who was a demon lover one night and a comforting teddy bear the next? The contrast, like so much about Kyle, kept her off-balance. So she simply ignored him and went back to eating the omelet Archer had prepared.

"That was good," she said, finishing the last bite.

Archer sat down across from her. "You sound surprised that a man can cook."

"Not at all. I'd be surprised if you could find a woman to cook for you."

Archer looked at Kyle. "I should have been giving you combat pay."

"Don't bother. I was putty for him," Lianne said before Kyle could speak.

"More like fire," Kyle muttered.

"I was referring to my brain," she said, watching Archer. "This would go faster without your brother."

"My name is Kyle, sweetheart, and I'm not going anywhere you don't go."

Lianne didn't answer, but Archer saw the subtle flinching of her eyelids, the slant of her body away from Kyle, and the bone white of her fingers clenching the coffee mug. For a bright woman—and Archer had no doubt that Lianne was very bright—she was real slow to follow up on the advantage she had by being Kyle's lover. She gave every impression of not wanting to touch him with anything softer than a knife, as though she really had been outraged to discover that he had had an ulterior motive for getting to know her.

Archer began to reassess his opinion of Lianne Blakely. Even as he did, he hoped it wasn't necessary. Life would be so much easier if she was a simple crook who could give Uncle Sam a nice, easy solution to the diplomatic hot potato of the jade burial shroud. If Lianne wasn't a crook, any solution that came down the road wouldn't be simple.

"Why were you following me around?" Kyle asked her after a moment. "And please, no stud-muffin routine. You aren't the type to pick up men."

"Type?"

"Brash, casual, party-loving, ready to have sex with any male who catches your eye," he said, reaching for the coffeepot.

She smiled thinly at him. After a few days, he knew her better than her father did after a lifetime. "Johnny asked me to pick you up and bring you home to the Tangs."

"Johnny? You mean your father?" Archer asked.

"After a fashion," she agreed sardonically.

"What did Johnny want with me?" Kyle asked.

"I don't know."

Archer didn't bother to conceal his impatience or his disbelief. "What did Johnny usually want when he sent you out to fetch a man?"

"This was the first time."

"Yeah. Right."

Lianne looked directly at Archer. Her face was calm. Her hands were aching from holding onto the coffee mug.

"Believe what you want to," she said evenly. "I'm telling you the truth."

"Do you have any idea why your father wanted to talk to me?" Kyle asked.

She frowned, trying to remember exactly what Johnny had said. "When I asked him, he said it was important, very important. And it was family business. That's all."

"Were you aware that Donovan International was approached by the Tang Consortium with an idea toward some kind of business alliance?" Archer asked.

Lianne shook her head.

"When?" Kyle asked his brother.

"Last year. We declined."

"Why?" Lianne asked. "Wasn't it a good match?"

Archer hesitated, then decided that the truth was more useful than any lie he could think of. "Same reason we turned down SunCo. Triads."

"What?" Kyle and Lianne said together.

"Both families—Sun and Tang—are heavily involved with Chinese gangs."

She frowned. "Many triads aren't gangs in the sense that you mean in America. Criminal. And in any case, China isn't a society of law in the same way America is. In China the state, whether Confucian, Communist, or capitalist, transcends the law. In America the law transcends the state."

"Even allowing for cultural differences," Archer said, "we found the triad connection with the Tangs—and especially the Suns—to be too close for our comfort."

"Is Johnny the Tang Consortium liaison with the gangs?" Kyle asked.

"No. His brother Harry is. Harry's number one mistress is the sister of a Red Phoenix overlord."

Lianne remembered the composed, intelligent woman who

had acted as unofficial hostess for the Tang post-auction party. "No wonder he could afford that bracelet for her."

"You noticed that, too?" Kyle asked dryly. "That central ruby must have been twenty carats." He turned back to Archer. "Red Phoenix again, huh? Those boys sure do get around."

"In the U.S. they do. They're Uncle's number one Asian headache."

Lianne set aside her coffee mug and focused on Archer. "So you believe that Johnny wanted me to pick up Kyle in order for the Tang family—and thus the Red Phoenix—to find a way into Donovan International?"

"You have a better idea?" Archer asked calmly.

"Not at the moment. But why would it be so urgent? Johnny was almost frightened the night of the auction. He said I had to meet Kyle before he and my mother went to Tahiti."

"Ask Johnny when he gets back," Archer suggested.

"What makes you think he'll be speaking to me?"

"He's your father," Kyle said, surprised.

"He's my mother's paramour," Lianne said coolly. "There's a difference. A big one. In any case, Johnny is a Tang. First, last, always."

"Why—" Archer began.

"I believe it's my turn," Lianne interrupted. "The government wanted Kyle to infiltrate the Tang family. Why?"

Kyle started to answer, then fell silent. He could always start talking if Archer didn't tell enough of the truth. Until then, Lianne seemed to do better with Archer.

That didn't make Kyle happy, but there wasn't much he could do about it until he got Lianne alone again. First he would get her naked and wrapped around him. Then he would try reason. If reason didn't work, he could always go back to a more hands-on approach.

"The U.S. government believes that the Tang family brokered the sale of the Jade Emperor's Tomb," Archer said.

Lianne opened her mouth, found nothing to say, and closed her mouth.

"No comment?" Archer asked.

"I'm . . . stunned," she said simply. "How would the Tangs get their hands on such a treasure trove? They haven't been powerful in mainland China for almost seventy years."

"The triads are," Archer said bluntly. "Red Phoenix, for example. Ever since China decided to try a semi-Socialist version of capitalism, Red Phoenix has gotten very, very wealthy on extortion, gambling, sex, and drugs. SunCo has made several billion dollars on money laundering alone. The Tang Consortium hasn't done as well. Wen isn't into gambling and has a moral aversion to drugs. He prefers straight import-export deals, influence peddling, immigrant smuggling, brand-name pirating for the folks back at home, and extortion."

Lianne let out a long breath. "If what you say is true, you know more about the Tang Consortium than I do."

"How do you see the consortium?" Kyle asked.

"All I know is that the Tangs have international business deals ranging from realty to trade goods to banks. Jade is more a passion for the consortium than a profit center."

"Are you saying that you've heard nothing about the Jade Emperor from the Tangs?" Archer demanded.

"Yes."

Archer muttered something under his breath and looked out at the awakening land. It was that magic time when the sky was new, radiant, and lights glittered like gemstones against the black satin body of the city.

"Whether or not you believe me, it's true," Lianne said. "I've heard speculation about the Jade Emperor, but not from the Tangs."

"Odd, isn't it?" Kyle asked. "Wen should have been fascinated by the idea."

"When the rumor mill started heating up a few months ago, I talked to Wen about it."

"What did he say?"

"That he was too old to believe in fairy tales. When I tried to pursue it, he was impatient. He said I had much to learn, he didn't have much time left to give me, and we should spend it on jades we could touch instead of setting snares for a phoenix."

"What about Johnny?" Archer asked. "What did he think about the Jade Emperor?"

"He knows less about jade than you do. Finance is his passion. Numbers and deals, buildings and banks. The only Tang who is interested in jade is Daniel."

"Your half brother?" Kyle asked.

"Johnny's son." Lianne's voice was clipped. "He has become Wen's apprentice."

"Shoving you out?" Archer asked.

"No shoving required. I left."

"Has Daniel mentioned the Jade Emperor?" Kyle asked quickly.

"I never spoke to Daniel until the day after the auction. He all but called me a thief and tried to keep me from seeing Wen."

"What did he accuse you of stealing?" Archer asked.

"Nothing directly." Lianne took a breath and said what she really didn't want to say. "I think . . . it's possible . . ." Her voice fragmented.

Archer waited.

Beneath the table, Kyle put his hand on her leg in a gesture that was comforting rather than provocative. Her flesh flinched but she didn't move away. She couldn't. There was nowhere left for her to go.

"What is it, sweetheart?"

"Don't call me that."

"Honey, darling, sugar, baby, love, *buttercup*," Kyle said. "What do you think is possible?"

Lianne wanted to scream or snarl at the lover's knowledge in Kyle's eyes and the gentle, implacable intimacy of his hand. The charade of mutual interest had been exposed, yet he wouldn't stop pretending it was real. Last night she had gone to sleep alone on the couch and awakened in the middle of the night in his bed, in his arms.

She could take the questions and the distrust, but not the offer of loving refuge where nothing existed but a need to pry knowledge out of her, knowledge that would be used against the only family she knew, the family that had betrayed her.

Betrayal. Everywhere she looked, everywhere she turned. Betrayal. But nowhere did it enrage her as much as in Kyle's beautiful, lying eyes.

Archer's eyes narrowed at the emotion vibrating in Lianne. Either she was a fine actress or she really wanted to take her coffee mug and cram it down Kyle's throat.

"The Neolithic blade and the camel aren't the only substitutions made in Wen's collection," Lianne said.

"We know that," Archer said. "Tell us something we don't know."

"Wen used to own the same jade suit that Farmer has now."

After a moment, Archer whistled through his teeth in shocked surprise. "You're certain?"

"Why didn't you tell me?" Kyle asked at the same time.

"Why should I?" she retorted. "You didn't tell me why you were screwing me."

"I was screwing you because you got me so hot I didn't know which end was up. I'm still picking splinters out of my butt from the dock. Wasn't I a gentleman, sweetheart? You only got splinters in your knees."

Archer lifted his eyebrows and smiled down into his coffee cup. He would have laughed out loud, but there was too much anger in Kyle's voice. His brother was baiting Lianne every way a man could. Only fair. She was baiting him the same way.

"I got *you* so hot," Lianne said, her voice rising. "You son of a bitch! I didn't even know people could do it that many ways, much less that it would feel so—" Abruptly she remembered that there was another person at the table, and that person was Kyle's brother. She flushed from her breasts to the top of her head. "Never mind," she muttered. "It has nothing to do with jade."

"Coffee, anyone?" Archer asked blandly.

No one answered. He poured the rest of the coffee into his cup, drank, and put the finishing touches on his reassessment of Lianne Blakely.

It didn't take long. Archer had his faults, but stupid wasn't one of them.

"You're sure about that jade suit?" he asked.

"Yes. I saw it twice in Wen's vault."

"Why didn't you mention it sooner?"

"I gave my word I would never speak about the burial suit to anyone except Wen. But now . . ." Lianne stared down at the yellow scraps of omelet scattered across her plate. A little piece of green pepper gleamed like precious jade against the stark white plate. "Jades are missing. Wen thinks I'm a thief. Somebody is stealing from Wen and blaming it on me."

Archer nodded. "Why didn't you tell this to the government? Mercer said the Feds know their case against you is circumstantial at best. They offered to cut you loose if you would cooperate with them about the Jade Emperor."

"I'm innocent. The Feds can go screw themselves."

Archer smiled slightly. "I admire the sentiment, if not the logic."

"No matter what Kyle's reasons," Lianne said, "he saved my life—"

"You fought for your life," Kyle said.

"—and then he got me out of jail," she finished, ignoring him. "If I can help out the Donovans, I will."

Archer's smile widened. This was a logic he understood, the logic of personal loyalty. Lianne might not like being in debt to the Donovans, but she accepted it.

"What do you know about Wen's suit, the one you say Farmer has?" Archer asked.

"It's styled after the Han burial suits, but since I've never examined it, I can't guarantee its age. The shroud is nephrite rather than serpentine."

"Back up," Archer said. "You lost me."

"Serpentine is softer, easier to carve, and not as rare as jade," Kyle explained, understanding what his brother wanted. "Before the nineteenth century, a lot of what the Chinese called jade wasn't even nephrite, but a bunch of other 'virtuous' stones."

"Okay. Go on, Lianne."

"Not all jade burial suits are made of nephrite. The imperial workshops had a monopoly on artisans and materials; only the upper crust of royalty was permitted the best. Serpentine was a common substitute for jade in burial shrouds because it was more easily carved and more readily available."

"But Wen's suit was the real thing," Archer said.

"Yes. The jade was extraordinary—a translucent, deep green with cloud markings over the most important organs of the body. A piece of art as well as a summation of Chinese beliefs in life, death, and the hereafter."

"You're certain that Farmer has the same suit that Wen did?" Kyle pressed.

She hesitated, then accepted what she knew to be true. "Yes."

"And that it's true jade?" Kyle asked.

"As certain as I can be without a chemical analysis. It felt right. Looked right. Took the right polish. There was none of the wear at the corners you would expect from softer stone. And Wen's attitude toward the suit was reverent. He had a modern preference for nephrite over other kinds of 'jade.' "

"Why would Wen sell Farmer that suit?" Kyle asked.

"Money," Archer said succinctly. "Millions."

"Not good enough," Kyle said. "Wen is a collector. Parting with that suit would be like selling his soul."

Archer looked at Lianne.

"He's right," she said simply. "Of course, if the family of

Tang was desperate . . ." Then she sighed and shook her head. "No. Wen would have used his entire jade collection as collateral on a loan before he would sell any of it, much less the jade shroud."

"Maybe he did take out a loan," Archer said. "Maybe he defaulted and the bank sold off the collateral."

Kyle got up and paced across the kitchen to the stove. Lianne watched him go from sunlight to shadow and back to sunlight again, and couldn't decide which was more beautiful to her—the golden-green blaze of his eyes in the darkness or the shimmering gold of his hair in the light. But in light or dark, what drew her was his intelligence, his humor, the promise of strength in his easy stride.

Too bad all he wanted from her was information and sex, Lianne thought bitterly. In that order. Yet, to be fair, he gave as good as he got. And he *had* saved her life.

"Lianne?" Archer said. "What do you think about the loan scenario?"

She blinked and forced herself to look away from Kyle. "Unlikely."

"Why?"

"It would be impossible to keep such a loan quiet. First, the collection would have to be appraised. That alone would start a furor in the jade world. Whoever appraised the pieces would have friends, associates, lovers, rivals. No matter what vows of silence were sworn to, word would get out simply because the Tang jades are unparalleled. It would be like . . ." She hesitated, trying to think of an analogy Archer would understand. "Like De Beers getting the contents of their London diamond vaults appraised for a loan."

Archer grunted. "That would set off shock waves."

Kyle looked up from measuring coffee. "Would anyone in the Tang family have a reason to set Farmer up for a fall?"

"I don't understand," Lianne said.

Archer did. He gave Kyle an approving look. The boy definitely was *not* thinking with his dick.

"Farmer is getting into bed with SunCo," Kyle said. "What does that do to the Tangs?"

"Nothing good," Lianne said, frowning. "The Suns have much better mainland access than the Tangs. Three of the Suns have married 'red princesses.' Sun Sen, the granddaughter of the Sun patriarch, is engaged to Deng Qiang, a grandnephew of the dead leader and one of the most powerful men in China today."

"The new aristocracy," Kyle said, disgusted. "The ultraprivileged children and grandchildren of Mao's cohort intermarrying with the most successful criminal entrepreneurs of the twenty-first century."

"In other words," Archer said, "the Tangs have ample reason to want to undermine the Suns' success."

"Yes, but what does that have to do with Farmer and the jade shroud?" Lianne asked.

"Remember the old saying, 'Grasp the stinging nettle firmly'?" Kyle said, coming back to the table.

She nodded.

"Well," he continued, "making a fist around the stingers is one way of doing it. Very direct. Very Western." He slid into the breakfast nook and sat close to her again. Hip to thigh. "Like me."

Lianne smiled in spite of herself.

"Better yet," Kyle said, smiling slowly at her in return, "you get someone else to grab the nettle for you. Then it doesn't matter how the damn thing is grasped. Nothing's stinging *you*."

"Very indirect. Very Eastern," Lianne said. "Quite clever, actually."

"Yeah, it's great . . . unless you're the guy stuck with a double handful of nettles."

She looked at her own hands, wrapped around the empty coffee mug as though it was some kind of lifeline. Slowly she forced herself to let go of it. Then she stared into the dregs as if she could read her future in it.

Archer started to speak, but stopped at a look from Kyle.

"You're saying that I was deliberately set up by the Tang family for the purpose of making Dick Farmer or SunCo lose face?" Lianne asked.

"I'm wondering if it's possible," Archer said.

"Why?" she asked starkly.

"I'm looking for a convincing motive for someone else to steal those jades."

Kyle's eyes narrowed. He studied his oldest brother as though he had never seen him before.

"Why?" Lianne asked again, surprised.

"Because he finally woke up and smelled the coffee," Kyle said. "He believes you didn't do it."

She stared at Kyle, then at Archer.

"Right," Archer said. "But believing isn't proving. We need something that will convince the Feds. That will let both her and us off the government hook."

"Why are you on the hook in the first place?" Lianne asked.

"It's a long story about Russian czars and amber," Kyle said. "I'll tell you later. Right now, our problem is finding a convincing suspect whose name isn't Lianne Blakely."

"There's a whole world out there," she retorted.

"We only want the ones who have motive, means, and opportunity," Kyle said.

"Always a good starting point," Archer said. "At the moment, the Feds know that Lianne had the means and opportunity to rifle the Tang vault."

"But no motive," she said.

"Wrong, sweetheart," Kyle said. "Revenge."

Her eyes widened. Then her expression closed down, revealing nothing except wary, whiskey-colored eyes watching him. "I see. Bastard daughter gets even with the legitimate Tangs by stealing them blind. Is that how the scenario goes?"

"Yes. But since you didn't do it, we need to look at everyone else who has access to the Tang vault."

"Wen, Joe, Daniel, me."

"That's it?" Archer asked. "No wives or girlfriends, no household staff, no lock maintenance people or pest inspectors or electricians or household security?"

Lianne shook her head. "No one. You have to understand; by American standards, the Tang family is paranoid about protecting itself and its wealth. By Chinese standards, the Tangs are simply prudent. Deeply secretive."

"What kind of security system does the vault have?" Kyle asked.

"The locks are old. Very solid, mind you. Just not high-tech. They're the kind you would find in late-nineteenth-century banks."

"Damn," Kyle said. "Tumblers and dials and no electricity. Sounds like your meat, Archer."

"Locks like that get cranky without maintenance. Who keeps them oiled?" Archer asked.

"Wen used to," Lianne said. "I assume he taught Joe, but Joe is rarely in Vancouver, so Daniel has been doing the maintenance."

"Are you sure?"

"Wen told Daniel when I mentioned that one of the locks was getting sticky."

"Daniel isn't real fond of you, is he?" Kyle asked quietly.

She lifted her chin and didn't answer.

Kyle brushed the back of his hand down her cheek in a gentle caress. "I know you don't want to point any fingers at your half brother, but who else is there? He had to be the one who told Wen about the missing jades."

Lianne fought the dry, hot burning behind her eyes. She didn't like to think of anyone setting her up. Thinking of Daniel doing it, Daniel with her father's eyes and smile . . . Her stomach rolled.

It was such an intimate betrayal.

"What about Wen himself?" Archer said. "Would he do it?"

"He's blind," Kyle said without looking away from Lianne.

"He's frail. I'll bet he can't even get into the vault without help, much less sort through the jade. Can he, sweetheart?"

She shook her head and tried not to lash out at the logic box that was being so carefully built for her. And the cage that had already been built.

Someone had stolen the jades and made certain that she took the blame.

"What about Joe?" Archer asked.

"He doesn't know the difference between nephrite and soapstone," Lianne said, her voice low. "Whoever did this had to know which pieces to steal, which to ignore, and how to find substitutes. Even if Joe had the knowledge, why would he do it? It's his own inheritance, his own personal wealth, the pride and soul of the Tangs. The Tang Consortium is held by the whole family. The jade vaults have been passed down to the First Son's First Son since the first piece was collected."

"Which leaves Daniel," Kyle said gently, relentlessly. "The third—or is it fourth?—son of Johnny, who is the third son of Wen Zhi Tang. Danny boy is a long way from inheriting the keys to the jade kingdom, isn't he?"

"Yes," she whispered unhappily.

"How long has he had the combination to the vault?" Archer asked.

"I don't know."

"Ten years? Five? Two?"

As though cold, Lianne pulled the silk lapels of her robe closer. "I . . . a year. Maybe less. Whenever Wen couldn't see or feel the combination anymore and Joe wasn't there to open the vault for him."

"In other words," Archer said, "Daniel has had plenty of time to cream the jades."

"Yes. But . . ."

"But what?" Kyle asked.

"Why would he hate me enough to set me up? I haven't done anything to deserve that."

"Wrong assumption," Archer said. "Hatred might have

nothing to do with it. Deserving sure as hell doesn't. Pragmatism would explain choosing you."

She looked at Kyle as though asking him to counter his brother's relentless logic.

"It's a lot easier for Daniel to pin a stinking rose on Johnny's illegitimate daughter than on Wen's Number One Son," Kyle said quietly. "Isn't it, sweetheart? There's no one to protect you, no patriarch to rise up in righteous fury if you're threatened. You've lived your whole life out on the end of a Tang limb. Now someone's sawing it off right next to the trunk."

Lianne's chin came up a notch. She didn't like Kyle's logic, but it made a horrible kind of sense. There was only one thing wrong with it.

"Daniel doesn't have the combination to the inner vault," she said. "The one that held the jade shroud."

"Can you prove that?" Kyle said instantly.

"No."

"Can Daniel prove that he didn't know the combination?" Archer asked.

"How do you prove a negative?" Lianne retorted with bitter satisfaction, for she was in the same position—trying to prove that she had *not* stolen any jades.

"You can't," Kyle said. Then he smiled as coldly as Archer ever had and turned to his older brother. "We don't have much, but it might be enough to shake something loose. Time to call Uncle?"

Archer's eyelids lowered until his eyes were no more than glittering, steel-colored slits. Then he got up and went to the phone.

twenty-one

Displayed by a television screen that was no thicker than a debit card and no smaller than a chair, three heads spoke in measured terms about the volatile international situation. Sitting in his circular work area, Dick Farmer watched PBS with part of his attention and scanned several computer screens with the rest.

"What effect do you think this will have on international monetary markets in the near, semi-near, and long term?" asked the host, Helen Coffmann, a woman of average looks, manly tweed jacket, and impressive cheekbones.

"In the short run, it's hard to say with total assurance," Ted Chung, the resident Asian specialist said. "A lot will depend on the reaction of overseas lenders and China's non-American trading partners. If trade barriers go back up, there is little chance of an economically painless resolution. The ripple effect will be very costly, especially in China."

"Then it's to China's best interest to find some means of defusing the situation," Helen said.

"Economically speaking, yes. But we must remember that China is and always has been ruled by symbols. It is very difficult for Westerners to understand, yet I have no doubt that China would sooner invite economic turmoil than be seen as bowing to America's will, much less to Taiwan's."

"Lev, what do you think?" Helen asked, turning toward the other man.

"It will be a disaster," Lev Kline, the guest economist, said bluntly. "China and the United States are at a crucial juncture in trade talks. Three days ago, we were at the point of agreeing on allotments of automobiles in exchange for clothing imports, among many other items, plus an agreement to ensure that Chinese banks follow international . . ."

Farmer switched all of his attention to the computer screens. The talking heads of public television knew less about the trade situation than he did. For one thing, they hadn't even mentioned China's brisk international arms trade. But even setting that aside, the brutal, overriding truth was that China's economy was based on exports of everything from guns to teething rings. Unless China climbed down off its ridiculous high horse, trade barriers would go up and the flood of Chinese exports to America's rich markets would squeeze down to a trickle.

When that happened, international bank loans made to China would be in jeopardy of default, because there would be no export profits to make payments on the loans. The West would lose some profit margin if China defaulted. China would lose a hell of a lot more.

Defaulting on international loans would set off a chain of consequences. Foremost among them would be China printing more money to cover its debts, money that had no true value to back it up. Inflation would quickly follow. Unless good money came in from somewhere else—not likely, if China was defaulting on international loans—inflation would get out of hand until Chinese money wasn't worth the match to burn it.

People would riot in the streets because a week's wages couldn't buy a cup of rice. Severe repression would be the order of the day. If that didn't get the job done, there would be a military coup, order would be restored, and a new state would be reborn within the burned-out shell of the old.

It had happened before. It would happen again. It was the way of the world.

Since Farmer didn't have anything on mainland China worth protecting, he didn't care about the value of Chinese currency or the cost of a bowl of rice. If he had been established in China, as he hoped to be in a decade, he would have fought with every bit of leverage and lies at his command to defuse the growing crisis, as China's other trading partners were no doubt doing, including the United States.

Farmer wasn't one of those partners. About all he had at risk was an overpriced jade suit. Whatever happened in China wouldn't particularly affect his lucrative South American markets, or his Russian ones. But in eight years—sixteen at most—those markets would be saturated.

He needed another low-tech, high-density population to sell electronics to, a country where the industrial revolution had taken place, but not the computer revolution. Africa, India, and China were the obvious choices. Africa didn't have the money to boot up for the twenty-first century. Even if Africa could get the loans, its future population density was problematic. Too many African states had denied or ignored AIDS for too long.

India had the population, and the money, to buy computers, but Farmer hadn't been strong enough to lock up that market when it emerged. Farmer Enterprises was struggling along on a 14.4 percent market share in India. It was bigger than anyone else's, but not nearly big enough to overpower the shifting coalition of international businesses that kept undercutting his prices.

China beckoned like a sweet, unspoiled dream. In China, Farmer's challenge had been to find a good, competitive edge over the rest of the international business wolves. He had tried the usual bribes, the usual kickbacks, and had got the usual results. Good, but not good enough.

To his surprise, the Jade Emperor's burial suit was becoming the very edge he had been searching for. All that remained was for China to bow to the inevitable and open up negotiations with him. If the government chose to be stiff-necked about it, Farmer would shift priorities and concentrate on how he could profit in China's coming economic ruin. Beginning now.

The day that had started before dawn had just become longer.

"Coffee, Mary Margaret. Black and strong."

"Cindi, you have the local angle on this crisis," the news anchor said.

Reluctantly Lianne turned away from Susa's paintings and faced the television set. Its screen was big enough for the travelogues that Susa enjoyed, but not big enough to dominate the airy room.

"Thanks, Carl." Wearing a tasteful burgundy suit, cream silk blouse, motionless hair, and a colorful scarf that lifted in the wind, Cindi turned toward the camera. Thanks to the deceptive miracle of digital TV, she appeared to be standing on I-5 overlooking the vast Boeing/McDonnell Douglas complex. "The atmosphere is tense here today at the Boeing plant. Workers who had been certain of employment from Chinese aircraft contracts are now grim, fearing layoffs or worse. Unless the trade situation is resolved, these men and women will be out of work before their kids are out of school for the summer. Back to you, Carl."

"Thanks, Cindi. Next, an update on the protest over the Nude Taco, the cafe that brought see-through dining to our Northwest cuisine."

Lianne punched a button on the remote, shutting off the TV. No matter how edgy she was, waiting to open her own negotiations with the U.S. government, there were some things she wouldn't waste time on. Afternoon "news" was one of them.

"No nude tacos?" Kyle asked from behind her.

She glanced over her shoulder. Kyle was across the room, leaning against the doorway, watching her with eyes that measured and desired.

"I'm into nude hot dogs," she said.

"You're in luck. I've got this—"

The front door opened. The teasing expression vanished from Kyle's face as a young, startlingly beautiful Chinese woman preceded Archer into the room.

Kyle had seen the woman before, at the Tang's post-auction party. She had been wearing less clothes and more hair then. Not that the tailored charcoal suit and red silk blouse made her look like a dog. Far from it.

With narrowed eyes, Lianne measured the young woman, wondering at the transformation from party bimbo to sleek, self-confident business person.

"Good behavior, boys and girls," Kyle said. "I do believe Uncle has just arrived."

The woman gave Kyle a look from glorious, polished jet eyes. "Bingo. This would have been a whole lot easier if you had used the telephone number I put in your pocket."

"My plate was full," he said dryly.

"April Joy, meet Lianne Blakely and my brother Kyle," Archer said.

"We've met," April said.

"April Joy?" Kyle's mouth turned up at one corner. "The name fit you better when you were wearing your hair down past the crack in your ass, and not much else."

Smiling, April walked closer to Kyle, giving that extra little swing and jiggle of hips and breasts that was guaranteed to bring a man's heart rate up. "How's your plate now, handsome?"

"Knock it off," Archer said impatiently to April before Kyle could answer. "You tried that approach already on him. It didn't work."

"Should I try it on you?" April asked, turning to Archer.

He smiled slowly, thinly. "Depends on how much time you have to waste."

"Forget it. I've read your file. You keep your cock in your pants like a regular priest." April looked at Lianne and spoke in rapid Cantonese. "Do not trust these men, sister. They will use you and forget you."

"Number Four Donovan Son saved my life," Lianne said in the same language. "It is his to do with as he pleases."

"You are American, not Chinese."

"Not in this."

"Shit," April said in heartfelt English. She turned to the men. "Give me a reason I shouldn't have the three of you locked up for obstructing a federal investigation."

"This is America, not China," Kyle said. "You need evidence to lock people up."

"Wrong," April said. "All you need is a pliant federal judge."

"If you had one that pliant, you wouldn't be here," Archer pointed out. "Any more gambits you're supposed to try before we get down to business?"

"Are you going to offer me coffee or are you going to be a prick?" she asked Archer.

"I'll get back to you on that."

"You're going to be a prick. This is my lucky day all the way to the wall." April looked at Lianne again. "Wash the stardust and sex out of your eyes and think. The government can help you more than the Donovans. We're the ones who put that triad assassin on a plane and sent him back to China."

"The government locked me up," Lianne said. "The Donovans set me free."

"You could have walked anytime you decided to roll over on your Chinese connection. That was all we wanted."

"That was the problem. I didn't have a 'Chinese connection.' I still don't."

"Bullshit. You couldn't have gotten something like that jade shroud out of China without mainland contacts. Lots of them.

We want them. Then we can confiscate the damned thing under the Cultural Antiquities Act, send it back where it belongs, and get on with the much more important business of Westernizing China."

"Good luck," Kyle muttered.

"Amen," Archer agreed. "More likely we'll be sinecized."

"Is that a word?" Kyle asked.

"Stand-up comics," April said scathingly. "Jesus. Keep it for the stage, slick. We've got serious business to do here."

"Are you slick?" Kyle asked Archer. "Or am I?"

"Must be you," Archer said. "I'm more an ass-kicker myself."

"If I had brought the suit into the U.S.," Lianne said before April could explode, "you're right, I would have needed a lot of help. But I didn't bring in the shroud. I don't have any mainland connections. Period."

"Believe her," Archer said. "I do."

April's anger faded as she looked right at him, running scenarios in her head, changing attacks in mid-stride because the attack she had been using wasn't any good.

"All right," she said, deciding. "Say I believe Lianne is innocent. Then what?"

"Then you get out of our face and let us clean up this mess."

"How will you do that?" April said quickly.

"Don't tell her," Kyle said, just as fast. "There's a leak somewhere on her side."

She turned on him, all acting gone. Nothing remained but a cold, polished agent who knew more than one way to kill. "Explain that."

"I couldn't figure out why the Feds were dragging their feet after Lianne put up bail," Kyle said. "The bureaucrat in charge did everything but make forms by hand."

"So civil service is a bitch," April said. "So what?"

"So someone called about Lianne making bail. Then someone else sent a triad hit man to her apartment."

"You're reaching," April said, turning back to Archer. "Okay. What's the deal?"

"I'll get back to you on that, too."

"You really believe our security is compromised?" April asked scornfully.

"It wouldn't be the first time, would it?"

Small, elegant fists shot up to rest on April's waist. The result was to outline her body very nicely, but for once she wasn't thinking of that.

"Okay, boys and girl," she said. "Listen up. Some really big elephants are at play. Right now, you're the grass underfoot, soon to be ground into mud. If the idea doesn't appeal to you, grab hold of Uncle Sam and climb up for the ride. You'll be a lot safer."

"What about Farmer?" Kyle demanded. "He bought the suit. Surely he can give you a lead."

"He says he got the suit from Taiwan."

"Then why are you leaning on Lianne?" Kyle asked.

April didn't answer.

Archer did. "Two reasons, I imagine. The first would be that our assets in Taiwan say that the jade shroud didn't come from there, but Taiwan is more than happy to twist the Chinese tiger's tail by saying it did and forcing the U.S. to choose sides. Uncle, of course, would rather not play that game."

"And the second reason?" Lianne asked.

"You're easier game than Dick Farmer. He has wires into enough Congressmen to light up Washington, D.C." Archer turned back to April. "Right, Ms. Joy?"

"Right or wrong, it's not my problem. It's yours." She watched Kyle with clear black eyes. "Last chance, handsome. I promise I'll be gentle with you."

Kyle gave April a genuine smile and shook his head.

She spoke to Lianne in rapid Cantonese. "No matter how strong and beautiful the tiger, it is always safer to walk than to ride."

"No doubt," Lianne said in English. "But I have to say, the ride is incredible."

"Yeah," April said, flicking Kyle a glance, "I'll just bet it is." She faced Archer. "Someone is going down for that jade shroud. We'd rather have the whole pipeline from here to China so this kind of thing won't happen again real soon. But if all we can get now is a small fish, we'll fry it crisp and pretend it's the whole damn feast. I'm sure you understand."

Archer nodded. He understood. It was what he would have done, once.

"Three days, slick," April said, looking from one Donovan brother to the other. "Then Farmer's museum opens and we start frying sweet little Lianne."

Maybe it was the artificial light outside Anna Blakely's condominium. Maybe it was the glittering jewelry and designer clothes she wore. At first glance, Kyle thought that Lianne didn't take after her blond, deliberately expensive mother very much. Then he took another, better, look and decided that the biological link was there in the tilt of her smile, the chin lifted to take on the world, the singing female allure of her walk, and the graceful length of her fingers as she reached for her daughter. They hugged as though it had been months rather than three days since they had last seen each other.

After repeated assurances that Lianne was all right, Anna pulled back and gave her daughter a long look.

"You should have called right away, baby," she said, her voice husky. "When Johnny told me, I went crazy."

"I left word at your hotel. When you didn't call back . . ." Lianne's voice died. The silence from her mother had been harder to bear than Wen's belief that she was a crook.

"The Tangs need a new travel agent," Anna said, her mouth turning down. "There was a mix-up in the reservations.

We had to change hotels. If Johnny hadn't thought to check with the original hotel for messages, we'd still be in Tahiti and you'd still be here alone."

"Let them come in," Johnny said, walking up behind Anna. "We can talk more safely inside."

Lianne stiffened and stepped away from her mother. She hadn't expected Johnny Tang to be here. She hadn't wanted him to be. She was afraid that he, like Wen, believed she was a thief.

"Inside," Johnny repeated, drawing Anna into the room.

Kyle shot him a look, but the older man was too busy staring past the women to the street to notice. Kyle had the distinct feeling that Johnny was worried.

We can talk more safely inside.

Maybe someone in the Tang family had told Johnny that his backdoor daughter was attracting the wrong kind of attention from the wrong kind of people. Or maybe Johnny hadn't had to be told. Maybe he had known all along.

And maybe he had known about the attack, too.

Cold rage shot through Kyle. He didn't like to think that Johnny had known in advance that Lianne was going to be arrested, so he packed up his mistress and took off for Tahiti, leaving Lianne to face the cops alone. The possibility that Johnny also might have known in advance about the attacker was enough to make Kyle killing mad.

Using a gentleness that was at odds with his thoughts, Kyle put his arm around Lianne's shoulders and urged her inside. Johnny and Anna were clear across the room, talking in low voices near the counter that separated the kitchen from the living area.

Even when the door shut behind him and automatic locks clicked into place, Kyle kept his arm around Lianne. She gave him a look that was surprise and something more, relief and yearning and wariness. She leaned against him for just a moment, then straightened instantly as though stung. When she would have stepped away from him entirely, his fingers tightened. His free hand came up under her stubborn chin and he kissed her very gently on the mouth.

"This is one you don't have to do alone," he said simply.

"Part of the stuffed-elephant escort service?" Lianne asked coolly, but her lips trembled.

"I met you because Archer asked me to," Kyle said. "I made love to you because I wanted you. I still do, and it has nothing to do with anything except us."

Lianne was too surprised to say anything. The hunger in Kyle's eyes was as real as his kiss had been tender. She was caught between the two, afraid to trust either, needing so much to believe in both. She told herself she would be a fool to believe in Kyle now, when she knew he was bound to his family just as Johnny was bound to his.

Then she was leaning into Kyle's arm and her own arm was stealing around his waist. No matter what had come before or what came after, she would take what he was offering to her now. She desperately needed it.

This is one you don't have to do alone.

When the ungiving leather and steel of Kyle's shoulder holster registered on Lianne's senses, she simply tightened her grip on him. Whatever happened tomorrow or the day after, she had to get through this day, this evening, the next hour. That came first. Everything else came last.

"Tea?" Anna asked, looking from Kyle to Lianne with a mother's sad, hopeful eyes.

"Sure," Kyle said. "Oolong, if you have it."

Anna smiled approvingly. "Lianne's favorite. Of course I have it. Johnny?"

"Brandy," he said. "I had enough Chinese tea on the flight back to last me a lifetime."

"Tea is good for you," Anna said, looking at the dark circles under his eyes and the brackets of fatigue on either side of his full mouth. For once, her lover showed every one of his years.

"Brandy is better." Johnny sat down on one of the low couches, leaned back against the silk cushion, closed his eyes, and said, "What the hell is going on, Lianne?"

"We were hoping you could tell us," Kyle said before Lianne could open her mouth.

She started to speak anyway, only to have Kyle's hand close with painful demand over her shoulder.

"Let your father talk," Kyle said calmly.

There was a crash from the open kitchen area as Anna dropped a brandy snifter.

Lianne jerked, but not because of the broken snifter. She wasn't used to hearing Johnny referred to as her father. Not out loud. Certainly not in Anna's presence, much less in Johnny's

"Sorry," Kyle said sardonically. "Did I point out that there's a lump the size of the Empire State Building under this fine Chinese rug?"

For the first time, Lianne realized that beneath his relaxed exterior, Kyle was furious. And the focus of his anger was Johnny Tang.

"Make that brandy a double," Johnny said. "Looks like Lianne has finally brought home a man who doesn't give a damn about the Tang Consortium."

"Oh, I care," Kyle said. "I need information. Tangs have it. One way or another, I'm going to get it."

Though Johnny's eyes were still closed, he sensed Anna leaning over the couch, a glass of brandy in her hand. He took the glass and a fast, healthy swallow. Then he opened his eyes, murmured something in Cantonese, and smiled gently when Anna flushed like a girl.

"Information from the Tangs," Johnny said idly. "Why? So Donovan International can get a leg up on Asian markets?"

"Fuck the markets. I want Lianne off the playing field. The only way I can do that is to get the truth about how Dick Farmer ended up with Wen Zhi Tang's jade shroud."

Johnny sat bolt upright, shock on his handsome face. "Jade shroud? What the hell are you talking about?"

For ten seconds Kyle stared. Then he muttered, "Shit Marie. Nothing about this is going to be easy, is it?"

twenty-two

"So someone has been taking jade out of the Tang vaults, selling it, and substituting junk in its place?" Johnny asked tiredly. As he spoke, he looked at his watch, hardly able to believe that less than half an hour had passed since Kyle had shattered precedent and named Lianne as Johnny Tang's daughter.

"That's one explanation," Lianne said. She reached for her second cup of tea. "Another is that Wen needs cash for some reason and is selling off jade to get it."

"He'd sooner sell his second and third sons," Johnny said. "And I mean that literally."

"What about his first son?" Kyle asked.

"Only an American would ask," Johnny said.

"Wen would sooner die than lose Joe," Lianne said in a calm voice. "The Chinese much prefer sons over daughters. First sons are greatly preferred over other sons, second sons are more valued than third, and so on. Correct, Johnny?"

Johnny shrugged. He had absorbed and accepted the consequences of sex and birth order long before he had words to describe any of it. For him, the cultural preference he had been raised in was as unremarkable, if sometimes as inconvenient, as getting older each year.

"Quit pacing, Anna," Johnny said. "Sit by me. The scent of your perfume helps me forget I've been awake for thirty-two hours."

Anna gave Lianne a searching glance and settled by Johnny's side. When he took her hand between his own, she couldn't conceal her surprise. For all his fluency in America's language and customs, Johnny had an old-fashioned Chinese reserve about touching Anna in public.

"If Wen didn't sell the jade," Kyle said evenly, "then it was stolen."

"Harsh word," Johnny said.

"You try seeing your woman in handcuffs, scared bloodless, and then tell me how tender you feel toward the world," Kyle retorted. "But, hey, I'm all for intercultural sensitivity, so how about I use the word *borrowed*. Does that make you feel better?"

"There's no need to be rude," Anna said. "This is Johnny's family we're talking about, not some stranger's."

"Correct me if I'm wrong, Ms. Blakely," Kyle said, giving Anna a cool look, "but one member of Johnny's family is sitting right next to me, which makes—"

"It doesn't matter," Lianne cut in. "The subject is jade, not family."

"The hell it is," Kyle retorted. "The subject is a Tang family dispute over how a batch of jade went missing. Various members of the family are pointing fingers at you, which makes me feel rude as Satan. From what I can see, you worked your ass off to please the Tangs, and in return you were set up to take the fall for a spot of family theft."

"Jade," Lianne said sharply. "Let's just stick to the damned jade."

"Christ," Kyle snarled. "Not you, too. Don't you ever get tired of tripping over everything that's been shoved under the carpet?"

She closed her eyes, hardly able to speak for the combination of humiliation, sadness, and anger sweeping over her.

"Yes! I get damned tired! But what does that have to do with getting the U.S. government off our backs? What—"

"Daughter."

Johnny's single word cut off the flow of angry words from Lianne. She opened her eyes and stared at the father who had never acknowledged her as his daughter. Until now. He was watching her with eyes that reflected her own seething emotions.

"I don't expect you to understand," Johnny said. "I value you as much as I value my legal daughters." He smiled sadly. "More, I'm afraid. There is so much of your mother in you. She is the only woman I have ever loved, and I will never marry her as long as my wife lives. Perhaps not even when she dies. It would be very, very difficult for Anna to be my wife. By then Wen would be dead. His Number One Son has no patience for Western women. Neither does Harry. Nor would I see my sons embittered by having to accept into their family the woman they have resented since they were old enough to know why I spent so much time in America."

Tears ran down Anna's face, shiny trails through her carefully applied makeup. She held her lover's hand between her own. Her eyes were unfocused, looking through everything, even the daughter of her love for Johnny Tang.

"Resentment," Kyle said. "Interesting. Like vengeance, resentment is an age-old human motive."

Johnny didn't disagree.

"How much do Lianne's half siblings resent her?" Kyle asked. "Enough to set her up for ten years in jail? Or would their vengeance be more personal and final? An assassin in a dingy hallway, for example."

"Don't be ridiculous," Johnny snapped.

"You have a better explanation as to why a triad hit man attacked Lianne yesterday?"

"*What?*" Johnny leaped to his feet. "Lianne, is that true?"

"Baby, are you all right?" Anna asked simultaneously, standing as swiftly as Johnny had.

"She's fine," Kyle said. "She has a nice karate kick." He looked at Lianne. "Didn't mention that little incident to your parents, huh?"

"What was the point?" Lianne's narrow eyes told him she wasn't happy that he had raised the subject. "It's over. The man has been shipped back to China."

"I'll tell you the point, sweetheart. A load of grief has come down on you lately, and it has come from the Tangs. I want to find out which Tang is responsible. Then I'll put an end to it."

"My sons resent Anna and, to some degree, Lianne," Johnny said after a moment. "They don't hate either one enough to kill."

"You sure about Daniel?"

"Kyle," Lianne said fiercely under her breath. "No!"

He ignored her. His odd, golden-green eyes were fixed on Johnny with the unflinching clarity of a big cat closing in on lunch.

"Daniel?" Johnny asked. "Why?"

"He knows jade," Kyle said succinctly.

Anger flattened Johnny's face and made his eyes opaque. "Are you saying that my son would steal from his family?"

"Someone in the Tang family is a thief, and it's not Lianne. If not Daniel, who? Who else knows jade, has the combination to the Tang vaults and a reason to wish Lianne a shitload of bad luck?"

"Daniel respects and loves his grandfather, his uncles, and his father too much to do such a thing."

"And Lianne doesn't?" Kyle shot back.

"But . . ." Slowly Johnny sat on the couch again. Jet lag weighed down his brain like melted lead. He made a sound that was more a groan than a sigh. "When I asked Lianne to meet you, I didn't think it would lead to this."

Worried by his sudden pallor, Anna sat next to Johnny and took his hand. It was cold.

"Which raises another interesting point," Kyle said

smoothly. "Just why did you want Lianne to pick me up? The Tang Consortium's overtures to the Donovan family were turned down months ago. Did the Tangs think I would be an easier Donovan mark than Archer? Or did you—"

"Stop bullying him!" Anna interrupted. "Can't you see that he's exhausted?"

Kyle gave her a cutting look. "What I keep seeing is your daughter in handcuffs. Unless your lover can help us, you'll get to see it, too."

Anna flinched as though Kyle had struck her. Johnny's cool hand touched her cheek.

"It's all right," he said tiredly. Then he turned to Kyle. "I wanted you because the Donovans don't need anything from the Tangs. Then there was that incident with the Russian amber. I don't know all the details, but what I found out suggested that you wouldn't turn and run at the first sign of trouble." He almost smiled. "I was right, wasn't I?"

"Kyle saved my life," Lianne said. "The assassin would have—"

"Bull," Kyle said. "The way I remember it, you saved *my* life."

"I did no such—"

"Sure you did," he said, talking over her. "You broke his knife arm. Now my life is yours. You can't get out of it, sweetheart. Old Chinese rules."

Lianne gave him a baffled look, then bent over and sniffed his teacup suspiciously. Nothing but oolong.

Kyle's knuckles slid down her cheek to the curve of her neck in a caress that was both casual and so infused with intimacy that her breath caught. She looked up and felt his smile like another gentle touch.

"No brandy," he said softly. "Just your perfume going to my head." But all gentleness left Kyle's expression when he faced Johnny again. "What were you planning for me and Lianne?"

"A healthy young man who is good in a fight, a beautiful

young woman who might need such a man on her side . . ."
Johnny shrugged. "There was no plan."

"What made you think that Lianne might need someone
like me?" Kyle asked. His voice was edgy, impatient. He
shouldn't have to drag answers out of Johnny like a cop cross-
examining a hostile suspect. It was Johnny's daughter they
were trying to help.

For a long time Johnny didn't say anything. He simply
focused on Anna's hand lying pale and beautiful on his arm.

"I am very uneasy about Han Seng," Johnny admitted finally. "My family . . . would like to ingratiate themselves
with him."

Lianne went cold. She stared at her father, hardly able to
believe what she was hearing.

"And Lianne was a little deal sweetener?" Kyle's tone was
neutral. But his whole body tightened.

"I told Joe that Lianne didn't like Seng, much less want to
become his lover," Johnny said.

"What about Wen?" Lianne asked, almost afraid to hear
the answer. "Did he expect me to be Seng's concubine?"

"He didn't understand the difference between you being
Chin's lover a while back and being Seng's now."

"Obviously Wen is blind," Kyle said. "Chin and Seng are
both snakes, but Chin is a damned pretty one."

Lianne ignored Kyle and spoke directly to her father. "I
thought I loved Chin. I thought he loved me. He didn't. He
loved only the family of Tang."

"Of course," Johnny said with faint impatience. "He is
Chinese-born, Chinese-raised. Did you really think Chin
wanted your body more than your family connections?"

"Yes."

Johnny shook his head. There were aspects of his American daughter that he would never understand. She was intelligent—very intelligent—quite fluent in Chinese art and
languages. Yet she couldn't seem to grasp the fundamental

dynamic of the Chinese culture: family. An individual's desires were as nothing against the needs of his family.

"So you were nervous about what Seng would do," Kyle said. "You were right, by the way. While you were flying to Tahiti, Harry told Lianne to take some jades for trade with good old Seng."

"It wasn't the first time such trades had been arranged," Johnny said calmly. "It was simply the Tang way of presenting Lianne with an opportunity to become intimate with Seng. The connection would have benefited the Tang family."

Kyle's eyes glittered with anger. " 'An opportunity to become intimate,' " he repeated savagely. "Well, that's one definition of rape, I suppose."

Johnny sighed. He had wanted an American protector for Lianne, one who wouldn't kowtow to the Tangs. He had gotten one, for better or for worse. "A liaison with Seng would have benefited Lianne greatly as well. He is a very wealthy, very influential man. His enthusiasms are brief, but he is known to be generous with his women. Since Lianne won't accept money from Anna, and the Tangs pay her barely enough to survive . . ." He shrugged.

The only thing that kept Lianne from jumping to her feet was the weight of Kyle's hand on her shoulder, holding her in place.

"So Seng is generous," Lianne said in a low, vicious tone. "Let me tell you how generous, Johnny. An appointment was set up for me to see his jades. The appointment was at night, on Farmer Island. Since there isn't any ferry service, arrangements had already been made for me to be picked up by the institute's launch. I was expected to spend the night. And I was to come alone, of course."

Johnny's eyelids flinched. It was what part of him had secretly feared but none of him had really believed. Wen was pragmatic and quick to defend or enlarge the interests of the Tang family, but he wasn't a cruel man. He wouldn't have set up his granddaughter's rape.

"When I showed up," Lianne continued, "Seng was wearing lounging pajamas and perfumed like a whore. Instead of the party I was told he was hosting, the place was empty except for his assistant and his armed bodyguard. Tell me, Johnny. If Kyle hadn't been with me, how much *choice* would I have had about becoming one of Seng's women?"

Johnny closed his eyes. "I'm sorry. I didn't know about that." He turned to Anna, who was watching him with pain thinning her full mouth. "Anna, it never occurred to the Tangs that Lianne wouldn't be open to Seng's offer. In Asia, women pursue Seng. As I said, he is generous. And it's not as though she was a virgin who had never taken a lover."

The nod Anna gave was tight, her eyes devastated. "I pity those women with nothing to sell but themselves. Lianne isn't that desperate. Tell your family. Immediately." She vibrated like a plucked string. "Never again, Johnny. Promise me. Lianne isn't what I was—homeless, rootless, forced to survive by—" Her voice shattered. *"Tell them."*

"I will."

Lianne let out a breath and pushed a wing of thick, black hair away from her cheek. "Don't worry, Mom. The Tang family won't be trying to fix me up with a generous rapist anymore. They're too busy hating me for pissing Seng off."

"By refusing him?" Johnny asked. "He'll simply buy a willing woman with three times your beauty."

"That could be tough," Kyle said dryly. "In case you hadn't noticed, Lianne is gorgeous."

Lianne ignored Kyle. "The only refusal Seng was truly upset by was my refusal to trade superior Tang jades for inferior Seng pieces."

"You refused a trade?" Johnny asked in disbelief.

"Yeah," Kyle said. "Seng didn't sic his guard dog on us until we headed out the door with Tang jades still wrapped and sealed in their boxes." He turned Lianne's face toward him. "You *are* gorgeous, you know."

"I know no such thing," she retorted. Then she smiled.

"But thanks anyway. Every woman likes to think that a drop-dead handsome man would see something gorgeous in her."

Kyle laughed and skimmed his thumb over her high, slanting cheekbone.

Frowning, Johnny sat without really listening, still caught by something about the trade that hadn't been consummated. "Those boxes . . ." he began.

Lianne turned toward her father. "What about them?"

"What was in them?"

"Three very fine pieces of the Tang erotica collection," she said. "There were other pieces as well, but I don't know what they were. The boxes were sealed when I picked them up in Vancouver."

Relief swept over Johnny, taking years off his appearance. "That explains it. Daniel said some of the erotica were missing, among other things. Obviously it's all a mistake. As soon as those boxes are returned to the Tangs, the charges will be dropped."

"You're not thinking very clearly," Lianne told him. "Wen packed the boxes and gave them to me himself. He knew about the trade. Why would he file charges saying those same pieces had been stolen?"

"Maybe because the trade didn't take place," Kyle said. "Wen was probably pissed."

"He was counting on Seng's goodwill," Johnny said reluctantly. "The Tang family needs a friend on the mainland."

"Putting Lianne in jail won't get you one," Kyle said, his voice rough.

"If Wen was so desperate for Seng to get those jades," Lianne said, "he should have passed them over himself. More importantly, Wen shouldn't have insisted that I put my name on three of the appraisal documents, as though I had seen and approved of the entire trade. Above all else, he shouldn't have told Daniel that I stole those jades."

"Are you sure Wen did?" Johnny asked.

"Someone did. Daniel looked at me the way you would at a thief. It was . . . painful. He has your eyes."

Johnny smiled sadly. "So do you."

Lianne's breath hitched, then smoothed out. She gave her father a strained smile in return.

"Don't worry," he said. "This has all been a misunderstanding. I'll talk with Wen. He'll drop the charges against you."

Kyle didn't think so. There was much more at stake than Seng's goodwill and a few cartons of stone erotica. But Johnny would have to find that out the hard way.

"Are you a betting man?" Kyle asked softly.

"I'm Chinese," Johnny said, grinning faintly.

"I'm betting that your family won't drop the charges against Lianne."

"But—"

Kyle kept talking. "If I'm wrong, I'll do everything in my power to convince Archer to accept a trial partnership with the Tang Consortium."

Johnny sat up straight. "Can you do this?"

"I give my word I'll try."

"Good. I'll set up a meeting between Joe and—"

"Not yet," Kyle interrupted. "You haven't heard what your stakes are."

"What do you want from me?"

"Access to the Tang jade vaults."

"Why?" Johnny asked.

"Yes or no," was Kyle's only answer.

Johnny measured him for several seconds, then said, "Yes."

"There's only one bed," Lianne said bluntly.

Kyle locked the door behind him and looked around his suite. The housekeeper had already been at work, which was why no dirty socks decorated the floor and no splash marks dimmed the shine of the bathroom. The bed that Lianne was objecting to was freshly made. It was also big enough to comfortably hold three Donovan brothers, if it came to that.

"That's okay," Kyle said. "You don't take up much room."

"I won't sleep with you."

"You slept with me just fine last night. You were yawning a few minutes ago, until Johnny called. You'll sleep."

"That wasn't what I meant."

"Then what did you mean?" Kyle's voice was muffled because he was peeling off his sweater.

Lianne rubbed her hands up and down her arms and thought of how warm his cast-off sweater would be, his body heat plus that of the wool. Her skin was cold. Even as she turned her back on Kyle, she wanted to burrow into his heat and strength, to pull him around her, to forget that it was almost midnight and that tomorrow was another day, another ordeal.

Wen had refused to drop the charges. Even though Lianne had expected it, part of her felt as though she had been slapped across the face.

"I won't have sex with you," Lianne said.

"Good."

She spun around. Kyle was smiling at her. Crookedly. There was passion in his eyes and gentleness in the hands reaching for her. His fingers skimmed over her hair, her eyelids, her cheekbones, her jaw, until her breath broke. His thumb caressed the rapidly beating pulse in her neck.

"I said I won't—"

"And I said good," he interrupted. "I don't want sex with you, Lianne. Sex is something that happens between people who need a lube job."

Without meaning to, Lianne looked from Kyle's eyes to the dark bronze hair on his chest, to the waistband of his jeans, and beyond, to the blunt bulge of his erection straining against the worn, faded denim.

"Who are you trying to kid?" she said. "You're rock-hard and ready to go."

He put his hand under her chin and tipped her head up. "I spent a lot of last night this way. It didn't interfere with your sleep then. It won't now." He searched her clear, cognac-colored eyes and saw that she believed him. "You want the bathroom first?"

Lianne shook her head slowly. Last night she had been shaken and furious with Kyle for taking advantage of her, for using her to get to the Tangs.

"Okay," he said. "I'll take it."

She shook her head again. Last night she had been a fool. Archer was right. She and Kyle had been using each other. And when all was said and done, he had given more than he got. She had never had a lover like him, tender and demanding by turns, as passionate as he was strong. She doubted if she would ever find a man who suited her in so many ways as Kyle Donovan.

And if she suited him only as a lover, then she would take it and not curse the fate that made women care so much when men only desired.

Lianne gave up trying to warm her hands on her cold arms and used Kyle's chest instead. Beneath her fingers his flesh tensed. Knowing she shouldn't, needing it too much to care, she lowered her mouth and nuzzled against the flat disk of his nipple.

Kyle's breath came out with a ripping sound. "Jesus. I didn't figure you for a tease."

Her tongue circled him with hot, wet deliberation.

"Lianne . . ."

Her answer was a husky, female sound of pleasure as she caught the nailhead of his nipple in her teeth and bit very, very gently.

When Kyle spoke, his voice strained, his mind a seething mix of hope and raw need. "Are you sure you know what you're doing?"

Her fingers slid between the snaps of his jeans, through the opening in his underwear, nuzzled him, testing him.

"You're right," he said hoarsely. "That's the dumbest question I ever asked. Put your tongue in my mouth before I say something really stupid."

Even as Kyle lifted her, Lianne was winding her legs around him, combing her fingers through his hair, seeking him with her open, eager mouth. She was shivering with hunger. Part of her was shocked that he could arouse her so easily, so completely. The rest of her cared only that he share her hunger, share her need, share her body. Tomorrow and its heartbreak were still one night away. She would take this night, this man, and damn all the rest.

She never knew how they got their clothes off. She knew only that she was astride him, riding him, and pleasure was a beautiful, savage beast clawing at her until she came apart. She would have screamed then, but she had no breath. He was slamming into her, driving her higher and higher until there was no air, no sensation, just blazing colors of ecstasy transfixing her.

When Lianne could bear it no longer, she collapsed on Kyle's chest. She was boneless, her breath tearing and shaking her. He lay sideways on the big bed, breathing deeply, evenly, like a long-distance runner just hitting his stride. He smiled at the ceiling, blew a lock of her hair away from his lips, and traced her spine with long, clever fingers.

"Sure glad you didn't want sex," Kyle said lazily. "I wouldn't have survived it."

Lianne felt too good to be embarrassed. "Bite me."

Then she bit him instead. Not hard or long—she needed her mouth to suck in enough air to survive. With a ragged breath she relaxed against him again.

"Come on, sweetheart. Time for a shower."

She made her grumpy cat sound and didn't move.

Still holding her, Kyle sat up, pivoted, and stood.

"I'll shower in the morning," she said.

"Okay. A person can't be too clean."

Lianne lifted her head from his shoulder. He was definitely

headed for the shower. It was a nice one, she remembered. Big enough to dance in, with tile benches built right in. But even so . . .

"I'd rather sleep," she said.

"Then you shouldn't have bitten me."

"It wasn't a hard bite."

"I'll keep that in mind."

She looked at his eyes, green and gold, surrounded by a knife-edge of black glittering like the ecstasy whose echoes still shivered through her . . . beautiful enough to take her breath away, to make her wish that she could die right here, right now.

"Take me back to bed and I'll apologize," she offered, smiling slowly.

"I'll look forward to it," he said, turning on the hot water in the shower. Hard.

"You're serious about this, aren't you?" Lianne asked.

"Dead serious."

"Why?"

"Simple. The suites are soundproofed, but Archer's bed is right on the opposite side of the wall from our bed. I figure if I turn the water on hard enough, he might not hear you scream."

"Scream? What are you talking about? You aren't into sadism, are you?"

Laughing, Kyle stepped into the shower, taking Lianne with him. "I'm into you, sweetheart. Can't you tell?"

"It would be impossible to miss."

Her breath caught as he tightened inside her, filling her until she shivered. His eyelids lowered and he flexed again. She was still hot, slick, swollen, and so sensitized that no matter how slight the movement, her breath broke each time he shifted inside her. Finally, reluctantly, he lifted her, separating their bodies.

Lianne's eyes dilated in surprise at the sudden stab of pleasure she felt even as Kyle withdrew. She sagged against the cold tile wall of the shower and braced her feet.

Turning his back to the torrent of water, shielding her from its force, Kyle bent and kissed her lips tenderly, teasing her with his tongue. When her mouth fit his, followed his, needed his as though it had been weeks rather than seconds since they had last loved, he ended the kiss as gently as it had begun.

"You okay standing up?" Kyle asked.

She nodded and reached up on tiptoe to kiss him again. He slid through her eager arms with an ease that reminded her just how strong he was. His mouth moved over each breast in turn, devouring her sweetly, thoroughly, sucking her nipples taut and then drawing them tighter still. When her hips began to twist against him, seeking him, he evaded her despite his thick erection and the heavy beating of his blood.

Lianne's breath fragmented as Kyle's hands and mouth slid down her body. He pressed her legs more widely apart, caressing and opening her with his thumbs, fitting his mouth over her, matching her sultry heat with his own, savoring her. She had never felt anything like it, never known she could be drenched and burning at the same time. Her knees shook. Her fingers clenched in his hair. She fought for balance, for breath, for understanding.

And she found only the searching, relentless, ravishing heat of his mouth. She tried to tell him to stop, she couldn't take any more pleasure. His fingers slid deep and his mouth shifted, closing around the wildly sensitive knot of flesh, sucking hard on her until she screamed and shattered into a thousand blind, glittering pieces.

Even then he didn't release her. He couldn't. He was as caught in the hot coils of sensuality as she was. By the time he could force himself to stop caressing her, her knees had given way and she was on the floor of the shower. He wanted her until his guts knotted, but her pupils were dilated so much there was no color, only black, her breath raked in and out of her lungs, and all that stood between her and drowning in the driving water of the shower was his broad back.

"Lianne?" Kyle managed, fighting to keep himself from taking her the way she was, open and dazed on the tile floor.

Slowly her eyes focused on him.

"Sweetheart?" he asked. "Are you all right?"

She nodded.

"Then you better get up."

She looked at the clouds of steam. "Is the hot water running out?"

"No. My control is. I'm about two seconds from taking you the way I did on the dock. Only this time you'd be on the bottom."

She licked her lips, counted off two seconds, and smiled slowly. "Okay."

twenty-three

Lianne stared at the concrete-and-steel building. It wasn't one of Seattle's many interesting architectural statements; it was a government-issue, get-it-done-on-budget, downscale high-rise. Even if she had never been inside, she would know from the building's exterior that the interior would be full of generic business offices with industrial-strength carpeting, plastic fig trees in dusty baskets, and middle-aged receptionists with too much dye in their hair. The only thing unusual about the building was the foyer, with its metal detector. A bored guard sat beside it.

"Don't look so unhappy," Kyle said to Lianne. "They won't keep you this time."

"How do you know?"

"We're using the front door. Or do you want to just forget the whole thing and go back to the condo?"

Kyle's words made Lianne realize that she was hanging back. Her chin came up and she quickened her stride. "Of course not."

"You sure? Johnny and I could take care of identifying the—"

"If you don't hurry up," she said, talking over Kyle, "we'll be late."

He glanced down at the small, slender woman striding next to him and smiled. Anyone looking at the black pantsuit, sensible shoes, and no-nonsense hair twisted at her nape wouldn't believe that the last time Lianne had been in the shower, it was a miracle that either of them had gotten out alive. Just thinking about the way she had looked when she said *Okay* was enough to make him hard all over again.

Lianne went through the metal detector without a hitch. So did Kyle, after he had emptied his pockets of change and car keys. The gun and holster were back in the safe, for now.

"I told you so," Lianne muttered as they walked up to the receptionist.

"What?"

"Too much dye."

Kyle looked at the receptionist's hair and thought of motorcycle helmets. But all he said was, "Donovan and Blakely to see Ms. Joy."

"Sixth floor," the receptionist said. "Take the elevator on your left."

A rolling cart stuffed with files got on the elevator at the second floor. Two more file carts got in on the third floor. The file jockeys traded sports statistics until they got off on the fifth floor, leaving Lianne and Kyle alone again.

"I thought that computers were supposed to do away with the need for paper," she said.

"Are you kidding? All computers did was make it easier to revise reports and send out revised copies to more people, who add more revisions, send out more copies, and—"

"Employ cart jockeys to haul the reports from floor to floor," Lianne finished.

"Uncle's answer to unemployment."

April Joy met them on the sixth floor. She was wearing a suit as understated as Lianne's. An ID card hung from a cheap metal chain around her neck.

"This better be good, Donovan," she said curtly.

"Anything is better than what you already have," Kyle said. "That's why we're here."

It was true. April just didn't like it. But then, the world was full of things that didn't make her smile. "Number five-eleven," she said. "Everything is there."

She turned and walked back down the hallway, not waiting to see if they followed. When she reached 511, she slid her ID card through a reader. A light glowed green. She opened the door and held it until Lianne and Kyle were inside.

Without a word Lianne headed for the steel conference table in the center of the room. On one end of the table sat two cartons wrapped in white paper, tied with twine whose knots looked like macramé, and covered with blotches of crimson wax. She bent over and examined the boxes closely. The knots were as complex and tight as the day they had been tied. The seals were intact. Each bore Wen's "chop" in the center.

"If anybody has been inside these boxes," Lianne said, "he didn't leave any signs."

April smiled thinly. "You should see the X-rays."

"I'd rather see the jades. I'll need scissors or a knife."

"In the center drawer."

Metal screeched when Lianne opened the drawer. The sound made her teeth ache. "Instead of pushing files around, why don't you have some of those eager young people oil drawers?"

"I'll bring it up at the next meeting," April said. Her voice said that she didn't care.

The scissors Lianne found were small, sharp enough, and had a plastic handle as red as the seals. She started cutting, working with swift, practiced motions. Very quickly, each carton grew a necklace of snipped twine and fancy knots. When she was through cutting the twine, seals, and paper, ready to open the first carton, Kyle put his hand on her arm, stopping her.

"Do you have that list she faxed you?" Kyle asked April. "Just to make sure there's no mistake?"

"Yes. If what you think is true, there will be some interesting stuff in these cartons."

"Go ahead," Kyle told Lianne.

She opened the first carton, pulled out something swathed in bubble wrap, and carefully began unrolling it. After a few moments, a lovely imperial jade penis dropped into her hand. Relief rushed through her so strongly that she felt light-headed. She grinned at the jade like a proud mother.

April's slim black eyebrows went up. "Art, huh?"

"Excellent color," Kyle said, deadpan.

"Only if the guy's dead," April retorted. "All right. One green hang-down checked off the list."

Lianne hoped her relief didn't show. Logic had told her that Seng was being bribed with upgrades on his collection of jade erotica—excellent pieces swapped for the so-so goods she had examined on Farmer Island. But logic wasn't as great as the fear that she could be wrong, that there might be another explanation for the substitutions she had seen in the Tang vault.

The next piece Lianne unwrapped had been made from a luminous white jade that was touched with faint blushes of lavender. The stone was carved so that the darker shade suggested folds in clothing, the curve of a limb, the shadow lying between a woman's thighs. The fluid line of the woman's body as she lay across her lover's lap evoked the essence of feminine surrender. The intensity of the man as he bent down to her summed up masculine urgency to possess.

The position of the figures made it impossible to see precisely what they were doing, yet the impact of the sculpture was such that it was impossible *not* to know exactly what they were doing.

April whistled. "I'd like to have that on my bedside table."

Reverently Lianne lifted the sculpture and turned it in her hands, savoring the satin weight of the jade. "Of the thousands of pieces of jade that the Tangs own, this is among the best. The stone is completely intact; there are no fractures, no pits, no variations in texture. This was carved by a master and polished by hand over unimaginable hours.

"The subject matter is worthy of the stone and the artist. Sexual union is the philosophical core of Taoism, the instant of fusion between yin and yang, when all forces are balanced and the sum total of harmony in the universe increases. To a Taoist, what we in the West think of as a merely physical joining of man and woman is profoundly metaphysical, an act which affects the balance of creation itself."

Gently Lianne set the jade on the table's scarred metal surface.

April looked from the jade to Lianne's face. The respect and love Lianne had for the sculpture and the tradition it represented was easy to read in her expression, in the way her fingertips traced and her palm cupped smooth stone. But there was no greed in her gestures, no hunger to possess, no bitterness that such a fine jade belonged to a man too old and blind to appreciate it.

Frowning, April glanced at Kyle. He was watching her with those odd, penetrating eyes. The look on his face said, *See? I told you. Lianne Blakely isn't a thief.*

For a time the only sound was that of Lianne unwrapping jades and making occasional comments.

"Excellent stone." "Superior artistry." "Look at this one carefully, Kyle. See how the veins of red coloring in the stone heighten instead of distract from the subject? A difficult thing to do with such pronounced color contrast." "Very fine polish." "Remarkable fluidity." "Ah, I haven't seen this one before. Exquisitely carved. Look at his expression, submission and ecstasy in one. Obviously she is a master of his jade flute."

Kyle knew it was juvenile of him—this was art, after all— but he couldn't help getting hard at the thought of having Lianne between his knees like that, his body corded and his head thrown back in blind, shattering climax.

"Yeah," he said. "Hell of a song she's playing."

April gave him a sideways look. "Getting to you, big boy?"

Lianne looked up from the sculpture. The smile she gave Kyle doubled his heart rate. "I'd worry about you if you didn't react. The purpose of these sculptures is to remind people that there are many roads to the metaphysical, and one of those roads is sublimely physical."

"Consider me reminded," he said. "How about you?"

"When you're around, I don't need reminders."

He turned to April. "Don't you want to get some coffee or something?"

"Tie a knot in it, Romeo." April glanced at her watch. "All right, let's say for the sake of argument that Lianne was sent off to make a swap with Han Seng, decided that she didn't like the smell of the deal, and left without unpacking the cartons."

"It would explain why she was arrested heading *back* into Canada with the Tang jades that were listed as missing," Kyle said, not for the first time.

"It wouldn't explain all of the missing jades. I've got a fax two pages long on my desk, and it's still growing. These are only part of what's on the list."

"Show me the fax," Lianne said instantly.

April ignored her. "Like I said, suppose we agree that Lianne was set up for the arrest and there's not enough evidence to hold her. What's in it for us?"

"A chance to make China happy and Farmer look like a fool," Kyle said.

In a heartbeat April went from casual to full alert. "The jade burial suit?"

Kyle nodded. "Interested?"

"Yes."

"Lianne has to be able to move freely. Drop the charges."

"You think Farmer has smuggled the damned shroud out of the States?" April asked quickly. "We know he took it to his island, but we didn't think he managed to get it over the border. Shit. That's all we need, piling the Canadian bureaucracy on top of everything else. What a Charlie Fox-trot."

Kyle didn't translate "Charlie Fox-trot" for Lianne. He was

too busy switching over to plan B, the one where the jade suit wasn't in Seattle. It wasn't his preferred plan. But then, nobody had asked him to approve.

"*Shit,*" April said again, with emphasis. She looked at Lianne, who had gone back to unwrapping jades. Then she glared at Kyle. "If you were anybody else's brother, I'd kick your tight butt out the door right now."

"I'll tell Archer you care."

April ignored him. She was sorting through possibilities with the speed of the well-trained, intelligent agent she was. It didn't take long to get to the bottom line.

None of the possibilities particularly appealed to her, and only one of them might lead to a fast solution. Speed was critical. The longer the standoff between Farmer and China went on, the greater the chance that China would unzip decades of zigzag economic progress in a rush to preserve national pride.

China's leaders wouldn't suffer in an economic downturn. They would still have their Western toys and Eastern aesthetics. Dick Farmer wouldn't suffer. There were other world markets to make another billion bucks in. The people who suffered would be the hundreds of millions of Chinese who would survive more gracefully in the twenty-first century, with all its drawbacks, than in the modern Bronze Age of rural China, where life was so brutally hard it stunted children in the womb.

With a mixture of bitterness and acceptance, April watched the last of the jades being unwrapped . . . the cream of a culture's artistic aspirations worked in stone that was as hard as a despot's heart. Even as she wondered how many millions had lived and died in poverty to support such an expensive, labor-intensive art, the pragmatic part of her knew it didn't matter. That was the past. The present was a jade artifact so important to China that her leaders were willing to kick off a trade war and self-destruct their own economy over it.

"What's your plan?" April asked.

"You don't want to know," Kyle said.

She stared at him without expression, but she was thinking of Archer Donovan. He had a legendary ability to drag the hottest chestnuts out of the fire and not burn down anybody's house in the process. "Slick, you better be as good as you think you are."

"I hear you."

"What do you need from us?" April said after another tense pause.

While Lianne listened to exactly what Kyle wanted from Uncle, she unwrapped the last jade. Very quickly, Bride Dreaming lay in her hands, as elemental and ethereal as her memories.

"Three rebreathers?" April asked. "You want the Navy SEALs to go with them? They'd love the exercise."

"If I need them, you'll be the first to know."

"What's a rebreather?" Lianne asked Kyle.

"Scuba gear that doesn't leave a trail of bubbles."

"Is one of those rebreathers for me?"

"No."

"Make it four," Lianne told April.

"Four it is."

Kyle started to argue, then shrugged. It wouldn't hurt to have an extra unit on hand in case something was defective in the first three. But if Lianne thought she was coming along, she was dead wrong.

"Anything else?" April asked.

"Get Farmer to agree to an expert appraisal of his burial shroud," Lianne said.

"He already has."

"Damn it. I'd like to have been there."

"It hasn't happened yet. China is sending its own expert." April gave Lianne her full attention. "Do you really think Farmer's shroud is fake?"

"I really think I'd like a close look at it," Lianne said smoothly. "But wouldn't it be nice if it was fake?"

"Only if China's expert agreed," April said. "If we had that, we wouldn't need to screw around with you two."

"Who is Uncle's expert?" Kyle asked.

"Me," April said, still looking at Lianne.

Somehow Kyle wasn't surprised.

"We're going to Farmer's private island the day before the museum opens," April added.

"Day after tomorrow?" Kyle asked.

"Yes. I'll arrange for Lianne to come with me on the appraisal," April said, turning to him. "I'm good, but she's better. That's assuming she's still out of jail. Big assumption." April turned back to Lianne. "Kyle got you close to the suit before the guards tossed you out. *Was it real?*"

"If you stay out of our face until the appraisal," Kyle said before Lianne could answer, "the shroud won't be a problem."

"What are you going to do?" April demanded again.

"You still don't want to know."

April put her fists on her hips. "If you get caught, we don't know you from skid marks on underwear."

Kyle nodded. "Whcn will I get the equipment?"

"It will be delivered to your condo by eighteen hundred."

"Six P.M.," he translated before Lianne could ask. "What about her passport?"

"I'll get it," April said.

"Take her off the immigration shit list, too. Just in case."

"I'll try, but . . ." April shrugged and headed out of the room. "This is a bureaucracy, Donovan. Better that her name never gets punched into a border computer in the first place."

As soon as the door closed behind April, Lianne said, "I don't need a passport to—"

The words ended in a muffled sound when Kyle kissed her firmly, shutting her up. After he lifted his mouth, all he said was, "Are you through here?"

Lianne looked down at the sculpture she still held. As eager as she was to see the last of the building where she had been handcuffed and locked in a room, she still was reluctant to part with Bride Dreaming.

Kyle took the sculpture from Lianne's hands. As he set it on the table, he looked at the jade for the first time. He whistled in a sliding, musical tribute to the artist's skill. The entire piece had been designed to take advantage of the remarkable chatoyance of the jade that lay between the woman's thighs, the physical door to a metaphysical experience.

"Is this the one you called Bride Dreaming?" Kyle asked without taking his eyes off the shimmering, gleaming jade.

"Yes."

"I see what you meant. This is much superior to the version Han Seng owned." As Kyle lifted his hands, he skimmed the ball of his thumb over the focus of the sculpture. "Extraordinary. But . . ."

"What?"

"Yours is prettier."

twenty-four

Two hours after the meeting with April, Lianne felt like a lion tamer without a whip or a chair. Everywhere she looked there were large, healthy, potentially dangerous animals sprawled on the floor of the Donovan condominium. The mass of muscle and bone made her feel beyond petite. She felt miniature.

"How does Susa stand it?" Lianne muttered. "All these big, overwhelming, overbearing *males*."

The males in question ignored her. They were debating various approaches to Farmer Island.

Faith looked up from a jewelry auction catalog and smiled. "You should see it when Dad, Justin, and Lawe are here."

"Frightening."

"Only if they're not on your side." Faith's mouth drew down in a frown. Her family's restrained dislike of her fiancé gnawed at her. Even Honor, who normally could be counted on for support, had to make an effort to look happy when Tony showed up.

As though Honor understood exactly what her twin was thinking, she asked Faith about Tony.

"Still in Tahiti," Faith said. "He's doing PR—oops, image

consulting—for one of the new pearl houses. When he called this morning, he said it might be another week before he could come home."

"Bet you wish you had gone with him," Honor said.

Faith's smile was strained. She had wanted to go, but she hadn't been invited. Tony was furious that she wouldn't approach Donovan International about switching its business to her future father-in-law's advertising firm. "Not much point in going," she said. "He'll be working sixteen-hour days."

That left the nights, but no one in the room mentioned it.

"Kyle," Lianne said, "what if—"

"No," he interrupted without looking up. "You're not going."

"Describe Farmer's jade shroud," she said.

"Green."

"What will you do if he's switched bad for good to fool China's expert?" she challenged. "We'll be back where we started as soon as the museum opens. Or what if I was wrong? What if the suit isn't Wen's? Then there would be a whole different can of worms to untangle and I'd be back in jail. You've never seen Wen's suit. I have."

One by one, three male heads came up. Lianne had their undivided attention. It wasn't comforting.

"You need me," she said.

"No," Kyle said flatly.

Archer and Jake looked at each other.

"Why shouldn't she go?" Honor asked Kyle with wide-eyed interest. "You and Jake have spent the last two hours telling me how *safe* this little jaunt will be. 'Just a walk in the park,' was what you said, Jake. Right?"

Jake grunted.

Archer rolled onto his side and faced Kyle, "She has a point."

"The hell she does," he said without looking away from Lianne. "Do you know how to dive?"

"No, but—"

"Exactly," Kyle cut in. "You're staying here."

"—the jade shroud isn't on the bottom of the ocean, either," Lianne said, talking over him.

"We can take the inflatable boat and run it up on the shore here," Archer said, pointing on the map to the east side of Farmer Island. "With the Zodiac, she won't even have to get her feet wet. By the time we go ashore, the guards will be tired of watching little lights go off on their consoles."

"No," Kyle snarled.

"Why?" Archer asked mildly.

"For God's sake, she's a—"

"GIRL," Lianne, Faith, and Honor chorused. Then they smiled at one another, pleased by their timing.

Kyle looked hunted. "If it was Honor," he said to Jake, "would you let her go?"

Amused, Jake smiled at his wife. "Would I let you go, honey?"

"I wouldn't ask," Honor retorted. "I'd just go like I did the last time you wanted me to stay ashore."

"That answer your question?" Jake asked Kyle.

"Shit."

"You were there when that thug jumped her," Jake pointed out. "Did she panic?"

"No. But she was damn near killed anyway!"

Archer sat up and watched Lianne with steady, silver-green eyes. "Running the Zodiac up on shore increases our risk," he said to her. "If necessary, could you suit up and swim for a hundred yards in dark water?"

"Yes."

He watched her for a few moments longer, nodded, and returned his attention to the map. "Four will fit in the Zodiac without a problem."

"Archer," Kyle said tightly, "don't do this to me."

"Think with your brain, not your dick," Archer said in a calm voice. "We need someone who can make a fast, expert appraisal of jade using only a trained eye, a flashlight, and nerve. You've got the nerve, I'll hold the flashlight, but we still won't be sure of the goods. We can't afford to fuck this one up. Uncle isn't in a forgiving mood."

"Which brings up another point," Kyle said. "Can we trust Uncle to stay out of this?"

"Once we get the jade suit off the island," Archer said, "it's open season. Uncle wants that suit. If some eager government boys steal it from us, who do we complain to?"

"That's what I thought." Kyle closed his eyes, thought of a few truly awful oaths, and asked, "Who do we have on the payroll that can fly small planes and keep his mouth shut?"

"Walker," Archer said instantly.

"Where is he?"

"Seattle. Just back from Australia. He was flying geologists around the outback for Donovan International."

"Okay, he can handle a plane," Kyle said. "What about the rest of it?"

"Are you talking about Owen Walker?" Jake asked.

Archer nodded.

"No worries," Jake said, turning back to the chart. "Walker used to bodyguard VIPs for Uncle. If it goes from sugar to shit, he'll know what to do."

"Aren't you going to ask what I want the plane for?" Kyle said to Archer.

"I'm more worried about getting a wet suit small enough for Lianne. Does that dive shop down on Fifth Street outfit kiddies?"

Lianne made an outraged sound and dove for Archer's back, but he had already rolled aside. Kyle caught her and tucked her along his side on the rug. "You'll get used to him, sweetheart. We have." He wrote quickly on a piece of paper before he looked up at Honor. "Okay, sis. It was your bright idea. You have three hours to shop for Lianne. Here's the list."

Faith, Honor, and Lianne walked into the condo, their arms overflowing with sacks.

"Took you long enough," Kyle said. "I was about to send out a search party."

"Listen, buttercup," Honor said sweetly. "You try getting a full set of acrylic nails and buying a wet suit, a Dolly Parton wig, size five shoes with five-inch heels, and sexy clothes in the kiddie department of Nordstrom, and see how fast *you* get home."

"It wasn't the kiddie department," Lianne said loudly. "Petite. Repeat after me. *Petite.*"

Faith winked at Lianne. "Honor's just jealous. Next to you and Susa, we feel like telephone poles."

Lianne looked at the tall, unmistakably female twins and rolled her eyes. "Yeah, right."

Archer came into the entryway wearing tan slacks and a black, silk-weave jacket. He looked casual and very, very expensive. "Twenty minutes."

As one, the women turned and rushed down the hall to Faith's suite.

"No perfume," Kyle called after them. "If I could recognize Lianne in the dark by her scent, someone else could."

"Sniffing around in the dark," Faith muttered. "Men are so primitive."

"Yeah," Honor said. "Isn't it grand?"

Nineteen minutes later, Lianne emerged from Faith's suite. The click of her high heels on marble was the only sound in the condominium.

Three men stared at her with a combination of shock and automatic male lust.

A red tube dress hugged Lianne like a hungry lover. Long sleeves and a V neck called attention to the shape of her breasts. The skirt cupped her rear and barely teased the top of her thighs. Smoky stockings made a long, sexy mystery of her legs. Faith's deft touch with makeup turned Lianne's eyes into a tawny challenge and gave an X-rated pout to her lips. She flipped back her curly, shoulder-length, frosted bronze hair, put one dagger-nailed hand on her hip, and said, "Ready when you are."

"Holy Christ," Kyle murmured. "That's the last time you go shopping with my sisters."

"You don't like the color?" Lianne asked innocently. "It matches my nails."

"There's more of it on your nails than on you! Where's the rest of the outfit?"

"What are you talking about? This is it."

"Wrong. You forgot the skirt."

"Quit bitching," Archer said, smiling as he looked Lianne over thoroughly. "She's supposed to be my date, not yours."

"That's what worries me," Kyle said sourly, glaring at his brother.

"Ignore him," Archer said, holding out his arm to Lianne. "I think you look good enough to eat. Twice."

"That's it," Kyle said flatly. "Lianne is sitting in the backseat with me."

"What are you complaining about?" Faith asked as she walked up with Honor. "You told us to make her over so that her own family wouldn't recognize her. We did. So put a sock in the rant and get going."

"You tell him," Honor said. And privately wished that Faith would show half as much sass with Tony. The man led her around like a poodle on a pink leash.

"Is Johnny here?" Lianne asked.

"Waiting in the lobby," Archer said. "Let's go."

As Archer's Mercedes pulled up to the Tang compound, light the color of Lianne's dress spilled across the sky. Johnny got out, spoke into the gate microphone, and climbed back in next to the driver. As he did, he glanced at the siren in the backseat and shook his head. Even at sixteen, Anna hadn't looked like that.

"Wen will see me in the family quarters," Johnny said. "I told him that I was taking the Donovan brothers to dinner in

Chinatown, that you were staying in Vancouver for a few days, and that you had made overtures on the subject of jade trading. Wen suggested a tour of the Tang vault, but it seems that Daniel is out on a date tonight. Wen's hands aren't up to opening the main vault door, and nobody else in the house knows the combination."

"That will make it easier," Archer said. "Unless he wants to see us along with you?"

"No. Daniel told me the exact truth. Wen hasn't left his bed for three days."

"How ill is he?" Lianne asked tightly.

"Not ill. Just old. Exhausted. This . . . all of it has been very hard on him."

Her chin lifted. "Go to him. I'll take Kyle and Archer to the vault."

No servants hovered in the kitchen. None were in the long hall leading to the vault wing of the compound. Lianne hadn't expected any. After five P.M., the servants went home to their rooms above Chinatown's shops and restaurants, or to one of the old apartment buildings where three families lived in space designed for one.

The men's footsteps and the click of Lianne's five-inch heels were the only sounds in the long hall. Kyle had a hard time taking his eyes off the twitch and sway of her butt. The short coat she wore left too much to the imagination.

And not enough.

Despite Lianne's distracting costume, Kyle made a low sound of appreciation when he saw the elegant jade screen that concealed the vault door. "I know museums that would commit grand theft to get their hands on a piece like that."

"It wouldn't be the first time museums accepted stolen goods," Lianne said dryly. She bent over the dial on the old vault door. "Every time another Old Master goes on display, some grandchild of World War Two claims that Hitler stole it from their family."

"Chances are he did," Archer said, watching Lianne spin the dial once, twice.

"Of course. But at what point do you say the statute has run out? One generation? Two? A century? Never? Pretty soon we'll be in the position Hong Kong—damn," she muttered and started over again on the combination. "We'll be in the position Hong Kong was when it reverted to China. Businesses, collectors, owners of all kinds of Chinese artifacts simply packed them up and shipped them to Vancouver or Seattle, San Francisco or L.A. or New York. Anywhere the mainland Chinese and their new rules couldn't confiscate them."

Frowning, Lianne fiddled yet again with the dial. "Incredible cultural treasures are simply gone, in hiding, because the rules of the game of provenance changed." She looked up. "Like now. Somebody has changed the rules. Or in this case, the combination."

"Excuse me," Archer said, gently pushing Lianne aside.

"Get out of his way, sweetheart," Kyle said. "This is why I let him come along."

Perplexed, she watched Archer reach into his jacket and pull out what looked like a very small tape player with earplugs attached. He tucked the plugs into his ears and pressed the box onto the vault door, near the dial. Eyes closed, face intent, he bent over the dial like a man over a lover, closing out everything else, living only for the next motion, the next sound, the next soft stirring that would tell him that his lover was responding.

In the silence, even Lianne's hushed breathing sounded loud. Archer caressed the dial with small movements of his fingertips, listening, listening, listening for the tiny noise that came when a tumbler fell into place and it was time for him to turn the dial the other way, find another number, another tumbler, and then another, until the last secret was known.

Ten minutes later the vault door softly opened.

"And I thought you were just another pretty face," Lianne said to his back.

"Live and learn." Archer wiped off the dial with a clean handkerchief. "After you, Lianne."

She looked at the Donovan brothers, one light, one dark, both alike in all the ways that mattered. "You two should come with a government warning label."

"Innocent until proven guilty," Kyle said. "Right, brother?"

"Yeah."

Kyle nudged her into the vault. Archer was on their heels. As soon as they were inside, Lianne pulled the heavy door shut and turned on the light. Kyle took one look at the white jade bowl sitting on the small mahogany table, let out a reverent oath, and went closer.

"Don't touch anything," Archer warned.

"Suck eggs," Kyle said absently. Hands in his pockets, he circled the table, devouring the bowl with his eyes.

Lianne walked quickly to the small room that held Wen's greatest prize. As always, the door was locked. She looked at the dial suspiciously, then at Archer. "I may need you again."

"I'll be right here, wiping Kyle's drool marks off the merchandise."

With fingers that were cold despite the warmth inside the vault, Lianne began turning the dial. She worked carefully, then let out a relieved sigh when the lock clicked open. As always, the door itself was stubborn. She tugged at it once, then again, harder.

"Let me," Kyle said, reaching past her.

The door opened with a grumble, as though awakened from sleep. Holding her breath without realizing it, terrified that she would see only emptiness, Lianne reached in and turned on the light.

A stone shroud lay on top of the coffin-sized table: motionless shades of green, the muted flash of gold threads beneath the overhead light.

"Well?" Kyle asked.

"It's not Wen's," Lianne said simply.

"How good is it?" Archer asked.

"It's perfect," she said on a rush of breath. "Just plain *perfect.*"

Kyle smiled like a wolf. "I'll get the suitcases."

Lianne watched Jake, Kyle, and Archer stow the last of the heavy suitcases aboard Kyle's boat, which was chuckling and rumbling with power as the big engine warmed. All twenty-seven feet of the *Tomorrow* rocked and tugged at the lines tying it to the dock below Kyle's cottage, which stood on a bluff. Strapped on top of the boat's white cabin, overhanging at both ends, a Zodiac lay facedown. The inflatable boat was blacker than the night.

The moon hadn't yet risen. Nothing brightened the dense lid of clouds except for two distant, separate glows where the city lights of Victoria and Vancouver bounced off the bottom of the clouds. The strait was a dark, subtly shimmering presence alive with the rush of wind.

There were no other boats at the dock, no other houses nearby. Kyle had chosen the cabin for two things: solitude and the private dock. It wasn't the first time that both had come in handy.

He stepped up out of the boat to the dock beside Lianne. He used only the colored reflections of the boat's running lights to find his way. No one had turned on the *Tomorrow*'s cabin lights. No one would. If anyone really wanted to see, there were night-vision goggles aboard.

Putting an arm around Lianne's waist, Kyle turned her toward him and tipped her face up to his. A ribbon of wind curled around them, bringing with it the scent of fir trees and the sea.

"You don't have to do this," he said quietly.

"I'm going. Nothing you can say or do will change my mind."

"I know," he whispered. "Damn it, I know."

He bent and kissed her, ignoring the stiffness that only slowly loosened beneath his caressing mouth.

But loosen it did. No matter how many times Lianne told herself that all she and Kyle had going was hot sex and cold business, she couldn't help responding to him. Adrenaline, nerves, plain old hormones, whatever. She didn't know. Right now, she didn't really care. She was hungry for him in ways she didn't even want to think about.

The intensity of her emotions frightened her more than anything else that had happened so far.

"You're shivering," Kyle said. He breathed warmth across Lianne's temples, her eyelids, her lips, her stubborn chin. "Do you want my jacket?"

She shook her head. Once she had changed out of the little red stretch dress and put on real clothes, she had warmed quickly enough.

"Scared?" he asked.

"About tomorrow? No."

"Then what?"

"It doesn't matter. This will all be over soon. And then . . . then it won't matter. I'll go back to my business and you'll go back to yours."

"What are you talking about?"

"Business," she whispered. "Just business, that's all."

Archer's voice rose from the stern of the boat. "We're at operating temperature. Jake says if we don't leave pretty quick, we'll run into some real chop in the passes."

"I'm ready," Lianne said.

Kyle started to hand her down into the stern well, but she pulled away from him, slipping like warm water through his fingers, leaving him cold. She went into the boat cabin without looking back to see if he was following.

Anger and an uneasy chill curled along Kyle's spine. Something was wrong. Not with the jade or tomorrow's dicey raid on Farmer Island, but with Lianne herself. She was acting as though she couldn't wait to say good-bye to him.

It doesn't matter. This will all be over soon. And then . . . then it won't matter.

He wanted to go after her and find out what the hell was going on in her quick, intensely intelligent, maddeningly female brain, but he didn't. Jake was right. They had to get going or they would hit wind against an ebbing tide in some of the passes. In terms of speed, it didn't matter; the SeaSport had plenty of power to outmuscle the tide. But if they got caught in razor waves, it would be a nasty bitch of a ride.

Kyle bent down and began undoing the *Tomorrow*'s lines. Voices floated out from the open door of the cabin.

"How long will it take to get to Jade Island?" Lianne asked Jake. He was standing in the aisle, calling up a program on Kyle's electronic chart plotter.

"Depends on what the water is like in the passes," Jake said, "and if the wind stays below fifteen knots." He punched another button on the plotter. "But unless it really sucks, we should anchor at Jade Island in time to get a decent night's sleep."

"Speak for yourself," Archer said. "I lost the toss for the bed. Such as it is."

"Yeah," Jake said, looking at the dinette, which converted into a bed of sorts. "Even if I sleep fetally, it will be a crunch."

"You can always sleep up in the notch with me," Archer offered. "Kyle said it was kind of comfortable."

"The last time Kyle camped out on Jade Island," Jake retorted, "he was wounded and half out of his mind with dehydration. I've seen the little ravine where he hid. If it rains, you'll be up to your ears in runoff."

"Maybe I'll just cut to the chase and sleep in my wet suit," Archer said.

The sound of the engine changed as Kyle throttled it down to idle. Archer stuck his head out the cabin door. Kyle was standing at the aft station, his hand on the gas lever.

"Want me to get the lines?" Archer asked.

"I got them," Kyle said. "Sit at the forward helm. I'll be along as soon as we're clear of the cove."

The dock began to fall away as Kyle eased the *Tomorrow* backward, turned, and put her bow toward Thatcher Pass.

"Take it," he called to Archer.

"I've got the helm," Archer answered.

While Kyle came forward and closed the door, Archer took the speed up to about fourteen knots. The boat could easily have done twice that, but there was no need. Too many logs, deadheads, and clumps of seaweed floated around the waters of the San Juan Islands for anyone to race off in the dark unless it was really necessary. Since no one was shooting at them, fourteen knots was plenty of speed.

Lianne pressed against the built-in dinette table to let Kyle pass by in the narrow, sunken aisle that ran from the rear of the cabin to the V berth. But instead of passing by her, he stopped, pinning her between the hard table and his equally hard body. His hands shot forward and gripped the edge of the table, caging her, cutting off any possibility that she could move aside.

She could barely breathe as she stared up at him. Rain spattered across the windows. Running lights turned the rain into melting green-and-red gems. His eyes glittered like shards of ice with slices of colored shadows caught between the sharp edges.

"I don't know what's gnawing on you," he said flatly, "but it will have to wait until we're finished getting Uncle off our backs. Understood?"

"No problem," she said, her lips stiff.

He just looked at her. "I don't believe you."

"You think I can't hold up my end of this?"

"You can do whatever you put your stubborn mind to," Kyle said in a low voice. "What worries me is what might be going on in what passes for your brain."

"Kyle," Archer said. "Is the back eddy along the point still loaded with trash from the high tide?"

"Yes. Want me to take the helm?" Kyle asked without taking his eyes off Lianne.

"Good idea. It will give you something to do besides intimidate our jade expert."

"Our? I hate to break it to you, brother dear, but Lianne isn't *ours*. She's mine."

Archer glanced over his shoulder. "Only if she wants to be. Right now, she looks like what she wants is to kick you in the balls."

"Save it," Jake said before Kyle could retort. "I've got better things to do than bruise my knuckles on you two hardheads. Hell, Archer, you know better than to pick a fight with a team member at this point."

"Yes," Archer said. "But apparently Kyle doesn't."

"What do you mean?" Kyle snarled. "I wasn't the one talking about—"

"You were baiting Lianne," Archer interrupted. "Like it or not, she's a member of our team. *Ours,* little brother. Not yours."

Kyle hissed a searing word and brushed past Lianne to take the helm. Before he got there, Archer crossed the aisle to the pilot seat and settled in next to Jake. Their wide shoulders overlapped, but otherwise the bench seat was quite comfortable.

Lianne let out a quiet breath and stepped up to one of the bench seats along the dinette. Kyle was too quick, too accurate in his reading of her. No sooner did she try to put some distance between them than he reached out and dragged her back.

It's business. Just business.

Only for her, it went deeper than business, deeper than lust. She was in danger of giving too much of herself to a man who didn't want anything more than sex. Closing her eyes, she wondered if she had been born to be stupid about men or if it was something she had perfected in the past thirty years.

Lianne folded her arms on the table, laid her head on them, and listened to the masculine rumble of voices discussing the weather, the water, and the occasional tugboat passing in the night. Gradually the subdued, muscular growl of the engine overcame the voices. She slept, but her dreams were fitful swirls of jade and accusations, fear and the black heart of an approaching storm.

"Is it time to go ashore?" Lianne asked, her voice foggy from sleep.

"No," Kyle said. "It's time to go to bed."

Before she could argue, he lifted her out of the dinette nook, put her on her feet, and half guided, half pushed her toward the bow. Behind him, Jake started muscling the table off its pedestal so that he could make up his bed.

"Watch your head," Kyle said.

Even with the warning, Lianne bumped her forehead as she stepped down into the V berth. She was so sleepy she didn't care. She just peeled off her shoes, jacket, and jeans and crawled beneath the specially made, V-shaped blanket.

Kyle stripped off everything and crawled in next to her.

"What are you—" she began.

"Scoot over," he said.

Lianne moved so far away from him that the blanket couldn't cover her, but even that wasn't far enough. Although plenty wide at one end, the pie-shaped bed didn't leave a lot of room for privacy at the other. The section of foam mattress she was lying on gave beneath Kyle's weight as he settled into the bed. Searching fingers of cold, damp air slid under the blanket.

She shivered and wished she hadn't taken off her jacket and jeans. The thong-bikini underwear and blouse she wore didn't offer much in the way of cover or warmth. But she made no move to get closer to the nearest source of heat— Kyle Donovan.

He made an impatient sound, rolled onto his side, and pulled Lianne close against his chest.

"I'm not cold," she muttered.

"I am."

It was a lie. The man radiated heat like the sun. She tried not to let his warmth seep into her, but it was impossible. Slowly her body began to soften against his.

"That's it, sweetheart," he said against her hair. "Sleep. It's going to be a long day tomorrow."

She sighed, relaxed more, then stiffened as her hips brushed against him. He was fully aroused.

"Don't worry," Kyle murmured against her ear, the words a bare thread of sound. "Much as I'd like to, Jake has ears like a fox. So just snuggle in here and we'll both make the best of a cold bed."

No longer worried about revealing his own arousal, he pulled her hips against his, wrapped his arms around her, and told himself he wasn't really torturing himself, he was just keeping her warm. The fact that one of his hands ended up tucked between her breasts was an accident.

The fact that her nipples were hard was a revelation.

Gently he skimmed them with his thumb, first one nipple, then the other, just for the sheer pleasure of hearing her breathing change, of having her body acknowledge the desire she wouldn't speak aloud. He didn't mean to spread his hand wide, to caress, to stroke, to unbutton and tease and arouse; but he did each of those things, over and over, while she remained motionless but for the wild beating of her heart.

Very, very slowly, his touch moved down her body like the sun sliding over a mountain peak and then down to the darkest valley, probing every shadow, even the deepest one. Especially the deepest one, the one that only his aching flesh could fill, the one that gave softly, generously as he parted her and pushed into the endless heat, the wellspring of feminine mystery that pulsed slowly, rhythmically, soundlessly around him even as he spilled into her, and they gave themselves in a prolonged, silent unraveling that was like nothing either had ever felt before.

They fell asleep that way, silent, motionless, joined.

twenty-five

The wind blew hard all morning, churning the water, bringing unpredictable bursts of rain. By the time the wind began to die down, it was raining steadily. Neither wind nor rain kept Kyle from showing Lianne how to handle the Zodiac, operate the short-range location system the divers would wear, and breathe underwater using the government's high-tech equipment.

While Kyle ran Lianne through her paces, Archer and Jake took turns scrambling up the narrow ridge that separated Jade Island into two unequal halves. The top of the ridge gave them a view of Farmer Island, just over three miles away. Braced against the wind, shielding the lenses from the rain, Archer and Jake traded off keeping watch through powerful binoculars.

They saw no unusual activity, no sign that Farmer was planning a party or hosting an unpublicized conference. Even after the wind dropped to a whisper, no boats arrived and no planes landed. Nor was there a plane tied down along the private runway. Apparently Dick Farmer was still in Seattle playing hardball with China and Uncle Sam.

"No change," Jake said, sliding down the last few feet of

the slope and handing the binoculars to Archer. "If anyone noticed us coming in last night, or the Zodiac zipping around earlier today, they're not worried enough to come looking."

Archer glanced at the angle of the sun and then at Kyle, who was methodically testing the rebreathers one last time. Unlike standard scuba gear, the rebreathing apparatus didn't let loose a stream of air bubbles every time the diver exhaled. It was a useful feature; if you happened to be diving in hostile waters on a clear, calm night, a trail of bubbles could get you killed.

"How does the water look between here and there?" Kyle asked Jake.

"Lively, but no problem."

Kyle looked at the sky. With luck, there would be a nice, steady drizzle to conceal the Zodiac while they played hide-and-seek with Farmer's guards.

"The gear is ready," Kyle said, standing and stretching.

"What about the electronics?" Archer asked.

"In a dry bag clipped to my dive belt."

"You sure that damned key works?" Jake asked.

"We'll find out soon enough," Archer said.

"Have a little faith," Kyle told his brother. "Remember the gizmo snitch. Not to mention Honor's alarm clock."

"Please, *don't* mention it," Jake muttered. "The first time I heard it go off, I thought someone was murdering her. I came running up from the dock to your cabin buck naked and waving my gun."

Kyle snickered. "I wish I could have seen Honor's face."

"It was dark."

Kyle looked at the sky again. The west was incandescent with colors. The east was a peaceful twilight blue condensing into night. "Let's suit up."

It was easier said than done, especially for Lianne, who had had little practice pulling on the clinging, stubborn neoprene. Even with the minimum underneath—a bikini swimsuit—she didn't think she would make it this time. But with a generous amount of talcum powder and a lot of wriggling, she finally got the suit on.

When she turned to take the path to the narrow, rocky strip of beach where the Zodiac had been hauled out of the water, Kyle was standing there, watching her with laughter and frank desire in his eyes.

"Sweetheart, that would make a hell of a nightclub act."

She ignored him. "Where's my rebreather?"

"In the Zodiac. But you won't have to use it. The rain will give us plenty of cover to beach the boat so you can walk ashore."

"You hope," she muttered.

And so did she. Driving the Zodiac around was a cinch. Climbing back into it after a dive wasn't. Karate training had given her coordination, but hadn't done much for the upper-body strength required to lever herself out of the water and into the Zodiac while wearing diving gear.

Jake and Archer were waiting by the Zodiac. Enough rain spit down to darken the sky, dampen the land, and dimple the surface of the water. In the late-day gloom, the men loomed huge in their unmarked black wet suits and scuba gear. Finding a pure black wet suit for Lianne had been impossible, so Kyle had taken black shoe polish to the bright coral slices of neoprene.

Lianne went to the bow, perched on the fat gunwale, and wrapped her neoprene-covered fingers around the straps, which would keep her from bouncing out at the first wave. She hoped.

The men waded into the dark gray ocean, taking the Zodiac with them. Archer and Jake rolled aboard with the ease of men who had done it hundreds of times before. Kyle quickly followed. Sitting on the flat red metal gas tank, he revved up the engine, checked that everyone was set, and headed for Farmer Island.

By the time they got there, it was dark and Lianne's hands ached from hanging onto the straps. Despite the sulky rain dribbling over his night goggles, Kyle didn't even need a compass to show the way. The rugged shape of Farmer Island was like a black beacon.

He checked his dive watch. Quarter of seven. Well within their time limits. Walker wouldn't even take off from Seattle until ten.

Kyle throttled the outboard back to a bare mutter and crept closer to the island. They were at the opposite end to the marina and the compound. Here there were no buildings, no lighted paths, no voices calling. The headland looked like a wall, which it was, unless the tide was out. Then a boat with a very shallow draft could reach one of the thin, rocky beaches that clung to either side of the headland.

The landing spot the men had chosen was lost in darkness, unless you happened to be the man wearing the night goggles. Just beyond the rocky rubble of the beach, the black mass of the forested headland rose steeply against the barely lighter sky.

"You're up," Kyle said to Archer in a voice that carried no farther than his brother.

"Sixty minutes," Archer answered in the same voice.

"Check the locator."

Archer switched on the miniature transmitter that would tell Kyle exactly where to pick him up in an hour.

The small receiver in Kyle's hand stirred to life and pointed toward Archer.

"It's hot," Kyle said. "Go."

Archer turned off the transmitter, lowered himself into the water, and began swimming toward the beach with powerful, invisible motions of his dive flippers.

Kyle turned the Zodiac and headed for the next drop-off point. It began to rain in earnest. No one in the open boat noticed. Wet suits were hard to get on or off, but they made world-class rain gear.

*　　*　　*

A light blinked on the console. When that wasn't enough to get the guard's attention, a beeper complained in rapidly rising tones.

"Now what?" the guard muttered, setting aside his magazine. "If that moron gardener is sneaking out in the bushes to ball the maid again, I'm going to personally rip off his cock and stuff it down her throat."

But the warning light wasn't in the servants' sector. It came from the dirt road at the far end of the island, near the runway. It could be deer. They had some on Farmer Island. Or it could be something on two legs.

The guard hit an intercom switch that connected him to staff quarters. When there wasn't a conference or a party scheduled, there were only two guards for the whole island. Usually it didn't matter, because the place was so quiet that the only danger was falling asleep on the job. The guards split the day into twelve-hour shifts, 6 A.M. to 6 P.M. When Murray was on duty, Steve was off—unless something happened.

Something had just happened.

"Steve!" Murray snapped. "Get your ass up here. We got a live one on the east side, sector six."

"Hell, Murray. You sure it isn't Lopez humping that lazy slut again?"

"Not unless they took a walk to the far end of the runway to do it."

"Five to one it's a deer."

"Five to one you're fired if you don't haul ass out there and take a look."

With a disgusted curse Steve pulled on a rain jacket and headed for the Jeep. Five minutes later he roared up to the far end of the island. His headlights and searchlight showed nothing but empty road and rain. He picked up the radio mike.

"Murray, this is Steve," he said curtly. "Nothing on the road. Not even deer tracks."

"Try the beach."

"It's raining cats and dogs."

"That's why you're getting paid fifteen bucks an hour."

Steve got out of the Jeep, slammed the door, and went to the point where the road fell away to the tiny beach thirty feet below. Using a powerful flashlight and slow, methodical sweeps of his arm, he lighted up swath after swath of night. Rocks gleamed wetly in the rain. A stunted pine clung to a ledge just out of reach of the salt water. No boat was hauled up on shore or anchored within reach of his light.

Rain trickled coldly down his jacket collar. His shoes were wet. So was his face. His leather gloves were getting clammy. He climbed back into the Jeep, slammed the door, and picked up the mike again. "Murray, Steve. Nothing but rain and rocks."

"That's what I figured. C'mon back."

As the lights of the Jeep vanished into the rain, Archer surfaced invisibly on the black breast of the sea. He checked the dial of his dive watch. Jake should be landing on the other side of the headland in a few minutes.

"I've got you on the grid," Kyle said softly to Jake. "Go."

"Fifty minutes."

"Check."

Jake rolled off the gunwale and into the water on the southwest side of the island, perhaps a roundabout thousand feet from the point where Archer had gone ashore. Even as Jake vanished into the rainy darkness, Kyle turned the Zodiac and headed out into the strait to watch the fun from a safe distance.

When the intercom came on again, water was still dripping off Steve's jacket, which was hung over the shower rod in his small quarters.

"Got a light again, Steve."

"Where?"

"Same sector."

"Same piece of it?"

"Nope. Other side of the headland. Southwest. Unless the sensors are getting cute. They do that sometimes in the rain."

Which, in the Pacific Northwest, meant the equipment wasn't really reliable.

"It's probably more of what was there the last time," Steve said. "Nothing."

"Fifteen bucks an hour, remember?"

"Crap. I'll call you when I get there."

Nervously Lianne watched Kyle prepare to go into the dark water. She clutched the receiver with its odd-shaped aerial and small, lighted dial.

"Test it," she said.

Kyle switched his transmitter on.

"Okay," she said. "You're on the grid."

He switched off.

"Twenty minutes," she said.

Kyle grabbed the back of Lianne's neck and swiftly kissed her mouth. It was the one part of both of them that wasn't covered with black neoprene. Then he rolled out of the Zodiac and into the cold water.

Lianne drove the Zodiac farther out into the sound. Alone on the restless, mysterious water, she settled in to wait for the longest twenty minutes of her life. Night-vision goggles helped her to make out the island. Once she even thought she might have seen something move across a patch of winter-killed grass that looked pale against the darker rocks and forest.

From her right came a sudden *whoosh-gasp,* as though a nearby diver had surfaced, blown out air suddenly, and sucked it back in just as fast. She turned toward the sound so quickly that she nearly lost her balance in the rocking Zodiac.

She saw nothing except the smooth surface of the water, oddly luminous through the night goggles. She heard nothing except the slap of water against the boat. Just when she thought she had been imagining things, the sound came again, closer this time. Her heart beat wildly as she imagined a diver stalking the Zodiac.

Silently a black shape rose out of the water, climbing higher and higher until it was a triangular fin taller than Lianne. The rapid gust and suck of air pulsed in the night. A twist of vapor, a whisper of white markings on black, and the killer whale disappeared into the sea with the same immense, mysterious power as when it had appeared.

Awe prickled over Lianne in a shower of tiny needles. She held her breath, listening, but the whale didn't surface again.

Headlights swept down the island toward the shallow, rocky cove where Kyle had gone ashore. Lianne strained forward, waiting for the headlights to stop. But the vehicle kept going to the far end of the island, where Jake and Archer were taking turns setting off sensors.

She let out her breath in a relieved sigh. Archer had guessed right. Dick Farmer hadn't thought the bleak little cove was inviting enough to be worth putting sensors in to warn of trespassers. After all, Farmer was worried about kayakers, bird-watchers, and picnickers parading around the island, not an armed invasion.

Twenty minutes after Lianne had dropped Kyle off, the locator lit up. She turned the Zodiac and headed at a sedate speed for the invisible piece of flotsam that was Kyle Donovan.

She came so close to him that she nearly ran him down and had to circle back, cut the engine, and drift. The Zodiac hesitated, then rocked hard as Kyle pulled himself aboard. Salt water cascaded off him.

"I'll take it," he said, reaching for the steering arm of the outboard. "Go to the bow."

In an hour the sensors recorded eleven hits, three of them while Steve was still parked on the headland. Nothing ever showed up when he ran his searchlight or flashlight over the landscape. By the time he got fed up with running back and forth, he was wet to his underwear, cold, and thoroughly disgusted.

When he returned to the compound, he didn't bother to go to his quarters. He went straight to the security room, where Murray sat dry and warm and watched Farmer's idiot electronics go *ftzz* in the night.

"There's gotta be a bug in the system," Steve said in disgust. "Water, probably. I'm sopping wet and haven't seen anything but rain."

"Get a cup of coffee. I'll have a report to Maintenance first thing in the morning." A light flashed on the console in front of him. "Well, shit."

"What?" Steve asked.

"Sector three just lit up."

"And you think I should check it out, just like I did four, five, and six."

"Fifteen bucks an—"

"Easy for you to say," Steve interrupted angrily, "sitting on your ass all warm and dry while I'm chasing my tail in the rain. If there isn't something in my flashlight beam this time, I'm going to bed and you can sit here and jack off all over the blinking lights."

When Steve got to sector three, nothing was there but rocks, trees, and an empty dirt road. No boats. No people. Not even a damned deer.

"Murray, Steve. Not a fucking thing out here but me. Why the hell didn't Farmer get some dogs? They don't go nuts from a little rain."

"Farmer hates dogs. Won't have them on the place."

Steve didn't bother to answer. He was on his way back to the compound and he was mad enough to kick something. Murray's lazy ass was first on his list.

By the time ten o'clock came, both guards were sitting at the console, betting on which sector would light up next. Neither man bothered to check out each hit physically anymore. After three hours of running around in the rain, both guards were ready to pull the plug on Dick Farmer's security system.

Fifteen bucks an hour wasn't nearly enough.

Archer came up out of the water and into the Zodiac with an easy motion that Lianne envied to the soles of her feet. She clung to the straps while the boat dipped and wallowed, balancing beneath the additional burden. Even with Jake, Kyle, and Lianne acting as counterweights, two hundred plus pounds of man climbing aboard was bound to make an impact on a small boat.

"Everything okay?" Kyle asked quickly.

"No problems. Either they shut down the system or they're ignoring it."

"That's my reading," Jake said.

"You cold?" Kyle asked Archer. He had recent personal knowledge of just how chilly the water could be.

"Not enough to slow me down," Archer said.

"Good. Let's beach this bastard and get to work."

twenty-six

From overhead came the grinding drone of a propeller plane circling Farmer Island's small, private runway. The sound cut out, picked up, stuttered, and steadied, only to cut out again.

Kyle looked at his watch. "Ten o'clock. Right on time." He turned to Archer. "Take care of Lianne."

"Every step of the way," Archer said. "Go. If you get into trouble—"

"Just get Lianne out," Kyle interrupted. "I'll take care of myself."

"Like hell," Jake muttered.

"I agree," Lianne said.

"The plan," Archer said before Kyle could argue any more, "is that all of us leave or none of us leave. You're wasting time."

Kyle turned and walked toward the compound, sliding from tree shadow to tree shadow, closing in on the secluded building that was Dick Farmer's personal residence. Glass gleamed weakly in the moonlight that managed to penetrate the windswept layers of clouds. Exterior lights triggered by motion sensors came on and off all over the compound, following invisible gusts of wind through the shrubs and trees.

Silently Kyle swore at the idiot lights. Their unpredictable flashing and dimming made the night goggles he had brought worse than useless. The illumination from just one light swamped the goggles' delicate light-gathering mechanism. The motion-sensing lights also made for jumps of pure adrenaline when they came on unexpectedly.

The only good news was that the guards obviously were accustomed to random lights flashing during windy times. And wind, like clouds and rain, wasn't exactly a stranger to the San Juan Islands. In any case, the guards would be too busy scrambling for the runway to warn off the uninvited plane. They wouldn't pay any attention to a few more security lights going on and off in the night.

At least, that was the plan.

Kyle didn't have to look around to know that Archer and Jake were following. And where Archer was, Lianne would be, too. It wasn't as safe as leaving her in Seattle, but it was as much safety as Kyle could arrange for his stubborn lover.

When Archer said he would take care of something, it got taken care of.

Even when wind gusted and lights flashed on, Kyle wasn't too worried about being spotted. He wore dark slacks, a dark waterproof jacket, and a fisherman's knit hat, also dark. Of course, if he got caught, he might have trouble explaining the heavy backpack and the neoprene dive suit under his street clothes, but he didn't plan on getting caught. Or if he got caught, he wouldn't stay that way for long. Archer and Jake were a lot better trained than Farmer's rent-a-cops.

The temptation to look over his shoulder every few steps and check on Lianne was like an itch Kyle couldn't scratch. But she was dressed in the same anonymous black as he was. She wouldn't stand out any more than a shadow.

The front door of Farmer's residence was made of fir carved in Haida totemic designs. There was no lock that Kyle could see, no handle. Very shortly, he would find out if he was nearly as clever with electronics as he thought he was.

Or if Farmer had changed the frequency on his personal electronic "key" in the past nine months.

Kyle reached into his jacket pocket to check that the key was in place. The slim little transmitter was powered by a Polaroid battery pack, just like the best letter bombs. Only this one didn't go boom; it quietly, discreetly, opened the compound's doors for Dick Farmer . . . or for anybody else who happened to be wearing it.

When he walked through the open, welcoming front door, Kyle discovered that the little unit also turned on lights, music, and wallpaper, giving him an adrenaline surge so sharp that his hands tingled. He looked around quickly, spotted a manual control panel, and killed the lights. The music continued, Dvorak's New World Symphony, all crashing notes and urgency. The wallpaper was Broadway at night, traffic patterns shifting and glowing realistically, crowds rushing, everything but horns honking—and the symphony supplied that.

Lianne hurried through the door. Archer and Jake were right on her heels. The heavy backpacks the men wore made odd, almost musical sounds as their loads shifted.

"Dial down the music," Jake muttered.

"As soon as I find the switch," Kyle agreed.

"Screw the music," Archer said. "The guards can't hear it. They're headed toward the runway. Find the shroud."

With Kyle in the lead, they went through door after door, carrying with them a cocoon of wallpaper and music doing ghostly transformations. None of the rooms that opened magically at Kyle's appearance held a Han burial shroud made of precious jade.

"What kind of ego needs this many bells and whistles?" Jake asked when the eighth door opened and *Thus Spake Zarathustra* poured from hidden speakers.

"Somebody with a tin-god complex," Kyle said, turning off the lights automatically. "But don't knock it. It's making our lives easy. One key fits all doors."

He started to turn away, then stopped. The room looked

like a plush college-lecture hall with a semicircle of seats rising steeply away from the podium. Forest-green curtains fell from ceiling to floor, shutting off the small stage.

Thoughtfully, Kyle pulled out a small pencil-beam flashlight.

"What are you doing?" Lianne asked.

"The curtains. Wonder what's behind them."

"You think he'd put something as valuable as the suit in an open *classroom?*" Lianne asked.

"Why not?" Kyle followed a thin beam of light down the central aisle. "As far as Farmer is concerned, this whole compound is a hell of a lot more secure than Wen's vault."

The curtains didn't spring apart at Kyle's appearance. He had to search the lectern before he found a series of switches. The first one turned on the podium light. The second was for the microphone. The third opened the curtains.

Lianne's breath caught in a wondering sound as the slim beam of Kyle's flashlight stroked gleaming shades of green from center stage. She ran down the aisle and up the stage stairs, her backpack bumping every step of the way. She hardly noticed the awkward weight. Her whole attention was fixed on the jade shroud that lay like a radiant, articulated suit of armor on top of a steel utility table.

Kyle was right on Lianne's heels. As she reached out to the shroud with reverent hands, he took the stage in a long leap that ignored the weight of his backpack.

"Is it a go?" Archer asked from behind his brother.

"Yes," Kyle said, not waiting for Lianne to answer. The look on her face said it all.

"Then let's get to work," Archer said, shucking off his own heavy backpack. "Walker will be taking off in an hour."

Kyle reached for Lianne's backpack. "Hold still, sweetheart. We'll start with the head."

By the time Murray and Steve arrived at the airstrip, Walker had the Piper Aztec's engine compartment open, a battery-operated work light clipped on, and a few greasy parts laid out on a tarp under the wing. Swirls of rain and wind danced across the tarmac, lifting the edges of the tarp. Bent over the engine, Walker presented the guards with a view of long legs and a lean, denim-clad butt.

"Hey," Murray yelled out of the Jeep's open window. "This is a private airstrip! You're trespassing!"

Walker took his time, straightening up and turning to the guards. Beneath the short, dark beard, his smile was welcoming— if you couldn't see his eyes. They were a blue as cold as it was clear. He looked at the men, cataloging them in a single quick glance. They were both under thirty, already going slack from their butt-broadening jobs, and not expecting any more trouble than they could handle.

"Sorry, boys," Walker said, deepening his normal West Texas drawl. "The engine started choking on me. No warning, just stuttered like a bitch. I was real glad to see this little ol' runway on my chart."

"This is private land," Murray said again.

"I hear you. I'll be glad to pay a tie-down fee or whatever, but I can't go anywhere until I straighten the kinks out. Fuel supply, is my guess."

"How long will that take?" Murray asked.

"I'm working on it."

Murray chewed on that while Walker bent over and began fiddling with the engine again.

" 'Course," Walker said after a minute, "if you boys were of a mind to help, it might go faster."

Wind and rain swirled again, plastering Walker's light-weight rain shell to his body and darkening his jeans.

"We're not mechanics," Murray said.

"Fucking-A," Steve muttered. "I'm not going out in this slop again."

But the guards didn't feel comfortable just driving off and leaving the trespasser on his own. Besides, they knew what was waiting for them back at the compound. Nothing. Murray rolled up his window, shut off the lights and the engine, and settled in to make sure that the stranger didn't steal any of Dick Farmer's private runway.

Walker didn't look at the guards again. Whistling tunelessly, he pulled out parts, wiped them off, stacked them on the tarp, and turned back to the engine. Making sure that his back was to the men, he checked his watch from time to time. His hands were cold and his face was so wet that rain dripped off his nose, but he never slowed the easy rhythm of take out, wipe off, set aside, and dive back into the residual warmth of the engine compartment.

Occasionally one of the guards rolled down a window to call out a question. Each time, Walker assured them that he was getting closer to the problem.

And he was. His watch was getting closer to eleven o'clock with every sweep of the second hand. When he judged the time was right, he began reassembling the pieces a good deal faster than he had taken them out in the first place. He unclipped the work light, folded the tarp, pulled the chocks away from the airplane's wheels, and stowed everything in its proper place. There was plenty of room. Where four passenger seats normally would be, there was nothing but blank space. Tonight the Aztec was a two-seater.

The guards watched while Walker climbed into his plane. They were bored, but boredom was a big part of their job.

"Don't suppose you could turn on the runway lights?" Walker called out.

"Only for Mr. Farmer," Steve yelled back. "You landed in the dark. You can take off the same way."

"Thanks, y'all," Walker said, smiling. He had expected just that answer from the lazy guards. "I sure do appreciate your help."

"Fuck you."

Walker started up the Aztec, listening carefully to the engine sound. He was accustomed to servicing the plane himself, but not in the middle of a strange runway at night in the rain.

The tough little plane growled with eagerness, straining to be up and doing what it did best.

With a last glance at the Jeep, Walker began to taxi down the runway. He went the complete length, turned, and paused for the final run-up. Holding the Aztec stationary, he increased the revs until the thunder of twin engines ripped through the night.

A figure slipped out of the wide drainage ditch that paralleled the runway. Walker opened the door of the plane in time to grab the dark backpack that came hurtling out of the darkness. Even though he had been prepared, he grunted as he caught the backpack.

"Heavy bastard," Walker muttered.

"Tell me about it," Kyle retorted. "I've been hauling it at a trot for the last fifteen minutes."

"Yeah, that Archer's a mean son of a bitch, isn't he?" Walker asked cheerfully.

"I heard that," Archer said. "Catch."

Walker snagged the second backpack and stowed it next to the first.

"Incoming," Jake said, shrugging out of his backpack.

"That you, Mallory?" Walker said.

"Yeah."

"Heard about your marriage. My condolences."

Jake gave a low crack of laughter. "Haven't changed, have you?"

"If it ain't broke, don't fix it. Shag your butts, boys. Those guards might get curious."

"Hold still, sweetheart," Kyle said.

"Sweetheart," Walker drawled. "Sugar boy, you're a real piece of work. We haven't even been formally introduced and already you're coming on to me."

"Screw you, Walker. I'm talking to Lianne."

She laughed and wriggled out of her backpack, only to gasp as Kyle tossed it up into the plane. "Be careful!"

From the far end of the runway, blades of white light sliced through rain and darkness, outlining the Aztec. Jake and Archer dove into the ditch. Kyle was a half step behind, dragging Lianne. They went down flat, but Kyle was up instantly, peering out at the runway. Archer was right beside him.

"We got problems, children," Walker said. "I can't take off with that Jeep on the runway, and there's no time to unload the backpacks. You want those two guards healthy or real quiet?"

"Healthy," Archer said. "If possible."

Lianne ripped off her jacket and began kicking out of her dark, loose slacks.

"Get the hell out of here before they see you," Walker said. "I'll think of something."

"I don't like it," Archer said.

"Come on," Kyle said to Lianne.

"Help me get out of the wet suit," Lianne said, dragging at the top.

"What?" Kyle said.

"Help me!"

He didn't know what she had in mind, but he knew a fast way to get out of neoprene. He yanked out his dive knife and started cutting. Within seconds Lianne was wearing nothing but rain and the bottom of her bikini swimsuit. She grabbed her jacket.

"Take everything else and go," she said urgently. When he hesitated she gave him a push. "Just do it! Hurry! They're almost here!"

"But—"

"I'll be all right," she interrupted. "Get out of here. Please, Kyle. Just go!"

He would have argued, but Archer and Jake were grabbing up pieces of wet suit and crawling off into the darkness. They knew there wasn't any time to object to or add to whatever Lianne had in mind.

With a savage curse, Kyle grabbed the slacks she had abandoned and followed the other two men into the darkness beyond the reach of lights.

Lianne gathered herself, shrugged into her lightweight jacket without zipping it, and climbed out of the ditch. Headlights silhouetted her, picking up the creamy length of her legs and turning the windblown jacket into a breathless striptease that revealed and then concealed her breasts and hips. Ignoring the guards scrambling out of the Jeep, she held her hands up to Walker.

"Okay," she called to him. "I'm done. Let's get a mile high real quick."

Walker pulled her into the plane with a strength that startled her.

"A mile high, huh?" he said. "They might go for it. Anything else I should know?"

"I had to pee."

"I figured that out. There's a tarp over the backpacks. Go decorate it. And don't fasten that jacket. Nothing like some bare tits to muddle a man's mind. Bare ass is even better."

"Some things are better left to the imagination," Lianne retorted as she scrambled by him.

Walker smiled. "Not that thing. It halves the male IQ in nothing flat."

"Hey!" Murray yelled, slapping the Aztec's wing with his palm. "What the hell is going on? I saw people out here!"

"You just saw me helping my little sugar girl take a pee," Walker drawled. "You know how it is with women. Can't pee in a beer bottle like men."

"Huh?" Murray said.

"Sugar girl, show your sweet little face."

"Baby," Lianne said, putting her best whine into it, "I'm cold. When are you going to get this piece of crud a mile high so we can fuck?"

Walker grinned at Murray like a proud parent. "That's my sweet thing. Wouldn't say shit if her mouth was full of it."

Murray leaned in past Walker and aimed his flashlight into

the back of the plane. He saw a mostly naked girl stretched out on what looked like a hastily made bed. Every time he started to think of a question, she breathed, her breasts shifted, and he was sure there was some bare pussy hanging out of the bottom of her jacket.

When the guard shifted the flashlight to get a better look, Walker moved, blocking the view.

"Mind moving that Jeep, buddy?" Walker asked easily. "I sure don't want to keep the little lady waiting. She might get out of the mood."

Reluctantly Murray pushed away from the plane and signaled for Steve to move the Jeep out of the way. Two minutes later the Aztec leaped off the runway and flew off into the rain-washed night. The Jeep followed.

Kyle watched from the dense shadows at the edge of the rocky bluff, straining up toward the plane as though he wished he, too, could fly.

"Relax," Archer said. "Walker will take care of her. He's as good as they get."

"That's what I'm afraid of."

After a final long look, Kyle eased his way down the bluff into the cove. Archer and Jake already had the Zodiac uncovered and were carrying it to the water. Kyle hurried after them.

As soon as they were aboard, Jake revved up the engine, Archer fixed a spotlight to a pole, and they took off toward Jade Island, no longer caring if anyone noticed them.

The first thing they saw when they crossed the passage between the two islands and circled around Jade Island's south side was the *Tomorrow*'s white hull. The second thing they saw was the matte-black Boston Whaler anchored nearby, the kind Navy SEALs used when they went out to play.

"Guess the boys couldn't wait to claim their rebreathers," Kyle said.

"Guess not." Archer smiled thinly.

Cabin lights aboard the *Tomorrow* came on. April Joy

opened the door and went to stand at the stern. Two very large black silhouettes joined her.

"Good thing you're not a trusting sort anymore," Jake told Kyle. "I'd hate to be sitting on backpacks full of jade right now."

"You wouldn't be sitting on them for long," Archer said sardonically. "I've got a feeling those boys are here to do some heavy lifting."

"Hello, the *Tomorrow,*" Kyle called out.

"Keep your hands in sight while you come alongside," April called back.

Jake tucked the Zodiac neatly along the *Tomorrow*'s hull. Kyle and Archer sat with their hands on their knees.

"Now I know you guys think you're hot shit," April said calmly, "but my SEALs are better. They'd be happy to prove it if I give—" The words stopped abruptly as she realized that there were only three people in the Zodiac. "Where's Lianne Blakely?"

"I don't know," Kyle said. It was the exact truth.

"Get out of the Zodiac," April ordered. "One at a time. You first, Archer. Then your brother. Then Jake."

As soon as the Zodiac was empty, two SEALs stepped down into it with the utter familiarity of men who spend their lives on small boats of various kinds. They began sorting through the stuff in the boat. It took them less than a minute to get to the bottom line.

"Four rebreathers, a cut-up dive suit, fuel tank, empty duffel bag. That's it, sir."

"Turn the boat over," April ordered.

It took some effort, but the SEALs managed to flip the Zodiac. The bottom was as clean as the sea.

Fists on her hips, April stalked up to Archer. "Where is it?"

"Where is what?" he asked.

"Don't get cute with me or I'll have your ass for a doormat. Where is the damned jade suit?"

Kyle came over and stood beside Archer. So did Jake. The SEALs closed in swiftly but kept their hands off.

"The last jade suit I saw was in Dick Farmer's compound," Kyle said casually. "You'll get to see it tomorrow. Ten o'clock, I believe?"

April turned and looked at Kyle with eyes that were like black ice. "If you've fucked this up, slick, you're going to have a long, unhappy life."

twenty-seven

"I'd just as soon not see this island ever again," Lianne muttered as the *Tomorrow* nosed up to Farmer's dock. "Or the guards. What if they recognize me? We were here just last night." She shivered, cold from the memory.

Kyle smiled rather grimly. "Don't worry. From what Walker told me, the bastards never looked at your face." Walker had mentioned some other things, too, like how much he admired Lianne's guts and quick mind . . . as well as her more traditional assets. Kyle hadn't liked hearing about any of it. He wasn't happy that Lianne had put herself at risk.

"Looks like Ms. Joy is already here," Lianne said, spotting the petite woman at the end of the dock. A man in a rumpled dark suit and large, black-rimmed glasses stood next to April. A cigarette smoldered between the middle and ring fingers of his right hand.

"That must be the Chinese jade expert with her," Kyle said.

"Is Farmer here yet?"

"If that was his plane we saw landing a few minutes ago, he should be in the classroom before we are. Of course, we don't know where we're going, do we?"

"Of course not."

Lianne straightened her jacket and repositioned the shoulder strap of her small red purse. It matched her shoes and picked up the scarlet trim of her black silk jacket. Slender black pants completed the outfit. Looking at her, no one would believe she was running on a few hours of sleep.

"All right, let's get it over with," she said. "I won't be able to draw a deep breath until this is settled and the suit is locked up in Vancouver again."

Kyle followed Lianne up the dock. He was dressed more casually than she was—jeans, olive-green turtleneck sweater, dark sport coat, and boat shoes. He looked more tired than she did. He had refused Faith's deft touch with cosmetics.

Farmer's personal assistant hurried down from the compound, waved the guard back to his post, and made introductions all around. With the speed of a good executive secretary, Mary Margaret herded them through the playful wind to Farmer's residence, escorted them to the "theater room," and turned them over to her boss with another flourish of introductions.

April and Sun Ming conferred in rapid Chinese at every break in the conversation.

"They say anything interesting yet?" Kyle asked Lianne under his breath.

"No. They're still at the fulsome-wishes-for-mutual-happiness stage. They won't talk business until they see the shroud."

"Thank you for taking the time to come to my island," Farmer said, pitching his voice to carry through the room. "Please, come forward." Smiling, he beckoned them down toward the stage.

Behind Farmer, the forest-green curtains were tightly closed, exactly the way Kyle had left them. He watched Farmer intently. The multibillionaire looked the same as he always did. Confident, even princely in his assurance. If

Farmer suspected anything was wrong, he was hiding it magnificently.

A chill prickled along Kyle's spine. He wondered what he would see when the curtain went up, if Farmer had somehow pulled off his own switch.

"I know you're as pressed for time as I am," Farmer said, "so I won't bore you with details from my own jade appraiser. If you wish, Mary Margaret will give you a copy of the detailed appraisal on your way out." He reached into the podium and flipped a switch. "Please, look as much as you like. I have an international conference call in four minutes. If you have any questions, I'll answer them to the best of my ability when I return."

The curtains whisked apart as Farmer spoke. He glanced at the stage, frowned, and went to a panel at the side of the stage. He fiddled with the lighting.

"Odd," he said. "The color still looks off. Yellowish."

Kyle glanced at the burial suit. "Some jade has a yellow cast to it."

So did most serpentine, but that wasn't something Kyle should point out. He was here as Lianne's assistant, not as an appraiser.

April and Sun Ming descended on the suit. Lianne was right beside them. Impatiently, Kyle listened to cascades of Chinese.

"English, please," he said to Lianne. "I can't help you in Chinese."

"Sorry," Lianne said without looking away from the suit. "The suit is serpentine, not jade. But that isn't what makes it . . . dubious."

The room's acoustics were very good. Though Farmer was halfway up the aisle, he stopped and spun toward the stage at Lianne's words.

"What really worries me is that the threads aren't spun from pure gold," she said. She flicked her fingertips at the dull threads that held the hundreds and hundreds of small stone plaques together. Time and weather wouldn't hurt gold, but they were hell on little threads of bronze.

"Are you sure?" Kyle asked.

"As sure as I can be without metallurgical tests," Lianne said. "Gold doesn't discolor, doesn't tarnish, doesn't corrode. It's immortal, like the dead princes and emperors wished to be. But some of these threads are darkened by corrosion. Look here, where the thread has broken."

Kyle started for the stage.

So did Farmer.

"Sir," Mary Margaret said, "your call."

"Reschedule it."

"But—yes, sir."

"Again," Lianne continued, ignoring Farmer's rush to the stage, "I would have to examine this more closely, but it appears that threads of copper or some metal were mixed in with the gold. Perhaps it's simply an inferior alloy, such as ten carat gold, or even eight. Which raises questions about the validity of the suit as a whole. Gold was rare in China, but not so rare that the imperial family had to skimp on its burial goods."

"I agree," April said. She twirled a twist of metal thread between her fingers, then dropped it on top of the stone suit. "If this is a modern fraud, whoever made it would be concerned about the quantity of pure gold required to sew the plaques together, not to mention the trim itself. The cost of gold would be considerable, particularly in China, where gold isn't common."

Lianne took a small, high-powered magnifying glass from her purse and bent over the stone shroud. She studied several plaques closely, paying special attention to the holes that had been drilled so that metal thread could bind the pieces of serpentine together.

"Machine-made," she said, "not handmade. Every hole is the same size and the same distance from its neighbor. Machine-polished, too. The marks are quite clear."

For the first time, Lianne looked at April. "I'll bet this shroud isn't old enough to vote. What do you think?"

"I agree." April turned to Sun and spoke rapidly. The jade expert answered just as rapidly.

Farmer didn't say a word, but if the red on his cheekbones was any indication, he wasn't a happy man.

"What are they saying?" Kyle asked Lianne.

"Sun Ming is reluctant to give up the idea of a genuine Han artifact," she said calmly, "but he will, no matter how much his government enjoys yanking Uncle Sam's chain. The visual evidence is compelling: the suit is fraudulent. With lab tests, it will be overwhelming." She glanced away from the shroud and appeared to notice Farmer for the first time. "This is very difficult, Mr. Farmer. Nothing is harder than telling a collector that some particularly prized item is, um, less than it seems."

Farmer stared at Lianne as if she had just farted. Then he turned back to watch the argument between April and Sun. Even not understanding a single word of Chinese, he knew that the jade expert was going to give up before Sun did.

With a hissing oath, Farmer turned and strode out of the theater. He didn't bother to say good-bye to his guests.

Wen sat in the Tang vault, arthritic hands resting on the carved jade dragon that crowned his walking stick. In his lap lay the magnificent Neolithic blade that Kyle had bought at auction and returned to its rightful owner, Wen Zhi Tang.

Even Wen's carefully tailored gray suit couldn't conceal the increasing frailty of his body. Next to him, within reach of his gnarled hands, the jade suit gleamed in shades of immortal green. Pure gold stitched through the shroud like sunlight. Wen couldn't see the colors, nor could his fingers discern the nuances of hand-polished jade. Yet the presence of the imperial burial suit comforted him, reminding him that the best of humanity transcended the worst.

Lianne watched Wen with concern darkening her eyes.

Kyle and Archer watched him with impassive faces. The past several days had been eventful for the family of Tang. The painful unraveling of the jade shroud's odyssey showed in the strain and weariness on Joe Tang's face.

"First Son, is everyone here?" Wen asked in Chinese. His voice was a quiet rustling, like wind through dry grass.

"Johnny stands at your left," Joe said.

As Lianne translated in a low voice for the Donovans, Kyle flicked a glance over the thinning white hair and fretful face of Number One Son. The handmade suit Joe wore was the same color as his father's. The son's frame was almost as slight, almost as stooped.

"Daniel is at your right," Joe continued. "I am in front of you. Lianne is behind me. Donald Donovan's First and Fourth Sons are also behind me."

"Harry?" Wen asked.

"He is in Shanghai," Joe said after a brief hesitation. "He has not responded to my messages."

Though Wen said not one word, his face seemed to age even more. A whispering sigh rattled his chest. He ran one hand over the jade shroud as though measuring it for size.

"Speak to your younger brother," Wen ordered.

Reluctantly Joe turned to Johnny. "I have brought shame and dishonor on my family and on my ancestors," he said, his voice strained.

Johnny's eyes widened. Whatever he had expected, it wasn't this. "I find that difficult to believe."

"I . . ." Joe's voice faded. He cleared his throat. "I have gambled too much."

Johnny looked perplexed. "You have always gambled too much. Wen has always scolded. The sun continued to rise and set in its usual way."

"Our father refused to give me more money," Joe said slowly. "I knew I could make it all back, all the wealth I had lost and more, much more. Just one race. One horse whose jockey also needed money. The Red Phoenix triad had it all arranged. I just needed funds to make a bet."

Kyle and Archer glanced at each other. Though Lianne was translating for the Donovans, she looked only at her grandfather. His face was impassive, but his eyes were as ancient and bleak as betrayal.

"Han Seng offered a way out of my dilemma," Joe said softly. "I would trade fine Tang jade for inferior pieces from Seng's collection. Not only would I pay off my old debts that way, I would have enough money left over to wager on future races where the Red Phoenix knew who would lose before the race was run. When I made enough money, I would be able to buy back the Tang jades. No one would ever know. . . ."

Johnny looked at his father. Wen looked neither right nor left nor even ahead. His eyes were blind, his hands crippled, his body brittle with age and betrayal.

"It did not happen that way," Joe continued, his voice barely a whisper. "The money that I won, I bet again, and I lost again. More Tang jades left the vault, replaced by Seng's less virtuous pieces."

"When did you decide to set up Lianne?" Kyle asked.

Lianne translated, her face as impassive as Wen's and her eyes as bleak.

Johnny flinched. Joe didn't. He had already shamed himself in front of his father and his ancestors. He had no pride left, simply a need to redeem himself however he could.

"I did not think of it," Joe said simply. "Harry did. Somehow he discovered my trading with Han Seng."

"Somehow?" Archer repeated coolly. "I'll tell you how. Harry, Han Seng, and the Red Phoenix triad are in bed together. That's why I advised my father against any partnership ventures between Donovan International and the Tang Consortium or SunCo."

Lianne's translation brought Wen's head around toward Archer. The old man squinted as though he could actually see.

Quick, choppy words poured out. Lianne didn't translate until Archer prodded her.

"Wen dislikes America's narrow view of the triads," she summarized.

"Really?" Archer said dryly. "Ask him why he has refused many Red Phoenix overtures for a closer partnership. To be precise, their scheme to launder drug money through Tang overseas financial institutions."

Lianne's eyes widened. "Is that true?"

"Ask him," Kyle said.

After she did, Wen positioned his head so that he might be looking at either Donovan. He spoke quietly. "Some triad business is inevitable. Some is avoidable. As long as I lead the family of Tang, the drug entanglement will be avoided."

"Good idea," Kyle said. Then he measured Joe with cold eyes. "So Harry caught you with your hand in the cookie jar. What happened next?"

Joe barely waited for Lianne to finish translating before he answered. "Harry started taking control of the trades. He made certain not only that Lianne was the go-between, but that no pieces of jade would be removed from the vault unless she had been there recently."

Joe gave Lianne a look that was strained, resentful, and apologetic at once. "I did as he wished. Then I did . . . more. The tips Han Seng gave me did not always work. Soon I was more in debt to him than ever. I doubled my bets and then I redoubled them. I was desperate to stop the flow of jade out of the Tang vault. Yet the more I wagered, the more deeply in debt I became."

Kyle watched slow tears well from Joe's dark eyes and down his lined cheeks. In a distant way Kyle felt sorry for the man; a gambling addict, easy prey for Harry and Han Seng. Yet Kyle's sympathy was inhibited by a simple fact: Joe had set up his niece to take the blame for his own thefts, and to go to jail in his place.

No tears, no apologies, no excuses about addiction could change that.

"Who planned the Jade Emperor charade?" Kyle asked coolly.

Joe sighed. "Han Seng."

"Figures," Kyle muttered.

"It was a way to explain the appearance on the market of such remarkable jades," Joe said sadly. "Seng sold many of the pieces. He kept only the erotica."

"I'll bet he made more on the deals than you did," Kyle said.

"I was not in a position to argue price. But yes, I never quite covered my losses."

"And good old Harry kept on helping you out. Why? What was in it for him?"

"He was protecting me."

"Bullshit. He was building his own empire." Kyle glanced at Archer.

"Go ahead," Archer said. "If anybody has a need to know, it's Wen."

"Harry knew he would never be Wen's Number One Son, but he had ambition," Kyle said. "He saw the Red Phoenix triad making money by the container load from drugs, gambling, extortion, and more drugs. He wanted some of the action. Han Seng was willing to oblige. But first, Harry would have to do something really special for Seng and the triad."

"The jade shroud," Lianne said.

"Yes," Kyle agreed. "SunCo, through Seng, had tried to woo Dick Farmer with a jade burial suit that was, shall we say, dubious. It didn't pass muster with Farmer's curator. SunCo tried to bribe a better suit out of one of the state museums, but China isn't like Russia yet. There's still enough civil government in China to protect state museums from being creamed by thieves and sold on the international market. Red Phoenix needed a real burial shroud. Harry Tang had one."

"So he traded the Tang jade suit for the fraudulent one

SunCo had," Lianne said. "He assumed Wen would never know the difference. But what about me? What about the inventory I would conduct at the end of the year?"

"You were a problem, sweetheart," Kyle said, brushing the backs of his fingers down her cheek. "That's why he arranged for the Red Phoenix to kill you, after he first had you arrested for theft."

Suddenly Johnny looked almost as old as Joe. "What? You can't know that!"

"Actually," Archer said, "we pretty much can. When it looked like Lianne was going to make bail, Harry's lawyer called Vancouver. A few hours later, two triad hit men were waiting for Lianne at her home. There was no sign of forced entry. The Tang Consortium owns the building. If Kyle hadn't been real close by, Lianne would be dead and every last jade theft would be laid at her door. Or her headstone, in this case."

Johnny turned to Wen, whose forehead was resting on his folded hands. "Father, do you believe this?"

"Have I a more sensible choice?" Wen asked, lifting his head. "It would be like Harry to stake everything on one bold, foolish plan. Number Two Son is clever, but not so clever as he thinks."

"He'd better be," Kyle said. "Farmer was well and truly pissed when he saw the wrong shroud on his altar. No doubt he recognized it for the fake Seng had already tried to sell him. Then he went straight to Seng and started screaming. Seng knows there's only one place that particular fake jade suit could have come from—the Tang vaults. Seng has a lot of explaining to do to the Red Phoenix boys. I'm sure he's looking for Harry to help him out."

"The triad won't be happy to lose a big fish like Farmer," Archer added. "All those juicy opportunities for graft, corruption, and money laundering in the New World. So if you hear from Harry, tell him to find a good, deep hole, dive in, and pull it in after him."

"It would be better if I didn't hear from him," Johnny said roughly. "I'm ashamed that he is my brother."

"In case you get to feeling sentimental, remember that Daniel likely was next on Harry's list of expendable relatives," Archer said. "Good old Harry wasn't going to take the fall for any missing jade."

Johnny went gray and looked at his youngest son.

For the first time, Daniel Tang spoke. "A few months ago, Harry told me to start checking the contents of the vault, using last year's inventory list. He didn't say why."

"So that you'd accuse Lianne of stealing," Kyle said. "Which you did."

"I had good reason."

"You had shit," Kyle said curtly. Lianne stopped translating, but he kept talking. "You were so jealous of Lianne's relationship with Wen that you couldn't wait to accuse her. The fact that she's the daughter of your father's lifelong lover just made revenge sweeter."

Daniel's eyelids flinched. "I have apologized to Wen and to my family."

"Not to all of it. You have a half sister—"

"Kyle," Lianne interrupted. "That's enough."

"—who refused to point a finger at you, even though it would have helped her at a time when she needed help very badly. You had the means, the motive, and the opportunity to steal jade, but she never said a word against you."

Anger darkened Daniel's face. "I wouldn't steal from my own grandfather!"

"Yet you assumed Lianne would steal from *her* own grandfather," Johnny said in a strained voice. "You assumed my daughter—your half sister—was a thief. Why? What has she done to you that you hate her so?"

Daniel had no answer except the one Kyle had already given. Jealousy.

Wen's voice rasped in a demand that needed no translation. Johnny spoke quickly in Chinese. Wen listened, then banged his walking stick on the floor for silence.

"Daniel misjudged his half sister," Wen said.

Joe and Johnny froze. Never had they heard their father speak of any blood relationship with Lianne Blakely.

"But the fault is mine," Wen continued. "The example was mine. I was content to use Lianne's inborn gift for jade and her natural hunger to be part of the Tang family."

Lianne's voice faltered. Johnny took up the translation without a pause.

"My first two sons followed my example," Wen said. "They used Lianne. But unlike me, they felt no affection for her. Nor did they worry what would happen if they sacrificed her for their own foolish ambitions. She was, after all, merely a woman, and a woman without family at that."

"She has a family," Kyle said fiercely. "Mine. There isn't a Donovan who wouldn't go to war for her. Pass the word through the Tang family, Wen. Lianne isn't alone anymore. Find your next sucker somewhere else."

Lianne turned toward Kyle, but he didn't notice. He was concentrating on Wen. Something very much like a smile was tugging on the old man's thin, pale lips.

"I wish I could see my granddaughter's defender," Wen said. "It would give me an idea of what my great-grandchildren will look like. Marry soon. I have little time left."

"Nothing has been said about a wedding," Lianne said over her father's translation.

"That's one way of keeping the Neolithic blade in the family," Kyle pointed out. "It would make a good wedding present."

Lianne stared at him like he had gone crazy.

"Haven't you figured it out yet, sweetheart?" Kyle asked, smiling gently at her. "Men know right away when they find their mate. It's women who need time to be convinced. How much more time do you think you'll take to add one and one and get two?"

Wen's dry laughter followed Johnny's translation. When Lianne started to speak, Wen smacked his walking stick on the floor in a command for silence.

"That virtuous blade will be the least of my gifts to you when you wed Kyle Donovan," Wen said to Lianne. "It is only fitting that the Jade Emperor's granddaughter go in wealth to her new family."

Lianne was too stunned to say anything.

Wen smiled as though he could see her face. "It is true, girl. Look around you and know that you have been privileged to shape and polish your jade skills among the greatest jade treasures ever gathered. Centuries ago, your Tang ancestors found the secret way into the Jade Emperor's Tomb." Wen lifted one frail, trembling hand in a gesture that took in the vault. "It became ours. All of it."

He thumped the walking stick on the floor once more. "Leave me, now. I am tired."

Kyle put his arm around Lianne and urged her out of the vault. "I owe you dinner at the Rain Lotus. It's a quiet place. We can talk."

"About what?"

"Upgrading my collection of erotica," he said blandly.

Lianne gave him a wary, sideways glance. "I didn't know you had one."

"I'm working on it." Kyle smiled at her. "And you're going to help me."

"I am?"

"Sure. Think about all those hours of jade training you owe me in exchange for the stuffed-elephant escort service."

"Ummm."

"And if I haven't convinced you by then that one and one makes two, I'm cashing in that third chance you promised me. But I'd rather keep it in reserve." Kyle leaned down and brushed a kiss over Lianne's mouth. "A lifetime is a long time to go without extra chances, sweetheart. Especially when two people are as stubborn as we are."

She looked into Kyle's clear, beautiful eyes and saw just how serious he was. Her heart turned over even as she smiled up at him.

"I don't know if I like being part of your, um, erotic collection," she said.

"How about if I'm part of yours instead?"

"I don't have one."

"Start one."

Smiling, Lianne put her arm around Kyle and leaned into his familiar strength. "Okay."